Graham Edward was born in Shepton Mallett, Somerset, in 1965, and brought up in Bournemouth. He attended art school in London and now works as a design studio manager. He lives in Nottingham with his wife Helen and their two children. *Dragonflame* is his third novel.

Voyager

GRAHAM EDWARDS

Dragonflame

HarperCollins*Publishers*

This novel is entirely a work of fiction. The names, characters and incidents portrayed in it are the work of the author's imagination. Any resemblance to actual persons, living or dead, events or localities is entirely coincidental.

Voyager
An Imprint of HarperCollins*Publishers*
77–85 Fulham Palace Road,
Hammersmith, London W6 8JB

The *Voyager* World Wide Web site address is
http://www.harpercollins.co.uk/voyager

A Paperback Original 1997
1 3 5 7 9 8 6 4 2

A catalogue record for this book
is available from the British Library

ISBN 0 00 648233 3

Set in Postscript Meridien by
Rowland Phototypesetting Ltd,
Bury St Edmunds, Suffolk

Printed and bound in Great Britain by
Caledonian International
Book Manufacturing Ltd, Glasgow

for C.A.E.

PROLOGUE

THE SOUND OF GRASS was constant as the sea. Savannah waves brought movement to this waterless ocean. The brush of stalk on stalk was a dry and ceaseless whispering of dryad voices, a soft, insistent undercurrent of thought and dream. It spoke as it moved, the grass, and its voice was warm and wholesome. Strong.

Wyrm listened to the grass as he lay on his back amid its currents. The perimeter of his vision was alive with the motion of the grain, bulging pods of seed dyed orange by the failing sun. As he settled the orange withered and was replaced by blue dusklight, which in turn gave way to the broad and fragile glow of the stars. The sky was clear and so were Wyrm's thoughts; he felt alert and alive, his mind and heart sharply attuned to the rhythms of the night. He felt no urge to sleep.

In all his short life, Wyrm had never slept.

Black dragon scales crackled faintly as he rolled briefly on to his side, using his long, agile tail to flick a few crumbs of soil away from his neck. Then he reclined once more, obsessively aware that his unprecedented lack of wings meant that he could lie like this more comfortably than any dragon in history had been able to before.

'Small comfort,' he whispered, to the stars.

What comfort he could not find in his own form he now – as he so frequently did – sought in the patterns of the night sky. The brighter stars had always borne names: for as long as dragons could remember bright Atros had turned in the heavens along with the great Northern Star, and many others whose names were older and more elaborate. Wyrm

3

knew them all, those old names, but he knew more, he *saw* more. He saw the shapes the stars made against the blackness.

There was the Unicorn, there Nistor, great and terrible cannibal dragon, there the simple curve of the Rose. Where most dragons saw only random scatterings of light Wyrm saw monumental characters dancing through fields of form, a tracery of lines which echoed in the void and made drama in the sky. There was the stab of the Lightning Fork, there dragon Destater, there the entwined fish shapes of Sapeth and Sor . . . so much life, so far away. Unattainable yet aglow with promise, with possibility.

They turned above Wyrm now, their rotation inexorably slow and as ceaseless as the waves in the grass which surrounded him and brushed his face like a mother's wing. They were his comfort, his friends in the sky; they alone consoled him when all seemed dark. In the darkness they were his one, true light.

And tonight, as he did every night, Wyrm began to search.

Wyrm was not aware that he was being observed, but had he realized he would not have been surprised, nor unduly concerned. Gaping behind him was the trollvein, the tunnel of charm which had brought him to this land of wavering grass. No dragon had tried to prevent him from leaving Mahl, not even his grandmother. Though she loved him, she, like all the others, found him . . . strange. He was not at ease with other dragons, nor were they with him; none of them understood his needs. And so, this very night, he had left.

Trollveins were hard to find now that the storms following the Turning had subsided, but the volatile geography of Mahl occasionally opened one up. This was the first that Wyrm had actually seen, and its appearance had reminded him that Mahl was no longer his home – if indeed it ever had been. The time had come to move more widely beneath the gaze of the stars, to leave the land which had for more than a year been home to all the dragons he had ever known. He would be missed, he supposed, but not by many. Some pleaded with him to stay, but wrapped inside their words he detected very clearly their relief, for no longer would they have to strive to understand this odd, black, wingless dragon. Besides, they were too concerned with other perils to fight against a young dragon's eagerness to strike out and explore the world. For his part, Wyrm felt no desire to save lives, not even that of his mother. Those tasks were for others to perform; he was no hero.

His grandmother followed him to the trollvein entrance, her white wings keeping time with his legs as Wyrm walked up to the ragged, pulsing circle standing open like a mouthless throat in the ravine wall. The far end of the tunnel was clearly visible, apparently a mere ten wing-widths away. But this was an illusion – stars twinkled there, and grass waved.

'A long way,' observed Gossamer, her voice tight, 'for a few, short steps.'

Wyrm nodded agreement in silence.

Gossamer cast her gaze across his young, slim body and he knew that she was struggling – as she had for so long – to reconcile the fact that, although he had lived little more than a year, already Wyrm was full grown. Indeed, he seemed a full ten years older than she. This time, as every other time, she gave up and simply shook her head, sighing.

'You move fast, Wyrm,' she said, infinite sadness casting shadows across her words.

'That is why I must go now, Gossamer,' he replied, disarming her by saying her name. His voice was – as it always was – dispassionate.

'Magic has touched you as it has touched no other dragon,' she whispered, embracing him once, awkwardly. 'Don't let it go to waste.'

'I have a long way to go,' he answered shortly. 'I shan't come back.'

'Goodbye, Wyrm.' Gossamer's voice was the gentlest murmur as she watched her grandson – a wingless dragon older than herself – enter the trollvein. His body shimmered into near-transparency, then elongated as troll charm transported him from the icy reaches of Mahl to the equator and beyond. She watched him step from the opposite end of the vein and out into long grass, then she turned and left.

5

Overwhelmed by this new land he had discovered, Wyrm did not move far from the exit. It was so hot! Even though it was night here the temperature far exceeded anything he had ever known on Mahl. So the stories about the shape of the world were true – not that he had ever really doubted them, for it was Wyrm's belief that all stories bear the truth somewhere at their core.

There will be new stories here, he thought eagerly. *Stories to lead me on, to bring me near. Stories to search by. Stories to take me into the light.*

So he rested, drinking in the intoxicating sky, conjuring names for the new patterns he saw, marvelling at the new stars lifting above the southern horizon.

It was towards dawn that the two dragons who had been watching finally came through the trollvein after him, although in the end it was not Wyrm's presence which attracted them. They emerged into the long grass amid the flurry of noise characteristic of dragons trying to be as quiet as possible.

'Shush, Vox,' hissed a female voice over the soft rushing of the savannah.

'Well,' snapped Vox by way of reply, 'are they or aren't they? By the skies, it's warm here!'

'Ask Wyrm,' urged Smoke, arching her neck as she squinted into the distance. 'He knows everything.'

Vox nervously approached their motionless companion, trying (without much success) not to disturb the shroud of grass which surrounded Wyrm's supine form. He cleared his throat.

'Ahem, er, Wyrm?'

'Yes, Vox?' responded Wyrm at once, his voice clear and calm and quite devoid of surprise.

'Oh, er, w-well – sorry to disturb you, by the way – we were just wondering if you could tell us whether those things over there are what we think they are.'

With a single, smooth movement Wyrm lifted himself from the ground and looked in the direction Vox's quivering wing was indicating. There was a pause as they all took in the view.

All was misty dark-blue but for where dawn light inflamed the horizon. Curiously flattened trees sprawled against the orange glow; far behind them great mountains began to shine before the waking sun. Shadows rippled in front of the trees.

'How interesting,' commented Wyrm. He could not have sounded less interested.

'Are they . . . ?' began Smoke, suddenly breaking off as the first arc of light cut through the mist and threw its rays over the world.

'They' were the shadows of animals, sheer and insubstantial in the morning haze. Slowed by distance, they galloped, their long legs slender, their heads held impossibly high on necks like those of the dragons who watched them. Dust plumed in their wake. The sound of their passage rumbled faintly through the ground and into the dragons' claws. There were thousands of them, but they were not yet real.

'They're transparent!' exclaimed Vox, but even as they watched the racing herd became more solid.

'It must be a trick of the light,' said Smoke, but Wyrm shook his head.

'No trick,' he announced. 'Vox is right, but they'll be real soon enough.'

On they galloped, turning away from the dragons towards a deep rock outcrop; soon they would be hidden from view. The distant trees were clearly visible behind them, *through* them. Their pale, transparent forms shimmered like ghosts above the savannah, flimsy as smoke. These great creatures of the grassland loped at last out of sight, the last of their number darkening, almost blotting out the trees as sun-golden flesh became translucent, then finally opaque.

'They have joined us now,' suggested Wyrm matter-of-factly.

'Were they . . . they looked like zirafae,' ventured Smoke.

Wyrm shrugged. 'Yes,' he agreed, 'or their heirs, at least. These creatures will be devoid of charm, of course, which will make them cruder than the zirafae were . . .'

'And we saw their creation,' breathed Smoke.

'The trollvein has closed,' noted Wyrm.

Aghast, Vox and Smoke whirled round. Sure enough, the

low plateau wall from which they had emerged was now seamless, all trace of the trollvein gone. But before they could cry out Wyrm went on, 'You must have known it was a risk.'

'Well, yes,' spluttered Vox. 'But . . .'

'But what?' Wyrm allowed himself an approximation of a smile.

'But . . . well, I'd just like to have had a choice.'

'Are you sorry to have left Mahl?' The tone of Wyrm's question gave no suggestion that he was at all interested in the nature of Vox's reply, nor even whether he replied at all.

'No,' broke in Smoke with sudden vehemence. 'No, we're not sorry at all, are we, my darling?'

Vox trembled for a moment, the orange of the rising sun painting strange colours across his bright purple scales, then his shoulders slumped. 'No,' he admitted, 'I think perhaps it's for the best, in the long run.'

'Of course it is,' agreed Smoke, forcing cheer into her voice. 'Well, Wyrm, which way are you headed? Because it looks like you've got yourself some companions, if you'll have us.'

The ten or so breaths during which Wyrm appraised them both felt like the longest of their lives. Later Vox would confess to Smoke that he felt as though those glistening, black eyes were taking him apart bone by bone. At length, Wyrm cocked his head to one side and demanded, 'Vox, you were outcast for many years, were you not?'

Vox glanced uncertainly at his partner, then nodded.

'And you, Smoke, you were . . . involved with Wraith?'

She shivered. 'Yes,' she whispered.

'Mmm. And now the zirafae have returned.'

Wyrm looked straight up and saw the last of the stars fading overhead – the constellation of Nistor, cannibal dragon. Then he looked down at the watching dragons and his face broke into a dazzling smile.

'Well, dragons,' he boomed, rearing up on to his hind legs and opening his forelegs wide. 'Welcome! Welcome to the great search for the hidden flame and the secret of the Last Circle! I am proud to have you join me and should be even prouder if, in time, you will consider me your friend! Now come, we have many lands to cover and we can go only at the speed of the slowest, and I'm afraid that's me! Come!'

Sweeping his tail round he launched himself at a brisk trot through the savannah grass, glancing back only once to urge his new companions on. 'Come,' he repeated. 'Time is shorter than you think. Believe me – I know!'

Smoke and Vox exchanged a glance, then shrugged.

'He's mad,' said Vox as they half-ran, half-glided after Wyrm.

'Maybe, but he knows some wonderful stories,' came Smoke's reply.

And above them the sky was bright.

PART ONE

CULT

CHAPTER 1

Into the Fissures

The two dragons were pale brown arrows against the white of the Kull Wall. Scant lines of vapour, almost invisible against the ice, described their shared path through the cold air towards the entrance tunnel. From daylight they flew into shadow. Into the shadow of the Fissures.

From his distant vantage point, Fortune could see little and hear nothing; it would have to be enough. If Scarn's sentries even sniffed a conspiracy then Aria would surely be lost forever, for there would be no second chance. For now he had to be content with this, but later . . . Glancing at the high sun he judged the time at a little after midday. Very well. They had until tomorrow night. Then the hard decisions would have to be made.

Just a reconnaissance, he reminded himself, but he could not help but think of Aria. *What if she really does want to stay – what if even half what Scarn says is true?*

On the other side of the valley Tallow and Anchre passed smoothly into the tunnel entrance. Flickers of green betrayed Scarn's sentries as they ushered the new arrivals into the darkness, the only points of colour on a barren landscape. Steep walls of brown rock and white ice; steam from the broad lake which hissed in the flat vale below; a cool and uninviting sky. *Land of contrasts*, considered Fortune as he lingered, hoping to catch one last glimpse of his friends on their journey underground, although they were quite gone from sight. *Land of fire and ice.*

Presently he turned and left the valley of the Kull, heading back south towards the coast and what remained of Mahl's original dragon settlement, become tiny now as

13

Scarn's influence increased. Nor was there any prospect of growth from within, now that all dragons were infertile. Cult dragons now outnumbered them by over ten to one and the trend showed no signs of losing its momentum. The collective decision to abandon Mahl before they too were sucked in had been an easy one in the end, although none could countenance leaving without at least offering freedom to any of Scarn's dragons prepared to take it.

And, for Fortune and Gossamer, there was Aria.

'If we go, she goes,' they had decided, each surprising the other with the simple power of their conviction; more surprising was the fact that it had taken them the best part of a year to reach this conclusion.

'And if she won't come?' It was Gossamer who dared to ask the question Fortune found so hard to face. 'Can we really bring her out by force?'

'It's for her own good.'

And so, they believed, it was.

Big-winged Tallow felt as though he were trying to squeeze back into the egg. A dragon most at home in the sky, he was distressed almost to the point of distraction by the narrow confines of the outer Kull tunnels. But then the guards would know that too, which made the fiction of his wanting to join the Cult all the more plausible. Only faith could bring such a giant to these catacombs, it would be judged – or so Tallow hoped.

It was not that Tallow had never been underground before, but here it was different. He tried to identify the source of his apprehension as he followed the leading guard through the high, narrow confines of the basalt corridors. Strands of daylight, brought from high above through the countless fissures which gave the deeper part of this underworld its name, slithered across his dorsal scales and blinked against his lowered, wary eyes. It was claustrophobic, to be sure, and his enormous wings proved the equally enormous hindrance he had known they would, but there was more.

He scented the air. Sulphur, steam contaminated by

14

countless strange substances he could not identify, certainly *heat*.

Tallow sighed. If there was more he could not isolate it, not yet. Pausing, he glanced up briefly, and was rewarded by a clear view of the infinite sky above, its brilliant light lancing down like a dragon's claw. He blinked, rubbing his watering eye with a folded wing membrane. When he looked again he made out that it was not truly sky that he was seeing but cloud, pure white cloud which undulated into shadowy grey as it passed over the steep-sided Kull valley and down towards the sea. *Cloud above*, he thought. *Darkness below*.

'The sooner we're out of here, the better,' he muttered to himself as the leading guard turned back to see what the delay was. 'Grit in my eye,' he explained conversationally. The guard gave a quizzical smile, behind which lurked scarcely concealed suspicion. 'I'm fine now – let's go on, please.' Behind him, Anchre grunted quiet encouragement and they set off again.

Tallow quickly discovered that his instinctive assumption that it would get darker the deeper they journeyed simply was not true. There were many corners where the shadows did indeed close in, leading the two newcomers to believe that *here* was the place where they would finally begin properly to descend, *here* was the real edge of Scarn's domain. But further ahead it would always brighten again, narrow shafts of light puncturing the rock, fanning out through spiralling rifts and long, vertical channels. The ceilings were a patchwork of light and shade, and soon the floors and walls began to display the same fragmentation. Presently they left the tunnels altogether. Now they were in the Fissures.

'Watch your step,' Tallow murmured to Anchre as they stumbled their way across a series of broken ridges. Between the slender steps yawned empty, black chasms, probably too narrow for a dragon to fall down – not that either of them wished to put this proposition to the test – but disconcerting nonetheless.

'No talking now, please,' suggested one of the guards smoothly. 'We are nearing the sacred boundary.'

15

'Of course,' came Anchre's warm, strangely forgettable voice from behind Tallow. 'Forgive us – we have much to learn.'

Tallow found himself trying to recall Anchre's features and failing. *A curious dragon, that one*, he reflected. *He sounds convincing though; I only hope I do as good a job.*

As they entered more tunnels, the dark basalt was changing to a strange, red rock neither of them recognized. Streaks of brown raced along its length, pointing towards a brilliant, white glow.

'The sacred boundary?' inquired Tallow.

'Indeed,' confirmed the leading guard.

The tunnel widened a little where the boundary was drawn with intersecting beams of light. Tallow and Anchre looked up, blinking, into the dazzle of thin clouds overhead – so far overhead. The huge shaft which rose from the broad place in the tunnel did so in a slowly widening spiral through jagged rock – as though scooped with some giant's finger. Its walls were lined with rusty splinters like loose teeth, prohibiting all thought of flight.

What I wouldn't give to be up there, thought Tallow wistfully.

What happened then took them both completely by surprise. From a secondary tunnel entrance which neither of them had spotted there swarmed a veritable flood of dragons. At the time it seemed that there were tens of the creatures, although looking back later Tallow decided that there could have been no more than six. In almost complete silence they descended on the two new recruits, separating them and hustling them off in opposite directions. An eerie fluidity accompanied their movements, as though the entire drama were being played out in the depths of some perfect, crystal pool. The last glimpse Tallow had of Anchre was of the narrow-winged dragon being squeezed without ceremony into the confines of the lesser tunnel from which the silent horde had sprung. He himself was hauled on beyond the wide place and the spiral of light, further along the tunnel. The leading guard remained at his head while two others flanked him, a fourth bringing up the rear and making escape impossible.

'But why should I wish to escape?' he muttered bitterly. 'I'm here voluntarily, after all.'

Then the tunnel system finally opened up. Tallow was ushered into a gloomy cavern whose only source of illumination was a single crack in the ceiling from which leaked a meagre drizzle of light. The dull glow served only to accentuate the forbidding nature of the many exit tunnels, but before Tallow had time even to count these he was marched onwards, through the cavern and into a cell which bubbled from its wall. His guards pushed him firmly – not roughly, not quite – into the small space and then left, melting through the vapid light and vanishing like ghosts. The scraping of their claws receded, leaving Tallow in silence. Then he heard breathing and realized he was not alone in here. Opposite, in the shadows, sat a dragon of the Cult of the Last Circle.

It waited, breathing gently and swaying slightly from side to side, as though some unfelt wind were blowing it. Tallow's fear rose briefly into his throat and he cast an anxious glance into the cave outside. Could he escape? The tunnel down which they had been brought had run a straightforward course – he was sure he could find his way out again. And there were always the light-bringing fissures themselves, one of which might just be wide enough to allow him to take flight and reach the clouds by more direct means.

Then he saw the other dragon's eyes and remembered the reason he was here. Those eyes: cold, impersonal. Watching him, suspecting him, hungry for him. He shivered, and knew he must stay.

'Welcome.' Her voice was young, strong, even seductive. Tallow could see only the glint of her eyes. 'Do not be afraid, Tallow. I once sat where you sit, and look at me now.'

I don't need to, shuddered Tallow. *I don't want to.*

'Look into my eyes,' said the dragon. 'And you will see.'

Tallow kept his eyes closed for what seemed to be a very long time, during which he forced himself to think ahead. *Tomorrow night. I only have to stay here today and tomorrow, then I get out and report back. Then we can decide what best to do – how many, if any, we can rescue. What can happen to me in just two days?* Reminding himself of his mission quelled his

17

rising panic and enabled him to look up, to regard his companion in this tiny cell of red stone. She shifted her weight slightly, allowing a bar of light to fall briefly across her face, and Tallow saw that she was indeed young, her eyes wide . . . had they been lively eyes, he might have considered her pretty. But she stared through Tallow, a thousand wing-widths beyond the wall of rock behind him. Her scales were a striking shade of russet, but they seemed to have no lustre: they were dull, like the expression on her face.

'I know how bad you must feel about yourself,' said the dragon. 'We all do, when we first come here. It's all right to have those feelings, Tallow, it really is.'

'It . . . is?' Tallow managed to mumble, unsure of where this was leading.

'Of course it is,' she replied, breaking into a smile. No doubt this was intended to be a warm and inviting smile, but it succeeded only in freezing the very scales of his face. *Heartless*, he thought before she went on, 'There is a way through for you, just as there was for me and for all the dragons of the Last Circle. But first we must find out what really drives you, Tallow. First you must lose yourself, so that you can be found again. First you must die, that you may be reborn.

'Lose yourself in me, Tallow. Die in me. Look into my eyes and do not look away until I ask you to.'

And Tallow did. *It's a test*, he decided. *Just like we used to play as infants. The dragon who looks away first is the loser. How long does she think she can hold my gaze, I wonder? How long can I hold hers, for that matter?*

So they stared, and even though he soon became uncomfortable, anxious to look away, Tallow stared on, fully aware that this was the first, and perhaps the most crucial, of Scarn's tests. And although he believed at first that he could hold on to his composure, as he looked deeper and deeper into his companion's curious gaze he began to see something, some fragment of the power which Scarn had unleashed in his underworld. Tallow's vision filled with this dragon's green eyes and his mind . . . his mind began to fill with the strangest things . . .

*   *   *

18

The dragon Tallow faced was one of Scarn's key first-contact dragons. Her name was Wist and she was devoted to the Cult, but something about this new dragon unsettled her. This *Tallow* . . . he seemed so strong, so self-aware – it quite took her breath away; indeed, it was as much as she could do to concentrate on the task at claw. She struggled through the test, finding the whole procedure far more difficult than she'd imagined it could be, even allowing for her relative inexperience. It was with the utmost relief that she finally sent him away with the splinter-talkers, pleased to observe in him the tell-tale signs of the soon-to-be-converted: Tallow left the cell with his head low, tail dragging, eyes vacant. Nevertheless, there was something about him . . .

His wings, she decided. *It was his wings*.

Scarn's teaching was quite clear on the subject of flight. 'The most important lesson for the new brother or sister to learn,' he had explained in his soft yet penetrating voice to Wist and the other eager pupils, 'is what you and I already know: that no dragon is strong. We are none of us worthy. We are all weak, we are all debased, we are constantly failing in all that we attempt. Only when a dragon realizes this may he or she be built anew. The first and greatest deceit is *flight*, for in trying to tame the sky we imagine we have powers that in truth lie far beyond our scope. Your task as first-contact dragons is to open minds deceived by unrestricted *flight* and its illusion of potency. You must uncover the true *weakness* hidden at the centre of all our spirits. Your role is vital. Perform it well.'

Alive in her memory, his words were compelling. They always stirred her, and she had only to recall Scarn's water-gentle eyes to know that he spoke from a deep well of understanding and wisdom. When the first three dragons she had personally 'interviewed' had all gone on to join the Cult of the Last Circle, she began to take pride in her work.

The 'interview' was, on the face of it, straightforward enough. First-contact dragons were required simply to sit with each prospective member and hold their gaze for the count of one thousand breaths. During that time no words were to be spoken, only that constant stare must be maintained. Simple enough to describe, the practice did in fact demand immense concentration and was laced with potential danger.

During the encounter, both dragons were likely to hallucinate images, usually in their peripheral vision. For some these images were frightening, and deep in the Fissures two dragons still lay in undisturbed catatonia, their condition a direct result of the unknown nightmares they had witnessed.

Wist herself experienced only minor visions, most of them mere flashes of colour, but several of her colleagues described – with trembling, awestruck voices – more exotic fantasies: ghost-dragons prowling at their sides, gouts of flame rushing towards them down long, winding tunnels, monstrous faces leering through cracks in the air. Scarn reassured them that this was an insignificant side-effect of what was essentially a reliable hypnotic process, and that the real work was being done in the mind of the watching dragon. Deep magic was being worked here, he explained, charm beyond the ken of mortal dragons.

The new recruits invariably left the encounters disorientated, stumbling away in the charge of the splinter-talkers who would coax them through the next stage of the process of breaking-down. Leaving the first-contact dragons to reassemble their own, quaking minds ready for the next time.

Now, just when it seemed that all possible dragons had been properly converted and her work was done, Tallow had come to Wist. He seemed to respond correctly, but Wist . . . Wist did not. Tallow weakened, certainly, but throughout the encounter he remained so *solid*. His face grew dull – of course, they all did – and his head drooped, but his *wings* remained so firm. Here was an individual who defied all of Scarn's claims that dragons were frail; here was a dragon with genuine power!

The image of Tallow's powerful wings haunted Wist as she made her way unsteadily back to the harem. Her own flimsy, rust-coloured wings were trembling uncontrollably and many of the dragons she passed regarded her with concern, some even reaching out to touch her, to reassure her. They knew of her place in Scarn's complex hierarchy and fell back respectfully as she stumbled past. She was a first-contact dragon, drained by her vital work yet fulfilled in the knowledge that she had helped to bring yet another dragon to the threshold of true self-awareness. Some even bowed their heads.

Wist staggered on. In her mind was a nightmare whirl of flickering lights – the remnants of the visions – bound up with thoughts of the raw, solid scales of Tallow's tan-coloured wings. The scales brought structure to the aethereal dance of light, brought structure to *everything* that was passing through Wist's mind, even the jumbled words of Scarn.

Through flight we once considered ourselves masters of the air and, in turn, masters of our own souls. Nothing could be further from the truth. We are not exalted by the use of our wings. Only when we have discovered our own inadequate hearts may we one day return to flight and, perhaps, recognize its cruel pretence.

Cult members were forbidden to fly. Only when all were worthy, Scarn said, would the dragons of the Cult take to the air again.

Tallow's wings!

The entrance to the harem was hidden beneath a low brow of rock tangled with a rough ivy which had dropped down from a cavity high above. Green-filtered sunlight washed through the fissure, turning the smooth basalt floor into a moving mosaic of light and shade. The concealment of the entrance was not deliberate – indeed, most if not all dragons knew exactly where it was – but its discretion was an important aspect of its nature. The harem was a refuge, a private place for Scarn's most valued acolytes to retire, to worship and to spend time with their master.

It's quiet in there this afternoon, thought Wist gratefully as she squeezed beneath the overhang, but no sooner had she wriggled through than she was grabbed forcibly by the wing and pushed against the wall. She looked up and saw her own face glaring back.

'Lessen!' she grimaced, shaking her wing membrane free.

Her twin sister continued to stare down at her, a sneer curling the corner of her mouth. 'What do you do to him?' she demanded without preamble. 'Tell me that, sister. What is it that makes you so special?'

'I don't know what you mean, Lessen, really I don't,' replied Wist angrily. 'I neither offer nor give him any more than you or any dragon else.' She felt her sister's fury nibbling at the corners of her mind and beat it back, caring little for the empathy.

' "I neither offer nor give . . ." ' mimicked Lessen scornfully. 'The sooner you learn to speak properly the better, little sister.' She regarded the dragon who had followed her out of their shared egg as she might an insect, then pushed her roughly aside. 'He's chosen you again tonight, as if you hadn't already guessed.' And with that she stalked off towards the water channel, tossing her head and snarling at any of the other concubines who dared to come near her.

Wist sighed. She supposed she should be grateful but all she really wanted to do tonight was to curl up as tight as she could – to imagine she was back inside that egg in fact, only this time on her own – and close her eyes against the storm of temptation Tallow had unleashed upon her.

Tallow is strong where Scarn says all are weak.

Tallow's wings are made for flying where Scarn says all who fly are unclean.

I want Tallow, where I should want only Scarn.

Confused, feeling tired and alone in a way no Cult dragon should, Wist dozed, awaiting the signal which would call her to Scarn's chamber where she would offer up the greatest gift she was able to give to the dragon who had brought new light to her world, to all their worlds.

She hugged herself close, ashamed of her weakness, for suddenly it was not Scarn she wanted. Nor, to her greater shame, was it the power of the Cult.

Fortune returned to a muted reception. The tiny settlement was shrouded with unease, its meagre population either pacing restlessly or staring blankly up into the sky. Even the distant cheer of the slender Raulla waterfall failed to instil any sense of hope into the scattering of nests and food caches. Temporary it was and temporary it looked, this strangely ramshackle camp of dragons, as though its creators had known from the start that they would not rest here, that sooner or later Mahl must be abandoned. The sky above

22

was full of clouds, pale here but darkening to the west; soon it would rain.

He glanced across the backs of his companions before furling his wings forward and stalling on to the broad ridge which they all used when flying. Wide and exposed, it caught the wind perfectly – an ideal launching and landing platform. There were the dragons he regarded as his family: Cumber and Velvet, Brace and Scoff and of course Gossamer. Beyond them the familiar wing-profiles of Volley and Ledra. And that was all. Wyrm, Vox and Smoke had disappeared through the trollvein the previous night; Tallow and Anchre were by now deep underground, embarked at last upon their mission. All their other friends: gone to the Cult.

That's all, he thought dismally. *We're all that's left now.*

A freshening of the wind bustled him down more quickly than he had anticipated, jarring his left wing against the platform. Overhead the clouds grew thick and predatory.

'Well,' he announced to the group at large. 'They're in.'

23

CHAPTER 2

The Chosen One

From behind the crack which she had opened between her closed wings, Aria watched as Wist settled herself down against the chamber wall. Now that Lessen had stalked off again this portion of the harem quarters was empty but for the two of them; the other concubines were either bathing or talking in the deeper reaches of the cave network. Just the two of them here, then, each a little island in a sea of confusion.

Like Wist, Aria felt as though her mind had been set adrift, although for her this was not an unusual state of affairs. It was no surprise that she had clung so tenaciously to the raft of promises Scarn had presented to her. Like the dazed, much-changed survivors of Aether's Cross, she was a prisoner of a debilitating insecurity, and it had taken very little coaxing by Scarn to gather her under his wing. Where her mother and father could offer her only love, Scarn had offered more: he had offered an *explanation*.

Aria still had little understanding of what had happened to her. When dragon Archan had unwrapped the charm held within the towers of the basilisk citadel the effect on the infant Aria had been devastating. She had no memory of the event, having learned of it (and here the riddles wound themselves ever tighter) from her own son, Wyrm. Time had distorted him as it had distorted her, so that Wyrm's body was ageing further and faster even than her own. And she had grown from infant to adult in the blink of a magic eye, in the citadel. Aria was like an empty gourd, ripe but quite hollow. She was devoid of experience, of memory, indeed of any sense of place or purpose. An empty space,

24

waiting to be filled. Whereas Wyrm . . . who had had even less time to comprehend the world . . . he knew things, stories, so much she had never even dreamed. And more than anything, Wyrm mystified her, so that she felt more empty than ever.

Scarn had been happy to fill Aria's mind with facts, and at first it had seemed to her that she was being educated. He could speak for an entire night, his words falling like seeds. Ideas took root in the very air, branching into promises, each promise becoming a truth, each truth a law and a guide for living which in turn would generate a new idea and so on until Scarn's vibrant tree of life assumed gigantic proportions, a living, thriving organism on which any dragon might alight and drink of its sweet sap.

Absent from his teachings was the warmth of her parents and their friends and she missed that, she supposed, but she was distanced from them by that one catastrophic night. Scarn offered her so many more *possibilities* than they ever had. Where they soothed and lulled and sang and hugged, Scarn *taught*. And his promises filled the aching emptiness of Aria's mind and heart.

But it is not *enough! Why does he never choose me?*

The question gnawed at her, incessantly. Many male dragons seemed to find her attractive, though she had as much sense of why they did so as she did of why she breathed. She considered her body inelegant and clumsy, but then had not Scarn told her that it was these things? Yet dragons' heads turned as she passed. The more she thought about it the more confused she became. She embraced facts as a coral embraces the sea which flows through it – without grasping any of them.

The question rose now like a spectre in her mind, and as she felt hot tears spread across the dark scales which covered her cheeks she saw Scarn. He appeared in the far entrance-way and came swiftly into the chamber. Always made nervous by the sight of him, her heart tumbled in her breast, prey to the complex emotions which surrounded and filled it whenever she was in his presence.

He strode past, the touch of his wing-arms silent on the smooth floor. His eyes, welcoming, turned towards her. The gesture tilted his broad and noble head into the light of an overhead fissure, making rich, olive-coloured scales shine with a lustre few Naturals were able to achieve. He was small and moved quickly, yet everything about him seemed somehow languid, as though his subtle speed and quiet approach were of no significance to him. His wings were short and broad, and Aria realized that she had never once seen him fly. She wondered what sound those wings would make on the air. Scarn fixed a kindly gaze on her as he slipped past, serving only to deepen her confusion.

He goes to her yet he has eyes only for me! Can I be so undesirable?

She closed her eyes and hid her face in her wings.

She had been here nearly as long as the others now, but Scarn had never once chosen her. He looked at her and there was something like lightning in his gaze whenever his eyes fell upon her body, and yet she had never spent the night with him. Contradiction. Confusion. She knew she should love him, but she had little idea of the meaning of the word, the emotion escaped her. She knew only that she did not know *anything*, not for certain.

As Scarn ushered Wist back across the low chamber, Aria sent her thoughts spiralling ahead into tomorrow. As she sent out her thoughts so Scarn sent out his gaze, embracing Wist physically yet caressing Aria with the touch of his eyes. She could feel the hunger in his look. In an effort to deflect it, to deny the overwhelming complexity of the signals he was sending, she spoke.

'Scarn,' she blurted, 'may I ask of you . . . that is . . . which dragon have you chosen for tomorrow's ceremony?'

Scarn paused, his wing membrane draped artfully so that Wist was effectively excluded from the conversation. 'The choice is not mine to make, dear Aria,' he answered smoothly. He always called her 'dear Aria'. 'I am merely the channel by which the decision is made manifest.'

'Yes, I know, but all the same . . .'

'Calm yourself, Aria dear. I know how concerned you are – as are we all – that we succeed tomorrow in our great ceremony, and be reassured that a choice has indeed been made. There is a dragon who is worthy. There is a dragon who is clean. There is a dragon who will lead us to the Last Circle.'

Aria found herself breathing hard. Scarn *had* chosen! She could not imagine what this meant for her own future, let alone the future of the Cult, but she did know that change was on the way and this excited her. Lately, her tiredness had grown. She was tired even of the taste of Scarn's words, and the shame this brought upon her was unfathomable, overwhelming. Yet she was relieved that at last her mind might be opened to new stimuli, new experiences. She, and the rest of the dragons of the Cult of the Last Circle, might soon be leaving Mahl!

Then, just as her thoughts were exploding further into a thousand promised tomorrows, Scarn brought her back to the present with an impact which jarred the very breath from her. After what seemed a lifetime of rejection she heard the words she now never thought she would hear from Scarn's lips. He fixed her with his gaze – so hungry, so gentle – and said,

'You are the chosen one, Aria. Tomorrow is your day, and that of no dragon else.'

And with that he whirled Wist out through the exit portal, leaving Aria alone, her ears bursting with the thunder of her heart, the tears like a river down her breast. She, Aria!

At last I have been chosen! Now I know what all the waiting was for. Now I understand!

Somewhere, deep inside her mind, truths began to lock into place.

Wist too found her mind reeling from the shock of Scarn's words. There had been much speculation over recent days about the ceremony Scarn was planning, the ceremony due to take place the very next day. Most of the preparation had been done in secret, but in his characteristic way Scarn had sown seeds of rumour among dragons he knew to be particularly talkative.

The rumours spoke of the end of an era. All the dragons who would be converted had been converted, and although latecomers Tallow and Anchre somewhat confounded this notion there was a general feeling that the phase of recruitment was indeed over and it was time for the Cult to move on, to re-enter the world from which it had remained in retreat for so long. Tomorrow's ceremony would mark the beginning of a journey into the unknown. Tomorrow they would begin their search for the location of the Last Circle, upon discovery of which the final, great exodus would be possible. The entire Cult would journey to their new home where true peace and enlightenment awaited them.

The Last Circle, thought Wist doubtfully as Scarn led her away to his private chamber. *I wonder if it really exists.*

Quite what the Last Circle was, or where it was, or what its powers – if any – were, Scarn had never actually explained, not to Wist and not, to her knowledge, to any dragon of the Cult. But Scarn had placed it at the centre of Cult life. Somewhere in the world, he claimed, was a circle of charm, the only circle left untouched by the Turning. It was waiting, he said, its power ready to be tapped, a vast store of magic. When released, it would restore peace and dignity to the shattered dragon world. Whether it was a stone circle like those which had played such an important part in the Heartland during the final events of the Turning, or whether it was some smaller or greater artefact, he could not say.

'I do not know,' he would answer, managing to sound both wise and ignorant. 'But I believe that a dragon will come who will lead us there. And when that day comes, we must all be ready. Everything turns, dragons, everything that was shall be again. We have only to be patient, and to love one another, and to have faith in the power of the Circle.'

So the myth promised true power to all dragons who gave up their old ways and joined Scarn's growing 'family'; Scarn himself invariably called the Cult his family. A day would come, Scarn said. Now it seemed that the day was here. *And the dragon is here too!* thought Wist, suddenly thinking of Aria, strange Aria who said so little yet who seemed to mean so much. She found herself curiously unsurprised that Aria was the dragon for whom they had all been waiting, that tomorrow she would play the crucial role in a mysterious ritual . . .

28

Tomorrow the journey will begin, and tonight, journey's eve, Scarn has chosen me for his partner! Despite her recent uncertainties Wist was humbled. On this most auspicious of nights Scarn had selected her, and for that she truly gave thanks.

But she could not rid her mind of Aria, she who was so unhappy, now to be the most exalted of them all.

He must have known all along, Wist realized, regarding their leader with sudden awe. *All these moons have passed, and he knew she was the one all the time. How can I have dared to doubt him?*

Wist moved closer to Scarn's cool flank and drove doubt from her mind. Yet, as they entered the fiery glow of Scarn's private quarters, she was distracted by a faint, almost inaudible thumping sound which echoed in the recesses of her mind. At first she thought it was the blood pumping through her body, but she could not match the rhythm of the sound to the pounding of her heart, itself a vibrant flame pulsing beneath her ribs.

Then she realized. It was the sound of powerful wings beating the air.

His wings!

Fortune woke abruptly into grainy, pre-dawn light. The swollen Raulla poured its melt waters over the distant falls, the sound echo-less, as dull as the surrounding landscape. The wide landing ridge, the woven nests, all seemed ill-formed and ghostly, as though their makers had been interrupted in the act of creation. In the flat-feeling gloom, he had the unsettling feeling that, were he to look too closely at his sleeping companions, he would find them to be faded away, and fading further with every slumbering breath they took.

Something's wrong!

He thumped his wing membrane against the arch of Gossamer's back, a dull thud of contact instantly swallowed by the unyielding air. She turned over, eyes wide: she had been awake for some time.

'Can you hear it?' she whispered. Her voice sounded as though it had travelled a tremendous distance to reach his straining ears. 'Fire!'

Fortune shook his head. He could hear nothing but the far-off hiss of the waterfall and the insistent beating of his own heart. Nevertheless, something was wrong.

'Tonight will be too late,' he said abruptly, seeing his insight reflected like a flame in Gossamer's eyes. 'They're in danger now. Aria's in danger *now*!'

Suddenly the sun rose.

For a brief moment, Tallow actually believed them.

Then he unhooked his eyes from the gaze of his inquisitor, whichever one of the three splinter-talkers it was – they were all bombarding him with questions – and sought in his mind's eye the memory of his very first flight.

Tallow had been young, younger than most dragons when they first took to the air. In spreading his wings he had finally, irrevocably come alive. Flight had been freedom, the lifting of his body from the clutter of the forest floor, on which most of his peers still scurried. Liberating elevation. It had intoxicated him then and intoxicated him still.

And now, these splinter-talkers telling him that flight was the enemy of the dragon, a harmful distraction from the true faith of the Cult. As their words crashed against his weakened spirit, Tallow found in his memory of that first flight the strength to resist their propaganda. He allowed the clean mountain air of his youth to tumble around him, bringing with it glorious sunlit cloud. The cloud hid the angry words, wrapping them and making them dull and meaningless. The cloud had a power all its own, Tallow discovered in those crucial moments, and it stayed with him long after he had been taken to rest in his low, dim cell.

In this way Tallow defied the first blows of the Cult against his heart, but despite the soothing presence of the cloud he wondered how long he might resist were he to stay.

But I'm not going to stay, he reminded himself later. He had been marched from the chamber where the splinter-talkers had confronted him and placed alone in a cell for the night. A strange tranquillity prevailed in the Fissures, and Tallow welclomed the quiet even more than he distrusted it. It was true, at first he had actually felt his will crumbling; already

30

disturbed by staring into Wist's green, lifeless eyes, he had been as vulnerable as any dragon. *I must be out by tomorrow night.*

The sounds of bustling dragons interrupted an uneasy dream in which leering heads floated before Tallow, disembodied and inflated many times greater than life-size. Their scales flickered through the rainbow and into indescribable colours beyond. Fire spouted from the rags of their necks. A cloud of vapour rolled in from nowhere and consumed them, then the cloud became the noise of activity in the corridor outside and Tallow awoke.

There was a tension in what he heard which alerted him immediately. He heard voices, many voices, speaking in whispers, and there was singing, somewhere nearby, the singing of prayers. Claws rattled in endless procession along the wide thoroughfare, throwing the occasional spark into Tallow's dim cell. The activity was in sharp contrast to the silence of the night and Tallow gained the impression that this was not just because it was morning: this particular morning was special.

The thought unnerved him. 'All dragons are weak, Tallow, deluded.' The shadowy splinter-talkers had intoned that like a prayer. 'And you are the weakest of all.' All at once he doubted what his instinct told him.

Cold, blue morning light, breaking through the fissures from the lightening sky above, brought Tallow to his senses. It was no comfort to him to know he was right, though. He now saw in the movement of many dragons the warning which Fortune and Gossamer had already perceived from their own, distant vantage: today *was* different. Tonight would be too late.

He must locate Anchre again, and quickly, and discover exactly what was going on. He and Anchre were on their own.

Wist left Scarn when it was still dark. All of Scarn's concubines had learned, one way or another, that it was not wise to be around their mentor when he woke up. Always he seemed to emerge from some dreadful nightmare, his tail lashing and his long claws raking the air. Wist herself bore

31

a set of rough, parallel scars down her right flank as testimony to this fact.

As she had been commanded, she bent her head in reverence towards the rearmost fissure of Scarn's extensive dormitory. This opening was in many ways *the* Fissure, the secret way to Scarn's own, private place where he said his most intimate prayers and performed the solitary rituals only he was blessed to know. Precisely what lay beyond this entrance Wist did not know, nor did she want to – at least, she had not wanted to until now. Now, this morning, she found herself hesitating, casting her gaze nervously between Scarn's prone form and the dark mouth of the Fissure.

Always there was the smell of sulphur emanating from the secret way. Today it was particularly strong, and there was more: yellow steam curled round in a tight spiral just beyond the entrance, enticing Wist with its sensuous dance.

Would it be so wrong just to peek?

Wist jumped, her jaw clamping shut on the involuntary moan which bleated out almost before she could stop it. What was she thinking? Enter Scarn's private chambers? What nonsense!

Scarn chose that moment to turn over, grunting and twitching his wings as though engaged in some furious airborne pursuit. That was enough for Wist. Gathering her own wings about her she sped from the dormitory and retreated into a dark corner of the harem, burying her face against her flank in an effort to silence her nervous breathing.

Slowly she recovered her composure, and was startled to see that two dragons were missing: Aria and Lessen. Then she remembered. *Of course, Aria is being prepared and Lessen has been chosen to stand at her wing during the ceremony; evidently she is being prepared too.*

Wist looked deep inside her heart to determine whether or not she was jealous of her twin sister. Did it not reflect their comparative worth in Scarn's eyes? She was rather surprised to find that she was not envious of Lessen, as she knew her sister was of her – quite the opposite in fact. She was relieved that Lessen had been selected over her; it was honour enough that Scarn had slept with her this night. All she desired now was to melt into the background, to let other dragons take the lead.

The ceremony will release us all from the icy grip of Mahl, she thought with excitement. *Then, at last, we shall be able to fly!*

Scarn awoke too.

The land of Mahl had dominated his dream. Bridges of black rock plaited themselves through the air as he flung his body up towards the sky. Below, in the great cracks which rent the dark soil, flames prowled, whispering to him that to fly was to blaspheme. As he pounded his wings it seemed that the entire land was conspiring to bring him down, for no sooner had he broken through the arching bridges than fresh mountains burst forth to each side, pressing in on him and forcing him higher and higher, all the while hurling gobbets of fire at his claws. The language of the dream was familiar but the narrative – this striving for escape – was wholly new, and Scarn knew that the time had come for change.

Scarn was probably the first of the Aether's Cross survivors to analyse what had happened to them during their incarceration. He, all but alone among that wretched band, had not been adversely affected by the period of stasis, but he observed closely those who had and perceived their weaknesses. And what he came to regard as their needs.

They need me, was Scarn's conclusion.

Before the stasis – before Wraith – when the west cliff of Aether's Cross had supported a thriving community of natural dragons, Scarn had been a storyteller. His skill with words had endeared him to the youngsters and, in later years, to many of the older dragons of the Cross. Before Scarn, stories had been merely a convenient way to occupy over-energetic infants – and most usefully to soothe them to sleep – but gradually the adult dragons who overheard his storytelling sessions began to be drawn into the tales of myth and legend. There was something compelling about Scarn, and whether it was the gentle tone of his voice or the skill with which he wove his words none could say. But they all listened.

His reputation secure, Scarn occupied a unique position in the Aether's Cross community. Under normal conditions, male dragons were duty bound to participate in the many and varied labours which living in such a precariously-positioned settlement demanded. The cliff was steep and prone to damage from weathering; food was relatively scarce; fresh water, though available in abundance, poured down at great velocity from the snow-covered upper slopes of the Low Mountains and so needed to be tamed before it could be conveniently stored. The days of the males were filled with terrace reconstructions, fishing expeditions, water cache excavations and the waging of the constant battle against erosion that characterized the terrain of the Cross. They kept the very fabric of the Cross together. All except Scarn.

He had to take his share of ridicule of course, especially from the younger, more aggressive dragons, but the dragons of Aether's Cross were nothing if not loyal, and the majority were fully in favour of Scarn's unique role. The females adored him, and even the least sympathetic of the generally chauvinistic males could not fail to be entranced by Scarn's easy manner and, of course, by his wealth of stories.

'Where does he get them all from?' they would ask, but no dragon really cared – they just wanted to listen.

If asked this question Scarn invariably avoided it, for the truth was that he did not really know himself. Many of the stories he remembered from his own infancy – he had a particularly good memory for narrative – but just as many seemed to pop into his mind practically fully-formed. It was strange, like magic. But Scarn, like his listeners, did not really care, because he enjoyed the stories too and feared that were he to delve too deeply into the wellspring which brought them forth then the spring might dry up and he would have nothing more to say. And with nothing to say, Scarn would be nothing.

Then everything changed. Wraith plundered the Cross, the canyon walls collapsed and the entire Natural population was imprisoned in a mesh of frozen charm. Outside their prison the world turned; in the stasis within, no time passed at all . . .

At first Scarn was surprised when, following their eventual release, the Cross dragons began to flock around him.

During the flight south from the crest of the world however he came to realize that their behaviour was quite natural. Whatever charm Wraith had laced into the stasis had robbed them of all confidence, leaving them confused and vulnerable – and desperate for a dragon to guide them. Scarn swiftly realized that he was that dragon. They were as infants again, and he knew how to deal with infants . . . At first he soothed these poor, regressive dragons with familiar tales, but as soon as they landed on Mahl the mood changed. The tales became grander, beginning to fit together, trying to describe greater things, greater powers. Quite soon, Scarn realized that within these entirely new stories was the power to describe the entire world, and once he had grasped that idea he could not let it go.

Soon the dreams began, and while his followers were clamouring for more of his increasingly elaborate tales Scarn was exploring, journeying both into his dreams and down beneath the surface of Mahl itself for what he knew to be there: the wellspring, the source of all the words he had ever spoken and of all the ideas which would ever be. And the day he found it was the greatest day of his life. On that day he was reborn, and even the surprise he felt when first he set eyes on that mighty source was nothing compared to the enormity of the ambition which overtook him. Here was a fountain of knowledge, in this place beneath the skin of the world was the single source of all that had been known and would be known. And it was Scarn's to drink from.

Ambition had followed at once on his initial surprise – that the wellspring was not a fountain of water at all.

It was a fountain of fire.

The chanting began shortly after sunrise and continued right up to the moment when Scarn appeared in the Flamehall. Dragons sang as they moved from cell to cell, sharing the good news of the day of revelation with their fellows, breaking off only to speculate nervously about what this auspicious day might bring for them both as a family and as individuals. Dragons wept openly as their emotions overflowed, then their tears turned to song and they rejoined

35

the chant, refreshing the constantly circulating melody with new rhythms. Lyrics never before heard in the Fissures slipped through the underground labyrinth like liquid fire, igniting dormant spirits and bringing light to those few dragons still untouched by the slow spiral of tension. Where the words came from none could say but all joined the song and all were glad.

Tallow wished he had Volley's company as he squirmed through the mêlée in search of Anchre. He hummed along self-consciously with the chanting, then smiled to himself to think that he was exhibiting the very nervousness he abhorred in these wretched, brain-washed dragons. *Volley could always pick out a tune better than me*, he thought wryly, *– better than most, in fact. What I wouldn't give to have him here right now.*

Just then he saw a familiar profile framed in a distant tunnel entrance. The dragon's snout and horns were silhouetted against pulsating red light illuminating the chamber beyond – the glow of some lava lake, Tallow assumed. Initial recognition became doubt as the dragon turned away, its features melting into the dark tunnel wall. Was it Anchre? Tallow thought so, but . . .

Anchre had always kept himself to himself on Mahl, and his companions had been happy to allow him to do so. He was, Gossamer once explained (for she remembered him from her early years on the cliff wall), one of the more specialized technicians of the former Aether's Cross community, responsible for the cutting of the primary water channels high on the upper cliffs. It was dangerous work, and Anchre was one of the few dragons who possessed the combination of brute strength and instinct necessary for this exacting task. He was not a native of the Cross, having flown in several summers before, but despite his solitary ways he was swiftly accepted into the community, for he contributed far more than he ever seemed to demand for himself.

Tallow took to Anchre soon after the Gathering. Solitary when living on the Cross, Anchre remained solitary now, as one of the minority unaffected by the stasis; later he would become unique, as his fellow survivors gradually drifted into the Cult. He was easy company for both Tallow and Volley, conversing little but appearing to enjoy their long flights – often lasting days at a time – across the turbulent landscape of Mahl. Together they surveyed the barren peaks, the shallow vales filled with steaming waters, the great cracks where veins of molten rock could be seen bubbling up from the underworld.

Anchre was first to volunteer for the reconnaissance mission and he seemed a good choice. One of his more unusual characteristics was his ability to *blend*: often a dragon might be basking for the best part of a day quite unaware that Anchre was resting only a few wingspans away. When asked, dragons found it hard to describe Anchre; from his dull brown scales to his bland face he was strangely featureless. Yet when Tallow looked hard into his eyes, there, masking the mystery of his past, was a cliff wall as impenetrable as that of the Cross itself. If ever a dragon was solid to the core, it was Anchre.

But now Tallow was beginning to have doubts. At first he thought it was the oppressive atmosphere of the Cult grinding away his confidence again, but as he pursued Anchre's fleeting outline – he was pretty sure it was Anchre – he changed his mind. Tails and scales rushed past him as he jostled his way through the crowd, being bounced painfully against the sharp rock walls. Chunks of pumice littered his trail as he made his clumsy way through the corridors, trying hard to keep his massive wings close against his body but failing most of the time. His half-hearted chant became a continuous stream of apologies as he stepped on feet and wings and slapped flanks with his tail. Still Anchre managed to evade him.

Perhaps that's just it, he thought. *Perhaps he's trying to evade me*. Suddenly, Anchre's willingness to participate in the mission felt wrong – an excuse perhaps, a reason finally to succumb to Scarn's influence. As he swept through the Fissures, Tallow became convinced that Anchre had been sucked into what he was coming to regard as the horror of the Cult.

He did not have to wait long to prove his theory. Up ahead, the narrow tunnel splayed out into a wide thoroughfare. Dragons marched down it three abreast, heading towards a sliver of bright, white light whose source Tallow could not make out. One of the splinter-talkers stood off to one side – with Anchre. The Cult official swiftly moved on, with a gesture to Anchre to stay. Anchre was breathing hard, looking back towards Tallow as though waiting for him. Even from this distance Tallow could see that his eyes were quite blank. His heart sinking, he approached his comrade and said cautiously,

'Anchre . . . are you prepared to finish what you have started?' He was reluctant to say any more. Dragons pressed close, among them splinter-talkers and first-contacters. Tallow felt sure that any display of hostility towards the Cult or Scarn would see the perpetrator transported to some isolated cell where his renegade spirit could properly be broken.

Anchre stared back at him, and even before he answered Tallow saw that the stone wall behind his eyes had grown even thicker and more indomitable. His words had no inflection, as though being spoken for him by some other dragon and relayed through his mouth.

'I have found the light, Tallow, I have found the fire. I rejoice that the day has come for us all.'

That said, with no fire nor joy in his voice, Anchre turned and joined the constant flow of dragons towards the far-off shard of light. Tallow made a brief lunge to stop him but checked himself. Further conversation would make them overly conspicuous amid this virtual stampede, and Anchre would only run from him again.

Which just leaves me, thought Tallow miserably. *And something very bad is going to happen any moment now.* How would he find Aria, in this crush?

In a way, Anchre's conversion – though he regretted it intensely – made it easier for Tallow, for now he only had himself to think about. Lowering his head and rejoining the chant, he entered the stream of dragons and made his way towards the light of the Flamehall and whatever unnatural ceremony Scarn had planned for this day.

In his own mind he chanted, *This time tomorrow you'll be clear of this forsaken place and flying free in the sky again, where you belong.*

CHAPTER 3

Fire and Faery

A vertical, silver plume of smoke spread upwards from the valley floor and into the still air. Clearly visible in the brilliant moonlight, it was a perfect betrayal of its maker's location. Stars danced behind it, their patterns disrupted by the beacon; the night was silent.

'Dragons?' inquired Vox, his wing raised towards the curling smoke.

'What else?' answered Smoke scornfully. 'What other creature could make a fire?'

'Then perhaps Wraith's campaign did not purge all lands of dragons,' Wyrm mused, half to himself it seemed. 'Yet this might be even more fascinating than it appears . . .'

Smoke was about to ask Wyrm quite what he meant by this when Vox butted in, 'What is this land, by the way, Wyrm? It's just occurred to me that I have no idea where we are. Do you, Smoke, my dear?'

Smoke shrugged. Though she was an accomplished pathfinder, the world-storm had practically wiped the face of the earth clean of all previous marks: now all continents were made anew and all lands were unknown. Until she could begin to get her bearings in this new terrain, she was as lost as Vox.

'I might guess,' she ventured, for although she did not know anything for certain she was beginning to feel old instincts pulling at her. Navigator instincts. Landmarks she knew were buried somewhere nearby; they called to her.

'Guess, then,' suggested Wyrm, a rare smile visiting his dark face.

'I'm probably wrong,' muttered Smoke, 'but I can't help feeling . . . well, that we're in the Heartland.'

'Nonsense!' chuckled Vox, but before he could continue the smile snapped onto Wyrm's face again and the young dragon emitted a short, barking laugh of his own.

'Quite right, dragon!' he cried, his voice ringing loud in the night. 'At least, as far as I can tell. This place was once the Heartland, or its eastern quarter at least. Far to the west the remains of the fabled Plated Mountain lie buried; this grassland is new. It has replaced what once was here . . . My guess is the Old Ice Peaks, or their foothills, at least.'

'Then Wraith did come here,' Smoke murmured. 'Or his army did, at least. It's said many of his strongest troops came from the eastern Heartland. He must have scoured this land. It should be empty of dragons now, surely.'

'Apparently not,' said Vox, indicating the smoke with an eloquent wing. A light breeze had found its way into the valley and the silver trail was beginning to fragment.

'Well,' came Wyrm's voice after a short pause. 'Should we investigate now, or shall we wait until first light?'

There was little argument. All were tired after their first day's trek across the open savannah. The sun had been hot and raw on their backs, forcing them to take shelter in the middle of the day beneath one of the huge, water-swollen trees growing in straggling clumps wherever the soil was deep enough. For Smoke and Vox it was especially hard work, since they found themselves walking far more than they normally would have done. Wyrm urged them to fly whenever they wanted to, and at intervals they did so, as much to exercise their wings as anything. But it seemed wrong to abandon their wingless companion to toil alone across the grassland and so for the most part they walked with him, feeling clumsy beside his natural, wide-legged gait.

Smoke had spent little time in Wyrm's company before this day, and she found herself thoroughly fascinated by him. Though wingless, he was an elegant dragon; his fore-limbs were proportioned more like those of a Charmed than a Natural, hence the ease of his gait on the ground. His scales were black, reminding her of Wraith . . .

'If we don't seem to be getting anywhere,' Vox whispered to Smoke as they turned lazy circles in the warm, afternoon air, idling on the breeze as they waited for Wyrm to catch up with them, 'we can always leave him to it.'

'Strike out on our own, you mean?' asked Smoke, nuzzling him briefly as their flight-paths coincided. 'Well, yes, I suppose we could, if we really wanted to.'

'Only if we wanted to,' echoed Vox, watching the slow, painful progress of their companion across the rich green of the landscape.

They passed the rest of the afternoon in Wyrm's company, walking with him towards the low ridge where, they had decided, they would spend the night. Shards of rock began to pierce the topsoil as they approached the undulating, grey spine. Beneath the spine, they hoped, were many places to shelter. By the time they reached it their hind legs were aching, and their wing-arms throbbed.

'I've been using some hidden muscles today,' gasped Vox as he finally flopped down in the shadow of a tall, over-reaching spire of rock. 'I don't get this tired flying, that's for sure.'

'Practice will help,' replied Wyrm distantly.

Neither Smoke nor Vox was yet used to Wyrm's swings of mood. He could change from being light and easy to glowering within the space of a single eye-blink, and seemed prone to long bouts of introspection. Woe betide any dragon who dared to speak to him then. It was mostly during these sessions that they had chosen to take to the air. Now, after bounding eagerly with his fellow travellers to the crest of the ridge, he faltered and retreated into himself.

'It's as if something's disappointed him,' commented Smoke in a whisper. 'Like he was expecting to find something here.'

'The rocks are nice,' panted Vox, more concerned to catch his breath and rest his weary limbs than in deciphering their temperamental companion's latest mood.

Later, when the twilight was at its richest and before the

moon had dusted its magic across the landscape, Wyrm rejoined the others, a wry smile on his face.

'If you can bear my company for another day, I think I can promise you some good eating tomorrow,' he said.

Uncertain of quite how to respond, both Smoke and Vox mumbled a few meaningless niceties. Then Vox asked Wyrm what he meant. Wyrm responded by inhaling a great draught of the warm, evening air. 'Can't you smell it?' he went on. 'Surely you can, Smoke?'

Smoke sniffed, cautiously at first but then with more relish.

'Mm,' she smiled. 'Water. Fresh water. And lots of it!'

'Freshwater fish!' exclaimed Vox in delight. 'I can't wait.' He craned his neck up over the outcroppings, intending to look out over the valley, but stopped short when several tiny bones crackled beneath his scales. 'Ouch. Well, maybe I can,' he concluded philosophically. 'I'll enjoy it all the more if I'm really hungry.'

Settling down beside his fellow dragons, Wyrm sighed, then smiled again. 'I know what will help take our minds off empty stomachs,' he announced suddenly. 'A story!'

Smoke and Vox exchanged a glance, then grinned at each other and huddled close. 'So long as it has a happy ending,' warned Smoke as they settled down to listen.

'Don't they all?' replied Wyrm with mock surprise.

Before there were dragons there was fire. Many creatures were born of fire in early times, and many knew the power of fire charm, but none was master of fire in the natural world until dragons came along. Not even the trolls could tame the heat in their veins. Not even the trolls.

When all dragons were charmed it was easy. Fire began in the Realm and dragons brought it into our world with the strength of their wills. There were contests between rival dragons: who could throw a fireball the furthest? Who could create the most brilliant of colours? Who could hold a flame in his claws the longest? Competition spawned skill and, eventually, wisdom.

Then came Cassel.

Until Cassel came fire was a phenomenon, a tool, a weapon. But Cassel took the flame and made it live.

When Cassel opened the Realm, he opened it not just into our world but into himself. He drew the fire with practised claw and absorbed it, letting it heat his blood as it had heated that of the trolls, but retaining the control which he had learned and they had not. Only then did he release it. Only then did he free it. Only then did he breathe *it.*

Fire-breather Cassel, the first of our kind to fill his throat with the flame. To his enemies his breath was disaster, to his friends it was beauty, for he could fill the sky with his song, painting with liquid flame the words he emptied into the air. Many dragons learned the craft from Cassel, and they in turn taught their young, until all charmed dragons held the power of fire charm in their throats, in their hearts.

And when Cassel died, it is said, the fire took his body from within, eating its flesh until only the scales remained, their joints ablaze. So it remained for a year and a day, and only after that time had passed did the fire finally die and allow the scales to part, drifting away like ash on the wind.

It is said that even today a dragon might find one of Cassel's scales buried in the soil, if only he knows where to look, but that such a scale, once found, can never be picked up.

For even after so many aeons they are hot still, and would burn whosoever might touch them.

Vox was about to complain that this was not a proper story when Smoke shushed him. 'That was beautiful, Wyrm,' she said, and she meant it. 'Thank you.'

'It's a favourite of mine,' replied Wyrm. He cocked his head thoughtfully on one side. 'But then they're all favourites, really.'

'Where did you learn them all?' asked Vox, inadequately stifling a yawn. He, like Smoke, knew of the strange dragon's reputation as a storyteller. *Such a mystery*, he mused as his thoughts drifted into sleep. *For a dragon who has known so little of life to know so much of the past. Where did he learn it all?*

But that particular enigma would have to remain unchallenged, for the moment at least. Vox drifted into a deep, perfect slumber, not to be woken until much later, when Wyrm first spotted the smoke.

*　　*　　*

43

The fire-maker – or makers – had gone by the time they reached the carefully concealed ashes early the following morning. Low light created a dusty, orange aura over the scar in the flattened grass where they had been buried. Though they looked around for clawmarks, or signs of passage through the deep grass, they found none. Only the hidden ashes.

'There's little enough we can do about it,' sighed Wyrm, obviously disappointed. 'If we press on we can reach the lake before noon.'

'He speaks as if he knows where he's going,' whispered Vox to Smoke as they watched Wyrm plod away towards the rising sun. Smoke shrugged.

'Perhaps he does,' she answered. 'Does it matter?'

Vox thought that it did, but he did not argue. Smoke seemed happy to tag along with Wyrm – indeed she was enjoying the enigmatic dragon's company in a way which made him feel quite jealous. When they had eventually taken each other as mates, Vox and Smoke had each healed a great wound in the other's heart: Smoke put memories of her brief liaison with Wraith in their proper place and Vox finally learned to bury his own, murdered Choliel. They were an odd couple, to be sure – Smoke neither Natural nor Charmed but somewhere between, and Vox a purple-scaled outcast, once Charmed, and wrongly accused of a murder the Black Dragon himself had committed. But with their pasts so closely intertwined, and their needs so perfectly matched, it was perhaps inevitable they should finally become joined.

But now? With the wounds mended and the bad memories defanged, was there anywhere for them to go? Had they used each other simply to move on? Vox saw the way Smoke looked at Wyrm and wondered . . .

By mid-morning they had reached the other side of the shallow vale and were climbing again, and shortly before noon they were rewarded by the sight of a glistening expanse of water. It shone a hard silver beneath a sky beginning to fill with clouds, a veritable ocean, so great that they could not see the far shore. Wyrm assured his fellow travellers that it was no ocean but an enormous lake, although how he knew this they could not imagine. They trusted him though, and believed him. He seemed incapable of lying.

'South of here lie the Towers of Nistor,' announced Wyrm. 'That is where we must go when we have eaten!'

Vox inhaled sharply, all fears about his relationship with Smoke driven from his mind by Wyrm's words. *Nistor!* Suddenly the past was not locked conveniently in the recesses of his heart but surging forward. The past, in the form of a dragon with scales like his own. *Purple.* Nistor! Wide-eyed and wide of jaw, a jaw which had definitely not been defanged.

'W-what has our journey to do with the Nistri?' he quavered, shrugging off the wingtip which Smoke offered to him. Wyrm raised his brows and studied his shaking companion.

'Hmm.' Wyrm's voice was dispassionate, like that of a judge. 'Yes, I did wonder how you might respond, Vox. That's why I waited until now – to give you less chance to back out.'

'Back out of what?'

'When you were outcast, Vox, when you were branded with the colour of the Nistri, how did you feel?'

Vox felt as though his scales were burning. Painful memories surfaced, memories of the dreadful day when the charm was drawn from his body and soul, when he was stripped of all rights and privileges normally due to a dragon of Covamere, when he was called *killer*. When his scales were stained purple. It was a long time before he answered. 'I felt . . . dirty,' he whispered. Smoke tried to hug him but again he shook her away.

'Of course,' agreed Wyrm reasonably. 'Wouldn't you like to find out more about the dragon tribe which first displayed the purple scale? Wouldn't you like to meet your brethren?'

'They're not my brethren,' Vox hissed angrily. 'And how could I meet with the dead?' He was shaking now, ashamed of his reaction but powerless to prevent it. Wyrm was shaking his head.

'Whether you like it or not you are linked to the tribe of Nistor, Vox. And there are many ways a dragon can commune with the past. Smoke, can you not convince him?'

'I don't know what you want,' she whispered. The

45

warmth she had begun to feel towards Wyrm had disappeared as if a sharp flurry of cold air had swept between them. All of a sudden he was an antagonist, a stranger.

Wyrm was frowning now, perhaps aware of the distress he was causing his companions. Yet something drove him on. 'The Nistri were not always evil, Vox, though they became so. South of this place lies their history, the memories they have left for us to see. I think your history lies there too. I think all our histories lie there.'

'We don't know what you mean,' replied Vox, drawing close to Smoke at last. Smoke pressed herself against him gratefully, glad of his support. Above them the clouds were gathering more swiftly.

Wyrm remained silent for a long while, his head bowed. The sky turned grey and a fine, warm rain began to fall around them. At length he looked up and spoke again. 'What it comes down to is this. I am going south to find the Towers of Nistor. You may come if you wish, but I shall go all the same. I do not know for certain what is waiting there, but I do believe that the future of all dragonkind depends upon what lies within. I want you to come with me, but I don't know how to ask you. I can only make words work for me when I tell a story, you see; I don't know how to say please . . .' His unhappiness was very apparent now. The rain coursed down his back, flattening the short, flimsy spines which ran its length and making him look lost and bedraggled. 'I don't know how to say please,' he repeated.

Vox appraised him for several eye-blinks then exhaled slowly. The bad memories had dropped away again, and although he was aware of their presence behind the veils in his mind he felt able to cope with them again, able to reason. 'I think you just did,' he sighed. 'I've no idea what you're up to, Wyrm, or even what we're doing following you . . . but I think we'll stick with you for just a bit longer, if you want us to.' Here he raised an inquiring brow at Smoke, who simply nodded her assent. Wyrm echoed the motion, then unleashed yet another surprise upon them.

'Did I tell you,' he announced, suddenly bright and cheerful, 'that I have a suspicion we're being followed?'

*   *   *

The nature of their alleged pursuer was, it turned out, no more definable than that of the mysterious, fire-lighting dragon who had gone ahead. All Wyrm could say was that he had sensed the gaze of some creature on him at intervals through the morning.

'Just on you, or on all of us?' asked Smoke.

'Just me,' replied Wyrm frankly.

'Sure of himself, isn't he?' came Vox's acidic whisper in Smoke's ear.

The rain turned out to be a welcome visitor, tempering the heat and freshening the air. Smoke and Vox pulled large numbers of huge, golden fish from the lake and they dined on the shore while the skies gradually cleared from the east, revealing a high afternoon moon. Then, as the sun emerged from behind the clouds, tilting from its zenith, they saw the smoke again, to the south now, a wavering trail of grey smudged against the line of the distant mountains.

'Looks like they're going our way,' commented Wyrm.

'Are we still being watched?' asked Smoke. Wyrm scented the air briefly before answering.

'No.' He moved away from his companions, his eyes fixed on the plain.

Vox held Smoke close as they watched. He tried to separate the thumping of their hearts and was unable to: they were beating in perfect rhythm. The swell of her body fitted inside his folded wing as though they were two pieces of a flawless puzzle.

How could I think we were not made for each other? he thought dreamily.

'Vox?'

'Yes, my dear?'

'Do you worry about us?'

Vox's heart stumbled, throwing the rhythm out of synchronization. He was about to bluster, to offer up a glib denial, but then he stopped himself: she deserved better than that. 'Yes,' he lamented. 'I see you with Wyrm and . . . and I don't know what to think.'

Smoke looked so crestfallen that he felt sure he had said entirely the wrong thing, but then a great smile broke across her face and she smothered a series of giggles. 'Oh, Vox, you idiot! Did you think . . . ? Wyrm is fascinating but I could never . . . oh, my dear! I love *you*. I thought you knew that.'

'Of course I did,' laughed Vox, holding her close. The embrace was warm and true, but he found that he was glad she could not see his face. The distant mountains seemed not so distant, and the trail of smoke which bisected them promised a fire he could not see, whose power he could not imagine. What lay ahead he did not know, but he feared it had the strength to tear them apart.

She wants me, not him, he thought as they set off into the afternoon. *But what do I want?*

They came upon the fire-makers quite unexpectedly, though by that time their fire was extinguished. The savannah afternoon began languorously as the dragons plodded laboriously through the deep grass ocean, the high sun baking the scales of their backs. The crescent moon was sharp and low, its shadow-half as blue as the sky. Beside it shone a star behind which trailed the faintest wisp of vapour.

'What is that?' asked Vox, spotting it suddenly.

'I don't know,' came Smoke's answer. 'I noticed it earlier. At first I thought it was one of the southern stars but I'm sure it wasn't there last night.'

'It was not.' Wyrm's voice cut through their exchange. 'But let us attend to more immediate concerns.'

Waving them low with his claws he crawled forward through the long, dry grass. Unable to prevent the stalks from rustling, he moved slowly, freezing often as he twisted his neck to try and see through the grass ahead. Presently he beckoned his companions forward. 'See?' he whispered. 'See how close we are?'

Smoke gasped as she parted a curtain of grass stems with her wing-arms and found herself looking out over a low cliff edge. Below them was a flat, dusty depression cut through by a narrow stream. Savannah grass crowded the perimeter of the bowl; sharp thorn bushes and patches of scrub sprouted from the grey dust, except where the stream ran. Here were lusher outcrops of foliage, including low shrubs bearing small, bright fruits. Saliva gathered in her mouth, and she was about to press forward when she saw the faery.

On the far side of the stream lay the remains of the fire whose smoke they had seen earlier. White ash stood proud of the darker grey dust and the area immediately surrounding the fire was littered with small bones and shreds of skin. Running water scattered the sunlight across the low vegetation.

The faery emerged from a hole in the far cliff. The smooth, grey wall was barely one tree high, its shadow still short beneath the afternoon sun. The interior of the cave was dark and gloomy, and as it walked out into the sunlight the faery seemed to glow brilliantly against the shadows within. Smoke inhaled sharply. Never had she seen such an aethereal being!

But then the faery turned and bent over, attending to the pile of cooling ashes. That initial flare of light diminished and Smoke could see what the creature really looked like, what it really was.

It was a faery . . . yet it was not. Though she had never seen one, Smoke knew what all dragons knew: faeries were small, translucent beings possessed of gossamer wings – wings which were not engines of flight but stores of charm. These elemental creatures manifested themselves only rarely in the physical world, preferring the rarefied environments of water and air through which they flitted practically unseen. Once they were virtually immortal, but the world had turned since then.

'It is a natural faery,' breathed Wyrm.

It was tall, as high at the shoulder as an average natural dragon. Like a faery it walked upright on two legs, leaving its arms free to work. But these were no faery limbs: they were crude, muscular things, dark and covered with hair. Sinews stretched at the creature's neck as it bent forward, scooping a hole in the dust in preparation for burying the ashes. Its moon face was hard and angular, a cruel parody of the faery's delicate visage. Bones seemed to jut from every angle of its heavy skull; bright, blue eyes peered out from beneath a deep brow.

The creature stopped, scented the air, glanced around. For

a moment it seemed to be looking directly into Smoke's eyes and she froze, but then its gaze travelled on and it bent forward again, completing its task of clearing away the remains of the fire and returning to the cave. Shortly afterwards it emerged once more, accompanied by many others – seven of them, two with infants clinging to their backs. The dragons watched the motley procession as it made its way up a gully in the far cliff wall and disappeared into the grass.

Wordlessly they crossed the dusty plain, stopping briefly to drink from the stream and marvel at the place where the fire had burned.

'It is no longer the dragon's place to be master of the flame,' commented Wyrm, his face hard.

Cautiously they entered the cave, curious to see what the faeries might have left there. Smoke followed her companions in through the low entrance, her heart thudding. This was no chance encounter, of that she was convinced. Half-Charmed, she could sense when magic was near and the dull pain behind her eyes betrayed its presence here.

Without looking round Wyrm nodded. 'You feel it too,' he stated, his voice flat and echoless despite the surrounding rock. Vox looked between the two of them, suspicious that some secret dialogue was being shared.

More bones lay on the dusty floor of the faery cave. Diligent with regard to fire, these creatures seemed unconcerned about the mess they left in their shelters. Rags of skin and oddly-shaped shards of stone were piled next to the bones. Fascinated, Vox examined the stones, turning several of them over with his claw. 'They have been worked,' he said at length, his voice full of admiration. 'Shaped, I mean. Do you think these faeries can still work charm?'

Wyrm shook his head. 'They have new skills,' he replied.

'Tidiness isn't one of them,' commented Smoke, regarding the piles of skin with some distaste. 'All this blood . . .'

'Oh, I'm sure they'll clear it up when they go for good,' said Wyrm airily, casting his gaze across the end wall.

'You mean . . . ?' started Smoke.

'. . . they're coming back!' Vox completed the sentence for

50

her, backing nervously away from the cave entrance.

'Come on,' Smoke urged. She did not want the faeries to find them here. 'Let's get out of here before . . .'

But Wyrm held them back, throwing his wing across their escape route. 'No! Wait!' he cried. 'These marks on the wall. Come and look at them. Look at them closely!'

Outside, the faeries had stopped at the top of the cliff wall and were gathered round some feature of interest they had found in the rock. Reluctant to stay but drawn back by Wyrm's sudden excitement, Vox and Smoke allowed themselves to be ushered down to the end of the cave where Vox pointed out a series of strange marks on the smooth rock. Awestruck, the dragons gazed in astonishment at the patterns, gradually piecing together the crude strokes which the faeries had formed there.

'Zirafae,' breathed Smoke, amazed. 'And that's a faery. What's that in its claws?'

'A branch?' hazarded Vox. 'This is remarkable. I've seen dragons scratch maps in the soil but this . . . and what do you make of this?' He pointed out a separate image, remote from the first collection of marks. The dragons agreed it was a representation of a hunting expedition. This second picture was more stylized, comprising a dark circle and a long, vertical scratch. The two were separated by a series of wavering horizontal lines. Above the circle was a small, white star. Vox grunted – this was rather easier for him to grasp.

'It's a map,' he asserted. 'But where of I haven't a . . .'

'It's a circle,' breathed Wyrm. '*The* circle. What Scarn wouldn't give to see this!'

'What do you mean?' demanded Smoke, but before Wyrm could respond their concentration was broken by a series of short, guttural sounds from behind them. They turned to see five of the faeries crowding the cave entrance, yellow teeth bared. In their clumsy hands they gripped long, straight branches to the ends of which were attached sharpened stones.

'Any ideas?' said Wyrm, brightly.

They glared at each other, these two groups of creatures, each uncertain of the other's intent. Although on the face of it the dragons were superior in strength, they were reluctant to attack. The faeries' stone-sticks looked dangerous, and the way the thick-set males were hefting them suggested a certain prowess in their use. So the dragons held back, eyeing their opposition warily.

The faeries were busy however. Behind the four males the smaller females were bent over something on the ground. The dragons craned their necks to see but there were too many bodies in the way. It looked as though they were bringing sticks, and one of the females was hunched over, moving her hands fast amid the growing pile. Suddenly there was flash of orange, then a tongue of flame leaped from the wood.

'Fire!' exclaimed Smoke, and the faeries recoiled at the sound of her voice. One of the males snarled and raised his stick. The dragons looked on in amazement as the faeries blew on the fire, encouraging it to burn. Though they had seen the smoke earlier, and observed the faery covering the ashes it had left, the full realization of what the discovery signified had not struck home. There were creatures other than dragons in the world who knew the secret of fire!

'They have inherited this from us,' whispered Wyrm, his thoughts mirroring those of his companions. 'The knowledge our race has lost has passed to another.'

Outside the cave the fire was blazing. The males retreated slowly, then turned and grasped the heavy animal pelts which their mates were holding out to them. The fur was dark and matted; the dragons did not know from what beast it came. Slowly the faeries began to fan the flames, and only now did their intentions become clear. Smoke billowed out from the fire: the wood was damp and gave off thick, acrid fumes. Swiftly the cave filled with the poisonous vapour and the dragons started to cough uncontrollably.

'We . . . we've got to get out of here!' spluttered Vox, cracking his horns against the wall as he blundered about, unable to see. 'They'll choke us to death otherwise.'

The entrance of the cave was just visible as a dim glow beyond the swirling clouds of smoke. Together they stumbled towards it, not caring what reception might await them outside, desperate only to rid their lungs of the smoke's searing bite.

'Wyrm?' cried Smoke suddenly, turning in the entrance as she realized that only Vox was at her side. 'What's wrong?'

Wyrm had not moved from his place at the back of the cave. The smoke descended around him, a black shroud across black scales, and he was lost from view. Behind them the faeries cried out in triumph.

CHAPTER 4

Smoke and Flame

Tallow drank in the spectacle of the Flamehall.

It was a cave, but one like no other Tallow had seen before. By nature uncomfortable in any underground environment, Tallow found himself instead positively inspired by the sheer vertical scale of it. Its horizontal dimension was not unusually large – the far side of the cave was perhaps ten tree-lengths away – but its height astonished him. The ceiling seemed so distant, it might as well have been as high as the sky, and down it reached, to a depth that gave even Tallow a tremor of vertigo. And still he could see no floor. The Flamehall was an immense, vertical fissure; it both soared and plunged; it was the very definition of the opposites high and low, and all the conflict and harmony between. And to its prodigious walls clung dragons.

Dragons of all sizes were perched on outcrops and ledges, dragons of all the colours allowed by the Natural palette – browns and greens, endless shades of autumn-red and evening-orange, ochres and umbers and piebald composites of them all. A living tapestry in full song. Their chanting combined to form a single, rushing voice which echoed first up then down the fissure, individual voices lost in the collective *sound*. But, as Tallow looked closer at the dragons nearest him, he was saddened to see that *all* identity was lost, that the eyes of each of these different dragons were the same: blank and soulless. The reminder was sobering; it dampened his awe. It was with a heavy heart that he took up position alone on a small ledge just to one side of the tunnel from which he had emerged.

What a place to fly! he thought as he turned his gaze back

54

to the cave, fascinated by the structure of this remarkable place. What a joy it would be to test the air currents here, to ride on the eddies, plunge on the vortices. He held his wings out, their primary elbow joints adjusted to tense the smooth membranes at a precise angle. By holding this position he turned his wings into delicate pressure detectors, sensitive to the tiniest movement of air through the chamber. Balanced like a statue, he closed his eyes and felt his surroundings.

Cool air above, but rolling down against the vertical walls as warm currents swept up from below. A constant exchange of pressure and temperature. Tiny draughts from flaws in the walls, stronger near the tunnels. Dampness within a low, wide tunnel mouth immediately opposite his perch. The gentle, palpable motion of the dragon song through the air. Hot at floor level though. Very hot.

He looked down but could see little. Scales of rock projected from the walls at intervals in the lower half of the cave, their arrangement conspiring to mask any view of the floor. They looked like caps of fungus on the inside of some tremendous hollow tree. Beneath them was a floor – the pressure waves told Tallow that – and it was unnaturally hot. A taint of sulphur mingled with the song, drifting up from the depths. *Volcanic heat*, he thought grimly. *Not the most stable of places, this Flamehall. I trust its name is not too appropriate.*

A rush of cool air disturbed his analysis and he snapped his eyes open in time to see dragon heads tilting in unison towards a gaping tunnel set higher than most. Abruptly the song stopped (Tallow's wings felt the slack vibration which signalled its end) and a hush descended over the watching dragons. Somewhere outside, high above, it was midday, but underground time had little meaning. Light filtered down as it did into most of the Fissures, through secret crevices, but it was flat and weak by the time it penetrated these depths. Silence accompanied the watery light; everything seemed thin and poorly defined. Waiting.

Tallow followed the gaze of the crowd up to a ledge immediately below the high tunnel and was unsurprised to see Scarn emerge. He had not changed since Tallow had last seen him – his grey-green scales still shone with a curious lustre and his honest, open face, with its deep eyes, still promised dreams fulfilled and fears thrown down. This, surely, was a dragon to be trusted. For a brief moment Tallow felt the visions he had experienced with Wist crowding the corners of his eyes, recalled the insecurities which had bunched around his heart as the splinter-talkers had later barraged him with their arguments, seeking to wear away at his self-esteem. For a brief moment, Tallow wanted to love him.

Then he saw Aria. She stood at Scarn's right wing, a striking figure set dark against darker rock. Her tail was long, her scales smooth and rich, but her face ... her face was quite, quite empty. And Tallow knew for certain that Scarn and all he had built here was evil to the core.

The realization was like a physical blow. Tallow would normally have defended the right of any dragon to make his or her own choices regardless of what their peers or society at large demanded of them. He himself had been something of a renegade, eschewing the safety of the forest floor for the wide, open sky; it was not for Tallow to pass judgement on the beliefs of any dragons.

But now, as he gazed up at Scarn he knew that this Cult was utterly wrong in everything it stood for, everything it preached. Not only did it deny dragons the basic freedom of flight but it emptied them of all identity and thus of all real hope. Whether Scarn's Last Circle existed or not, Tallow could not bear the thought of all these dragons giving up their very souls in its pursuit. Even were they to reach their paradise they would take with them empty hearts and closed minds. Scarn's so-called Golden Age would be an era of enslavement, will-less dragons playing out their leader's misguided dream against an alien and empty sky.

Is he just crazy for power, or is there more? Tallow wondered suddenly. *What can he possibly gain from all this?*

That question, like so many others, would have to wait, for Scarn was leaning forward, ready to speak. Tallow caught his breath as he saw the face of the third dragon on the rostrum which the ledge had become – it was the first-contact dragon who had shared the hallucinations with him, whose name he did not know. *But*, he wondered, *is it her?* for something about her seemed different . . . But then Scarn blocked his view and Tallow closed his wings, ready to hear the leader of the Cult of the Last Circle begin his oration.

For the first time since arriving on Mahl, Scarn felt that he was taking a risk. The Flame had shown him many things, but still it had not revealed to him the location of the Last Circle itself. That the place did exist he had no doubt, and he was wholly convinced that he would be greatly rewarded when he led his followers there, but time flew so fast and still he was no nearer to finding it. To have called this meeting was, therefore, a risk, for he had permitted the rumours to spread that this was the great day, the day of the unveiling, the day on which the great mysteries would begin to fall away revealing enlightenment and the pathway to salvation. Revealing the route to the Last Circle.

He prayed that this was indeed that day, and his prayers were sincere; Scarn genuinely believed every word he preached.

A risk, then, but a calculated one. Aria was the key, that much he knew. The Flame had brought visions of Aria taking flight with Scarn at her side. A cloud had enveloped them both and from the cloud had burst thousands of dragons. Reflected in Aria's eyes Scarn had seen a line of light moving swiftly through the sky. And at its end: a circle of fire. *The Last Circle!* On each of the last five nights this vision had visited him and its interpretation was clear: whether or not she was aware of it herself, Aria held inside her the directions to paradise. She and Scarn, together, were the future incarnate; together they would lead all dragons into the light.

Now she must grow into her new role, thought Scarn with satisfaction as he looked down upon the throng. *This is how I shall place my trust in the Flame, on this day of beginnings.*

The urge to pray was overpowering and, bending his head, he intoned, 'Guide me into your Flame of enlightenment. Make my words live, that all may be enriched by them. Show me the way . . . show us all the way.'

A rumble of 'yeas' pitched its way round the huge

chamber. As with all Scarn's prayers, it was not clear to whom, or to what, his words were directed. The Flame was Scarn's most closely guarded secret, and consequently most dragons assumed that their prayers were spoken to the Last Circle itself – or some strange personification of that mystical place. But dragons close to Scarn, like Wist and Lessen and Aria, knew of the existence of secret fissures which led from Scarn's private chamber. These initiates believed – though they did not know – that the real power behind their faith was nothing less than Scarn's Flame. It was a mysterious source of power and wisdom which none but Scarn was permitted to see. The Last Circle was merely a junction from which they would finally strike out into that Flame, when its glory would be revealed to all dragons, not just the chosen one. When the world was finally illuminated, it would be Scarn's Flame that would bring the light.

Scarn opened his mouth to begin, knowing that somehow or other the words would come . . . then he stopped. The Cult was agog, anxious to know what miracle their leader was about to perform.

Scarn lowered his head as if to stare down into the hot and shadowy depths of the Flamehall, then a slender smile lifted the corners of his mouth. Looking to his left he shook free the membrane of one short wing, then did the same with the right. A gasp raced around the chamber. Raising his head now he opened his wings fully and straightened his hind legs to lift his body clear of the ledge. His neck stiffened, then rolled back to press against his dorsal spines.

'He's going to fly,' came a frightened whisper from the gallery of rock below.

'It's forbidden,' blurted another anxious dragon.

'But he's Scarn,' hissed a third.

Scarn held his pose for a breath, two breaths, three, while every dragon in the chamber gazed fixedly on his immobile form. Then he relaxed again, folded his wings neatly against his sides and began to speak.

'Yes.' His calm, reasonable voice carried perfectly down through the cave, reaching every corner, every outcrop. 'To fly is forbidden. But our creed promises that one day we shall fly again, and that day is near, dragons, so very near.

In fact, I say to you now that *on this very day* there shall be some among us who will be called upon to fly!' He waited for the inevitable hubbub to subside before continuing.

'Dragons, I am especially humbled in your presence today because I know that before the sun sets I shall be able to reveal to you the knowledge you all yearn for.' More gasps, some ecstatic. 'First, I must formally introduce my companions.'

As Scarn ushered Lessen forward, Tallow saw that although the face was the same, the dragon was not. This had to be the twin sister of the first-contacter who had interviewed him: the features matched but the eyes . . . the eyes were totally different. Lessen's were the blank and soulless eyes of the Cult dragon, and Tallow now realized that the other's eyes (how he wished he knew her name!) had not been empty. His heart raced with the discovery – though he had not seen it at the time, Lessen's sister had retained some measure of spirit, of independence, and if she had done so then surely others must have done so too!

There is room here for rebellion, he thought icily, *if only we can free the will.*

Having introduced Lessen, Scarn turned his attention to Aria. Tallow watched intently, feeling revulsion as he saw what none of the Cult dragons seemed to see: the raw lust in the gaze Scarn cast upon Fortune's daughter. Yet Tallow saw too that Scarn was restrained, though by what he could not judge. Scarn was in awe of Aria – and that brought Tallow no small measure of satisfaction. *Her adores her . . . yet he is afraid of her too.* But Scarn was speaking again, and Tallow had to listen.

'The greatness of this day begins here,' Scarn was saying, brushing his wingtip across Aria's breast. Tallow shook with rage as he saw Aria close her eyes in response to his touch. *She is hypnotized by him*, he thought angrily. Scarn continued, 'Here, in the heart of this ravaged dragon is the pathway by which we shall all find peace. We need only look into Aria's heart to see the future.'

With a flourish he opened his wings again. His cue was picked up at once by the two females at his side, then more hesitantly by the rest of the dragons in the Flamehall.

Instinctively Tallow measured the punches of air as wing after wing was unfurled up and down the chamber's giddying height; these wings were unpractised, he noted, hesitant in their movement. Once more Scarn stood frozen to the spot . . . and lowered his wings again. He was teasing them, rousing them for some climax yet to come. Tallow wondered what that might be.

'And now,' whispered Scarn, his voice carrying despite its lowered pitch, 'do you want to see where the future comes from? Do you really want to see what it is that will drive us on to become great again? Do you really want to see the fire?'

His voice gathered in strength as sudden inspiration seized him and for the final time he opened his wings and this time he did jump from the ledge. Tucking his neck against his back, he launched himself down into the chasm, swooping past the astonished faces of the followers he had told to regard flight as filthy, perverted, a useless distraction from the inexorable process of enlightenment. Cries of horror merged with shouts of joy and all watched him dive into the heat that swelled from the Flamehall's depths. All watched him turn, flicking his tail against the rising thermals and striking high across the top surface of one of the rock plates which masked the floor from view.

Tallow leaned over to get a better view: clearly this dragon could fly, and fly well. From Tallow's vantage it seemed as though Scarn was flying over a huge mushroom, a semi-circular fungal canopy rooted fast to the cave wall. What was he planning?

Judging space, measuring the angle of the chamber wall against the rush of the air, Scarn accelerated towards the sheer rock face which rose from the base of the mushroom-like formation. Dragons called out warnings – could he turn clear in time? – until at the last possible breath he clamped his wings against the wind and executed a wrenching stall-and-turn which stopped him dead a mere claw's width from the wall. The vortex caused by his aerobatics sucked at a wedge of scree which lay balanced against the root of the blade of rock, bringing it thundering down. More debris followed, a veritable mountain of loose stone and wrecked

60

pumice, tier upon tier sliding and slithering down to form a growing mound on top of the curved rock canopy. Groaning sounds issued forth and a tremendous crack raced up the wall. With a roaring, screaming concussion the mushroom detached itself from the side of the chamber and crashed on to the other outcrops further down. One after another the layers of false floor broke away, each one adding to the momentum until at last the final one gave way and they all succumbed to a titanic impact as they met the floor of the Flamehall.

No floor of rock was this, however. Here it was that the Flamehall betrayed its true nature, and the origin of its name.

The falling rocks fell to a floor made entirely of fire. Heat rushed upwards unimpeded.

All was movement as tremendous gouts of flame belched up from the sea of lava that bubbled beneath the astonished dragons. Taboos were forgotten in an instant as they dropped from their ledges and pumped the hot, writhing air to climb above it and escape to safety. They hurled themselves into tunnels, scrabbling over each other in panic. Dragon bodies dyed red by the overwhelming glow of the sea of fire danced in turmoil, their frantic shadows made huge far up the face of the rock. Yet for all the desperation in the frenzied activity there was almost complete silence. Eerily, somewhere beneath the fear, there was faith.

Tallow was one of the few dragons who remained motionless. There was a clear tunnel exit a mere wingspan to his left down which he could escape in the blink of an eye if necessary. But he did not think it was necessary. The punch of hot air which had scattered the Cult dragons was the inevitable result of so much rock falling into the lava, but the lava had evidently been there for some time and there was no reason it should threaten them now. Soon perhaps, tomorrow, or next year it would rise, there would be an eruption and the Fissures would be thrown open to the sky, but Tallow felt that the odds were good for the moment at least. Instead he observed, and by keeping calm he managed to see Scarn's own return from the depths.

Scarn flew close to Tallow as he ascended, black soot

61

adhering to his underbelly scales as he stroked the air with tight, economical thrusts. He frowned briefly, meeting Tallow's eye for an instant and seeming puzzled by his unruffled air. Then he was gone. Tallow watched him round up his most reliable sentries and begin to gather together the scared dragons who were clustered high in the upper reaches of the Flamehall. Gradually they descended, fearful still but willing to trust their leader. So too did their companions emerge from the tunnels again, exchanging nervous, awestruck glances and taking up their former stations. Within a few hundred breaths they were crowded exactly as they had been before, gazing adoringly at Scarn, now perched once more on his chosen ledge.

Red light glinted in all their eyes, and the heat was a palpable presence in the cave, breathing and lighting with a life all its own. The lava rumbled quietly, crackling and popping as its level began to settle again. The slabs of rock which had fallen into it had almost completely vanished, consumed by the fire. A dense cloud of smoke rose from a cluster of boulders which had fallen against one of the walls, prevented from dropping completely into the lava by some hidden shelf; a tangle of wood was visible amid the rocks, the remains of a nest which some untidy dragon had thrown down into the depths rather than dispose of it properly. The heat blistered the timber and a series of tiny explosions ran the entire length of one of the larger pieces as a trail of knots gave way. One by one the logs and screens flared, throwing up brilliant orange flames and yet more smoke.

Up through the Flamehall the smoke drifted, now seeming to dissipate, now whirling in tight, sudden strands as eddies interfered with its passage higher, always higher. Somehow the column of smoke kept its integrity, refusing to disperse, and by the time it reached Tallow's level dragons were hypnotized by it, tilting their heads slowly as the dense, black twine filtered upwards before their eyes. Then it reached Scarn's perch.

Tallow felt the new breeze which turned the smoke round. As the head of the smoke trail drew level with Scarn, it curled over as though it had struck some invisible overhang, then billowed out and around Scarn and Aria, covering them like a shroud. It was too much for Lessen, who leaped screaming from the ledge. Even her hectic wingbeats did not disturb the cloud enough to drive it from around her companions. The moment did not last long but, for a breath or two, Scarn and Aria were utterly hidden from view.

Tallow felt his heart racing. Events had taken a decidedly unusual turn and he was worried. The truth was he wanted to get out of here, and to get out of here right now. But he had already decided that he would not leave without Aria. He could not bear to see her in the company of the vile Scarn for a single breath longer. As for the other wretched dragons of the Cult . . . maybe with Aria gone some might follow, or she might at least provide some clue as to how they could break Scarn's hold on them all.

He flicked his gaze up and to his left, seeking out what he knew had to be there. Rock, shadow . . . there! A tiny slit of light, barely visible but there all the same. Here was where the new breeze was coming from, the breeze which Tallow's wings had not felt until the fire had been revealed. The rockfall had shaken the upper walls sufficiently to open a crack to the sky beyond. A crack wide enough for a dragon to fly through. And none but Tallow had noticed it.

Before he could think further the smoke expanded, spreading out into the chamber and dispersing with astonishing speed. Three scant breaths later it was almost completely gone, only its scent lingering like a charred after-image.

Scarn and Aria were revealed, stanced exactly as they had been when the smoke had enfolded them, yet Aria looked somehow *greater* than she had before. The illusion lasted only briefly – indeed she seemed visibly to shrink as clear air reclaimed the pair. The expression on her face was unreadable as she announced to the dragons of the Cult,

'I have spoken with my son, and he has shown me the way.'

There is much that I do not understand, yet I must not fear ignorance, for only from ignorance can we journey towards knowledge. Ignorance is like a birth, a pure beginning from which we can achieve . . . anything!

These new faeries – they seem so rude, so ill-formed. What place

can there be for them in this natural world? Despite this I see in their eyes the promise of knowledge and, more importantly, the awareness of their own ignorance. They know something which we dragons do not know: they know they have a future. One day, they may be wise. I wonder – will they remember us? They want to kill us now, to choke us with their fire; are we simply monsters to their eyes?

But the smoke brings me knowledge in my ignorance! My mind expands, it fills the feeble prison of this cave and travels on the wind. I see the sky, the stars, the patterns on the rock, the glow of the fire. The flame!

I see my mother!

'Wyrm. A cloud surrounds you. Are you here?'

'You are with me, Aria, and I am with you. The cloud has brought us together.'

'You have the knowledge I need, my son.'

'I can offer you only my ignorance, Aria.'

'Will you not call me mother?'

'I use your name, Aria, for that is who you are. What is this knowledge?'

'Give me your eyes, Wyrm, that I may see it for myself.'

I close my eyes and then open them to see a lake of fire almost obscured by a great cloud of smoke. To my left stands a dragon – Scarn, I think – but more important seems the dragon perched on a ledge some way below. Tallow! He is looking up at a crack in the cave wall.

Free her! I call with my mother's mind, then she returns, her eyes filled with the patterns which the faeries have drawn on the wall of the cave. Filled with the map.

'Thank you, my son.'

'Do you know what this map is? Do you have the knowledge which I lack?'

'I do know, Wyrm, as perhaps one day you shall.'

And she is gone.

The cave, and the smoke.

Cries of pain from outside.

The air seared Vox's lungs as he burst free of the cloying smoke. Coughing uncontrollably, he spat what felt like tiny embers out through his mouth, a telling reminder of how cold his breath was – as was that of all dragons now. *But my fire was taken sooner than most*, he thought bitterly. *There is no ice like that in the heart of the outcast.*

The angry thoughts boiled in him, strange visitors, but before he could trace their origin he felt the thud of meat against his lowered horns. Raking his claws into the dust he stumbled to a halt and threw his head to the side, suddenly aware of the dreadful weight which it bore. Blinking away the floods of tears which the smoke had stimulated he stared out through a watery veil at the faery corpse he had just flung to the ground. In his haste to escape from the cave he had ploughed heedlessly into their midst, evidently taking them by surprise. The dead faery was a female, quite old as near as he could judge. A trail of straggling, red hair was pooled across the crude angles of her face; to Vox she seemed all bones, a rough parody of the aethereal faery form.

But dead, he realized in anguish. *And I killed her!*

Guttural cries broke from the ranks of the remaining faeries. They feinted blows against the dragon who had exploded into their midst but they seemed reluctant actually to engage him. They taunted Vox, slapping his flank with their blade-sharp sticks, snarling and posturing. One of the younger females bent to attend to her fallen companion. Water dripped from her eyes.

Vox backed away from the horde, horror at his carelessness overwhelming his instincts. To flee or to attack: neither seemed right and so he simply retreated, fending off the largely ineffectual blows as best he could. Suddenly Smoke's voice rang out.

'Leave him alone!' she bellowed, springing between Vox and the advancing line of faeries. They faced each other in the broad, dusty arena, with the afternoon sun glinting off dragon scale and faery spear. The two dragons stood close, reluctant to attack the creatures which had tried to choke them to death, for was it not they themselves who had been trespassing? And these were faeries: whatever their outward appearance, whatever changes nature had wrought upon their bodies, they were *faeries*, heirs to the magic of the Old Earth Dwellers, the Gentle Ones, the Makers of the Rings. Who were they, mere dragons, to assault them?

65

Smoke, ever the peace-maker, took a tentative step forward but was halted in her tracks by the largest of the faeries, a tall male with broad shoulders and a great swathe of chestnut hair which ran down his back to his waist. Tiny bones hung suspended from his ears and his face was striped with pale mud. His teeth were small and square, but he bared them as though they were the sharpest of fangs. Clearly furious, he grunted and gestured, his language quite alien yet clear in its meaning: the dragons were to leave now, before the confrontation brought more bloodshed.

'But our friend . . .' began Smoke, indicating the smoking cave entrance with her wing.

But the faery raised his spear and jabbed at her flank. The blow was hard enough to pierce the soft skin between her scales and a thin trail of blood trickled down her side. The faery stepped back with a hiss as Vox lunged towards him but Smoke herself intervened. 'No,' she said. 'Come on, Vox, we need to go. Now.'

'But Wyrm!' protested Vox as Smoke jostled him away towards the stream. The faeries stalked after them, encouraging their retreat with raised spears and hoarse cries.

'Wait,' answered Smoke shortly. 'There's still time, but we have to deal with this first.'

When they reached the foot of the low cliff which surrounded the flattened, dusty bowl, Smoke caught the eye of the tall male. They stared at each other long and hard. The faery looked from the tip of his spear to Smoke, and then back to his spear again, then lowered his weapon and grunted once. His low brow was ferociously creased, and though she could not read the expression on his strange, moon-like face Smoke fancied she saw there both anger and awe.

They fear us, she thought. *Yet there is something about us they envy.*

The faery leader watched as the two dragons spread their wings and ascended gracefully to the clifftop, disappearing into the grass. Then he turned to attend to the burial of his fallen comrade.

There were ten trees of clear space between the faeries and the cave.

Smoke and Vox exploded from the cover of the tall grass, wings spread and pumping the air. Dust lifted in their wake, obscuring the faeries from view, not that their eyes were fixed on anything but the pall of smoke still issuing from the vicinity of the entrance-way. The black cloud expanded before them like a ravening mouth. Smoke fanned her wings wide, opening a path through the cloud and simultaneously dropping behind Vox, whose wings were tucked tight and close to increase his speed.

Vox's eyes were tight shut as he entered the choking confines of the faery cave – he had closed them when approaching the corpse of the female he had killed. Instead of sight he was reaching out with a more subtle sense: charm sense, or what was left of it.

During his long years without charm, when he had survived as cripple and outcast on the periphery of Covamere society, Vox had been able to hone his charm sense – not his ability to work charm but his ability to detect it – to an astonishing degree of sensitivity. Like the blind dragon who discovers he has an enhanced sense of hearing, or of smell, Vox became a virtual antenna for charm. Now, even with most charm gone from the world, he was still able to feel its echoes where most dragons sensed nothing. And there was, he knew, much that was magical about Wyrm.

So much charm! he thought, astounded, as he forged his way into the cave.

It blazed, a beacon in the darkness. The faery map, the threads drawn through the surface of the rock ... and Wyrm! He glowed, a bold dragon shape thrown like a living sun against the smoke-filled void. Vox arrowed towards him, ignoring all else, even the sparks of magic which were flying from the marks the faeries had left – the wavering lines, the pale ring of chalk. He moved fast; Wyrm's form, bright though it shone, was slumped.

Claws extended, he crashed his wings open and executed a wrenching turn, grazing his wingtips against the cave ceiling. No room for error, not that he intended to make any; a faery already lay dead outside because of his clumsiness. Swiftly he gathered up Wyrm (black scales invisible, brilliant white light shining from within) and punched his way through to the fresh air outside. He had not taken a breath since entering the cave. Smoke followed him up into the sky, staying close on his tail but slightly below, just in case he should lose his grip. Vox's claws remained firm about Wyrm's limp body; there was no way he was going to let go.

As they passed back over the arena the dust began to settle and the faces of the faeries seemed to float upturned, gazing up at them as they crossed the sky. For that brief instant they appeared aethereal again, their crude features softened both by the haze and by the strange markings they had painted across them.

They like to mark their world, thought Smoke abstractly as the faeries passed out of sight once more.

They flew for longer than they would have liked, keen to put plenty of ground between them and the faeries. Finally they landed in the shelter of a small thicket of fat-trunked trees which, they knew, would yield both water and a sweet, sticky resin which was good to eat. There they bent their heads to the task of reviving Wyrm.

Tallow heard the sound of the other dragon's approach before he felt the soft pulse of air from the tunnel. Instinctively he bunched his wings, ready to jump but anxious not to miss any part of the proceedings if he could help it. Aria was speaking.

'What Scarn promised you has come true,' she cried, her voice loud but quite empty of emotion. Where Scarn spoke of feeling, she spoke fact. 'The power of the fire has revealed to me the way to the Last Circle. I have seen the path across the world. Now we can fly, dragons, and soon we will all be gathered into the light. Then our lives can truly begin; then we can at last be reborn.'

Tallow reviewed this last statement: was not the process of joining the Cult regarded as a rebirth? Surely these dragons did not consider themselves hatched anew only to go through the same thing again? No, something about Aria's words did not ring true. But before he could begin to puzzle it out Tallow was interrupted by an urgent whisper; the dragon he had heard a few breaths before had finally emerged from the tunnel. For some curious reason, he was not at all surprised to find that it was the first-contacter, the very dragon who had interviewed him the day before and tried to enrol him into the Cult of the Last Circle.

'Hello again,' she said, her voice low and nervous. 'My name is Wist, and I want to help you.'

CHAPTER 5

Seeking the Sky

Scarn took up smoothly where Aria left off. The Cult dragons were nervous and excited now; clearly this *was* the long-promised day of days. The volume of their chatter increased steadily and many of them were openly exercising their wings. Not until this moment had they realized how stiff their muscles had become, and how weak. Scarn was fully aware of this fact, and soothed them with prayers, urging the dragons to come to him one by one and receive his blessing. Soon a great trail of dragons moved through the Flamehall, some along ledges, others bravely hovering in the hot air despite the extra effort that required. Scarn touched each of them in turn, whispering reassuringly to them. As they turned away from him Lessen ushered them into the main exit tunnel that opened into the Flamehall, a broad corridor which led up into the dragons' living spaces. Aria stood at Scarn's side, her face blank.

Tallow watched the goings-on with interest and a certain amount of relief: clearly this process of blessing would take some considerable time, valuable time during which he could think and plan. Two dragons were foremost in his mind: Aria and Fortune. Instinct told him that Fortune and Gossamer might well have sensed the strange magic he had just witnessed in the Flamehall, and might even be on their way here now. He hesitated – it was a big assumption . . . but it tasted right, and he rarely had reason not to trust his instincts.

That something magical had occurred here Tallow had no doubt, and Aria had been at its centre. He firmly believed that if Aria could be rescued then other dragons would

70

follow her out of the Fissures, a belief which balanced his fear that he was singling her out and, by planning to rescue only her, abandoning all the others to their fate. *She's your friend's daughter*, he berated himself. *Of course she's important!*

Tallow looked down at the dragon who stood watching from the tunnel beside him. The first-contacter: did she want rescuing too?

'I'm Wist,' she repeated. 'Tallow, I think you are in a position to aid the dragons of the Cult of the Last Circle, and I want to do everything I can to assist you in that objective.' Her voice was clear and sweet, her words careful and considered. Tallow looked closely at her face – the same face as that borne by Scarn's assistant Lessen. But the eyes . . . now he saw, *these* eyes shone like gemstones!

'My twin sister,' confirmed Wist, nodding at her sibling. 'We differ in all respects other than our outward appearance. Most dragons can tell us apart however, although I am not certain how they are able to do this.'

Your eyes, thought Tallow, momentarily hypnotized.

'Your wings,' blurted Wist. She looked away shyly, suddenly seeming very young. 'What I mean is, it was your wings that made me think about what it was we are doing here. Scarn is a great dragon, Tallow, and he has shown us many great things, but I no longer believe that he has all the answers.'

'Who does?' asked Tallow, intrigued and enraptured. He was listening closely in an effort to detect any hint of subterfuge. After all, was this dragon not one of Scarn's key agents? What wiles might she be trying on him?

'Each one of us,' she answered immediately. 'Me, you, and Scarn of course. The Last Circle exists, Tallow, that you should believe, but this is not the way to find it. The sky is where we should be, not this underground gaol. Wraith kept us imprisoned for long enough; it is not right that another should do the same, however good his intentions.'

'Scarn seems to be mellowing on that score,' suggested Tallow, indicating the line of flying dragons.

'Yes, and that may be a good thing,' came Wist's abrupt reply. 'Now, may I help you, or shall I simply journey on my own?'

71

'Who said anything about journeys?' responded Tallow. 'And why should I trust you?'

Wist appraised the big dragon for a moment. He towered over her, sleek and perfect despite his tremendous bulk. 'I think you are a dragon who likes journeys,' she smiled, 'and as for trust, well, in time you'll learn why it is you are able to trust me. Because you are going to trust me, are you not?'

Again there was that sensation of being hypnotized. *Does she have power over me?* wondered Tallow, but when he pressed down the dizziness he found his instinct on this matter as strong as any, and he allowed himself a broad smile. 'Since you seem to know me better than I know myself, I suppose I'll have to. Now listen closely.'

Wist trembled as she made her way cautiously through the outlying tunnels. The confidence she had projected when talking to Tallow had been largely a bluff and now it had all but evaporated. What had possessed her to reject Scarn all at once, so forcibly? Scarn, the dragon who had pulled her as he had pulled so many from the near-coma which had enveloped them since the Turning; Scarn, who had chosen her to join his élite; Scarn, with whom she had spent many pleasurable nights . . .

He hears so much, but he does not hear the beat of his own wings.

All that he preached she believed, with one important exception: she no longer believed that dragons should be restrained from flying. This conclusion she had reached shortly after leaving Scarn this morning, and she had spent the rest of the time tracking Tallow down. That Scarn seemed now to have changed his approach and to be actively advocating flight made her nervous for a breath or two – had he detected her treachery somehow and devised this as some elaborate lesson? But as she watched the ceremony in the Flamehall she knew that his fundamental beliefs had not shifted by a single claw's width. To Scarn, flight was still evil. Necessary now perhaps, but still essentially abhorrent.

And that was something she could not agree with. Flight

was not something for dragons to use, it was something for dragons to *be*.

The rest of it she still believed devoutly: the quest for Last Circle, its promise of illumination for all dragons. She pitied Scarn now, for his own belief had evidently become an obsession. She prayed that one day, when she had finally reached the light, she might be able to turn back and save him. Until then she needed other dragons at her side.

She passed through the outer tunnels without incident and soon found herself scurrying towards a brilliant circle of daylight. As she had expected, a guard opened his wings wide to bar her passage, but as soon as he saw that it was one of Scarn's élite approaching he stepped back and bowed his head respectfully.

'Important work,' she muttered as she brushed past him. 'The Circle calls.' *Well, it's not so far from the truth!*

As soon as she was out of sight of the exit she stopped and, unable to restrain herself, spread her wings wide. At once a spasm of pain clamped down on her right shoulder and she nearly shrieked with agony. Slowly the cramp subsided and she tentatively flexed her wings again. Unused muscles protested, but as she worked them against the stiff southerly breeze they loosened deliciously. Blood warmed their rich red membranes and soon she felt ready to fly.

Briefly she was back at Aether's Cross. The steep rock walls of the Kull Valley echoed the terrain of her home and she yearned for the days when she had raced her friends through the cold, damp air above the rapids. She had not been the best flyer, but she had been one of the fastest. How she missed it!

She stood poised on a low outcrop of volcanic rock, waiting for the wind she knew would come. Cold air swept over her wings, lifting her, but not quite enough. Then . . . *now!* . . . came a gust more gentle but angled perfectly. It sped across the upper surfaces of her wings and at the same time curled more slowly beneath them. Her ears sensed the sudden shift in pressure and she flicked an array of bony blades forward from the leading edges of her wing-arms, reducing the likelihood of an early stall. The lift was immediate and exhilarating and before she could blink she was hovering at the height of a mature oak. A single flap doubled that and then she was above the distant ridge which was fragmenting the wind and soaring high in a stream of clear, cool air. She howled with ecstasy and dived towards the ground, pulling clear at the last moment to turn skywards again. 'Racing Wist' she had been once, and so she was again.

Presently she turned away from the Kull Wall, picking out the bearings which would take her towards Fortune's settlement, but no sooner had she fixed her position between two landmarks than she saw specks in the air which could only be dragons. They descended, gathering and landing, and as she accelerated towards them she closed her eyes in brief concentration, reviewing what Tallow had said to her, what she must convince Fortune to do. As she flew Wist imagined Tallow was at her side, the beat of his wings like the rhythm of the world itself.

The rush of the Raulla falls was an insistent voice behind Fortune's words as he called his friends together in the shadow of the Twin Bridges. Here, in the misty air above the drinking pool, two arches of dark grey volcanic rock reached out across the water like fallen trees fused with the land. As well as providing a challenging set of aerial obstacles through which a playful dragon might fly, the bridges were the open wings in whose embrace they met as a formal group. This was their Great Chamber, open to the skies but no less imposing for that. Spray laced the air and doused the rock, and the high sun scintillated off a million droplets of mist. If there was no magic here, then Fortune was no dragon.

He looked at his friends as they waited for him to speak, recalling their trials, their triumphs. Gossamer and Brace, still with such holes in their lives – he hoped desperately that their parents, Rarch and Jevell, could be saved along with Aria. Cumber and Velvet, such an odd couple, and so devoted to each other. They seemed old though, as if they had been through too much already; how they *leaned* on each other. Volley, looking lost without Tallow. And Ledra: what a revelation she had been. After the Gathering she had blossomed into a determined, caring dragon, quite the opposite of the vain power-seeker she had once been. Scoff, of course, dear Scoff who had guided Fortune so well through his most difficult times.

They looked to him for leadership, as so many dragons had looked to him in the past, and he was aware of a difference within himself, a new confidence through which he looked back at them. Though he was only eleven years old – still a whole summer short of traditional dragon maturity – he felt grown at last. *Drama pulls a dragon out of his youth*, he thought with a private smile. *And I've certainly had my fair share of drama!* And growth had brought with it a new sensation: power. But not the power of a dragon like Wraith or Shatter or Archan or Scarn, no, this power was what Fortune could only describe as *good* power. When he spoke about it to Gossamer she would smile knowingly and say, 'It is the Cloud that you sense, Fortune,' and he would shake his head . . . and wonder.

The Cloud had entered Gossamer's life at almost the exact instant her daughter had been taken by Archan. Tallow had taken up her belief – somehow he associated it with the thrill he experienced when flying – as had Ledra. Gossamer's faith in the Cloud was her power, but it was a power Fortune did not claim to understand. His own strength was, he felt, an inner strength born of experience; Gossamer's Cloud he perceived as an outside presence, an intruder into this world.

And when he said this to his beloved, again she would smile that secret smile and say, 'You'll see the truth of it one day, I know you will.'

Whatever its source, he could feel the good power at work now, sharpening his mind and tuning his wings. Instinct was scratching at him too, working with it . . .

'Something's happening in the Fissures,' he announced, his voice as cool and measured as the flow of the water down the steeply-sloping bed of the Raulla. 'I don't know if any of you can feel it, but there's something going on and the time has come for us to act.' The others automatically looked across at Gossamer for confirmation of this; she nodded, just once, and the group relaxed: if these two dragons agreed then there was no doubt this was for real. Then Fortune grinned and they relaxed further.

'You should know by now that I don't hold much with plans,' he went on. A chuckle ran round the small audience. He was about to continue when he saw Scoff squinting into the bright sky. 'What is it, Scoff?' he asked quickly.

'Dragon,' came the terse reply. 'Don't recognize her. Scarn's?'

They watched apprehensively as the dragon drew near, finally hovering over the Twin Bridges with long, confident strokes of her earth-red wings. Fortune found himself analysing the rhythm of her wingbeats, a technique he had learned from Tallow and one which could betray much about a dragon. She was a good flier, fast if not skilled in aerobatics, but the stiffness of her wings suggested a lack of recent practice.

Yes, thought Fortune, *they are forbidden to fly!*

The newcomer twisted her neck from one side to the other, picking her spot to land. In the end she alighted a short distance from them, stepping forward cautiously only after a long pause as she appraised each of them in turn. Her confidence in flight was transformed into nervousness on the ground, but with a shrug she finally gathered herself and spoke.

'You must be Fortune,' she said, walking straight up to him. He nodded, surprised: they had never met, and there was no way she could have known who he was. Her next statement went some way towards explaining her insight. 'Tallow described you. There's no mistaking you.'

'You've met Tallow?' Fortune asked carefully. The stranger nodded.

'My name is Wist,' she explained, 'and I've left the Cult.'

There were intakes of breath all around the group – no dragon had ever left the Cult of the Last Circle. Sensing their suspicion Wist went on, 'Tallow has found reason to trust me. He sent me with a message – he needs your help. Now,' she added forcibly, glancing back over her shoulder in the direction of the Kull Valley.

'How do we know you have Tallow's confidence?' asked Fortune kindly. With an imperceptible nod of his head he directed Scoff and Volley to position themselves behind Wist, ready to cut off her escape should it prove necessary. He saw her eyes flick to the side as they moved.

'He told me you would be suspicious.' Wist smiled disarmingly. 'You might be interested to know that I am very close to Scarn.'

Now Brace moved in. Fortune looked out into the sky. Was this some kind of elaborate trap? What Scarn would gain by attacking them he could not imagine, but fear had reared suddenly and he was unable to suppress it.

'Tallow told me to tell you,' Wist continued, 'that he has a plan. He told me to tell you this, because you don't like plans. He thought it might amuse you.'

Fortune exchanged a glance with Gossamer. Her face was unreadable.

'And,' concluded Wist, 'he said to remember the flying lessons. He said to trust your wings.'

Fortune felt his heart pause for the briefest of intervals, then it galloped with relief. 'Wist!' he exclaimed. 'You don't know how happy I am to see you! Now tell me everything that Tallow has told you, and quickly please – we may not have much time.'

Tallow's instructions were concise and they all listened intently. Critical to his plan's success was Tallow's ability to get Aria clear of Scarn, a difficult feat but one which he was confident of achieving.

'She'll struggle,' observed Gossamer.

'Undoubtedly,' answered Fortune. 'But Tallow can deal with it. He's twice her size. Will dragons follow her, Wist?'

'Tallow believes they will,' she answered cautiously.

Fortune regarded her closely. 'But you don't?' he suggested. She shook her head in agreement.

'Tallow wants to do it in full view of the Cult, but they are already leaving the Flamehall. That's why he wants us to hurry, before Scarn takes her back to the harem. But you must remember that it is Scarn they follow, not Aria, however much importance he has placed upon her.'

'How will Scarn react if we abduct her?'

Wist thought for a moment. Her face grew hard. 'He will be furious. He will try to get her back.'

'Then we'll just have to make sure he doesn't succeed,' replied Fortune grimly.

The sun was still high as they flew across the steaming lake. Ahead of them the Kull Wall was a low brow of rock, but that was not their destination. Tallow's directions were clear, so clear that some of the group had expressed doubt as to their accuracy.

'How can he be so precise?' Brace had protested as they had sketched maps in the sand under Wist's direction. 'There he is, stuck deep underground, telling us how to reach him from the air!'

'He knows what he's talking about,' Fortune had answered firmly. 'Tallow sees the way the world fits together, as you should well know, Brace. Rock is no more an obstacle to him than fog or blizzard. Believe me, he knows exactly where he is, and exactly how to guide us there.'

They flew wide around the entrance to the Fissures, rising up over the Kull Wall and into the icy domain beyond. Here sprawled the outer fringes of the great, nameless glacier which dominated the central part of Mahl, a slab of ice as great as a mountain whose voice ground out its mournful song in the deep dark of the night. If Tallow's directions were correct – and Fortune knew that they were – beside the nearest of the fingers of ice was a hidden fissure leading down into the rock, down into Scarn's underworld, down in fact to meet the outer wall of the Flamehall itself. Scarn's spectacular aerobatics had opened a crack in that wall through which they would enter and, Fortune hoped, escape with his daughter.

The ice flashed beneath them, throwing the sun back in waves of scintillating light and then suddenly there it was. Their shadows raced across the dust-blackened curve of the ice, accelerating and growing as they dived towards the fissure. Swiftly they passed into darkness.

Tallow was counting. Having not had the benefit of seeing Wist fly, he was forced to make a series of assumptions about her speed in the air. At peak fitness she would have been, he guessed, a remarkably fast flier, but a year under-ground would undoubtedly have taken its toll. Still, she was young and looked reasonably fit – she would make good time.

He imagined her wings in his mind, filling his thoughts with what he had observed about their shape and size, their texture, then he put them in motion, sending her flying across his imagination towards Fortune. He counted the strokes as she neared the settlement, then counted breaths and decisions as she presented Tallow's plans to his friends. He measured the beat of indecision, calculated the rhythm of mistrust. Then, when he was as sure as he could be that Wist had convinced the others to come, he counted the collective wingbeats of the group as they flew across the Kull Valley and veered west towards the secret fissure he knew would lead them down here. The longer he counted the more room for error was creeping in, the less he could trust the numbers in his head, but they were close enough. Tallow counted nearly as well as he flew.

They had found the way into the fissure; now they were descending, a straggling line of dragons; now they were close. Very close.

His mind continued to count as he scrutinized the ledge where Scarn still stood, graciously blessing the dragons who flowed steadily past him. He was over half way through the process now and the Flamehall was beginning to feel empty. Aria was stood next to Lessen, a little way to the right of their master, having fallen back to allow his ministry to take place. Lessen was rather too near for Tallow's liking but there was nothing he could do about it. Both dragons were relaxed, unsuspecting, and that was good.

Now. The numbers met in his head and he looked up at the hole in the wall. Stray shards of sunlight crowded through the gap, so dim that they could scarcely be seen. As he watched they flickered, a shadowy vibration on the high and distant wall. Despite the tension he found himself able to bask in the accuracy of his guesswork. Luck was a factor, of course, but Tallow considered that a dragon created his own luck, good or bad. Either way they were here, now, outside the opening. *And coming in.*

Tallow's wings opened like the petals of some tremendous flower greeting the rising sun. A torrent of air whipped around beneath their leading edges as he tipped himself forward off the ledge, the angle of his launch precisely set so that his forward motion generated the greatest possible lift. Air bunched itself under his outspread wing membranes and bounced back off the wall behind him to create a surging wave of pressure that thrust his body upwards and outwards even before he had taken a single stroke. As he powered his mighty wings down into that first, crucial beat he was so sure of his position in space that he kept his eyes tight shut, opening them only when he was clear of the ledge and accelerating up towards Scarn.

Heads turned and looked, carrying a ripple of motion back down the line of hovering dragons. Tallow seemed to fill the very air as he pumped his way across the short distance with three great wingbeats. Despite his colossal power, he flew in complete silence.

Scarn's puzzled face turned down to look at the large, tan-coloured dragon rising up before him. Tallow executed a tight roll to the left, tucking his wings close to avoid contact with the jagged ledge. Tallow expected Scarn to flinch, for he had angled his approach to make Scarn himself appear to be his target. But there was no fear, no retreat: just curiosity. This unsettled Tallow, but not enough to drive him off course. Lessen helped matters by cringing down against the rock, leaving Aria exposed and alone. She too was staring at Tallow, but her expression was not one of curiosity – it was one of naked fury.

The silence in which Tallow had flown was made to seem all the greater when the sound of his impact with Aria echoed through the Flamehall. With a resounding thud he grappled his hind legs around her body, knocking all the wind from her as he spun completely around in the air, thumping his wings as though trying to beat back an insistent enemy. The blow was shocking enough to completely incapacitate Aria without actually harming her; again, Tallow's calculations were measured to perfection.

Wheeling hard, thin lines of vapour shrieking from his speeding wingtips, Tallow poured all his energy into the climb as he lifted himself and the limp Aria clear of the ledge and thundered up towards the opening where his friends were waiting. The faint pattern of the light rays in that gloomy corner of the wall flickered again and he fancied he could see faces peering through. Fortune? And was it Brace?

He glanced down, half-expecting to see Scarn flying in furious pursuit, and found himself looking into the sun.

Searing pain burned into his eyes. Had he shut them a fraction of a breath later he would almost certainly have been blinded. He flew on automatically, his body carrying him upwards with sightless precision while his thoughts sprinted ahead. What was happening? The light dimmed beyond his closed lids and he squinted them open, fearing attack.

What he saw he did not immediately understand. Movement attracted his eyes. Far below, below even Scarn and the straggling line of shocked dragons, was the river of lava which flowed across the floor of the Flamehall. Except it was no longer confined to the floor. Tendrils of fire were lifting themselves up from the bubbling surface, faint strands like fragments of glowing spiders' webs. One by one they pulled themselves clear, entwining with their neighbours as they ascended and beginning to turn about a common centre. Swiftly this fiery vortex rose through the chamber, opening out at the top until it resembled a flaming whirlwind, spinning faster and faster, casting sparks and splashes of light across the walls as it came. Up towards Tallow it came and he opened his mouth to cry out.

But it did not touch him. It looped over, its mouth tightening again as it rolled over and down towards the ledge where Scarn stood watching with that same, curious expression with which he had observed Tallow's approach. Dragons scattered as it came, all except Scarn. Tallow watched aghast as Scarn opened his wings to receive the flames.

The instant the fire touched Scarn it vanished. There was a dull popping sound, like the breaking of damp twigs. Then there was utter silence. Tallow's wings continued to beat. He was nearly at the opening now; he could hear someone urging him on, telling him not to look down.

But he couldn't help himself.

Now he saw where the fire had gone. It was inside Scarn, illuminating his throat from within as he gaped wide and punched a great jet of flame up towards him. Scarn's neck was stretched taut, the scales dark against a maze of fiery lines which marked their joins. The inside of his mouth was a furnace. He was a natural dragon, yet he was breathing fire.

The flame, a tight, controlled line of brilliant orange, scorched Tallow's back as he ducked beneath it, then dodged to the side to avoid a second jet which came in rapid pursuit. Each time he tried to approach the opening Scarn launched another salvo, gradually forcing him down again. Tallow looked up helplessly; with each evasive manoeuvre his escape route drew further away. In his claws he felt Aria twitch and begin to struggle. He could not hold her like this for much longer.

By now all was pandemonium in the Flamehall. Dragons were fleeing in every direction, taking every available tunnel in their search for safety. Tallow cast his gaze wildly about, trying desperately to locate some other way out of this chamber. A ball of fire rolled across his right wing, burning the skin and throwing him even further down. Now he was almost level with Scarn again. He could see Lessen cowering in the tunnel behind her master. The air was filled with the scent of the fire, the bite of the smoke.

Then Tallow remembered something, something he had scented here earlier. He sniffed, inhaling a great draught of air. Scarn spat flame once more, its blast knocking Tallow lower still. Aria's wings opened, unbalancing the big dragon. He lurched towards Scarn, his own wings flailing as he tried to keep them both level.

There it was: moisture! A breath of warm, moist air coming from a tunnel entrance a little way below Scarn's ledge. No dragons had come this way. Why was that? Was it a dead end? Tallow made for it anyway: it was at least partly sheltered from Scarn's incredible attack. He peered into its depths and scented again, and this time his mind was made up. Fresh air – he was convinced of it. This tunnel led to the surface. This was the way out now. He glanced up, hoping to catch sight of his friends waiting at the other opening, but all he could see was the lacework of fire which Scarn was constructing above him, a flaming net which it would be impossible to breach.

Tallow paused for an eye-blink, hovering with powerful strokes of his wings, Aria thumping his breastbone with her head as she tried to shake herself clear. Then he decided – it was this or defeat.

'If you don't stop struggling you'll knock yourself out on the walls,' he warned as he arrowed towards the wide tunnel entrance. Aria continued to writhe for a moment, then her eyes grew wide as she registered the tremendous speed at which Tallow was approaching the opening. She screamed and tucked her head in. Warm, sticky air wrapped itself round them and then Scarn's fire was nothing but a circle of orange receding in their wake. Tallow felt the size of the tunnel in the pressure of the air which rushed past them as he flew through its generous confines, and he was cautiously optimistic that it would remain large enough to fly in for some time.

He wondered why no other dragon had chosen this as an escape route.

CHAPTER 6

Water in the Air

Fortune's view of events in the Flamehall was confused. No sooner had he balanced himself on one of the ragged series of outcrops outside the opening, through which he had to extend his neck uncomfortably in order to see within, than he was momentarily blinded by a great flash of orange light. Brace scrabbled at his side, pressing his own head through the gap and gasping in astonishment as he looked down into the burgeoning fire. They both looked on aghast as Tallow flew towards them only to be forced back down – he had been so close! – and then Wist pressed herself between them, her slender neck filling the cramped space almost completely.

'He's found another way out!' cried Brace as they watched Tallow's fire-lit form disappear into the tunnel, Aria's struggling body clamped close to his chest.

'Where does that way lead?' demanded Fortune, some detached part of his mind fascinated by the ludicrous position in which he found himself. *What if we get stuck fast in this gap?* he wondered. 'Does it lead to the surface?'

'I suppose so,' answered Wist after the briefest of pauses, 'but . . .'

'No "buts",' snapped Fortune. 'Take us to its exit, now!' He jerked himself free of the hole, no longer interested in whatever events were unfolding in the Flamehall. *Scarn breathed fire!* a small voice pestered, but it was drowned by a greater imperative. *Tallow is coming. He has Aria!*

'Shouldn't someone stay and watch the cave?' came Brace's muffled voice. Wist too had pulled herself clear but

84

Brace's head remained pressed into the cavity, his neck taut and strained. Fortune considered this for a breath.

'Very well.' He called over his shoulder, 'Ledra, you stay with Brace. Watch what goes on but don't get involved, do you understand? And don't move from this spot: if Tallow reappears he'll most likely come to you.'

Brace muttered an unintelligible reply as Ledra joined him, thrusting her pale neck in through the hole beside his. Fortune pushed awkwardly away from the precipitous outcrop to which he had been clinging and called to his companions who were waiting on the opposite side of the fissure. 'Follow Wist! And hurry – Tallow's flying faster than I've ever seen him!'

'In a tunnel?' exclaimed Velvet, opening long white wings.

'Not likely to stop him,' came Volley's dry comment as they launched themselves in pursuit of Wist, who had already rediscovered much of her former speed. Fortune allowed them all to precede him, turning at the last instant to shout to Brace again.

But Brace had gone!

Ledra's face gaped back at him, withdrawn from the opening and mouthing something he could not hear. 'What?' he cried, flying closer.

'He's gone inside!' she repeated. 'He just jumped!'

Fortune faltered. His mind's eye was filled with another time, another cave – the Great Chamber of South Point. There he had seen his dear friend Wood plunge in just such a way into the flames. Now it was happening all over again. His eyes burned with the pain of it.

'Go after him!' he commanded. Ledra nodded, just once, before throwing herself through the opening and into the darkness beyond. The darkness was illuminated by a flicker of red and Fortune heard a dull concussion from within the chamber. His heart screaming, he arrowed upwards in pursuit of his friends.

Scarn was in ecstasy. Not only was the Flamehall now truly worthy of its name, but the fire had at last chosen him as its vessel. Vanity precluded any surprise at this extraordinary turn of events but that did not mean Scarn was not overwhelmed by his new-found abilities. It was in a virtual stupor that he sent the flames boiling out into the chamber from his mouth, targeting the blasphemous dragon who had dared to take Aria from his very claws: Aria, who now held the secret knowledge for which he had searched for so long! The blasphemer must be punished – and Aria must be restored to her place at Scarn's side.

But as soon as he observed the interloper entering the wide Strokk Corridor the heat dissipated from his breast, replaced by an immense peace. Looking down and around he saw that the chamber was utterly deserted, and so it was upon emptiness that he turned his back as he marched purposefully down the tunnel towards his private quarters in the Fissures. Towards *the* Fissure.

He saw few dragons on his short journey. Those he did pass cowered back, dipping their heads and mumbling awestruck prayers as this miracle among dragons walked past. The harem chambers were crowded but even these dragons, who were closer to him than any others, cringed against the walls, not daring even to meet his eye. The sensation of power was intoxicating. Into the privacy of his caves he swept, descending towards the one place in the whole of the Fissures system to which only he had access.

His quarters were spare, undecorated chambers. Scarn slept on bare rock and desired little in the way of comfort. The caves and linking tunnels were lit by the usual cracks through which tired chinks of sunlight fell, all except one. This one – *the* Fissure – was different. Here no daylight ever penetrated, sealed as it was by a threefold twist in the approach tunnel which trapped all light from outside.

Scarn negotiated that triple turn now, winding his body through the tight spiral which rotated almost to meet itself then dropped alarmingly and turned again, this time in the opposite direction. His legs and wing-arms – their short membranes furled protectively – moved seemingly without his direction. His conscious mind was engrossed with the memory of the fire in his breast, his throat, the way it had spurted from between his teeth. Already he could feel it building inside him again, though he knew he was not fully recovered from that first salvo.

Yet I am a Natural! his reason protested, but it was beaten down by sheer joy. *The Flame has chosen me after all!*

So it was in joy that he entered the Fissure.

The rock here was as dark and craggy as anywhere in the system, but what transformed it was the light. Not sunlight, but firelight. Here was Scarn's wellspring, the source of all his inspiration, all his prayers.

The cave was long and narrow and so low that Scarn was forced to crouch. Across its far end ran a river of lava, a miniature twin of the one which he had revealed in the Flamehall and undoubtedly a tributary of that greater stream. The heat was intense but bearable, and the orange glow of the molten rock created a perfect backdrop for the exquisite beauty of the Flame itself.

A stalagmite erupted from the rough, pumice floor, its parent stalactite long since broken off. Its conical form had split, shattered by some subterranean pressure, and now from the crack separating the two halves there danced a brilliant flame of perfect blue. Almost to the ceiling it reached, drawn there by an invisible draught which fed it the vital air it needed to stay alive, the result of lightless fissures which reached even here. This was Scarn's greatest discovery, and his greatest secret; here resided all his faith and all his power. Now even more so.

He bent his head in brief prayer then lifted his eyes to the Flame, drinking its glory, feeling its heat growing inside his body. Orange lava filtered through the blue glow of the Flame, opposing colours cascading across his vision. He could hear the steady rumble and hiss of the two sources of fire, one so raw, one so beautiful. Both so powerful. Both his.

He had intended this moment of worship to be brief. Though there was no way the interloper could escape through the Strokk Corridor he must nevertheless have him tracked down and Aria returned to his side. Yet something kept him here, something in the flickering glow of the Flame ... Scarn looked closer, stretching his neck forward as shapes began to appear in the blue, no, *through* the blue. It

87

was as though the Flame were a portal through which he was able to observe . . . something. Some other place, he decided, as the image coalesced.

He was looking out through a cave entrance. Beyond, in the light, he could see dim, upright shapes silhouetted against the sky. Smoke billowed in front of him, obscuring his view and then suddenly the perspective shifted and he was looking inwards, towards the rear of the cave. All was tinted blue, a magical, moonlight hue. A dragon was slumped against the wall but it was not the dragon he was interested in – it was the patterns on the rock.

So it was that Scarn saw what Aria had seen. So it was that just as Wyrm had opened the way for Aria so the Flame opened the way for Scarn, and he saw in a single burst of insight the shapes inscribed on the wall of the faery dwelling. A pattern of undulating lines; patches of white, one of them a circle. The Last Circle.

Scarn watched, absorbed, learned. Learned the pathway to enlightenment.

The image of the map burned itself into Scarn's mind with such an agonizing pain that he cried out as if he had been clawed by some ravening beast. When he recovered himself he found that the Flame was a flame again, the images it had thrown at him gone except for the vivid tracks they had seared across his mind. He would not forget.

Nor would he forget Aria. Accompanying the revelation of the *way* was the realization that he no longer had need of her. Nevertheless he felt there was still a ceremony to be performed. The knowledge he now bore was too important for any dragon to carry other than himself. He must be the sole bearer now, with all others superfluous. Here his era truly began. Here others ended.

The Flame flickered, signalling its agreement and urging Scarn out of the Fissure towards the wide reaches of the Strokk Corridor where Tallow would even now be turning back in despair. Trickles of fire leaked from between Scarn's teeth as he departed in furious delight, adding their own glow to the mosaic of colour which illuminated his underworld.

*　　*　　*

Tallow reached the end of the tunnel in fifty sharp strokes of his mighty wings. Towards the end he was forced to concentrate ever more closely on keeping his flight-line straight and true, so close were the tunnel walls to his wing-tips. The final hundred or so trees of the corridor narrowed and curved gently to the left, forcing him to bunch his straining shoulder muscles and reduce his wingspan, an awkward manoeuvre for a dragon flying at speed. Thankfully Aria remained still in his grasp, clearly aware that any undue movement could be disastrous for them both.

When he rounded the last of the bends Tallow flattened his wing membranes wide and fanned himself to an abrupt halt, landing heavily on the rough floor of the tunnel. Aria tumbled from his embrace, scrabbling clear and pulling herself upright hastily. She darted to the side but Tallow blocked her way, his wings still open. She regarded him with hostile, guarded eyes.

'Don't think about it,' suggested Tallow conversationally, his breathing steady despite the flight.

'Or what?' retorted Aria, tossing her head.

'Or you'll be asleep the rest of the way. And you'll wake up with a headache.'

The tunnel ended abruptly, opening into a broad lime-scaled chimney. Daylight cascaded from its upper reaches; steam rose from below. Keeping his wings open he inspected this wide, vertical shaft. The air was hot and damp, full of tiny particles of mist brilliantly lit from above by welcome sunlight. A rumbling sound echoed in the depths of the shaft. Cautiously Tallow squinted over the edge of the chasm in an effort to confirm how deep it really was.

'I shouldn't bother,' said Aria. 'Oh, and you might want to stand back a bit.'

Tallow was about to ask what she knew of this place when suddenly the rumbling sound took on more menacing overtones. A huge billow of steam rolled up out of the shaft, wafting into the tunnel and surrounding the two dragons.

'Please,' cried Aria, fear falling across her face. She pressed against Tallow, trying to force him back the way they had come. He resisted for a breath or two then relented as he

89

saw her genuine terror. He took several paces backwards. Then they were both blown off their feet.

The shaft turned white as a piston of superheated water exploded up from its deepest reaches. The steam surged then retreated as the suction drew it up with the column of water. The noise was overwhelming, a sound like an avalanche compressed into a single passageway beneath the rock; it roared like a drowning troll. On and on it roared until gradually the sound began to abate and the solid wall of white took on flecks of blue. With no clue as to when the transition had occurred, it now became apparent that the water was descending again, crashing back down into the shaft and fragmenting as it fell. Most of it would be on the surface now, or floating high in the air above the blowhole, but some returned to the fires below, ready for the next eruption. Finally the sound dropped to a rumble and the far wall of the shaft reappeared, veiled by a scintillating cloud of tiny droplets suspended in a cloud of steam.

Strokk, the greatest geyser on Mahl, had sounded again.

Tallow blinked into the dissipating vapour, unable to believe he had escaped this far only to be foiled at the last. How could he escape safely through such a passage? And with a reluctant prisoner too?

Too late he remembered Aria. He whirled to see her gathering her dark wings and beginning her leap into the damp air of the corridor. Wrongfooted, he cried out his frustration as he stumbled on a treacherous ridge of pumice and crashed to the floor. Briefly she flicked her head round, her eyes flashing in the broken daylight. Then Scarn walked out in front of her. Behind him loomed the menacing silhouettes of guard dragons. Between them they blocked the corridor entirely.

As Aria rushed into Scarn's open, welcoming wings, Tallow groaned aloud. Behind him the rumble built again towards its crescendo as Strokk readied itself for another of its outbursts.

Scarn's guards prowled behind him as he wrapped his wings around Aria, looming dragon forms shifting in the

90

gloom of the broad corridor. Tallow finally resolved this mountain of flesh into six distinct shapes, each heavily built and broad of wing. He looked up: the corridor was high, but not nearly high enough for him to sprint over their heads. They would bat him from the air as easily as they might a drifting thistledown seed. No escape that way then. Behind him the water erupted again through the shaft on its recurrent journey to the surface. Surely that way was far too dangerous.

'It's a poor gamble,' came Scarn's voice, clear and loud in the wide tunnel. 'The surges come at random, you see, so there is no way to predict when the next might occur.' As if to confirm his words, Strokk belched forth another column of water even before the last had abated, resulting in a series of shock waves which knocked superheated air in a great pulse over Tallow's head. Slowly the vapour cleared again and Tallow saw, to his surprise, that Scarn was pushing Aria away. He watched carefully, while that detached part of his mind performed the feat which made him the champion flier he was – it counted.

Strokk roared again as Aria tilted her head upwards to see in Scarn's face not benevolence, nor that scarce-restrained desire which Tallow had noticed earlier, but raw anger. She cringed as he lifted his wing as though to strike her, but he halted the motion before carrying it out. Beads of water which had fallen across his scales steamed with a faint, hissing sound while orange fire flickered somewhere in his throat.

'A dragon may exist for many reasons,' Scarn announced suddenly. 'A dragon may exist to serve, for instance, or perhaps to lead. And a dragon may exist to tempt another!' This last phrase he spat out with unrestrained venom and it was on a tongue of yellow flame that the words rolled free. Aria shrank back even further, barely escaping the tip of the flame as it lashed across her face. The fire illuminated the tunnel and the faces of the guards were revealed if only briefly; all were impassive, without expression.

'Temptress!' repeated Scarn, striding forward and forcing Aria back towards the narrower part of the tunnel where Tallow stood like a rock. Now Aria was confused and upset, beginning to cry as she cast her eyes from side to side, seeking a means of escape, or perhaps an explanation for Scarn's peculiar behaviour.

'But I know the way now, Scarn,' she pleaded. 'Let me come back to you, I beg you. Just tell me what I've done and I'll . . .'

'What you've done?' thundered Scarn. 'For a year you have distracted me from the one, true path – the path to illumination. Well, no more, temptress! I too know the way to the Last Circle, and my knowledge shines with the pure light of the Flame itself. Your pitiful claims are dead and cold, evil one. Only my way promises the true enlightenment only the Flame can provide.'

'But I saw it,' wept Aria. Now her quivering tail met Tallow's outstretched wing. The big dragon shifted his weight as yet again the geyser roared behind them. His eyes did not leave the advancing Scarn. 'I saw it,' she repeated, 'I saw the Last Circle. I want to take you there, Scarn. I want to lead us all there. Please . . .'

'No more temptation!' bellowed Scarn, and at last Tallow recognized the source of his wrath. Whatever new knowledge the Cult leader had gained – and what it was Tallow had only the vaguest of ideas – had made Aria redundant in his eyes. *But he still desired her!* That hidden desire, that secret wanting which Tallow had first seen in the Flamehall had now become a monster fanning the miraculous fires in Scarn's twisted heart.

He has been saving her for this moment, thought Tallow, *and now he finds he cannot let himself have her. No wonder he's furious!*

These thoughts moved across his mind with the speed of a single wingbeat. Just as fast, the numbers moved through a web of calculation. Scarn was close now, all but blocking them from the sightlines of the guards behind him. Water crashed back down the shaft into the hidden shadows.

'Don't you touch her!' warned Tallow. The words were heartfelt but really he was playing for time. He was not ready to move, not yet. Aria held herself away from his wings, shrinking in upon herself as she found herself trapped between two dangerous dragons.

'Touch her?' sneered Scarn, leaning close and extending a wingtip to brush Aria's cheek. Then he withdrew suddenly, taking two steps back and pulling his wing away as though he had been burned. Smoke leaked from the gaps between his teeth. 'I would not soil myself. You are cast out, Aria, do you understand? You are no longer welcome in this family.'

'Then she's free to go?' demanded Tallow, seizing on a chance he had not expected. Aria was shaking now, curling up and withdrawing from events. That was good, he decided.

'Oh no,' answered Scarn at once, his eyes glinting with the flames which spilled from his open jaws. 'Quite the contrary, dragon. She, like you, will never leave this place again. After all,' he added, his face drawn in a mask of regret, 'we wouldn't want the journey to the Last Circle to become a race, now would we?'

Thunder. Water gouted up the shaft and retreated yet again. Tallow's mind was a blur of sounds and measures and guesses, a melange on which he was about to gamble the lives of both himself and Aria. Vapour all around, a warm cloud which enveloped him and lent him strength.

'The Cloud,' he whispered to himself.

For the second time that day he gathered Aria up with his claws. This time she was limp, compliant, and for that he was grateful. Sparks skidded into Scarn's face as Tallow whipped around on the damp rock and slashed his tail across the astonished dragon's exposed flank. With a cry of outrage and pain Scarn called his guards forward, but they stumbled in the narrower confines of the dead end, colliding with their master in their haste and knocking him forwards towards the place where Tallow had stood only an eye-blink before.

But Tallow was no longer there. Gripping Aria in a tight bundle like a great, dark egg beneath his breast, he swooped low across the floor then turned upwards, entering the mist-filled shaft of the Strokk with an agonized, hopeful bellow. The backdraught from his wings scattered the flames Scarn was hurling in his wake, taming their searing heat and throwing waves of steam across Scarn's face.

Then they were gone. Below the geyser screamed as it launched another jet of superheated water on its journey to the surface.

'After them!' howled Scarn, beside himself with rage. The six guards looked at each other uncertainly and then, incredibly, two of their number, the devoutest of believers in Scarn's Cult and loyal only to their master, leaped up the shaft in pursuit of the fleeing dragons.

'Here it is!' exclaimed Wist as they approached the blowhole. Water was pooled around it, steaming gently in the afternoon sun. Crystal surrounded the dark cavity in concentric rings. The plain which surrounded the waterlogged rock was flat and wide and seemed utterly tranquil.

Then the geyser blew. A jet of water fully fifteen trees high exploded before the flying dragons, scattering them into the ensuing clouds of steam. Gradually they flocked together again and took up a position hovering upwind at what they considered to be a safe distance. Hot rain fell to the east, blown there by the strong breeze. The sound of the geyser was like thunder.

'They'll never make it.' Volley's voice was deep and final. 'I've seen Tallow pull off some things in his time, but this . . .'

For once, Volley's silence was more eloquent than his rich baritone.

Tallow knew they would be followed. His eyes were closed. Here in the confines of the shaft his ears and nose were of more use. Pressure troughs and blasts of steam signalled turns and narrowings better than vision in the swirling turbulence of the steam-filled passage. For his pursuers he had little care – if they were stupid enough to come after him then they were stupid enough to die. The coldness of his thoughts scared him and he focused in on the numbers churning through his head.

It was going to be very close.

Beneath him the air bulged as the water exploded once more. He fancied he could hear screams from down there, but of course he could hear nothing now but the overwhelming sound of the geyser. The voice of Strokk. All subtlety of flight was gone now, all notion of pressure and finesse. Now it was raw power.

Aria weighed heavy in his claws, unbalancing him, the extra load drawing great ribbons of pain through his shoulders and back every time he expanded his wings. The air beneath their straining membranes was hot and angry now, but the pressure itself was helping to force them upwards. Strokk was spitting them out of its gullet on a column of superheated steam.

Still his eyes remained closed. He had no desire to see how far he was from the surface. That was the most dangerous guess. The rhythm of Strokk was erratic but rhythm it had, despite Scarn's assurance to the contrary. He had counted enough of its eruptions – he hoped – to make accurate enough measure of it. The distance to the sky was another matter, for that he could calculate only by matching his memory of the tunnels through which he had travelled against the pressure of the air . . . but an error the width of a sapling's trunk could make all the difference. Scalding air washed over his fleeting form. Thunder filled his head.

The thunder expanded, rushed clear of Tallow's mind with a deafening concussion. Vacuum sucked at him from every side as his eyelids glowed orange and yellow. A new wind pounded him sideways. The head of the geyser met the tip of his tail.

No dragon should have been able to turn as quickly as Tallow turned then. His watching friends swore later that there had been no transition between his headlong vertical flight and the clean horizontal line which took him clear of the exploding column of boiling water. His breastbone cracked against the lip of the geyser funnel with a dreadful sound that raced ahead of the roar of the water. Tiny bones splintered along the leading edge of his wings as he wrenched them outwards, flipping his body on to his back and rolling upright only when he was well away from the towering geyser. His wake drew streamers of steam after him, some of them stained red with the blood of his luckless pursuers. Into the afternoon sun he flew, Aria safely bundled still beneath his massive wingspan, slowing only gradually, turning back towards his friends in a long, lazy spiral towards the waiting group. He was breathing heavily, and for the first time in his life his wings were labouring out of rhythm, their beating jerky.

His smile was pained but broad as he approached and if his wings lacked style they still had strength, and his own unshakeable confidence took himself and his passenger down to the steaming ground. Fortune led his companions down to greet him, and all were torn between congratulating Tallow and welcoming Aria back to their family, for the look of relief on her face when she saw that she was safe and with dragons who loved her was one which could not be misinterpreted. Gossamer was first with the embrace, swiftly followed by Fortune and Velvet until the plain of the Strokk geyser was graced with a single, loving, dragon-mountain surrounded by a gently-descending cloud of warm, comforting steam.

Then Strokk erupted again, and this time it was not water which emerged. It was fire.

CHAPTER 7

Wings of Fire

Brace and Ledra too were witness to this second wave of fire, but from rather closer quarters than their companions on the surface.

It was in the glare of the first wave – the fire which had beaten Tallow back – that Ledra had finally caught up with Brace and hustled him down on to a secluded ledge. There they had lain together, panting and watching as the Flamehall had emptied. Presently Scarn's flames stopped, leaving only the flickering orange light from the glowing lava floor and the narrow shaft of blue which marked the place by which they had gained access to the chamber. Silence, but for their breathing.

'Tallow went down there,' whispered Ledra, indicating the wide mouth of the Strokk corridor. 'Should we follow him? Fortune wanted . . .'

'I've dragons to find of my own,' said Brace, the tremble in his voice betraying the conflict in his heart. 'It didn't look to me as if Scarn followed Tallow directly – we've still got some time.'

'What do you mean?'

Brace turned to Ledra, clasping her hard with outstretched wings.

'Long ago I made a promise,' he said urgently. 'And this could be my last chance to keep it. Will you help me?'

Ledra looked hard at this intense young dragon and found that she liked what she saw in his eyes. 'Yes,' she nodded. 'But you'd better be quick about it, whatever it is.'

'Rarch,' said Brace. 'Jevell. My parents' names. Shout them!'

So through the bustling corridors of the Fissures they forced their way, each crying out the names over and over again. They paid no heed to the curious looks they attracted, nor did they fear the attention of Scarn's guard dragons; confusion reigned in the tunnels now and the constant chanting of the Cult had been replaced by the buzz of fear. Scarn's fiery display and subsequent disappearance into his chambers had left his dragons lost and full of doubt. They clung to each other as they awaited their leader's next revelation, and cared little about two fools wandering in search of lost companions.

'Rarch! Jevell!'

On they hurried, passing in a great loop through the tunnel system until suddenly and quite unexpectedly they broke through into the Flamehall again. By now several dragons had re-entered the massive chamber and were circling warily, talking in low voices. Brace looked at Ledra in surprise, and was about to double back when a cry rang out, 'Brace!' It was Jevell, his mother.

She swooped down from the circling group, the orange light of the lava rippling across her wrinkled underbelly. Softly she alighted next to her son, saying nothing but leaning close, searching his eyes. Brace too remained silent, returning her gaze with an intense scrutiny of his own. Then, slowly, a broad smile broke across his face.

'It's really you!' he exclaimed. 'You're no Cult dragon, mother. You never were!' Jevell nodded enthusiastically. The same rich ochres and umbers which had once adorned Gossamer's scales shone from her gnarled hide in the warm glow of the lava. 'And father?' Brace continued excitedly.

But here his mother lowered her eyes. After a long pause she began to speak.

'It was your father who first came to Scarn,' she sighed. 'But then you knew that.'

Brace nodded. He remembered only too well the day his father had joined the Cult. They had argued, father and son, and in the end Rarch had simply flown away to the Fissures, his eyes cold and empty. Brace had pleaded with his mother not to follow but ten days later she had. 'I'll bring him back,' she had said. But, of course, she had not.

98

'I wanted to come back to you,' she groaned, 'but your father was . . . changed. They call it "first contact" – it was the first and last for him. I had to stay with him. I believed that a moment would come when he would open himself to me again; I had to believe that, or else I would have gone mad.' Her voice turned cold and bitter, and again she looked away.

'So I stayed too, hiding my lack of faith behind false prayers. The longer I stayed the harder it was to leave him – I couldn't bear the thought of leaving only to find I had missed my one chance to rescue him. Can you understand that, Brace my dear? Not a day went by that I didn't think of you and Gossamer. Aria is here, of course . . . but she is beyond my reach now. My granddaughter . . .

'The shell of your father remains, Brace, but I fear that the dragon you remember may have gone forever.'

Brace's tears were as soft as his mother's voice, but his wings and shoulders heaved in great spasms as his breath caught in his throat. His joy at finding his mother – and finding her unaffected by the almost universal compulsion to follow Scarn – had been utterly swept aside by this dreadful news. It was more than he could take in; his mind closed up like a flower at dusk. His mother sobbed quietly while, at his side, Ledra proffered a wing, then drew it back, uncertain of what to do or say. Temporarily the chamber and its circling dragons seemed to have disappeared: these three dragons existed in a void of sorrow.

Then, as Scarn vented his fury in the Strokk corridor, the backlash sent more fire blasting its way into the Flamehall.

Crimson fire lashed across the Flamehall. Flying dragons exploded into flame. Some fell, into the incandescent pit below . . . but those directly in the path of the flame seemed to *vanish*. The flames struck the far wall – and melted it! Over the rock the fire blazed then splashed backwards like a jet of water, bearing down on the dragons on the ledge. It was dimmed now but looked dangerous enough. Brace cowered down, closing his eyes against the heat. Ledra too was curled up, her wings forming a protective shell. Jevell was hunched over with her back turned towards the onslaught. The fire rolled across their backs, biting into their scales with its hot and magical touch . . .

There was a fourth dragon there, too.

She was lurking in the shadows at the back of the ledge. She had already been secret witness to the reunion between Brace and his mother but now she was witness to much, much more. Unlike the others, she raised her head and opened her wings into the rushing fire.

Above ground, the show of flame from the mouth of Strokk was brief but no less impressive for that. Vivid crimson fire leaped clear of the rock-swamp which surrounded the blow-hole, at its peak reaching fully as high as the water had scant breaths before. The noise it made was high and sharp, a keen whistling sound which cut the dragons' ears like ice. Then, abruptly, it stopped, flashing back into the ground in the blink of an eye and leaving only a thin wisp of orange smoke trailing in the wind. No further flames emerged, although the ground trembled momentarily as the fire receded. Patiently the dragons waited for the geyser to erupt again. It did not.

'What do you think, Tallow?' asked Fortune, raising an eyebrow at his friend. But the big dragon could only shake his head, wincing at the agony it drew across his breast and shoulders as he did so.

'Wouldn't like to say,' he replied. 'Something big has happened down there though, Fortune. That geyser was a mighty force – for it to have been stilled . . .'

'A mighty force,' echoed Fortune.

They watched in vain for the water to emerge once more, unable to articulate the fear its absence invoked. The sun was growing cooler now as it dropped towards the mountainous heartland of Mahl, its rays carving deep rifts into the uncompromising landscape of rock and ice, crag and chasm. It was Gossamer's voice that broke the silence.

'Your decision, Fortune?' she said simply, her white wings casting a long and intricate shadow across the crystalline plain. Fortune's answer made it clear what she was asking.

'We go back in,' he replied. 'Brace is there. Ledra is there.

Many dragons in there are in need of help. We cannot abandon them, not yet.'

There were nods all around the group, until a cackling laugh disrupted the murmurs of agreement.

'In need of help?' laughed Aria. Then her voice became suddenly low and full of hate. 'Yes, they may *need* help, but they don't *want* it. Scarn has seen to that. I shan't go back, not ever. My course is clear to me now. I can't stop you following me so I won't try, but I'm flying west, towards the Last Circle. I won't wait here to be drawn back into slavery.' So saying she spread her long wings wide and made as if to take off, but Gossamer rushed against her, battening her wings against her body and urging her to stop. Aria struggled, but only a little, as though reluctant to disobey her mother.

'Of course you must go, my dear,' soothed Gossamer as though she were talking to a tiny hatchling. 'And you're right, we will come with you. But there is something your father must do here first. Can you not at least wait for him? I suspect your journey is a long one – can you not wait just one night so that we may fly together, all of us?'

Fortune saw the conflict in his daughter's dark and troubled eyes. 'We could catch you up,' he began, reluctant to upset Aria, fearful that she really would fly off and leave them, this time forever.

'You don't know the way,' replied mother and daughter in unison. The pitch of their voices was identical, the matched expression of amused scorn worthy of twins. They looked at each other, shocked, and shared a nervous, investigatory laugh.

'Then tell me,' suggested Fortune, his spirits raised to absurd heights by this simple exchange between his mate and their daughter. In that instant he realized how little he knew his own daughter, and how precious was this opportunity to recapture the family which had been torn from him. Aria was a stranger, but in that laugh he had heard the sound of redemption, and it was sweet.

'I can't tell you the way,' answered Aria, frowning. 'I can only fly it.' She thought hard, the frown deepening. Then she nodded, a decision reached. 'I will wait until sundown.

101

Then I shall go west. I won't wait longer,' she added defiantly. Then she looked at her mother as though for approval and again Fortune's heart soared. *She needs her mother!*

'That's all the time I need,' he replied. 'Gossamer – you'll stay with her?'

Gossamer nodded. 'We'll wait beneath the Twin Bridges,' she confirmed. 'Tallow, will you come with us? I think you've earned a rest.'

Tallow had no hesitation in agreeing. Rather more difficult was the breaking up of the rest of the party.

'I want no more than four,' Fortune maintained. 'Cumber, because he's ex-Charmed and knows a thing or two about tunnels; Wist because she knows these particular tunnels backwards; Scoff, because he knew Aether's Cross and might know how to get at some of these dragons; and me . . . because I say so.'

First to protest was Velvet. 'You don't want me because I'm a female,' she scowled, 'but I can fly faster than most of you and what's more . . .'

'It's not that, Velvet dear,' interrupted Fortune kindly. 'It's just that I don't want too many of us going down there.'

'Yes, but . . .'

'No "buts" now, my darling,' said Cumber, bustling his mate away towards Gossamer despite her protests, 'but Fortune's right, because we really can't have too many of us blundering around in those tunnels . . .' His voice faded as he ushered her away.

'I always get left out of the real adventures,' grumbled Volley as he went to join his old friend Tallow at Gossamer's side.

'If you're late just head west out to sea,' shouted Tallow. 'I'll look out for you.'

'We won't be,' called Fortune as he led his small band towards the blowhole. The long shadows from their wings combined to form a single, elaborate entity which flowed across the harsh landscape like running water. They descended and the shadow drew near to them, breaking into its component parts as they separated to make their final approach.

'I hope this geyser's really gone quiet,' announced Cumber cheerfully.

Fortune doubted only briefly the wisdom of his decision to enter the Fissures through the geyser's exit shaft. He felt confident that this was the last place Scarn would expect to find them, if he were expecting them at all (though Fortune believed that somehow he would be); any lingering concerns about their safety in terms of the geyser itself were gone as soon as they penetrated the shaft.

It was ruined, simply. Scarn's fire, or whatever it was that had emerged from the blowhole, had utterly melted the sides of the shaft, causing them to sag downwards like resin. What power could cause rock to flow in this way Fortune could not imagine, for already it was cool to the touch. Conventional volcanic activity would surely have left the walls molten for some considerable time, and normal fire would scarcely have marked them. Something new then, something unnatural. *Something charmed!*

The melting rock had pooled only a few wingspans below the exit into the horizontal Strokk Corridor, effectively sealing the shaft. Whether water still broiled beneath this new floor the hovering dragons could not tell; they did not linger in the shaft, swooping one by one through the distorted oval of the opening and alighting in the tunnel beyond.

Here too the rock seemed melted. Normally rough pumice had been transformed into glossy curves of jet, smooth and shining in the dim light which had followed them down the shaft. Here and there along the length of the tunnel the ceiling drooped as though a giant had pressed his weight against it from above. Runnels of a strange, dark substance clung to the walls, looking for all the world like trails of hot, sticky sap, yet when the dragons touched them they found them barely warm and quite hard.

'Have you ever seen anything like it, Cumber?' whispered Fortune. His voice rang like metal off the bulging walls, echoing around the curve of the corridor.

'I have not,' came Cumber's uncharacteristically terse reply.

Their claws ticked along the undulating floor as they made

103

their way back along the route Tallow had flown, the only sound in a tunnel otherwise completely silent. Wist commented on this fact, for during her time here she had never heard it so quiet.

'There was always some dragon chanting or talking,' she explained. 'It's very odd.'

'Not really,' said Scoff. 'Dragons in tunnels. Fire in tunnels.' He paused for effect. 'No more dragons.'

'Do you really think they're all dead?' exclaimed Wist, unable to control herself. Her voice resounded, bouncing about their heads like a wild, flying thing, but she could not help herself. 'My sister is down here. And dragons I've known all my life.'

'I don't think they're dead,' cut in Cumber. His remark was not gauged to calm Wist but it had that effect nonetheless.

'Why do you say that?' demanded Fortune. A glance ahead confirmed that the tunnel was opening out: they were about to enter the Flamehall.

'I can't smell burned meat,' came Cumber's matter-of-fact reply. Wist was about to cry out when she stopped herself, clamping her jaw shut so hard that she bit into the end of her tongue with her teeth. Through her tears of pain she managed to say,

'Cumber, I'm afraid you're wrong.'

And they looked out into the Flamehall.

The light was quite different to when she had been here last, and to when Fortune had peered in through the secret opening. Indeed, that opening had now become a great gash running nearly the full height of the chamber and admitting a veritable flood of daylight, reflected in from the lower reaches of the canyon beyond. The fiery floor was gone, buried beneath an avalanche of fallen, melted rock as had been the waters of Strokk; gone too was its garish orange light. Every surface was black and shiny, smooth as ice, sculpted.

Fortune cast his gaze across the high walls, trying to identify what it was Wist had seen. Something made him uneasy here but he could not isolate it. The melting of the rock was strange, certainly, and disturbing in its own way, but there

104

was something more. He scented the air, remembering Cumber's remark.

The walls were striated, with great, flowing grooves running from top to bottom. The walls spread and pooled near the floor, as though too heavy to support their own tremendous weight; they, like the shaft of the Strokk, sagged. Impressed upon the grooves was a pattern of lighter shapes. Fortune regarded this: it was pleasing, he decided, like the shadows thrown by falling leaves on the ground.

Then he realized what he was looking at.

'By the Cloud!' he breathed. Then he bent forward and coughed violently, nearly vomiting as the horror of what had happened here dawned on him.

'Dragons,' said Scoff, grimly regarding the broken, leafy silhouettes on the walls.

'They were completely vaporized,' murmured Cumber with dreadful fascination, 'and these are the shadows left behind, the parts of the wall the fire couldn't reach because their bodies were in the way.'

Suddenly Wist opened her wings. Fortune made a grab for her but she was too quick, accelerating out into the middle of the chamber and whirling round, her neck whipping from side to side as she looked now high, now low, as though searching. He was about to call out to her, to try to calm her, when he saw that she *was* calm, surprisingly so.

'It's not as bad as it looks,' she announced, rejoining them on the ledge. 'I count only thirteen . . . markings. That must mean the majority are somewhere else.'

'The majority of the markings, do you mean, or the majority of the dragons?' asked Cumber. 'Because if you mean the dragons, you see, it's entirely possible . . .'

'I think what Wist is trying to say,' interrupted Fortune, smiling at his friend's astonishing lack of tact, 'is that not all of them were caught here.'

'But they might have been caught somewhere else,' countered Cumber brightly.

'Or they might have survived,' said Wist, her voice allowing no further argument on the subject. Cumber was about to pursue it when Scoff nudged him hard in the ribs.

'Let's stay optimistic,' he suggested.

'What? Oh, yes, I see what you mean,' blurted Cumber in an exaggerated whisper. 'Mustn't upset the poor dear, of course.'

'Why should I be upset?' answered Wist conversationally. Cumber shuffled his claws in embarrassment when he realized she had heard him. 'Every dragon I've ever known could be dead – why should I worry?'

'Oh dear, I'm sorry, I mean, well, what I meant was . . .'

'I know exactly what you meant, Cumber, and I appreciate your concern. But you must understand that my faith in the Last Circle brings me strength. Perhaps one day you too will understand. Enlightenment will come for all dragons, Cumber, even those who have died.'

It was Wist in the end who suggested that they make for the harem. 'It is the heart of the Cult, if it can be said to possess a heart. There must be dragons somewhere.'

The Fissures system did indeed appear to be deserted. They scoured the corridors and cells and all was silent and empty. Wist talked about the harem as they explored, and was rather surprised at the reaction of her companions to her explanation of its function, and indeed of Scarn's attitude towards the female dragons under his influence.

'It's barbaric,' exclaimed Cumber indignantly.

'It's the way it is,' shrugged Wist, feeling unexpectedly defensive. She motioned them to halt: they had arrived.

'You're sure there will be dragons here?' asked Fortune sharply as he peered through into the darkness beyond the low, arched entrance. Here, as everywhere else, the rock was smooth, black and liquid. There was certainly heat within, and he fancied he could hear a faint sound – breathing, perhaps. Or was it his imagination?

'Of course I'm not sure,' snapped Wist, instantly regretting her caustic tone. Fortune graced her with a brief smile which acknowledged the tension they all shared, then he ducked through into the harem. One by one the others followed.

The darkness was overwhelming, a crushing presence which seemed to have dispelled all air from the chamber. Wist hissed in surprise, for nothing felt familiar here: it was too hot, too dark, it smelt wrong . . . *everything* was wrong. They clustered together near the centre of the entrance chamber, waiting for their eyes to adjust to the gloom.

Gradually shapes began to appear. Directly ahead was a dim circle of red light – the opening through to Scarn's private chambers beyond, Wist explained. Around them the walls, dimly visible now, closed in, rising into a domed ceiling like up-reaching wings. They glistened in the dull, red light. Fortune was convinced that he could hear breathing now, pale and shallow, the breaths of many dragons. Then Scoff's voice broke the silence.

'Look,' he hissed. Then he elaborated, 'Up.'

They did so, and at first none could take in the sight. Fortune found his eyes straining to find contrasts in this red gloom, to find edges where all seemed flat and blurred. Gradually he began to see shapes in the patterns of light and shade which spread themselves across the walls and ceiling, until at last he could identify what it was that had spread itself across the entire inner surface of Scarn's harem chamber.

Dragons. Red dragons, clinging to the rock so close to each other as to form a living skin. At first he thought their redness came from the light, but soon he realized that this was not so: these dragons were actually red, every one of them – their scales, their skin, even their eyes. Red wings fell across red flanks, tails draped around neighbours' necks, horns interlocked, faces pressed close against one another. The rock was quite masked by these plaited bodies; how they clung there Fortune could not guess, but he was already beginning to accept that strange charm, new charm was at work in this underworld.

It was difficult to make out faces in this living mosaic but Fortune still found himself searching for dragons he knew, friends perhaps. As he scanned this dragon ceiling, these dragon walls, he sensed a change in the light – it grew swiftly darker then a long, hard shadow expanded across the arch of red scales. Claws clicked on the rock. A deeper, more guttural breathing joined the susurration of the throng. Fortune looked down and saw Scarn.

He stood, framed in the glow of the opening in the wall. Yellow light played across his back and flanks as though reflected from the moving water of a stream, but only when

107

he looked again did Fortune discover the source of the light. Scarn too was red, like all his followers, but unlike them he bore wings of acid yellow. They wavered, translucent and alive, those wings. And they were made of fire.

A stifled gasp at his side revealed that Wist too had recognized Scarn's transformation. Instinctively Fortune stepped forwards, opening his wings slightly to protect his companions. 'Be wary,' came Scoff's voice in his ear. Fortune nodded imperceptibly, locking his eyes with Scarn's. Scarn's eyes, like his wings, were yellow. *Like Wraith's*, thought Fortune with a shudder.

'Why have you come?' asked Scarn, his voice soft and reasonable. Fortune flinched; to hear such a pleasing tone from the mouth of what was surely a monster was somehow worse than hearing a snarl. Scarn's words stroked, they soothed. They might, Fortune judged warily, hypnotize.

'We came to find our friends,' he answered cautiously. 'Nothing more.'

'Nothing more.' Scarn seemed to ponder this for a while before replying, 'If they are here, you are at liberty to speak with them, of course. But do not expect them to follow you out of here.'

And what am I to make of that? wondered Fortune. Would any of them be permitted to leave? What powers did this new Scarn really possess?

'Brace!' he called, feigning confidence. 'Are you here? Brace? Ledra!'

All breathing stopped in the silence that followed, then Scarn's warm and flowing laughter rippled through the still, red air. 'Well, that appears to be that,' he chuckled. His fiery wings flexed, shedding tiny sparks as they kissed the edges of the opening. The rock smouldered where they made contact.

Fortune turned abruptly, bending his head to consult with Scoff and Cumber, both of whom had pressed close against his flanks. Wist stood to one side, transfixed by the sight of her master.

'You might enjoy a special place with me again, Wist,' announced Scarn as the others whispered hurriedly. 'Our family, as you see, has moved on, whereas I have not – at

108

least, not yet. You are a dragon as yet untouched by the fire and such a dragon might be considered, ah, desirable. Come back to me, Wist, and I will show you wonders you have never seen before.'

Wist stumbled forwards in response to Scarn's oily entreaties, only to find her way blocked by one of Scoff's outstretched, rainbow-hued wings. She shook her head and blinked her eyes frantically as though trying to free them of grit.

'Wait,' advised Scoff in an undertone. 'One breath.'

Fortune turned back towards Scarn and was about to speak again when a dragon neck uncoiled itself from the canopy of red scales above them. The light from Scarn's wings sculpted the dragon's features, unmistakable despite their recent change of colour. It was Brace.

'Fortune, let me speak.' Fortune tried to interrupt but Brace was adamant. 'Time is short, Fortune. Listen to what I have to say, and be sure to listen to every word, for I have considered them all with the utmost care.'

Brace's tone put Fortune instantly on his guard, for it sounded so stilted, so unnatural. Yet his eyes looked the same. Was this still the Brace he knew?

'Fortune, you of all dragons know the importance of home, of belonging. Well, here I have at last been reunited with my parents. Here again is Jevell, my mother.' Directly beside Brace, Fortune could just make out her face, the face which had reminded him so much of his beloved Gossamer when first he had seen it nearly a year ago. 'And here too is my father.'

Jevell's eyes, like Brace's, were sharp and alive, but those of Rarch were utterly vacant. *Living dead*, thought Fortune. A single glance around the chamber confirmed that most of the dragons clinging to the rock shared that look. The look of desolation. Were Brace's eyes really any different, or was it just wishful thinking?

'I have found my home, Fortune, here among the dragons of Aether's Cross. If you want to understand, just imagine how you would feel if you could fly again over your own beloved West Point and taste the cold mountain air of your home. We must stay, Fortune – and Ledra too, for she shares

109

my feelings. There is so much for us to do here with Scarn. Go, and we will stay. Do it for us all.'

Now Ledra's head descended from a mass of bodies almost directly above Fortune's head. Her eyes were almost closed but she nodded imperceptibly before retreating once more.

Brace's blunt, red face stared impassively at his friend's.

'Come on,' muttered Fortune, bustling his companions towards the exit.

'But . . .' protested Cumber as he was pummelled through the opening, 'but what Brace said back there. I mean, didn't you hear what he . . .'

'Enough!' barked Scoff, eyeing Fortune curiously as they stumbled into the corridor outside. 'Trust Fortune.'

'Wist!' called Fortune abruptly. 'Are you coming with us?'

Laughter brayed from the harem chamber. Yellow and red light flickered violently as shadows threw themselves across the floor. Dragon wings – Wist's – opened briefly against the light then folded again. Then there was a sudden flurry and Wist burst out into the tunnel, nearly knocking Cumber over in the process. Relentlessly, Scarn's laughter followed her.

'You were always cold, Wist!' came his taunt. 'Do you not wish the fire to enter you too?'

'Are you all right?' asked Fortune quietly as Wist dusted herself off; when she had done so she kept her wings closed protectively against her body. She shook her head.

'Let's get out of this place,' she said.

'Flamehall?' suggested Scoff. They all agreed.

Fortune's last glance back into the interior of the harem was like looking into a fiery sky: dragon eyes glinted like stars against a glowing red firmament. No individuals were discernible except one. At first he thought it was Brace, but just before turning away Fortune recognized the vague, inscrutable face of Anchre, Tallow's companion on that first sortie into the caves. Then he was gone.

Fortune fully expected Scarn to pursue them and so urged his companions to move at speed through the distorted corridors, but no pursuit came. They reached the Flamehall without incident, indeed without seeing any other dragon. To their left gaped the enormous crack which the landslides and blasts of fire had opened in the wall; a shred of sky was just visible at the top of the cliffs beyond. The cool draught was welcome and they spread their wings with relief.

'We can slow down,' puffed Cumber. 'They're not coming after us, you know. It's such a pity about Brace, though – he's clearly been brainwashed by that fanatic and his cronies.' He was surprised to hear Scoff and Fortune chuckle.

'Think, Cumber,' rumbled Scoff as they soared towards the gash in the rock.

'Didn't you listen to what Brace was saying?' explained Fortune. 'He did tell us to listen to every word, after all.'

'Oh, well,' blustered Cumber, 'some nonsense about home and, and . . . and he got it wrong. West Point, indeed! And in the mountains. Why, every dragon knows . . .'

'That we came from *South* Point? By the sea?' Fortune laughed. 'But every dragon *doesn't* know that, Cumber. And that's precisely the point.'

There was a long, tortuous silence as Cumber's thoughts caught up with those of his friends. 'You mean . . . it was a message? He's not been brainwashed after all?' Cumber shook his wings irritably. 'Hmph, well, if I were sending a secret message I would have made it a good deal plainer than that.'

Fortune smiled. 'But I think I understood him. As soon as I saw his eyes I was hopeful he hadn't been turned.'

'And the message?' demanded Cumber haughtily, still put out that he alone had missed the point.

'Simply this: he and Ledra are all right – and so is Jevell, I suspect. And he thinks they'll be of more use where they are than coming with us.'

Together they passed out of the confines of the Flamehall and rose into the canyon which would lead them up to the sky once more. Escape had been easy, strangely anti-climactic . . . but their curious encounter with Scarn and Brace had left them all puzzled and suspicious by turns. Suddenly it seemed that leaving was not simply a matter of striking out west over the sea: now there were friends abandoned and enemies left unthwarted.

Wist caught up with them and Fortune found himself

thinking of Wyrm. With Aria rescued, his grandson's fate was now, suddenly, of great concern to him. As the sky expanded around them Fortune felt the tug of the wind pulling him onwards but also *away*: away from Brace and Ledra and all the wretched dragons of the Cult, away from yet another temporary home ... and away from Wyrm. *Where shall we find rest?* he mourned. *Where do we dragons truly belong?*

Once all dragons had been charmed, but the world had turned away from charm and in doing so it had all but shaken dragons from its skin. Magic was still to be found, loitering in hidden pools and pockets, as powerful dragons such as Archan had already shown. But the power of the abandoned charm was slowly dying. And Scarn – what had he stumbled upon, this natural dragon who breathed fire and bore wings of yellow flame? Was it charm, or was it something else? Something new? 'Do it for us all,' Brace had said. What did that mean?

Fortune did not know, but as he flew to rejoin Gossamer and Aria, as he contemplated the vastness of the ocean which lay before them, he could not shake of his sense of abandonment. *Away*, he thought, the word sticking like a bramble in his mind. *Away*.

One dragon remained in the Fissures who had not been absorbed into Scarn's gathering at the harem. She watched the dragons as they flew out of the Flamehall; four dragons – three male, one female. The female: her twin sister.

Whether it was by sight that Lessen tracked their flight, or by hearing, or even scent she could not say. Her senses, like her body and mind, had been irrevocably changed by the crimson fire which had engulfed her. While the others – Brace and Ledra and Jevell – had cowered on the ledge she had allowed the fire to enter her and in doing so she had discovered the fire within the fire, the secret heart.

The fire had changed Lessen as it had all the dragons it struck, save those unfortunate few who caught the full impact of its blast. But her change was different. Although she had been reddened like the rest of the Cult dragons who clung now to the rock in the harem, she alone had received the blessing of the secret light. That coiling serpent had pierced her and threaded its way into her every vessel, her every pore, until her mind was ablaze with its power. While her thoughts exploded her body shrank, hardening and drying, shrinking back against the rock and eventually fusing with it. A dark ruby she became, set against the blackness of the chamber wall, an approximation of a dragon, a formation of crystal with a fire in its heart.

She was still Lessen, and in that flaming heart she still felt the insistent tug of her sister's life-force, that secret bond which they alone knew and neither could express. Yet now she was so much more, for inside her were depths immeasurable, including a way through to the source of the fire itself. Scarn's fire, she realized.

The fire licked at her soul, pleased at last to have a new channel through which to work its power in the world. First Scarn, now Lessen; together they would herald the new age of the world. First had come charm, then the world had turned. Now, now would come the fire.

PART TWO

FLAME

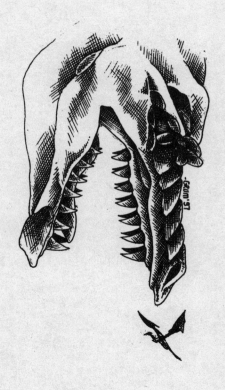

CHAPTER 8

The Pursuer

Smoke tended Wyrm with quiet fear; his body was
unmarked except with grime and soot but his breathing was
shallow and ragged. Clearly he had inhaled a huge amount
of smoke, enough to kill any normal dragon, but then . . .

Is Wyrm normal? She stroked a wingtip gently across his
dark brow, then sighed and gazed up into the clear, night
sky. The ring of fat, savannah trees soared into an enclosing
canopy, a circular frame within which the star-speckled
blackness was perfectly framed.

Vox knew that Smoke loved him, but he could not help but
feel jealous whenever she was near Wyrm. While she tended
to their enigmatic companion he wandered between the
smooth trunks of the mighty trees, seeking the source of his
jealousy; but there seemed to be too many distractions.

Not least of these was the loom of the mountains to the
south. Grey and broken they were, a random army of spears
and precipices marching across the horizon. Somewhere
amid that confusion stood the Towers of Nistor. What they
would find there Vox could not begin to guess, but looking
now at those angry peaks he felt nothing but dread. *If Wyrm
does not recover, we might never know.*

And then there was the matter of their pursuer. In the
drama of the events at the faery cave Vox had quite forgotten Wyrm's assertion that they were being followed; now
he himself felt the touch of another's gaze. Hidden away
inside the twinklings and rustlings of the night were signals
he could not ignore. Someone – or something, for Vox was
sure it was no dragon – was observing them, and from

117

nearby. Yet no sooner did he seem to pinpoint its location than all trace of the interloper vanished, only to reassert itself on the opposite side of the thicket. Several times he thought he heard a long, guttural breath, but the instant he turned there was silence.

Indeed, there had been silence for some time now, Vox realized. Cautiously he permitted himself to wonder whether their pursuer had given up for the night. Finding himself at the outer perimeter of the broad ring of trees he turned back wearily towards the central glade where Smoke and Wyrm lay, looking up into the starry sky as he did so. His eyes widened in surprise.

There, near the moon, was a star – perhaps the same star he and Smoke had noticed before, only now it was grown to tremendous size. Fully one tenth of the breadth of the moon it was now, a huge splash of light in the heavens. It trailed a tenuous, gossamer veil, a trail of glowing, white smoke – or so it seemed to be to Vox as he stared open-mouthed at its beauty.

'A comet!' he breathed, dredging the name from some infant's tale he could scarcely remember. No dragon in his lifetime, nor even his parents', had seen such a phenomenon; here was a wonder indeed! With head raised aloft and eyes entirely diverted from the trail along which he walked Vox made his way clumsily back towards his companions, calling out as he stumbled, 'Smoke, can you see it? Isn't it beautiful?'

A branch glanced against his brow and his claws crashed into something lying directly in his path; he toppled forward, bruising his snout on an outreaching root. He looked around sharply at whatever it was that had caused him to fall. Whatever it was, it spoke.

'Your companion is dying, dragon. Ocher will help him on his way.' The voice was scratchy and hesitant, and at first Vox imagined the tree itself had spoken to him; if a tree were to speak then surely its voice would sound like this – dry and rough like bark. Then he saw the creature.

It was pale, clad in creamy scales which glimmered in the moonlight. Its blunt body trailed swiftly into a long, sinuous tail. Two muscular arms sprang from its flanks, each tipped with long, silvery claws. Its eyes were silver too, and feature-less – bottomless mirrors in which Vox could read neither expression nor intent. But he did recognize the creature, for he had seen its kind once before, at the World's Crest. It looked just as he remembered it but . . . older?

It was a basilisk. For what seemed an age Vox goggled at the creature, scarcely able to believe his eyes. The basilisk stared back, although the direction of its gaze was impossible to gauge, so bland were its eyes: it might just as well have been looking into the heavens at the suddenly-appeared comet as returning Vox's gaze. The air about its gnarled face was clouded and Vox remembered tales of how a basilisk could kill with its breath. His heart stuttered and suddenly he was afraid.

'Wh-what do you want?' he managed to say.

But the basilisk, its appraisal of this particular dragon finished, tipped its head down and began to crawl through the short, dry grass towards the clearing. Vox followed it through the scrub, hoping that it was not making for his friends, but soon it became apparent that that was exactly where it was going. Spreading his wings he overtook the basilisk with a single leap and twisted upon landing to con-front it once more.

It has lost most of its magic, he decided, frantically measuring the feel of the charm which surrounded the creature like an aura – for charm there was, tenuous though it felt. *Has it lost its power to kill?*

'What do you want from us?' he repeated, pronouncing the words carefully and slowly. The basilisk's first, croaking statement had been as clumsy as its walk – perhaps it was having trouble with their language.

But the basilisk, ignoring Vox completely, simply waded on through the grass. Vox's desire to protect his companions – especially the injured Wyrm – forced him to assume this ancient creature was hostile; the ambiguity of its greeting had done nothing to assure him that it was not. So he planted himself squarely in its path and opened his wings wide. 'P-please wait,' he said, his heartbeat like thunder.

The basilisk did not even hesitate. With heavy, muscular sweeps of its long arms and sideways lunges of its tail it continued to lurch towards the dragon who blocked its way. Vox stood his ground, trembling – although the basilisk was much smaller than he, Vox feared it all the same. Deep inside the creature's metal eyes the stars – and the comet – glinted with cold, hard light.

Ocher's wrinkled head met Vox's belly. The impact was soft but irresistible. Without the slightest pause, Vox found himself slipping backwards through the grass, propelled by the basilisk's relentless momentum. He dug his claws into the dry soil to no avail; he lashed his tail around a tall sapling but the young wood broke and his tail was flung free, burned by the friction. A long trail of dragon claw-marks opened up in the leaf-littered ground: parallel grooves marking his unlikely passage. At once horrified and amused, for the situation was as absurd as any he might have imagined, he lunged and scrabbled in vain as the basilisk trudged on, apparently oblivious to his presence. Realizing the futility of his efforts he kicked free with his hind legs and flew backwards towards the clearing, pumping his wings hard and fast as he raced low across the ground.

Smoke was wide-eyed and alert as he landed next to her. 'Is that what I think it is?' she asked. Vox nodded. 'It must be the last one,' she went on, fascinated by its steady progress towards them. 'Don't you remember, one survived.'

'I wonder if it's still immortal.'

'I doubt it. Fortune and Cumber believed that Archan got her wish in the end. She is immortal now, they say, though without a body I don't know how that can be. No, I suspect this . . . this thing is as mortal as you or I.'

'That's as may be, but I wouldn't know how to kill it – I can't even move it!'

'Who says we should kill it?' murmured Smoke, taking a pace towards the oncoming creature.

Ocher emerged from the dappled shade into the eldritch light of the moon, the stars and the comet. It paused there, sniffing at the air with natural senses – and what little charm was left to it.

Once, when it had been immortal, it had owned millions of senses, millions of outlooks, millions of memories. Now only the memories were left. Fragments of charm still clung to it but Ocher no longer enjoyed symbiosis with the countless companion senses which had given it immortality. Those companions had held the power to recreate a basilisk's body if ever it were destroyed, to sustain it forever, however hostile the environment. But the Gathering had blown them away with a single stroke, the last great stroke of charm in the world, and now only Ocher remained, the last of the Deathless.

Deathless no more, the basilisk thought as it contemplated the light of the comet. *This body feels old now. Every day the death for which Ocher yearned comes closer.*

Ocher had wandered far after the Gathering of the Deathless. Suicide whispered its false promises many times, and many times Ocher came close to ending its new life. But always it pulled back from the cliff edge, it turned away from the white water. If it died, would that truly be an end? Or were its five siblings waiting on the other side of some cosmic barrier? So long – indeed forever – had Ocher lived as an immortal that it could not conceive of its life simply ending any more than it could bring itself to actually end it. And always a question chuckled mischievously in the back of its mind: *what is the natural lifespan of a basilisk anyway?*

But other mysteries occupied its mind, not least of them the unanswered puzzle of what would replace charm in the world. Nature had superseded magic to be sure, but *replaced* it? Ocher did not believe so.

Ocher had been witness to many Turnings, and in none of them had any power ever been destroyed. Creation was rife throughout all the histories, as was mutation, but destruction – true destruction – had never in its memory occurred. Its memory was faulty, to be sure, still afflicted by great swathes of darkness where the aeons had worn away its mind, but if there was one universal law which seemed constant through all the myriad changes the basilisk had seen, it was this: *nothing disappears.*

During the years running up to the latest Turning, the laws of nature had been formed, the newest creation of an ever-imaginative cosmos. Nature's predecessor, charm, had enjoyed an uneasy alliance with its soon-to-be-usurper right up to the moment of the Turning itself, when the Realm had separated from the world and magic had seemed to be sucked into oblivion in the blink of an eye. *But* not *into oblivion*, worried Ocher obsessively. *Charm cannot simply go. It must become something else.*

Nothing vanishes.

The magic was scattered across the universe now, broken and transparent, the laws by which it had been woven twisted entirely out of shape, but it lingered still in some form, an ethereal presence which Ocher could still detect at the outside edges of its consciousness. It was not the abandoned charm it was sensing here but rather a background murmur, a whisper through the sky. A memory, even. And soon it would become something new.

Ocher looked into the night sky and saw the comet blazing in the darkness. It looked at the two dragons standing protectively on either side of their fallen companion. The light of the comet thrust its way deep into the prone dragon's dark and shining scales, seeming to gather there, to focus. The dragon's eyes flicked open, locking with the gaze of the basilisk with fearless strength. Ocher began to move forward again.

Both dragons recoiled as the basilisk leaned over Wyrm. Smoke's flinch was one of real pain: a quirk of her half-charmed parentage had made her highly sensitive to charm. Vox too could feel the threads of magic which were flowing from the basilisk around Wyrm, and he prepared to repel the creature.

'No,' said Smoke, her voice sudden and loud in the still night. 'I think it's all right.'

'You think . . .' was as far as Vox got before basilisk charm enveloped their friend.

The magic was delicate, sensitive. Tiny spirals of light darted from the basilisk's outstretched claws, embedding themselves not into Wyrm but into the ground all around him. The long grass glowed yellow and seemed to retract briefly before redirecting the charm in the form of thousands of slender needles into Wyrm's body. Vox strained against

Smoke's open wing as the basilisk brought its face right up against Wyrm's, but still she held him back. Her expression was one of mixed hope and fear, for she was relying entirely on some hidden instinct, trusting that this strange and ancient creature meant them no harm.

The basilisk opened its cavernous mouth, revealing silver fangs.

Throughout the basilisk's approach Wyrm had kept his eyes wide open, tracking the creature's every move. Now he too opened his mouth, and closed his eyes. Basilisk kissed dragon.

Ocher inhaled slowly, a long, deep breath which pulled air not only from Wyrm's lungs but from all around the clearing. Vox and Smoke dug their claws into the ground as a flurry of dust and litter scattered past them. The giant trees swayed inwards, their mighty trunks creaking and groaning in protest. Wyrm's body jerked and a spasm ran down his flanks, then he slumped again and lay very still. There was an audible pop as the basilisk separated its mouth from that of the dragon. The wind dropped as suddenly as it had begun. The basilisk sat back on its coiled tail and regarded Vox and Smoke with a baleful glare.

'Ocher,' it announced, its voice dry as sand.

As if on cue Wyrm coughed and lurched up on to his claws. He spat cloudy fluid on to the ground, then turned bright-eyed to face his companions.

'Well,' he announced, 'I suppose we might call that a spectacular recovery!'

Even the brilliance of the rising sun could not wholly extinguish the light of the comet. Long shadows lay across the motionless forms of Wyrm and Ocher; dragon and basilisk lay together in low, creeping mist, watched by their two dragon companions. The air was dusty and substantial, and Smoke had to suppress an urge to take a bite out of it, so nutritious did it smell.

'Are you awake?' she asked, nudging Vox in the ribs. He grunted, waking from his doze.

'What?'

'The air – it's wonderful. What a fabulous morning!'

Vox sniffed unenthusiastically and offered a non-committal shake of his head. 'I suppose so. I wonder what they've been talking about all night.'

Immediately after the miraculous healing, Wyrm and Ocher had entered into a tight huddle. Muttered words had drifted out but Vox and Smoke had not lingered – they knew when they were not wanted. They had retreated to the shelter of the trees, leaving dragon and basilisk to talk the night away. Now, in the rich, morning light, they watched as friend and strange newcomer turned their heads simultaneously in their direction. Wyrm stretched, arching his back against the stiffness which had set in, and then they both made their way through the shadow-lines to where Vox and Smoke were waiting.

'Are you . . . are you all right?' asked Smoke, reaching her wing out to Wyrm. She stopped short, afraid to touch him.

'Never better. Ocher will be travelling with us now.'

Vox grimaced, then looked pleadingly at Smoke, who just smiled and shrugged.

'Our destination?' she prompted.

'Remains unchanged.' Wyrm nodded towards the west. 'The Towers of Nistor. Ocher can help us to find them: it has been there before.'

Vox and Smoke regarded the pale creature, expecting a contribution to the conversation, but the basilisk remained utterly inscrutable. In its eyes the comet flew high and white in the brightening sky.

They breakfasted on a crop of tubers which Ocher dug up from the base of one of the huge trees. A sweet, fleshy fungus which clung beneath the lowest branches refreshed their palates after the knotty textures of the vegetables; Ocher's final surprise came when it slashed a claw through the thick bark (Smoke shuddered as she saw the immense strength of the beast), unleashing a flood of water stored within. It gathered in the trench from which they had dug the tubers, creating a temporary waterhole which was more than sufficient to slake their thirst. Slowly the water drained away into the hard-packed soil, and as one they turned their heads west.

124

'The mountains are not what they seem,' announced Wyrm. 'In fact, if Ocher is to be believed, they are not mountains at all but an optical illusion.'

'What do you mean?' asked Smoke, intrigued. But Wyrm only smiled.

'Let's find out, shall we?'

The trek was much shorter than they had anticipated. The savannah swiftly gave way to dried mud, which in turn yielded to the cracked bed of a great salt lake. It extended as far as they could see to each side, but was bounded ahead by a long line of salt ridges. The ridges were large to be sure – the tallest was surely thirty trees high at its peak – but mountains they were not.

'So this is your optical illusion,' commented Smoke as they picked their way across this narrow ribbon of land. The ground was quite flat except for the broad hexagonal mesh of ridges which patterned its surface, from which their claws chipped tiny shards of hardened cement.

'When the rains come,' explained Wyrm, 'this whole area is awash, if only briefly. When the sun dries it out again the salt contracts and breaks into these six-sided shapes. The wind brings desert sand and dust which fills the cracks and hardens; as the salt continues to shrink downwards it leaves the cement standing proud. Eventually sandstorms will come and wear the entire surface smooth again, ready for the next rains. It is an elegant process.'

'You seem very well informed,' commented Vox, gazing ahead at the strange, twisted peaks.

'Ocher has been here before. It told me about this place last night.'

'Oh.' Vox's tone changed instantly. Wyrm and Ocher carried on, seemingly oblivious to the sudden coldness in his voice. Smoke frowned at Vox, pulling him back and allowing the others to go on ahead.

'What's the matter with you?' she hissed. 'You've done everything but spit on that creature since we started this morning. Wyrm obviously trusts it – why can't you?' She found herself shaking with unexpected rage. Vox had indeed been unnecessarily rude to the basilisk during their journey, his behaviour ranging from insulting the taciturn creature to actually marching across its path and causing it to stumble. 'Last night you were afraid of it – now you're trying to pick a fight.'

'I don't like basilisks!' snapped Vox, shaking himself free from her grip. But Smoke was not about to give up.

'No, Vox,' she continued, grabbing his wing again, 'you won't get away with it that easily. Tell me – what's the matter?'

'Nothing! Leave me alone!'

Wyrm and Ocher had wandered far enough ahead now to be quite out of earshot. White dust plumed in their wake, making their forms ghostly.

'It's the Nistri isn't it?' Smoke sighed. 'Look, I know all this is stirring up a lot of old pain for you, Vox my dear, but Wyrm thinks . . .'

' "Wyrm thinks",' mimicked Vox. 'Who cares what Wyrm thinks, much less that monster?'

'What's happened to you?' whispered Smoke, finally pulling away from him. It was then that Vox started to cry, softly at first, then with great, heaving sobs. He fell into Smoke's embrace, no longer resisting her touch, mumbling incoherently and only gradually regaining his composure. Then he talked.

'Of course I love Wyrm dearly, and I do trust him when he says we must find the Towers of Nistor. I don't know what he plans to do when we get there, and I don't mind admitting I'm scared – don't ask me why because I don't know, I just am. But the basilisk – Ocher . . . I don't know what to make of it. It probably is as harmless as you and Wyrm seem to think it is but all I see when I look at it is the memory of a dragon I thought I had forgotten.'

'Wraith!' Smoke nodded her understanding. 'I should have guessed.' Indeed, Ocher had once been *joined* with Wraith, physically, by the power of the Black Dragon's ambition. 'But Wraith is dead, Vox. You must place him in your past, just as I have done. I loved him once, briefly, before he was what he became – but now he is gone and I have moved on. You must move on, Vox.'

'I can't,' Vox said through clenched teeth. 'Wraith murdered my love, my Choliel, and I paid the price for his crime.

126

But the revenge I dreamed of was never mine, Smoke – I was cheated of it. And now ... now I find myself in the company of the very basilisk Wraith took into himself. It reeks of him, Smoke.'

'You can't know this is the same ...'

'Fortune told us the story many times. It *is* the same basilisk – I know it in my heart.'

'What do you want, Vox?' whispered Smoke, fresh tears running from her own eyes.

'Peace. I do believe the answers lie where Wyrm says they do. With the Nistri, with their past. And perhaps with the basilisk too. But the past torments me, Smoke, and the future, too.'

'I know, my darling.'

From the cracked salt beds sprang the strange spires of the Never Mountains – for so Wyrm christened this weird terrain. What looked like heavily sculpted rock was in fact crystallized salt, formed into rough slopes and lumpy towers. It meandered uneasily across the barren landscape, this miniature mountain range, the darkness nestling below its salt-encrusted spires promising hidden depths. Steam rose gently from fumaroles; rich green water pooled in a maze of secret clefts. A dragon might have flown over it without so much as losing breath, yet it seemed to the approaching dragons that it held much within its confines. Its scale was small, but its formidable presence was undeniable; it was *concentrated*.

'They yearn to be mountains,' pronounced Wyrm, looking up at the bright yellow pinnacles, 'but their lives are too short.'

'What do you mean?' asked Smoke. The landscape made her uneasy – it was like nothing she had seen before.

'Each year this place changes beyond recognition. Each moon cycle sees smaller changes; even the passage of a day might observe the loss of another peak, the birth of another tower. Constant change, death and rebirth.'

As if to confirm Wyrm's assessment a great dome of salt exploded as hot spring water surged up beneath it. Steam and spray showered across the coarse slopes and chunks of crystal clattered down towards the dragons. Smoke regarded the spectacle without enthusiasm.

'Are these your Towers of Nistor then?' she demanded.

Wyrm shook his head, a frown creasing his brow. After exchanging an inscrutable glance with the basilisk, he replied, 'No, but the Towers lie within the perimeter of the Never Mountains. We are in the right place, Smoke, you can be sure of that.'

Ocher led the way silently into the salt mountains, picking a safe path up through the network of spires and steaming pools. Some parts of the incline were fragile, crumbling away beneath their claws as they passed, but for the most part the Never Mountains were rather more durable than they seemed – and than Wyrm's description had led the dragons to believe. Wind and weather might erode them in time, but a few journeying dragons would make little impact.

As they ascended the landscape gradually changed colour from yellow to grey. The individual towers were much taller here, separated by a veritable labyrinth of passages and deep ravines. High above the dragons could see the caps of pale gypsum which protected these older, stronger spires from the erosion which was eating steadily away at their flanks. The roots of some seemed impossibly narrow, supporting great slabs of crystal many times their breadth and mass; in many places they found tremendous piles of salt and gypsum – the remains of those towers whose roots had finally given way.

For a long time none of them questioned Ocher's route, until, with the sun high and hot, they found themselves in a dead end. Hard-packed salt rose sharply on three sides: the only way out was back the way they had come. Smoke sat against one of the pale, grey walls and squinted up into the midday sky.

'Well,' she gasped, 'I'm thirsty.'

'Yes,' agreed Wyrm. 'Would you mind very much returning to that waterhole, Smoke? We would all benefit from a brief rest.'

'I'll come with you,' called Vox as she took to the air, rising vertically out of the canyon. Together the two winged dragons flew back across the salt flats, covering in a fraction of the time the terrain which it had taken them the whole morning – at the slower, earth-bound pace of Wyrm and Ocher – to cross. Broad leaves culled from the ubiquitous fat savannah trees were swiftly fashioned into water carriers, and between them they managed to scoop up sufficient drinking water to quench the thirst of a dozen hot dragons. They sped back towards the Never Mountains in easy silence, neither wishing to speak and both appreciating the absence of any need to do so. This brief sojourn was like a sudden release, and they both realized how much they had missed flying.

'Poor Wyrm,' lamented Smoke as they dropped back towards the square canyon. 'He will never know the joy of flight.'

As they swooped in with their precious load, they were surprised to find the canyon where they had left their two companions quite empty.

'They can't have gone far,' said Vox, beating at the warm, salty air with his wings. He led Smoke back down the path and into the maze of towers and passages. Of Wyrm and Ocher there was no sign.

'I don't like this, Vox,' murmured Smoke, pressing close against him as they dropped finally to the ground. Tiny, six-sided crystals chipped beneath their claws, glinting in the hard, noon light. Steam loitered around corners, reaching out inquiring tendrils.

Then the ground trembled and a deep, resonant groan broke across them like a wave. Salt showered across their scales, a gentle hailstorm, then all was still. Shadows shifted deep in the heart of the maze.

Between the pinnacles of the Never Mountains, something big was beginning to move.

CHAPTER 9

Grell

The rumbling went on for only a few breaths, then all was still. The hiss of steam escaping from some hidden fumarole continued with quiet insistence; no other sound penetrated the canyon until suddenly Vox heard a steady click-click. He jumped, a reflex action, then relaxed again as he recognized the familiar sound of dragon claws. Moments later Wyrm poked his head around a salt pillar.

'Our apologies,' he said. 'We did not intend to abandon you. We heard a sound.'

'So did we!' exclaimed Smoke with feeling.

'We've brought water,' added Vox.

Ocher appeared and approached the carefully wrapped and knotted leaves with some curiosity. It nudged the nearest of them and nodded, apparently impressed by the watertight seam the dragons had managed to achieve.

'Thank you,' replied Smoke, assuming that a compliment had been paid. Vox scowled.

Two of the parcels of water were unfolded enough to allow the dragons and their silent basilisk companion to drain their contents. The remaining two were tucked safely into a crevice in the canyon wall and left there while they went to investigate the source of the rumbling sound.

A narrow passage had opened up just beyond the entrance to the canyon. Wyrm and Ocher had ventured only a short way in before hearing their companions' return. Now its shadowy depths beckoned once more.

Wyrm entered first, followed by his dragon friends and finally the basilisk. The walls of the passage were tight, white salt, packed hard and scored by thousands of thin, vertical channels. Wyrm explained about the rainwater which percolated through the crystals, opening these minute tunnels; Vox and Smoke did not really listen, being more concerned with the flickering light visible at the end of the corridor. As the corridor widened this was revealed to be simple sunlight, pouring down through a great chimney which pierced the gypsum ceiling. The flickering was the result of something moving on the far side of the chamber thus revealed. Something large.

The air was bright and full of crystal flakes, but the moving shape stood out from the haze in sharp contrast. A hard, black silhouette, at first it appeared quite featureless; then it turned to face them. Rising up as it spun ponderously around, the thing appeared to grow before their astonished eyes, though in reality it was merely standing up. Fully erect, it stood three times the height of Vox, the largest of the watching dragons.

It was a giant, clearly, but not like any giant the dragons had seen before. Ocher had seen its kind – of course, the Deathless had seen most of the world's spawn through eternity – but it too was fascinated; it had thought these creatures long gone, claimed by the brutal cleansing which had surrounded the turning of the world. Ordinary earth giants had remained relatively common in many lands right up to the moment of the Turning, but their more exotic cousins had been rare indeed, now even more so. And few were more exotic than the salt giants.

She towered over them all, a broad, lumbering creature with a flat moon face and chubby paws capped with long, mobile fingers. Her claws were short and blunt, quite unlike those of either dragon or basilisk. Folds of fat drooped about her waist, while her breasts dangled like two pendulous orbs of flesh. Black, salt-caked skin sagged towards the ground, glinting as the brilliant sunlight was scattered by the crystals which were embedded in it; sections of skin looked badly scarred, especially around her trunk-like left leg. There it was not so much scarred as ruined, hanging off in pathetic folds. The leg itself was riddled with holes, some of which pierced the limb completely, revealing clear air behind. The left foot was missing.

No sooner had the salt giant pulled herself to her full —
and undeniably impressive — height than she lurched heavily
to one side, regaining her balance only by thrusting her arm
out against the salt wall. The whole chamber shook and
more crystals showered down across the dragons' backs. She
looked down at her leg and waggled the stump experimen-
tally; had they not been so nervous the dragons might have
found her perplexed expression amusing.

Then she saw them.

'Url kall . . .' she began to say, her voice deep and rich,
almost melodic. It was odd that a sound so pleasing could
come from such a ruined creature. Then she stopped and
seemed to consider the onlookers. 'Dra . . . gun,' she boomed
eventually, working her massive jaw extravagantly as she
struggled with the unpractised syllables. 'Dra-gon,' she
repeated more successfully. Then she frowned. 'You disturb
me!' she thundered, her voice like a trapped storm.

'Excuse me,' retorted Wyrm at once, 'but we did nothing
of the sort.' Smoke threw him a shocked glance: *What are
you doing — trying to get us killed?* Wyrm winked infuriatingly:
Trust me!

The giant too looked surprised. She blinked slowly, night-
black lids rolling over pale yellow eyes like tiny wings.
'Something disturb me,' she suggested, her tone uncertain.
She frowned again. 'You'll do!'

It was then that she noticed Ocher for the first time. Those
yellow eyes widened, exposing big, round pupils. 'Deathless,' she murmured, backing away.

'It's all right,' soothed Wyrm, advancing as the giant
retreated. 'I can personally vouch for Ocher — you're safe.'

'Who you?' came the rumbling voice.

'My name is Wyrm.' The most dazzling of smiles lit up
Wyrm's face.

As the crystal dust settled down so did the salt giant. Ocher
kept its distance, prowling the corridor beyond the sunlit
chamber while the three dragons listened to her halting
words. They learned that her name was Grell, and that she
was, as far as she was aware, the last salt giant alive on the
face of the world.

'This our home,' she explained with slow thunder. 'All

come back sooner or later. None now. Not for long, long.'

'I have heard of your kind,' prompted Wyrm when her words slowed. 'Pardon my ignorance, Grell, but I thought salt giants were, well . . . white. Like salt.'

Grell shrugged, the sound of her mighty shoulders like a small landslide. 'I may tell. Or may not,' she offered unhelpfully. 'I may sleep. I wish it.'

Wyrm looked to his friends, both of whom nodded their encouragement. He turned back to Grell only to see her lolling back against the chamber wall, eyes drooping. 'Forgive me,' he said loudly. Grell started, knocking lumps of crystal from the wall. Her brow lowered and she growled. 'Please,' Wyrm went on, his voice soothing again, 'we are searching for the Towers of Nistor. Can you help us.'

The salt giant regarded Wyrm for such a long time that the dragons began to wonder if she had frozen to the spot. At length she spoke. Her voice was flat and final.

'No,' she replied. 'I shall not sleep. Help I might – that is up to you.'

With that she turned her back on them, shoulders slumped, ruined leg pressed against an outcrop of gypsum so that her tremendous weight was fully supported. The sun tipped past its zenith and a thin line of shadow skated down the sheer wall of the chamber.

The dragons left the giant and spent the afternoon exploring the complex heights of the Never Mountains. Ocher did not participate, preferring for its own inscrutable reasons to loiter near the salt giant's chamber. Wyrm spent a few moments in a whispered conversation with it – no words of which were heard by Smoke or Vox – after which he rejoined his companions.

'Feeling tired, is it?' sneered Vox, glowering at the basilisk.

'Ocher wishes to observe the giant,' Wyrm replied, ignoring Vox's sarcasm. 'Come.'

At first their enthusiasm was high; only later did listlessness overtake them. Vox and Smoke alternated flying shifts, soaring over the peaks and spying out likely routes, information which they would then return to the others on the ground. The terrain was impossible to map completely from the air, so intertwined were the passages, many of which might just as well have been underground tunnels for all the access they offered to the sky. But, elaborate though the maze was, it was soon revealed to be relatively small and ultimately frustrating: passages either finished in dead-ends or wrapped around to meet their neighbours. None led below the surface and none showed any trace of hidden entrance or even directional marking. The Never Mountains were, it seemed, quite barren.

'I-I suppose it's only to be expected,' stammered Vox as they traipsed back towards the chamber to meet up with Ocher. 'If the salt is constantly getting worn away and built up again, it's no wonder there's no trace of the Nistri. It must be thousands of years since they were here. All sign of them must be long g-gone.'

What is he really so frightened of, Smoke wondered. Wyrm said nothing.

Ocher was squatting motionless at the entrance to the chamber. Grell did not appear to have moved. The dragons fidgeted in the corridor, none of them sure what to do next.

'Perhaps your basilisk friend has a bright idea,' suggested Vox, his voice still tight. But Wyrm shook his head.

'Come,' he said quietly. 'Sit with me a while.'

He led them to the middle of the chamber. Deep shadows filled the space now, among which the motionless form of Grell was the greatest shadow of all. He began to tell a story.

Once dragons were few. In those times, in the times of charm, there were points of focus on the skin of the world. Here the spawn of the world came forth. One such place was the Never Mountains.

Sterilized by salt, these nearly-mountains were nevertheless abundant in charm. Little enough life clung to their slopes, but dragons were born here. Early dragons, young dragons alive with ambition. Dragons with dreams. The Nistri.

So possessive were they of the charm which brought them life, the Nistri sought its power even after death: they became cannibals, consuming their brethren in an effort to recycle the magic they had left behind. Nistor, the leader for whom they were named, ritualized the practice and made it their faith. Each time the moon grew fat, a young, male dragon was butchered on the yellow stone at the heart of the Towers of Nistor. His still-warm body was devoured by his fellow dragons. The choicest delicacies were reserved for Nistor himself. Most revered were the eyes.

One dragon dared to rebel against the creed. His name was Duress, and he saw things of greater worth than mere bloodletting in the culture of the Nistri. He saw the elegance of their halls and palaces, the power of their charm, and its greatest expression in the beauty of the dazzling flame which burned over the sacrificial stone. He preached his beliefs, he consulted with Nistor himself. 'Why should we not move out into the world?' he demanded. 'Is there not more to our life than death?'

Then the moon grew fat again and Duress himself was chosen.

He was brought to the stone still singing his song of life. When Nistor held him down and lowered the flame towards his shining eyes, still Duress asked, 'Why?'

Then Nistor stopped.

Nistor said Duress must go free, and all the dragons of the Nistri watched as he flew from the Never Mountains out into the world where disparate dragon clans were spreading across land and sky. He was outcast. Always would he be known among his new family by the colour of his scales, the colour all of Nistor's clan bore, young and old alike: purple.

From that day on the Nistri dwindled. The flame grew colder day by day and each new sacrifice saw it grow colder still, until finally it withered and died. When dragons ceased to die so the faith of the Nistri ceased to live, and Nistor himself passed on from the world. Some of their number fled in pursuit of Duress, but none of them found sanctuary as he had done. Stories of their lust for blood had preceded them, and now their colour revolted others of their kind. As they had once cast Duress out, so now were they outcasts themselves.

Soon only Duress remained of their number, accepted among dragons despite the colour of his scales for he alone had rejected the Nistri in his heart. And he alone knew the true power at the heart of the clan, the true purpose of the sacrifice. That secret he carried to his death, for though he boasted much he explained little.

Duress boasted that the shining pools of blood at the stone of Nistor reflected only one thing: the future.

135

Duress boasted that some day all dragons would come to under-stand the power of the flame.

Duress boasted that some day the purple scale of the outcast would become the shining scale of enlightenment.

Duress sired many sons. His bloodline is rich in the dragon clans. Perhaps some day his boasts will be proved false ... or true. Perhaps some day the true purpose of the sacrifice will be known.

Perhaps some day dragons will look again into the flame.

Smoke shivered. 'I didn't like that as much as your other stories, Wyrm,' she said. She glanced up at the soaring walls, grey now in the long afternoon light. 'I think this place must be making me nervous.'

Vox too was shivering, although he was looking at the ground, and would not say what he made of the story. Behind the dragons Ocher remained motionless; whether the basilisk had been listening, or indeed had heard anything at all, none could say.

But there was one there who had listened with relish. During the pause after Smoke's words the air was filled with a low, slapping sound, a steady thump-thump coming from the vicinity of the salt giant. For the second time that day Grell turned to face the dragons, and as they looked up at her they saw that she was clapping. Crystals of salt sprayed up into her broadly beaming face, sticking to her jet-like skin, but she did not seem to mind. Approaching Wyrm, she bent forward, casting a great shadow across his already dark scales. 'Well told, little dragon,' she boomed. 'You know more?'

Smoke saw Wyrm suppressing a smile of triumph and felt her heart tumble in her chest. Suddenly, much as she loved him, Wyrm seemed somehow alien. *He knew the giant would respond to that story! How could he know? How does he know all these things, all these stories?*

But there was no time to dwell on these imponderables. Already Wyrm was reaching up and beckoning Grell to sit with them. This she did, crashing on to the pale floor like an avalanche and raising the inevitable cloud of fine, white powder as she did so.

'Of course I know more,' answered Wyrm. 'But I think it's your turn first.'

Grell's tale was no less strange than Wyrm's. She told it in slow, steady measure, addressing herself primarily to Wyrm, whom she now regarded, it seemed, with some measure of respect, not unmixed with suspicion. Dusk light threw shades of blue into the drifting salt haze as her story unfolded.

Salt giants had always been rare. They were more fragile than their close cousins, the earth giants, relying heavily on a skeleton of almost pure charm to sustain their friable bodies against the ravages of the weather. Here in the Never Mountains they gathered, here where the raw charm of the Nistri kept reserves of salt constantly renewed. Here there were always enough crystals to reconstitute themselves when the need arose and here they found a role.

The Nistri were secretive dragons, hiding themselves and their deeply-held beliefs from the outside world in their tunnels and caverns, practising their extravagant magic and roaming the world only with their minds. At first they ignored the presence of the lumbering giants who roamed the ephemeral landscape above their heads, but gradually they became intrigued by the slow and easy lives of the newcomers. The salt giants possessed charm unique to their species; nowhere else could the Nistri find magic with quite the same flavour, though they often sent their minds abroad, culling spells from the darkest corners of the world. The empathy the giants enjoyed with the land was of particular interest to Nistor himself, for not even in the earth giants had he ever seen such subtlety of charm, such a fusion of animate and inanimate. They fascinated him.

So they struck a bargain. The Nistri taught the salt giants some of their own magical techniques in return for the chance to study the charms of transformation which, every night, allowed their gigantic neighbours to become the land.

'Shape-shifters they were,' shuddered Grell, yellow eyes glazed.

'Weren't all charmed dragons?' suggested Smoke. 'For that matter, isn't that just what you are?'

'Not like the Nistri,' replied Grell emphatically. 'And my charm is not the same as dragon charm. Not at all.'

But the charm did not last. It leaked away as the world accelerated towards the Turning, and the salt giants simply dissolved. Grell watched her kind melt away one by one. One night her three brothers lay down together to sleep. In the manner of their kind, their bodies merged with the ground during their slumber; backbone became hillside, stretched legs became long, salt ridges. In sleep, they *were* the land. But that night a rainstorm lashed the hills. In the morning, with insufficient charm around to remake their living bodies, her brothers were no more.

So died all but two of the salt giants. Only Grell and her mate, Troo, remained.

'What happened to him?' interrupted Smoke again. She had become engrossed in the giant's tale and suspected that Troo's fate had been rather different to that of the others. She pressed herself close against Vox as Grell went on, feeling him shiver as a slice of cool air descended upon them through the open roof of the chamber. Overhead the sky was growing darker with surprising speed.

As giants died, those remaining grew stronger, for there was less demand on the shrinking store of charm. By the time Grell and Troo found themselves alone, the store was small indeed but substantial enough to sustain them for some years. Still, they both knew that it was only a matter of time . . .

Troo resolved to find an answer, a way to fight their doom. The Nistri too had dwindled; now all that remained of them were the long, empty spaces of their haunted caves. In recent times no giant had dared to venture within, though all knew the depth of charm locked up within was immeasurable. Ghosts prowled in the deep, it was said.

'The Towers of the Nistri are towers of death,' murmured Grell as she focused on some hidden memory.

'I don't understand,' said Vox suddenly. 'Are they towers or caves? Surely they can't be both.'

'Let her talk,' hissed Smoke.

Troo resolved to enter the Towers of Nistor. Grell pleaded with her love but he would not be turned. She did everything in her power to prevent him from entering the haunted caves but it was not enough.

'I could not stay awake,' she explained, pausing in her narrative.

'You mean he slipped away while you were asleep?' prompted Smoke.

'Yes.' Grell's voice was a whisper.

Troo vanished into the caves and never returned. Whether he lived still Grell could not say, did not dare to speculate. Long years passed during which she awaited his return, until finally she gave up hope and lay herself down to sleep for the last time. As she turned herself over, tucking herself against the land, she prayed for rain.

'Then you came,' she concluded mournfully. 'You woke me.'

Silence fell, cooling the evening air still further. Above them the first fragments of the stars were beginning to pierce the blue-black heavens. At last Vox relaxed into Smoke's embrace, holding her close and sighing quietly. Wyrm watched the salt giant with a sharp, electric gaze. Even the basilisk had come close, circling the huddled group, its tail trailing through the crystal-strewn floor.

'You did not wish to follow him?' asked Wyrm eventually, his voice soft as snow.

'Of course.' Grell shook her head as she spoke. Her voice too was soft, though deeper than Wyrm's and coarse with emotion. 'But it is not the way of things.'

'Might we follow him?' Wyrm was leaning forward now, his eyes wide.

'Of course,' Grell repeated.

Wyrm paused, then whispered, 'Can you show us the way to the Towers of Nistor?'

Grell hesitated, then sketched a hand down her huge, black body in a curious gesture. She lumbered back, unidentifiable emotions fighting for control of her massive features. Tipping her head back, she howled mournfully at the stars.

'Can you show us the way?' asked Wyrm again.

Grell looked at the dragons one by one, then repeated the strange gesture. Then she sighed, and in a voice as fragile

139

as the salt from which she was made, whispered, 'Dragon, I am the way.'

Wyrm blinked.

'I am tired,' murmured Grell. 'Let me sleep and you shall see.'

So saying she lowered herself slowly to the ground, curling up against the chamber wall as she did so. At first she did not shut her eyes, then slowly her lids closed, wiping featureless black over yellow orbs. Her breathing slowed, then seemed to stop altogether. Then the dragons were witness to a miracle.

At first her body was clearly defined, a great, black slab pressed against a wall of salt, still pale despite the dimness of the waning light. Then the boundaries began to merge. Threads of salt infiltrated the contour of her shoulder, snaking down across her breast and vanishing into the shadows beneath. The ragged end of her ruined leg melted into the ground, whitening and blending with the pile of crystals into which it had been thrust. The heat of her body receded, replaced by night-coolness. Slowly, steadily, Grell joined with the land.

The dragons watched in awe, and for a long time Grell's form lingered, even when it was so changed that it had neither head nor recognizable limbs. Something of her essential solidity remained, something of her soul, perhaps. Then she changed further.

Where her body had loomed now it receded; the blackness of her skin, still visible against the pale salt wall, collapsed. Where she had been presence now she was void.

Grell the salt giant had joined with the land, but she had not *become* the land: she had become an entrance into it.

The entrance to the Towers of Nistor.

CHAPTER 10

Landfall

Two days after Fortune's party left the shores of Mahl, nine dragon shadows swarmed over a sea of white cloud. Far beneath the cloud rolled the sea itself, the rolling expanse of the great Western Ocean. Above it, the weather was fine. The cloud stretched as far as any of them could see, a solid, comforting presence which reassured them that they could do this, they could make the great crossing and reach the other side of the mighty water. As long as the cloud remained they could forget about the sea, and as long as they could do that they could fly.

But Tallow had concealed the severity of his injuries. His dramatic rescue of Aria from the geyser had broken more bones in his body than even he realized, though he knew he was gravely hurt. The pain in his wings he could tolerate easily; the cracks in their supporting bones and spines were relatively minor and would heal quickly – or rather they would have done had they been allowed to rest. Anyway, Tallow's wings refused to let him down. But they were not the problem.

It was Fortune who first saw him struggling for breath. Tallow was trailing behind the rest of the group, and this in itself was unusual. When Fortune dropped back he saw that his friend was labouring in the air, his wingbeats fast and shallow, their rhythm erratic.

'Can't catch . . . breath,' gasped Tallow.

But he seemed to recover and banished most of Fortune's fears with a cheerful smile. Even so, they flew together for a while, Fortune casting an occasional worried glance sideways at the big Natural who had taught him the glory

141

of flight. Later on, Gossamer called Fortune forward to discuss the pressing problem of food (water was not a concern
for the moment as they had been able to descend into heavy
rain showers on both of the previous days). Telling Tallow
to take it easy, he moved swiftly up through the group. As
he went, he threw a single look back and shivered: Tallow
looked suddenly small, a tiny dragon-mote adrift in the
empty sky.

Don't be silly, he scolded himself. *This is Tallow, big Tallow.*
No sooner had he looked away again than he heard Velvet's cry.

A breath after her scream came another, more dreadful
sound. It was a cracking sound, almost an explosion,
although later Fortune wondered if his memory had not
amplified it. His first thought was of falling trees, but how
could there be such a noise here, high above a landless
ocean? In the time it took his thoughts to sort out their
confusion he managed to lock his gaze on Tallow and
realized where the sound had come from.

Tallow's body had folded. A spear of blood arced from
just beneath his neck, fanning into the air with awful deli-
cacy. His wings spasmed and his long neck curled back. It
seemed to Fortune at the time that Tallow's face was con-
torting in agony but he thought later that he was probably
already dead.

The crack had been the sound of Tallow's breastbone shat-
tering. The impact with the lip of the geyser crater had
caused far more damage than any of them had guessed.
How he had flown at all with such an injury would later
be the cause of much sorrowful debate, but for now all
Fortune and his companions could do was watch in abject
horror as their strong and faithful companion turned over
and fell from the sky. Tallow's breastbone, the deep keel to
which all his powerful flight muscles were anchored, had
simply disintegrated, sending shards of bone into his heart
and lungs and out through his skin. His wings flapped
loosely, caught by the wind, but they did not support his
substantial weight. He dropped like a stone.

'Catch him!' screamed Velvet and they dived after him.
The futility of their gesture was demonstrated when the

clouds swallowed Tallow, and all except Fortune and Volley pulled back.

'Leave them!' barked Gossamer through her tears.

Fortune and Volley plunged side by side through the thick cloud, wings tucked tight against their flanks. Both knew they could dive faster than Tallow's body would fall, and this was borne out when they emerged – only five trees above sea level – some breaths before the ragged, broken body of their friend broke through the cloud. They had time to flatten out into a hover, to scan the underside of the lowering cloud with hot, grief-stricken eyes.

Volley saw him first, and he blundered in front of Fortune, holding back his younger companion's instinctive lunge towards the falling shape. Together they watched Tallow tumble from the grey shroud, dragging wisps of vapour in his wake; they saw his pale shadow open its wings to meet him, they saw the shocking plume of water as he finally struck the waters of the Western Ocean. Cold spray showered across them both, joining with their unrestrained tears. When the water settled back to its slow, steady swell there was no trace of the body. Tallow had gone.

'We must go on,' said Volley, his normally smooth baritone sounding dry and cracked. Fortune protested weakly that they should remain circling here for a while but Volley was adamant and so they went on. Once more above the cloud, they struck out south-westwards beneath the noon sun.

They all looked to Volley now, to this quiet, unassuming dragon who had been Tallow's friend for so many years. They had grown up together in the forests of the Plated Mountain, and together they had vowed to seek adventure, to journey far across the world. They had journeyed far, to be sure, but this flight was to have been their greatest adventure. Not for Tallow, not now. Only Volley remained of the group of four who had once roamed the mountain slopes; charm had taken Weft and Piper and now the adventure itself had claimed big Tallow. Only Volley remained. Volley and his songs. His companions all looked to him, sharing his grief and knowing that his grief was greater, and all he could think of to do was sing . . .

Time betrays the struggle to be free
River buries love inside the sea
Tide returns with echoes of the day
Night conceals the grief I cannot say
Shore begins the hunt for struggles new
Whisper leads the way from me to you
Memories find life within the clay
Night conceals the grief I cannot say
Heart believes the struggling is right
Cloud reveals the peaceful inner light
Star reminds us all there is a way
Night conceals the grief I cannot say

The night was appalling. Here above the clouds both stars and moon were brilliant. Their light was augmented by the new comet; Fortune and Cumber wondered privately if its appearance might be some kind of omen, but its beauty – and indeed the beauty of all the night sky – was wholly unwelcome in the face of their grief. They clustered together in tiny groups, except for Volley who flew alone. None knew how to approach him, all were unable to console even themselves let alone Tallow's closest friend. Their moon-shadows were long and blue on the billowing cloud, but they did not notice them.

Morning saw them descend through the cloud in search of rain, which they found with relative ease. Drinking rain in flight was a slow and difficult process but one with which they had become quite familiar since setting out from Mahl. As they glided low over the waves, heads turned up, mouths gaping, they studiously ignored the waters of the ocean which had claimed their friend. But everywhere they looked they were reminded of his face, his smile, the steady, reliable beat of his wings . . .

Fortune had just finished drinking his fill when Gossamer swooped up next to him. 'Tired?' he asked. She nodded.

'Of course. We knew what to expect.' She grimaced as she said this.

'No, we didn't,' whispered Fortune.

'Tallow estimated it would take us five days to reach the continent of North Ocea,' Gossamer pressed on, closing her eyes briefly as she spoke his name. 'What if he was wrong?'

'He wasn't wrong,' Fortune snapped, his sudden anger clean and somehow welcome. It was gone as soon as it had come. 'No, you're right, my dear. All lands have changed since the world was last mapped by dragons, and few enough had made this journey even then.'

'The sea was much wider in those days,' agreed Gossamer. 'Tallow believes – believed – the journey is shorter than it ever was before.'

'Five days in the air without rest is hardly a short journey!'

Their conversation proceeded in circles, with neither dragon reaching any conclusion about what they should do. Fishing was possible but hazardous given the titanic swell of the ocean – this would be their recourse were the journey to prove longer than Tallow had hoped. They could survive for many days without food, but the constant flight was wearying. They slept on the wing – brief periods of shallow sleep snatched in shifts – but the cumulative effect of too much exertion and too little rest had caught up with them all. That and the sorrow.

'We go on,' sighed Fortune at length. Gossamer simply nodded, the tragic set of her features eloquent enough.

On the seventh day they sighted land. The coast was ragged and icy, depressingly like that which they had left behind on Mahl. After a short discussion they turned south, instinctively following the edge of the new continent towards what they hoped were warmer waters. Another night passed, during which the omnipresent clouds began to fragment, finally disappearing altogether. The coastline started to undulate in the dimness and sunrise fulfilled the promise which the moonlight had made: below them were grey rocks and stiff pine trees, while to the south and west a land of brilliant green expanded to touch the haze obscuring the horizon.

Hope filled the veins of these weak and hungry dragons, chasing away at least a little of their sadness. The mighty forest nudged the shoreline, its bristling canopy patterned with dark indentations which shadowed the tracks of rivers far beneath. The outpouring of these rivers was evident at the shore itself, where deep gullies etched the cliffs.

Everywhere vegetation bloomed, and the misty sound of the ocean surf falling against the land was like the welcome voice of a forgotten friend. Tree, river, life. A new land, a new world.

They spread apart for a time, separating into couples or splitting off alone according to their needs. Fortune found himself gliding some wingspans behind Gossamer and Aria, able to hear their conversation but for some reason reluctant to join it. Feeling like an eavesdropper yet compelled to listen all the same, he caught their words as they tumbled through the brilliant blue sky, falling past him and out across the sea.

'What do you believe?' Gossamer was asking, her voice kind but intense, probing. Aria paused before answering, and for a breath or two Fortune thought she would fly away without responding at all. During the flight from Mahl Aria had remained aloof, saying little and tending to fly alone at the edge of their flock. Something was different about her today though, a change signalled by the set of her wings, the line of her long tail.

'I believe in the Last Circle, mother. And I believe in the light.'

'Do you mean Scarn's precious Flame?'

'I mean the light.'

The wind gusted then, turning their words to meaningless fragments. When Fortune managed to pick up the conversation again Aria was still talking, talking hard as though to make up for her former silence.

'. . . had it half-right. There is power in the Flame, but the real power lies within the Last Circle itself. That is where the light is, or will be, that is where the Flame's power has its origin. And that is where I must go. This new land holds the answers, all the answers to all the riddles. Every question a dragon has ever asked – the answers lie here, mother, don't you see?'

'I see that you believe it, my dear,' replied Gossamer.

'Because it is true. When the world turned, all the circles of charm – the stone circles, the faery circles, all of them – were destroyed. You know that, mother, you were there. All circles except one. Its ruins remain, and its power remains too. Scarn was right when he said we must find it,

146

and he was right to wait for the sign. But *I* was the one who saw the sign, *I* am the one who knows the way to the Last Circle, the way to the future.' Here Aria faltered, and Fortune had to struggle to catch her words. 'I . . . I don't know what it is. But I know where it is: it's out there, over the horizon. But . . . I don't know what it looks like, or what it might do. And that makes me afraid, I think. Is it all right to be afraid, mother?'

Fortune felt his heart turn over. Here was his daughter, robbed of her infancy by the evil charm of Archan and thrown into adulthood with no knowledge of either the meaning or value of emotion. And what guiles Scarn had worked upon her he could not begin to guess. She was at the same time so old . . . and yet so very young.

'Scarn called me a temptress,' Aria went on, her voice trembling with rage and confusion and fear. 'He wanted me – I *know* he did, I could see it in his eyes – yet he never once . . . Why was I so different to all the others? Why did he turn against me so, mother? Why? I thought I could lead him here, but he saw the way too and as soon as he realized he didn't need me any more he . . . he . . .' At this point her words dissolved into sobs and moans, and Fortune could only watch in anger and pity as Gossamer brushed her wings against their daughter's flank in an inadequate attempt to comfort her. They angled downwards, mother and daughter, aiming for an empty spot on the rough shore, leading the small group of adventurers down at last to touch the new land.

Night on the beach brought a wealth of memories rolling into Fortune's mind. Memories of other shores, other nights. The gold sands of Haven, that idyllic lull before the great storm which had wrenched the world towards the Gathering; dream-time, or so he thought of it now. And his own, beloved South Point, of course. The beach of rock where, as Wood had so often told him, his father Welkin had rested on nights such as this, watching the night dragons play in the dark sky. The line between land and sea, that zone of constant change where nothing rests, nothing abides, everything moves on.

Everything turns, thought Fortune as he lay back on the

grey shingle. Low cliffs supported the forest bulk, a sheer wall of pines, their trunks straight and perfect; the sea was a deep, moonlit blue. A searing line of pure white cut through the field of stars and vanished into the tail of the comet.

'A shooting star!' exclaimed Wist excitedly. After the best part of a year spent in the Fissures with Scarn, the young Natural still found wonder in the sky. *And such pleasure in flight*, thought Fortune appreciatively. *Just like Tallow . . .* But that thought was too painful to dwell on and he called out in reply.

'Once they would have been called night dragons.'

'I think shooting stars are nicer,' laughed Wist. She cut herself short, suddenly embarrassed, but a glance around the group revealed approving looks. Her laughter was welcome, those looks said, despite the circumstances.

'What *are* you doing, Cumber?' said Fortune, forcing his voice to stay light. His ex-Charmed friend had been busy for some time now, dragging branches and clumps of brushwood down from a winding gully a little way up-shore. The pile he had accumulated on the beach was now about as tall as a big dragon. Cumber continued in silence and as the heap of sticks and stumps grew its purpose became obvious; eventually Velvet voiced the question on everybody's mind.

'It's impressive, my dear,' she admitted as Cumber flopped down beside her, clearly pleased with the result of his labour, 'but how are you going to light it?'

'Fire without charm, Cumber,' added Fortune. 'It can't be done.'

Cumber shrugged, a little out of breath. Uncharacteristically quiet, he lowered his head, breathed hard several times, then walked across to the wood pile.

'We learned the inadequacy of the old ceremonies when Thaw and Ratchet died,' he began.

'And Mokishi,' put in Velvet.

'And the chitraka, yes,' agreed Cumber. 'In the end we cast them into the waterfall beside the basilisk citadel – I'm sure Gossamer would tell us we cast them into the Cloud.' Gossamer nodded, a slight frown troubling her features. 'Well, I've brought something with me from Mahl, something which I found near the geyser after Tallow rescued Aria. I didn't know why I brought it, or even why I kept it secret, but I think now perhaps I do.'

Bending forward, Cumber lifted his snout slightly and parted his teeth. A tiny flash of light illuminated the interior of his mouth, shining through his tongue and making it seem translucent. It projected orange across his gleaming white scales. He curled his tongue back then flicked it forward, sending the light darting into the pyre where it vanished briefly before flaring into brilliant, luminous life. Flames leaped skywards, enveloping the branches in a single, beautiful explosion. Cumber did not step back; the fire fell across him but lapped harmlessly at his claws.

Awestruck, his companions came forward one by one and gathered around the pyre, forming a large circle with their outstretched wings. Tipping their heads back they watched the embers fall upwards to join the watching stars. An orange halo ascended, embracing the perfect whiteness of the comet. They wept again for Tallow, and for all the friends they had lost. The rising tide reached their claws but came no further, as if conscious of the shared privacy of their sorrow. Instead it retreated again, while above the stars wheeled in their course and on the beach the dragons held their station and the fire lived for a time then slowly died, as all things eventually die.

Volley's song echoed again.

'It was just a tiny shred of abandoned charm,' explained Cumber to Fortune later when the dragons had retired to various shelters beneath the cliffs. Sleep eluded these two old friends and the simple comfort of company was enough to warm them even though the fire had long since guttered. 'There's so little of it left now, you see.'

'Is there any here on Ocea?' asked Fortune. Cumber closed his eyes for several breaths and frowned. He nodded non-committally.

'Perhaps,' he replied. 'There's a tickle to the west.'

'A tickle to the west?' Fortune could not help sniggering. 'Oh, Cumber, you cheer me up like no other dragon can.'

'Do I?' snorted Cumber, feigning offence. 'Well, I really don't see how; after all, I was only trying to answer your

149

question in the most helpful way . . .' He stopped, grinning along with Fortune. Then both of them sighed. 'Your Aria,' Cumber said suddenly, 'what do you make of her?'

'What do I *make* of her?' For a moment Fortune did not know how to reply. 'She's my daughter, Cumber.'

'Yes, yes, I know that, but what I mean is what do you think is driving her? Why has she brought us here, of all places?'

Fortune pondered this for a while. 'I think we would have come here anyway,' he suggested. 'Poor Tallow wanted to see the world, and we all wanted rid of Mahl. None of us wanted to return to the Spine or whatever's left of the Heartland – too many bad memories there. I suppose Ocea is a fresh start for all of us.'

'Yes, but does Aria strike you as a dragon looking for a fresh start?'

'I don't know what you . . .'

'Of course you don't.' Cumber looked suddenly tired. 'Look, Fortune old fellow, I shouldn't be asking you these questions. As you say, she is your daughter and you love her and that's an end to it. I'm sorry for bringing it up.'

'It's all right, Cumber,' Fortune yawned. 'You know, I think I might actually sleep for a while now, if that's all right with you.'

Fortune fell asleep to the sound of the ebb tide stealing away into the night, and to the steady click of his friend's claws as they tapped an uncertain rhythm on the shingle.

Gossamer watched Aria sleep. Soon she would dare to believe that her daughter had truly returned to her. Too many times in the past she had been cheated of that reunion – first when Archan had stolen Aria away, then when Scarn had claimed her mind, if not her body, for his own. And now? Now it was just her and Aria together – could it be their time had come at last? Gossamer asked the Cloud that it would be so, and in it she put her trust.

The Cloud, the strange presence which had first come to Gossamer in the basilisk tower just before Aria was captured by Archan . . . time had stopped in the basilisk tower during that fateful moment, of that she was convinced. And into its limbo, a wedge of unreality, had slipped the Cloud.

A visitor from the future!

The thought was a new one but it seemed to echo something the Cloud's gentle, hypnotic voice had said to her: 'This world is not ready for me . . .' Had those been its words? Gossamer remembered better the sense of power, the sense of *destiny* which had accompanied the voice. 'Do not despair,' the Cloud had said. 'It is important that dragon heirs survive in the natural world.' And the final, enigmatic promise: 'The answer lies within your wings.'

Gossamer looked pensively up into the star-decked blackness. The moon had set; the comet was swiftly dropping towards the sea. *Until the sky falls . . .*

Her faith in the power of the Cloud, in its essential *goodness* had grown as time went by but as it grew it also became more fragile. After all, the Cloud had spoken to her only once, and had intervened in her affairs only once more since then, when it had frozen Archan into immobility at the crest of the world, allowing Fortune to rescue Aria's egg – the egg which brought Wyrm into the world. The void which followed had forced upon her a long and difficult exploration of her beliefs, not least of her trust that good would triumph over evil.

The two were sharply delineated in her own mind: the evil of the Flame, the good of the Cloud, but was that merely her inadequate dragon sensibility imposing order where there was none? Having lived through such times of chaos, was she simply seeking a stability she had never really known? Doubt plagued her even now. But her faith remained, aided by signs of the same faith in some of her companions, including poor Tallow. The Cloud had promised her nothing, but she trusted it would bring the light and the hope for which she yearned, which would make sense of the chaos. Still, she could not help wondering when and how it would manifest itself again. Except lately her mind insisted on using a different word: *how will it create itself next time?* she wondered as another shooting star raced across the heavens.

Whenever she thought about the words of the Cloud her mind turned inevitably to Wyrm. What was he if not a dragon heir? *The* dragon heir, if truth be told. She remembered how he had always called her by her first name, and how that had disarmed her. She remembered his strangeness, the intensity of his gaze, the curiously magical aura surrounding his patently natural, wingless body. The coldness Aria had shown to him after the initial thrill of motherhood, her inability to cope with even the simplest dragon emotion let alone the complex relationship between parent and offspring. Aria had retreated from Wyrm as she had retreated from the world, and if at first Gossamer had blamed Scarn for that she knew better now. In the end it all came back to Archan.

I hope you did achieve the immortality you sought, thought Gossamer bitterly, *because that means there will always be the possibility of retribution. Even when I and my kin are long dead, justice will live on. You will pay, Archan. Some day, you will pay.*

Aria turned over in her sleep. Without thinking Gossamer stroked her with one white wing and murmured a soothing song. As she sang it she acknowledged that her daughter's life was more precious to her than her own. That if she needed to sacrifice herself for Aria's sake, she would do so with wings open and head raised high. A tingle travelled the length of her outstretched wing and pierced her heart. Charm, barely perceptible, trickled through the air and she looked to the west. Though the cliffs and the forest blocked her view, she knew that beyond the horizon lay their destination: Aria's Last Circle.

And she knew there was magic there. Not much, but it was there. And it was waiting.

And the Cloud? She prayed that it would come to her again soon.

The sun rose and Volley sang again. This time the tune was a lilting, optimistic refrain, a song of mountain springs and fast flight to meet old friends. His face was drawn as he sang but his voice was strong and sure. When he had finished he called his companions around.

'Scarn will pay for Tallow's death,' he announced. 'Justice will be served. Justice cannot die.'

Smiling, he led them into the air.

CHAPTER 11

Nistor's Tunnel

Smoke glanced back as they passed into the darkness of the tunnel and saw the basilisk pause in the entrance, its head lowered. She fancied she heard its voice scratching at her ears, but she could not be sure. Then it entered the shadows directly behind her and disappeared; she did not see it again for some time.

The sensation of penetrating Grell's sleeping form was a curious one: Smoke's eyes told her that she was simply walking into a hole in the sheer salt wall, but her stomach recoiled as she crossed the boundary from outside to within. Lingering shreds of her charm sense warned her that this was a living threshold, not a hole but a being, warm and vibrant. *Does this hurt the giant?* wondered Smoke anxiously. *Just as charm hurts me?*

It was a fleeting sensation however – once in the tunnel Smoke wondered if she had not imagined it, and it was driven from her mind altogether when she finally understood the tragedy of Grell's story.

'Of course she couldn't follow him in!' she blurted, her words stopping Wyrm and Vox in their tracks.

'What do you mean?' called Vox, his voice echoing strangely in the dimly lit tunnel.

'Grell's mate came here too, don't you remember? He waited until she was asleep. And she couldn't follow. How could she?' Smoke felt so sad for the wretched giant that she could say no more. At the same time she found herself wondering what had happened to giant Troo. What lay down here that was so terrible, now that the Nistri were gone?

153

Wyrm led them through the wide, descending tunnel, picking his way slowly down the sharp incline of smooth crystal. The way was slippery – they all had to keep their claws located in the numerous cracks crazing the floor – and led ever downwards into blackness. Soon they were blind. The tunnel did not turn, it simply continued on, on, on . . .

After some time the walls revealed themselves again, reflecting a distant, white glow. The dragons stopped, partly to catch their breath but also to examine the walls, for they were most odd.

The tunnel here was exactly square in section. The floor remained a smooth slope but the walls were studded with hard crystalline deposits, each one a flawless cube. The ceiling was flat, but unlike the cracked floor it was polished to a dazzling gloss, as perfect a mirror as an undisturbed pool of spring water. Smoke gazed up at her reflection, wondering what this place must have been like years ago, when the voices of the Nistri had filled its passageways. A gust of wind glanced against her brow and she turned quickly, fancying she had caught sight of a movement behind them out of the corner of her eye. But there was nothing. The basilisk, perhaps . . .

Wyrm was examining the pattern of cubes, bobbing his head up and down as he slipped sideways down the corridor towards the glow. Every so often he would pause and backtrack slightly, peering alternately high and low as though searching for a particular feature. Smoke exchanged a glance with Vox who simply shrugged – he had no more idea what Wyrm was up to than she did.

'What do you make of it, Wyrm?' called Smoke at last, a little impatiently. Wyrm started at the sound of her voice, and seemed surprised to see them both standing there.

'Oh, I'm sorry,' he said, rather sheepishly. 'I was getting somewhat carried away. It is a fascinating piece, you see, very involving.'

'It looks like a lot of blocks to me,' put in Vox. Beneath his petulance Smoke thought she detected the curiosity he would once have displayed in a situation such as this. What did he fear that had made him so cynical?

'It is a record,' continued Wyrm, ignoring Vox's interruption. 'A story, if you will, sculpted long ago by a skilled artisan, one of Nistor's élite I suspect. These shapes were once bound up with charm – they were practically alive – and in their movement they told the story they were designed to hold.'

'What story?' demanded Vox, intrigued yet stubborn in his refusal to open himself to this experience. Smoke watched as his eyes darted first to the sculpted wall, then to the shadows behind them, then to Wyrm's eyes. He was more tense than she had ever seen him.

Wyrm sighed. 'I don't know. The charm is dead, of course, and even if it were still alive it would probably take me months to decipher their language. Once this wall would have been full of words and pictures and emotions, a vibrant thing, spilling some epic tale out into the corridor, impossible to ignore as you made your way towards the inner chambers.'

'Chambers?' queried Smoke. 'Or towers?'

Now it was Wyrm's turn to shrug. 'I don't know,' he smiled. 'Shall we find out?'

The glow strengthened as they approached its source until it suffused the air, spilling across the complex relief of the cubes and glaring down from the mirror-like ceiling. The maze of cracks in the translucent crystal floor were etched deep by the low angle of the light so that the tunnel seemed about to fragment. It was impossible to make out its source, so dazzling was it; it was like walking into luminous mist.

Then, as they took their next steps gingerly forward, the light abandoned them one by one, winking out as though it had never existed. The dragons cried out in astonishment, so abrupt was the transition. Only Vox thought to stop and take a few steps backwards, whereupon his companions saw him suddenly bathed in the light again. 'I see it,' he said, moving forward again and raising a wing upwards.

Only now did they register what had happened to the tunnel here. At some time in the past there had been a cave-in or landslide or some minor catastrophe. A section of the ceiling had separated, releasing a long slab of mirror which must have swung down in a perfect arc before finally coming to rest at an angle on the floor, an inclined ramp of distorted, reflective material. A chimney had opened in the salt strata above it – perhaps this opening had actually caused the collapse in the first place – through which the night sky was clearly visible. Directly above the chimney hung the comet, throwing its light down into the tunnels of the Nistri. The fallen mirror had captured the light and was focusing it along the length of the tunnel. Particles of salt still drifted down through the roughly circular channel, filling the air and scintillating in the light beam. As they watched, the comet passed slowly out of view and the salt motes darkened. Darkness descended once more.

But it was not total darkness. The tunnel beyond the broken section was brightly illuminated by the very structures Wyrm had been studying. The wall panels in this deeper part had retained something of their magic, it seemed; their light was warm and yellow and welcoming. Unfortunately there was no way to reach it.

No sooner had the dragons picked their way past the broken mirror than they encountered a tremendous rip in the floor. The matrix of cracks had exploded here, and now an apparently bottomless chasm gaped in the floor. The temptingly illuminated section of wall commenced on the opposite side of this gulf: clearly the chasm marked the boundary of whatever remained of the power of the Nistri.

Vox quickly established that it was impossible for them to jump across, or even fly: the tunnel was especially narrow here. He could barely lift his wings, let alone open them enough to fly, much less fly and carry the wingless Wyrm across the abyss. They squirmed in the confined place, trying to devise a way by which they might cross, but to no avail.

'I wonder how deep it is,' ventured Smoke, peering cautiously over the ragged edge of the chasm. 'It can't really be bottomless.'

'Nothing would surprise me down here,' muttered Vox darkly.

'Perhaps we could climb down and then up again the other side,' Smoke persisted. 'I'm just trying to think positively, Vox.' *Unlike some I could mention*, she said to herself.

Vox snorted and squeezed past her, taking up station

beside the mirror where he stood, angrily tapping his claws. Smoke took one last look down into the blackness then shuffled around herself, intending to join him. Instead she found herself face to face with the basilisk.

'O-Ocher,' she blurted. Her own face stared back at her, a double reflection in the ancient creature's blank, silver eyes. 'Can you help us?'

The basilisk did not reply. It moved aside, allowing Smoke to pass, then coiled its long, muscular tail beneath its body and closed its inscrutable eyes.

'Fine time to sleep,' commented Vox. At first he resisted Smoke's embrace, then he allowed himself to relax into it. 'I'm fighting it, my darling,' he murmured at last. 'I don't know what it is but I don't like what it's doing to me any more than you do. But I think . . . I think that once we get through to the Towers I'll know what it is, why I'm here. Why we're all here.'

'Will you still be afraid?'

But Vox did not answer.

Smoke came to abruptly, amazed that she had fallen asleep. Vox snored against her flank, a warm dragon shape which seemed so familiar, so real to Smoke in the midst of all this strangeness that she almost found herself crying. She eased herself out from under him, eyeing the basilisk – itself asleep, apparently – with caution and trying to locate Wyrm.

The sky, just visible at the top of the narrow chimney, was a deep, pre-dawn blue. The sloping mirror was caught between the dim blue of the heavens and the bright yellow light which awaited them beyond the chasm, and on it sat Wyrm.

His dark scales looked black in the peculiar light. His wingless body seemed suddenly alien to Smoke. He was so poised, so *right* – it occurred to Smoke then that Wyrm seemed *right* wherever he was, whatever he was doing. Fortune sometimes joked that his mother had called him an 'economical' dragon, a phrase she had never understood until now. Wyrm possessed an economy which surpassed even that of Fortune: an economy of form, of muscle, of thought, a sense that nothing about this dragon was wasted, that

157

everything he did and said and believed had purpose and meaning.

Oh, Wyrm, Smoke thought with sudden awe. *Why have you brought us here?* Then she heard the sound which had woken her. It was a heavy sound, an ominous scraping which quickened her heart and widened her eyes. Grell had spoken of these tunnels as being haunted, and Smoke's experience of them so far had done nothing to reassure her that they were not. *The ghosts of the Nistri indeed!* she scolded herself. *The very idea of it!* But still her heart pounded.

The tunnel they had passed through looked black and dreadful. It was from there that the noise was emanating. Smoke shrank back, aware that Wyrm remained unmoved; he seemed confident, even. Was that a smile playing at the corners of his mouth? But she found only fear in her heart, irrational fear that the ghost of Nistor himself had come to claim them for his own, come to perform his final act of sacrifice and they were his victims. She backed clumsily against Vox, waking him from his slumber. He heard the noise at once and, alerted to the danger, pushed roughly past Smoke, calling out, 'Come out where we can see you. I've had enough. I'm here now – tell me what you want of me.'

Something monstrous lumbered in the blackness.

Smoke's eyes widened yet further as she struggled to make out what was approaching them through the shadows. Vox half-opened a wing in front of her, offering a shield, but she brushed it down again. The basilisk was awake now, too – if it had ever been asleep – and had joined Wyrm on the slab of mirror. Together they watched the monster emerge from the darkness and into the light.

It was Grell. The huge, black salt giant was crawling on all fours through the narrow tunnel, her flat face raised painfully forward so that she could see where she was going. An expression of almost comic relief crossed her blunt features as she realized she had found a place where she could stretch her limbs at least a little, only to be replaced by an equally exaggerated look of dismay as she saw the cramped area where the dragons stood, and the peril of the chasm beyond.

'Couldn't resist it,' she explained as she squeezed out of the tunnel and into the relative comfort of the landslip, where one of the walls had subsided to create a cavity into which she could press her massive body. Her huge hands scraped the floor, brushing against her good foot and the stump of its ruined partner; her knees hugged her cheeks. 'Not when the ancient one told me what to do.' Here she shook a lazy finger at the basilisk, which regarded her dispassionately with its cool, once-lethal gaze.

'Ocher knew the right magic, didn't it?' said Wyrm happily. 'It knew there was a way for you to enter through your own body.'

'Should be impossible,' agreed Grell, 'but the Deathless know many things.'

Smoke could scarcely believe her eyes. 'But how did you do it?' she asked. 'I mean . . . if you need to be asleep before your body turns itself into the entrance, how can you possibly . . .'

'This is my dream,' answered Grell, her heavy brow crashing down across her yellow eyes. 'I am here, but I am not here. Is that right?'

The basilisk nodded imperceptibly. Smoke was not sure if she had merely imagined the motion.

'So your body is still back there?' Smoke ventured, voicing a fear which had suddenly come to her. 'What I mean is, could we still get out if we wanted to?'

'So long as I continue to dream, there is always a way out,' Grell agreed.

Looking closely, Smoke realized she could partially see through the salt giant's mighty form. Grell was clearly a solid enough presence in this confined space – her hands brushed salt from the walls, and the shadow she cast was real enough – but some elaborate charm was keeping her sleeping body entirely separate from this dream-self, this tangible ghost . . .

'So the Towers of the Nistri are haunted after all,' she smiled.

Grell thought about this for a moment, then a broad grin cracked her face wide open and she laughed. A great wave of bellowing laughter filled the tunnel, bringing yet more

159

salt cascading down across them all and subsiding only gradually as Grell regained control of herself.

'So,' she chuckled, wiping tears from her craggy cheeks, 'do you need some help?'

It did not take Grell long to scoop away sufficient salt to widen the constriction in the tunnel. As soon as she reached the abyss she turned to face the watching dragons and their basilisk companion and eased herself backwards over the edge. Her face was a mask of concentration as her legs scrabbled against the friable wall of the chasm, then a look of satisfaction appeared as she located first her foot and then her injured leg in some safe crevice. Then, moving with a suppleness her real body might not have been able to match, she swivelled her torso around to face across the gap.

'Here goes,' she grunted, and she fell forward.

Smoke cried out and lunged forward, but Vox held her back. There was a tremendous thud and a cloud of white powder billowed up out of the chasm. Nervously they edged towards it.

As the dust settled they saw that Grell's gamble had paid off – for them at least. Her great, black body was stretched across the chasm, thick arms extended so that their muscles bulged like seed pods about to burst. Her back was arched, her head was lowered almost out of sight; she was breathing short and fast. 'Quickly!' she gasped.

The dragons did not need to be told twice. Hurriedly they scampered across Grell's back, pushing with their wings against both wall and air as best they could in an effort to keep their weight to a minimum. Smoke went first, followed by Vox and Wyrm and finally Ocher. The basilisk seemed to glide across almost without touching the salt giant and Smoke found herself wondering if it needed this living bridge at all. Once on the other side they turned in unison to face their helper.

Grunts and moans echoed in the tunnel as Grell tried to lever herself back upright. The muscles in her back shook with the effort. Her fingers clutched at the salt ledge on to which they had lodged themselves, just below this far lip.

She swayed her hips, looking for purchase as the walls of the chasm began to crumble away all around her.

'Hurry!' called Smoke, angry and frustrated. There was nothing they could do to help this gentle giant; all they could do was watch her struggle.

The far cliff, the one in which Grell's foot and leg were buried, was starting to slide into the darkness, slithering down in huge chunks. White dust filled the air once more. The noise was like waves on the shore. Grell's shoulder lurched and she fell back. One hand jerked free and clawed at emptiness. Smoke shrieked. Grell's face lifted and they saw her scared eyes slowly falling away from them.

Ocher's tail whipped out, slamming against the giant's outstretched hand. Grell's fingers closed instinctively, gripping so tight that a tiny cloud of basilisk scales puffed outwards, joining the salt mist. Ocher was pulled backwards but then, just when it should have been hauled into empty space by the falling giant, it stopped dead. It stared mildly at the astonished dragons, fixing them one by one with its silver eyes and settling finally on Vox. They all remembered how Vox had been unable to stop the basilisk's relentless progress through the trees towards Wyrm when it had first appeared. What strength, what tremendous *mass* did it have that it could do such things? Was it simply the weight of history, of memory?

Flickers of charm splintered beneath Ocher's claws and the dragons saw very clearly from where the basilisk's power came. Magic – abandoned by the Turning, all but destroyed in the explosive Gathering of the Deathless, yet lingering still, here and there, tattered but quick enough to work miracles even in this changed, natural world. Flashes of red light scintillated across the cracked floor as Ocher leaned into its task and pulled the salt giant clear of what had promised to be her grave.

That initial tug was all it really took: her momentum checked, Grell was able to push against the far wall with her legs and propel herself with sufficient speed to lift her body clear of the edge of the precipice. The hand which was not clutching Ocher's tail found a particularly wide crack in the floor and the dragons were forced to scramble backwards as an avalanche-sized salt giant lunged at them from the black shadows and white mist which had so nearly claimed her. She landed at their scrabbling claw-tips, grinning broadly and coughing out a shower of salt debris.

'He won't get away from me!' she spluttered. 'That Troo's got a lot to answer for. Useful travelling companion, a Deathless One.'

Ocher pulled its tail free of her relaxing grasp. If it was pleased with itself it did not show it. The white dust settled across its creamy scales but it did not stay to help Grell to her feet. As the dragons clustered around the giant, Ocher lashed its tail and sped away down the corridor more quickly than they had ever seen it move before.

'It has its own goals,' said Wyrm reflectively. 'Some of them may coincide with ours – some may not.'

'Troo,' announced Grell, bent almost double in the square Nistri corridor. The yellow light made her eyes bright but they were sad now, quite empty of the exhilaration which had accompanied her rescue from the chasm. 'I want to find him now, please.'

The tunnel did not descend as steeply but widened rapidly and before long Grell could walk comfortably. The yellow light was an unpleasant glare but at least they could see where they were going well enough. Both Vox and Smoke retained sufficient charm sense to confirm that it was indeed some vestige of the Nistri's former magic illuminating the tunnel. Wyrm continued to marvel at what this corridor must once have been like when the charm was at full strength.

'Do you remember the Nistri?' Wyrm asked Grell as they plodded steadily on.

'Not really.' The more she talked the better Grell's speech was becoming. 'My mother kept the entrance to this tunnel in Nistor's time, but he was long dead by the time I took on her role.'

' "Kept the entrance",' said Vox. 'You mean she *was* the entrance, just like you are now.'

'We shared much with the Nistri,' agreed Grell. 'Though it was always their choice, not ours. They learned the shape-shifting ways of our kind and turned them to their own use.

162

They mixed earth charm with fire charm, and the results were often . . . unpleasant.'

'What do you mean?' Smoke was relieved to find Vox beginning to relax. Ever since they had crossed the chasm he was acting more and more like his old self.

'Earth charm is gentle,' explained Grell, ducking her head to avoid a projecting outcrop of glowing yellow cubes. 'When I change I do so in sympathy with the form I share with the land. I love the land, as all the earth-charmed love the land, and the land loves us in return. But fire charm – or dragon charm as I think of it – knows little of love. It is brutal. Your Realm was a place of anger and thunder. It was not even of this world.

'What Nistor did was to take the simplest spell by which our kind and our cousins all across the world achieve fusion with the soil and sea, and he threw it out into the Realm. There it was consumed, and it remained hidden for a long time before finally it was spat out by some errant magic. And it was changed, horribly changed. Nistor leapt upon this new, changing charm and made it his own. Every fire charm which ever changed a dragon's shape from one thing to another came from that one, original earth charm. Without the magic of the giants, you dragons would have been lesser creatures.'

Vox and Smoke were stunned into silence by this speech of Grell's, but Wyrm continued to question her. 'You said it was horribly changed. Yet many charmed dragons were beautiful. They used this "changing charm" as you call it for good things as well as bad. What was so dreadful about it?'

'Earth charm is never bad!' snapped Grell abruptly. 'Nistor unleashed the evil of the fire as soon as he stole our magic.'

'You shared it with him,' murmured Wyrm.

'Fire is evil, and that is that. You would not doubt my words if you knew what Nistor did with the changing charm.'

'And what precisely did he do?'

Grell stopped and raised one, heavy hand upwards, finger extended. As she did so her whole body seemed to waver slightly. The brightness of the wall showed briefly through her flesh and the dragons were reminded that she was here only by virtue of some strange charm of Ocher's. Solid though she appeared, this giant was simply a dream . . .

Where Grell was pointing the tunnel ended in a huge, round chamber aglow with beams of the same yellow light. Vertical lines of shadow streaked the dappled glow, towers of salt sculpted into strange and – from this distance – unidentifiable shapes.

'The Towers of Nistor,' said Grell.

Feeling tiny, like crawling insects, the dragons made their way reverently into the tower chamber. It was vast and white, and big enough to hold a small dragon army. Bell-shaped, walls soared up from the spacious circle of the smooth floor, narrowing as they rose towards the chamber's apex. The floor was marred only by a tremendous pile of broken blocks and chunks of crystal at its centre. All around the perimeter, set perhaps one wing's width in from the walls, were placed the Towers of Nistor. Each one was a dragon.

There were hundreds of them, tall, white sculptures arrayed round the chamber – although clearly the great task of filling the chamber with these edifices had never been completed, for fully one quarter of the circumference was empty. Strangely elongated, these stylized dragons stood erect, their tails coiled back upon themselves, their wings folded close to their stretched flanks, their necks rigid and tense as though reaching for the sky which was hidden from them. Each dragon was different, an individual; Vox knew at once that these were portraits.

The dragon towers led the eye inevitably upwards towards the chamber's crowning glory. Vox stumbled as his eyes took it in: he had expected nothing like this.

A dragon's head glared down from the apex of the cone. It was giant, many times larger than life-size. Unlike the sculptures it was carved from some rich, purple stone and looked durable enough to see out many a Turning. Not a scratch marked its surface; it reflected the beams of yellow light with a glorious gloss. Nose down, horns melding into the converging walls, it glared down into the tower chamber with featureless eyes. It was familiar. It was Vox.

Smoke followed Vox's trembling wing as he directed her attention upwards. At first she could not make out what she was seeing – she thought there was a hole in the ceiling – but then her perception shifted and she found herself staring into the eyes of the dragon she loved. She gasped and her legs and wings gave way; she struck the floor with an indelicate thump. Wyrm too looked up, and even he gasped, astonished.

Grell pushed her way past the goggling dragons, her eyes focused on something different. Two thirds of the way up the walls, ringing the entire chamber, was a wide ledge. There was no visible way to reach it (the walls were over-hanging and the dragon sculptures were far too fragile to provide a means of ascent) and yet there was something lying on the ledge which she knew at once.

'Troo!' she cried. There, impossibly high in the chamber of the Towers of Nistor, lay the motionless body of the salt giant's lost mate.

CHAPTER 12

The Towers

Vox's thinking, which had grown increasingly muddled since Ocher had joined their company, suddenly sprang back into focus. It was like a bubble bursting inside his mind, and as it burst he found he was able to trace back the confusion further even than the basilisk's arrival. *It happened when we came through the trollvein on to the savannah and found Wyrm,* he thought, revelation like an explosion of light in his head. But then he went still further, riding backwards into the past on waves of insight, identifying moments, turning points, crucial passages in his life until the motion was dizzying. A sound built in his mind, the whir of memory. It reached a crescendo, and as the critical moment drew near he felt himself shying from it, struggling to avoid its inexorable approach. With a crash he stopped.

Here was the moment, here was where everything had started to go wrong. This was the point where Vox's life had been broken, and here was where he had to begin if there was to be any real hope of his rebuilding it. It was a truth he had always known, an absurdly obvious one now he saw it laid bare before him. It was the moment when Wraith had killed his love.

Those dreadful events he had replayed time and time again, endlessly. He had spoken to his friends about them, he had wept in Smoke's wings more often than he cared to remember, each time believing that another wisp of the ghost his Choliel had become had been exorcised. But now he saw the truth: that all his talking had been in vain. That despite all the years, all the pain, all the love that had passed since then, still he had advanced no further. The truth knocked his breath away and in a state of shock he saw the murder again.

Wraith looming over the cowering Choliel. His claws slicing through the air. Her head separated from her slender body. The blood.

Vox's long years in exile, convicted of the crime only he – and perhaps, in his heart, Halcyon – knew Wraith to have committed. The years spent planning his revenge. The turning of the world, and the news that Wraith had died. The knowledge that vengeance could never be his.

Smoke. Even though he loved Smoke he bore the open wound from which Choliel's blood still flowed, after all these years. It would not let him rest. Not yet.

But here in the chamber of the Towers of Nistor, here Vox began to believe there might be an answer to the horror that had dominated his life for so long. Here, where dragons had first worn the purple scales which were to become the mark of the outcast, here where blood sacrifice had been not a crime but a way of life, here perhaps Vox might at last find peace.

How this might be he could not say, but his heart was howling the truth of it and he could not ignore its wail. He stared up at a stone dragon which stared straight back down at him. It was as though he were looking into a perfect, crystal mirror: he was the stone dragon, every one of its etched scales was a replica of his own. In some way he did not yet understand, he had come home.

He was surprised that Grell was not weeping, for it was obvious to them all that Troo was dead. Instead the towering salt giant, her coarse, black skin gleaming in the yellow haze of the multiple beams of light, was standing tall and proud, casting her gaze about the walls. Evidently she was seeking a way up to join her fallen mate. As Vox watched her he felt a sharp jab in his ribs.

'Vox,' whispered Smoke in a voice pitched for him alone. 'Can I believe my eyes? Have you come back to me at last?'

He looked at her and saw her – *really* saw her – for the first time in what felt like an aeon. The clarity of his vision was as astonishing as the vividness of his memory; it was like waking from a dream. In the contours of her face he saw all the concern she had lavished on him, all the worry he had caused her over recent days, and he felt immeasurably guilty. Unable to find words of apology he hugged her tight, squeezing her with his wings until she gasped.

'Yes,' he murmured in reply. 'Yes, my dear. I'm back. There's something I have to do here. I don't know what it is yet, but I have an idea or two.'

Smoke pulled herself free of his embrace and held him at wing's length, appraising him closely. She cocked her head to one side and smiled hesitantly. 'The shadow has gone from you, Vox,' she said cautiously, 'but something has taken its place. You seem ... I don't know, serious somehow.'

Much of her fear had been swept away but something was worrying at her still. Vox's eyes were bright, as bright as she had ever seen them, and he had a sense of purpose about him which had been long absent. In the same instant she felt a dull throbbing at the base of her skull, the familiar ache of charm. *Vox has felt it too*, she thought. *What spell is it working upon him?*

Her fears could not dampen her joy however, for she knew Vox well enough to see that he truly was himself again. Doubtless whatever sense of purpose had gripped him would be revealed soon enough. She smiled warmly and embraced him once more before stepping back.

'Well,' she asked, 'how can we help Grell?'

Wyrm was strangely subdued and had little help to offer. He insisted on performing a meticulous search of the huge chamber floor, partly to gather as much information about this place as possible and also to search for Ocher; the basilisk had not been seen since its dramatic rescue of Grell and Wyrm seemed to be missing it.

Smoke elected to stay with Grell while Vox toured the airspace. He was far more adept at dealing with charm than she was and insisted that it was foolish to risk both of their lives. They did not yet know how Troo had died; it made sense to be cautious. She curled her wings in close as a draught of cold air touched her back and was gone.

Ghosts, she shivered.

'Troo was right,' announced Grell happily as Vox circled slowly, just above their heads. 'Much charm here still, the charm of Nistor.'

'You feel it too?' inquired Smoke. Grell nodded. She had forgotten that the salt giant was ex-Charmed too. *Earth charm seems to linger*, she pondered. *Perhaps it is more powerful than fire charm after all.* Together they watched as Vox gradually flew higher and higher, scanning the walls constantly as he did so.

Vox's spiralling ascent was painstaking. He circled round at low level initially, climbing only gradually as he reassured himself that there were no magical triggers set in the air. Then, just as he reached the level of the ledge on which Troo lay, he managed to locate the source of the charm they could feel: a short distance above the ledge was a narrow slit in the wall running the entire circumference of the chamber. The air in its vicinity was thick and salty, somehow stagnant. Ancient charm leaked from it, creating a perilous zone of unknown magic into which Vox had no desire to ascend.

Thereafter he kept low. His sweeping flight took him near to the sculpted towers, the tops of which stopped more or less level with the ledge. Dragon faces stared back at him as he glided silently on his arc, salt eyes cradled beneath salt brows, salt wings furled and stretched into abstract white shrouds. All of them were strangers and he could not help casting his eyes occasionally upwards to where his own face glared down from the convergence of the ceiling. His – its – mouth was open, teeth bared as though ready to descend on any luckless dragon who flew beneath it.

He returned to the ledge, taking care not to lift his wingtips any higher than the spines on his back lest he should stray into the zone of threatening charm. Landing next to Troo's massive body he waved to his companions. Even Grell looked tiny on the ground from this height.

Troo, unlike his mate, was pure white. Vox was beginning to appreciate the curious relationship between the sexes of this ancient race, how Grell's blackness complemented Troo's whiteness, how the males were one with the salt itself, the females with the spaces between the crystals, the tunnels and cavities in the rock. Though he did not fully understand it he found it elegant, and this new-found empathy with the giants brought tears to his eyes as he viewed the shattered remains of the once-mighty Troo.

The giant was lying prone, his body half-melted into the ledge. The characteristic shape-changing which occurred whenever a giant fell asleep had evidently been halted at the moment of death, and as a result it was hard to make out what was giant and what was rock. *Perhaps there is really no difference at all*, thought Vox as he observed the way one out-flung arm simply blended into the smooth chamber wall. Parts of this curious corpse were encrusted with spikes of crystal, others were globular as though frozen in the act of melting. Some pieces had broken away altogether, exposing a complex crystal lattice – the remains of the giant's inner workings. Vox examined the entire body and stopped exactly where he had expected to stop: at the head. Here too there was fragmentation, but a single wound stood out over all the others. Troo's neck had been severed – his head had been cut from his body.

It was Nistor's charm that had killed the luckless salt giant, at the very moment he had been reaching for his prize.

Vox could see it as clearly as if he had been there: the giant, crouched on the ledge, adjusting his balance. The sculpted dragon head hanging from the ceiling, its mouth open, challenging him to reach up. Troo standing erect, arms balanced wide, his head passing smoothly up past the line of the slit and into the zone of charm. The sheet of fire charm lancing out from the cavity, decapitating him. The graceless fall of his body to the ledge, the futile attempts of the gentle earth charm to merge him for the final time with the land.

He contemplated the garish wound in poor Troo's neck, then glanced down at Grell and Smoke. Vox reached a decision.

Extending his tail he nudged the head a little to the side, grimacing as a fan of crystals dissolved to powder beneath it. The friable salt which defined the sheer line of the neck wound collapsed, then the head itself tipped back against the body, revealing a single drooping eye socket devoid of the orb it had once held. The small cloud of dust this tiny movement created settled and Vox was satisfied to see that he had destroyed all evidence that Troo had been murdered by Nistor's ancient charm. Now Troo's entire upper half was a random mass of fragments, innocent and quite without order. The crime had been erased.

'He fell,' Vox called. 'He must have been reaching for the dragon.' He pointed at the giant replica of his own face.

'He was always clumsy.' Grell gave Smoke a half-smile.

'Forgive me,' said Smoke hesitantly, 'but you don't seem surprised to find him here like this. You don't even seem . . .'

'To care?' suggested Grell. Her smile faded. 'Oh, I care, dragon. I care very much. But you see, Troo was dead to me the instant he entered Nistor's tunnel. No salt giant has ever come out alive. I knew then I was the last of my kind. I wanted only to find his place of rest, and to satisfy myself that he was not killed by dragon charm at least. That means a lot to me, you see.'

'The last salt giant,' sighed Smoke. 'What will you do now?'

'Join him, of course. I am dying, in case you had not noticed.' Grell raised her leg and indicated her ruined foot. 'I am more tired than you can ever know, and the next time I go to sleep I shall not wake again. All I want now is to lie down next to my love.'

By the time Vox returned to the ground Wyrm had joined them again, though he remained aloof.

'He must have climbed up the central pedestal,' Vox said to Grell, indicating the pile of rubble in the middle of the chamber with one purple wing. 'He managed to jump on to the ledge, but the pedestal collapsed under him as he did so.'

'What did he want up there?' asked Grell quietly.

Raising his wing now so as to point directly upwards, Vox pointed to the huge dragon head. 'The Flame,' he said simply. 'I think the dragon head must have been the source of Nistor's fire charm.'

'He wanted to cheat death for just a little longer,' Grell sighed. 'As did we all.'

'Did he crave immortality?' asked Smoke cautiously. She

had little sympathy for creatures who yearned for such a goal; the evil it had worked on Archan and Thaw had proved to her the falseness of its promises.

'No,' chuckled Grell, shaking her massive head. Again Smoke was reminded that the giant was not entirely here, as she glimpsed the sculpted towers through the contours of her skull. 'Troo just wanted to stay awake a little longer. You see,' she continued, staring wistfully up at her lover's body, 'our kind finds little glory in death. For us, sleep is as much a part of our active lives as wakefulness. Awake, we feed off the land; asleep, we replenish what we have taken. When a salt giant dies, she finds neither triumph nor tragedy – she simply falls asleep for the last time, and the waking half of her life is over. The sleeping part goes on forever.

'So you see,' she concluded with a half-smile, 'we are immortal, in a way.'

The dragons slowly nodded their understanding. Then Vox broke the silence by asking, 'What do you want most now, Grell?'

'To sleep,' she answered at once. 'To sleep in the arms of my love, for the last time. I would give anything to be with him when I close my eyes.'

'There is no way you can reach him,' said Smoke gently. 'We would help you if we could, but . . .' Once more she felt the touch of cold air against her skin and she shuddered. The pain of the charm had increased and she found that her wings were shaking.

An odd series of expressions passed across Vox's face then, beginning with shock and ending with determination. Somewhere in the middle, Smoke saw fear. His eyes had turned inward though, as though these were old emotions, very old . . .

'What is it, Vox?' she asked cautiously, glancing at Grell. '*Can* we help her?'

Vox came to a decision.

He spread his wings wide and took to the air again. He began to circle the chamber, quickly this time and flying faster with every breath. Soon he was a blur in Smoke's vision, completing each circuit so fast that she could scarcely keep up with him.

'What are you doing!' she shouted, terror suddenly swelling in her breast like a bubble of hot metal. 'Are you crazy?'

Vox did not reply, and even if he had spoken his words would almost certainly have been lost in his slipstream. Smoke darted frantically across the floor. Wyrm called after her, 'Leave him now, Smoke. This is something he has to do for himself, and for Grell,' but his words succeeded only in frightening her more. She opened her own wings, making ready to pursue her mate into the air, but Vox himself, swooping low, beat her down.

'. . . too high . . . Flame . . .' Vox's disjointed words fluttered down as he whipped ever faster, drawing strands of vapour from the air '. . . fire is coming . . . fire in the sky . . .'

But that was all she heard. Vox abandoned his whirlwind circuit to dive towards the rubble and at that precise instant the pain of the charm in her head escalated to an overwhelming agony, an almost audible blindness which shrieked at her and felled her like a tree in a tornado. She collapsed whimpering, eyes wide and unseeing, ears deaf to the howl of the wind as Vox dived low then pulled out to accelerate vertically towards the mouth of the dragon sculpture.

If Smoke had fallen prey to pain and confusion then Vox had achieved a kind of purity of thought. It seemed to him that the very air through which he flew was pouring into his mind and bursting out through the cracks between his scales, cleansing and illuminating as it went so that his direction, his purpose, was as clear as a crystal spring. So acutely refined was his perception that it transcended the distortions of the tremendous speed at which he was travelling and revealed to him a perfect, gestalt view of the chamber's interior.

Smoke, fallen; Wyrm gazing up expectantly; Grell likewise, her broad face confused and hopeful.

The body of Troo on the ledge, his poor head so many broken pieces; the fierce glow of the charm building behind the slit in the wall.

The basilisk entering the chamber from a hidden tunnel.

Memories too: the black of Grell's skin carrying echoes of Wraith; the round chamber like the Map Room in the basilisk citadel; Troo, prone and headless, like Choliel . . . Choliel . . . Choliel . . .

Grell, alone. Like Vox.

Vox's own head drawing near, a giant edifice of stone. The barrier of the charm protecting it.

The peril was clean and sharp, blown as it was on the gale which had cleared his mind. His uncanny vision perceived the first claws of charm twitching in the shadows behind the slit, then saw the burst of fire as yellow light turned livid orange and great limbs of flame launched themselves at him through the air. He beat down the screams of his companions; all he needed was the sound of the fire, the sight of it. His wings thumped, increasing his already searing speed. He entered the zone of charm.

A circular sheet of fire erupted from the slit. It sliced through the air a mere scale's width from where Vox had just been. Grell's exclamation was one of both relief and sudden understanding as she simultaneously rejoiced at Vox's escape and shuddered at the realization of what had really happened to Troo. But the relief was short-lived, for no sooner had Vox surpassed the plane of the fire than it began to elevate towards him. Smoke, peering through a red haze, cried out as she realized that this was what he had intended all along.

At the centre of the thin disc of fire was a boiling concentration of charm. This focus Vox had cleared with almost nothing to spare, but now it was pursuing him, drawing the disc up into a cone of orange light which gained on the tiny dragon shape which had so far eluded it. Vox flapped harder, stepping up his speed further than any of them thought possible. The fire cast his shadow on the sculpture towards which he raced, a dragon shape in frantic motion on a wall of scales. With a twist of his wings he side-slipped and turned into the gaping jaws of his own, looming visage. The fire-disc hesitated, its central focus opening and peeling back for the briefest of moments, a predatory mouth. Vox emerged from between a cluster of teeth and slithered upwards, his body wrapped close against the sculpture's enormous cheekbone with only a breath of air to separate them. He looked as though he was made of liquid.

Now he was level with the eyes. Twin, moulded horns reared back from the giant dragon's skull to merge with the ceiling. There was nowhere for Vox to go. He turned sharply, lashing his tail downwards as though to fend off the advancing fire. Smoke screamed.

The sheet of fire bit into the dragon head. There was an explosion, a ball of dirty flames laced with splinters of rock and flakes of salt. A wave of sound preceded the falling debris, a shock wave which thundered in the air, shook the ground. For a breath or two all was confusion, the site of the explosion a mass of fragments and licks of flame. Then something larger moved through the cloud: the dragon head itself, descending.

It ripped free from the ceiling which had held it suspended for aeons, the centrepiece of Nistor's Tower Chamber free in the air at last, if only for the briefest time. A tremendous groaning issued from the wound which had opened up at its base, a low and baleful moan like a sighing troll. Air whistled through the shattered remains of its teeth as the sculpture gathered speed, tipping forwards as it fell. Down into the chamber it plunged, tumbling now through a mist of salt dust and rock shards. The fire which had liberated it had winked out; the air was quiet and empty but for the slow rumble of the falling edifice. Yellow light flickered behind the treacherous slit but the charm had fled.

The onlookers scrambled to safety as the dragon head plunged towards and finally struck the ground. The impact was strangely anti-climactic: instead of breaking apart the sculpture simply landed like a clumsy infant unrehearsed at flight. It had rotated half a turn during its descent so that now its mouth was gaping up towards the broken ceiling, and when it impacted the back-swept horns and the base of the skull were crushed into an unrecognizable mass of crumpled rock. The entire rear half of the sculpture sagged, absorbing the impact as it distorted, but the overall structure remained intact. As the dust settled, the huge replica of Vox's head was revealed standing proud of the salt-strewn floor, gazing up into the heights of the chamber, jaws wide and waiting.

Grell lunged forward, and at last Smoke saw what it was

175

Vox had done. The giant effortlessly climbed the rack of teeth which the sculpture now presented to her and repeated Troo's leap across to the ledge. Smoke searched the hazy air for some sign of Vox, but she found none. Some cruel part of her mind threw up the speculation that the very dust obscuring her vision might be all that was left of Vox, but she shouted it down and turned instead to Wyrm, her eyes pleading for some explanation, for some hope. He could offer none, only the warmth of his embrace, which she accepted.

They huddled together, oblivious to the steady approach of the basilisk towards the fallen edifice, watching as Grell stepped cautiously towards the body of Troo.

On the ledge the giant leaned forward tentatively, then looked down at the two dragons and waved, a curious, shy gesture. Then she lay down and embraced the remains, a black cloak thrown across shards of white. The dragons watched for a while as she grew more transparent, then there was a whisper of wind from the tunnel entrance and a long, soft rumble, like thunder on the other side of the world. The instant it stopped Grell's body became solid again, and as it did so its breathing slowed until its pulse could no longer be detected. The black salt giant flowed around her white companion until their forms could not be separated; for the last time, Grell slept. Perhaps one day she would die.

A voice carried on the whisper of air: *thank you* . . .

Smoke looked away, unable to bear it. They were trapped here now, but the fact seemed to have no meaning. Smoke could not conceive what had happened to Grell's physical body – and hence to the exterior tunnel entrance – now that the giant had entered the chamber and passed on. Somehow it did not seem to matter. All that mattered to her now was Vox. What had happened to him?

Wyrm pressed against her, turning her head into the chamber. She braced herself, expecting to see Vox's body tumbling to earth. Instead she saw a light inside the mouth of the fallen head. A flickering, blue light which danced and crackled even as it grew bright and tall.

A flame, alive in the broken replica of her lover's jaws.

The flame, which had once burned upside down over the sacrificial stone, the pedestal which Troo had unwittingly destroyed. The Towers of Nistor, those weird, elongated dragon shapes, shimmered in the eerie glow as if they were about to take flight.

It was Nistor's flame, long thought to have died. The dragon flame.

CHAPTER 13

Scales of Red

In what he imagined to be the secrecy of the Fissure, Scarn looked deep into the Flame. Lurid patterns danced across his face; his features were drawn tight with concentration, the random blue flashing of the light their only source of animation. What he could see inside the fire Brace could not guess, but it was clear there was something . . .

The massive detonation of charm in the Flamehall, and the tremors caused by the final, cataclysmic eruption of the geyser, had opened many new cracks in the already fragile structure of the Fissures cave complex. Brace and Ledra had swiftly managed to separate themselves from the rest of Scarn's dragons, finding anonymity in the fact that they all now bore scales of red, the new uniform of the dragons of the Cult. Brace's mother, Jevell, had remained with the others – in particular with her catatonic mate Rarch. Like Brace, she prayed there might be a way out of this nightmare even for him.

Over the days that followed Brace and Ledra found many places to hide, moving frequently to avoid Scarn's regular patrols. Ledra commented that Scarn's paranoia must be overwhelming if he found it necessary to mount such an intense vigil when all the signs were that every dragon in the Fissures adored him.

'We are proof that his suspicion is justified. And therefore that Scarn is smarter than he seems,' commented Brace dryly, and Ledra could only agree.

Both dragons were huddled in their latest hiding place. This tiny cave was positioned at the end of a long, narrow tunnel which wound through the rock at such a

178

steep angle that it was almost impassable. Almost. Brace had excavated enough of the claustrophobic space to make it possible for them both to conceal themselves in its depths. The cave at the end was a bonus, as was the discovery that a minute crack in the cave floor opened on to Scarn's secret Fissure. The chamber in which burned the Flame itself.

'Doesn't look like much to me,' Ledra had grumbled when first they had laid eyes upon it. The blue of the Flame danced beneath them, pulsing from the broken stalagmite from which it burned with a steady rhythm, like a heartbeat. Orange lava burned away to the side, casting hot shadows down the length of the narrow cave.

'It could be everything,' answered Brace.

This thought occurred to him again as he looked for the second time on the scene. When they had first arrived the Fissure had been empty; now Scarn was there, staring into the Flame as though he were watching some drama unfold within. Taking care not to let his claws scratch on the thin rock – and praying that the floor was substantial enough to bear their combined weight for at least a little longer – Brace bent forward and squinted into the crack. However hard he tried he could make out nothing but the ever-changing ripple of the blue fire; if Scarn could see something then it was for his eyes alone.

'We should talk to your mother again,' whispered Ledra. Brace jumped, cursing silently.

'Don't do that,' he scolded. Ledra smiled and glanced down at the red scales on her breast, luxuriating in her resplendent new colouring.

'I don't suppose you feel like . . .' she began.

'Not here,' chuckled Brace.

Ledra sighed, stretching her neck as gracefully as the confined space allowed. 'We've been skulking around for too long,' she said. 'If we're going to do something we have to do it soon.'

Brace lifted his head carefully from the crack. 'All right,' he said, heavily, 'I can tell you've come up with an idea. Let's hear it.'

*　　*　　*

Brace could not easily leave these dragons of the Cult. His thoughts still echoed with the promise he had sworn long before: that he would free the dragons of Aether's Cross.

'But you did free them,' Ledra had protested at first. 'You freed them when you found them still trapped by Wraith's charm, when you all escaped through the trollvein. Scarn happened later – for the sky's sake, Scarn was one of the ones you saved.'

'Then I'm responsible for all this.'

'Don't be absurd – you're not responsible for any of it – or any of these dragons.'

'But I *feel* responsible.'

'Brace,' said Ledra softly, touching his wing with hers, 'you have to let go sooner or later.'

It was then, during their first night hiding in the Fissures, that they found comfort together. Brace, hopelessly naive when it came to love and its many expressions, was guided by the more experienced Ledra, and between them they found some spark of joy in the darkness. Ledra wept later, for until now all her affairs – of which her liaison with cruel Hesper had been the last – had been cold and fleeting. She had used dragons for pleasure, and this aspect of her past was one she bitterly regretted.

But now Brace had released in her a passion she had never known existed, a way of loving which was more to do with caring for her partner than pleasuring herself. For his part Brace was simply overjoyed to have been accepted by such a beautiful and – as he saw it – mature dragon; together they called it love.

The following morning Brace came to a decision.

'You're right, Ledra,' he announced. 'I am not responsible for these dragons. But I cannot leave without trying to help my parents. My mother is as opposed to Scarn as we are, but she will not leave my father and he cannot leave of his own accord. I have to get them both away.' He thought for a moment, then added, 'And Scarn needs watching. As long as he is alive Fortune and the others are in grave danger, no matter how far away they may be.'

How he knew this Brace would not say – perhaps he did not really know himself. But Ledra believed him, so convincing were his words, the tone of his voice. She found it hard to believe he had once been scorned and bullied, that others had found him an object of ridicule. She found, to her surprise, that she adored him.

Ledra was happy to share Brace's goals, even if she did not fully understand their origins. For her part she believed Scarn to be wholly evil and now that he had gained access to some kind of charm she feared him all the more. She had grown to love Fortune and Gossamer, and now Brace, and if this surrogate family were put in any danger she would defend it with her life.

To this end, she joined Brace in his self-appointed mission: to find a way to free both Rarch and Jevell – and themselves of course – from the captivity of the Cult. The problem of Rarch's catatonia they would tackle when they were clear of the Fissures. If any other dragons wished to join them they would be welcomed, but they would not go out of their way to help those who would not be helped.

So they prowled and delved, seeking hidden exits and testing defences. Scarn had increased the level of his patrols dramatically. It was almost impossible to roam the corridors of the Fissures without being accosted and questioned in considerable detail about the ways of the Cult. Several close escapes forced them to lie low more and more often, until they began to despair that they would ever find a way out.

'I think we should try to beat Scarn at his own game,' announced Ledra bravely as Brace looked up from the crack.

'What do you mean?'

'Just this: we know where Rarch and Jevell are – in the former harem.'

'Close to Scarn,' pointed out Brace.

'Ssh and listen. What I mean is getting to them isn't really a problem. What we can't seem to do is find a decent escape route. For all the cracks and crevices running through this place there are very few that actually lead to the surface, and Scarn has those heavily guarded.'

Brace agreed with a shudder. Not only had Scarn posted sentries but he had somehow constructed sealing charms across all the exits. And Brace could not help but remember

181

the similar magic which had so nearly killed him during the escape from Aether's Cross. *Before the Turning*, he realized in wonder. *Was that so long ago?*

Ledra went on, 'Well, now it looks like we've found a way to the heart of Scarn's power. So why don't we use it?'

Brace blinked, not understanding for a moment. Then he glanced down at the crack in the floor, at the flicker of blue light which lined its ragged edge.

'You mean . . .'

'I mean the Flame,' affirmed Ledra, vigorously nodding her head.

'But . . . we don't know the first thing about this charm Scarn claims to have found. We don't even know what the Flame is, or what it can do. And we're Naturals, both of us, what could we possibly know about charm?'

Ledra smiled the slow, seductive smile Brace had come to love.

'Both Naturals, you say?' she purred. 'Ah, but that's where you're wrong.'

They had to wait some time before Scarn finally vacated the Fissure. Ledra hurried to the other end of the narrow tunnel and was fortunate enough to overhear a passing sentry telling his colleague that Scarn had called a prayer meeting in the Flamehall. It would continue for the rest of the afternoon.

'Perfect,' said Brace grimly when Ledra returned with the good news. 'He won't be back for ages. It's now or never!'

It did not take them long to widen the crack sufficiently for Brace to reach a claw through, and soon it was big enough to allow them to drop through one by one. Both were relieved that the ceiling remained otherwise intact – the sound of so much collapsing rock would certainly have brought dragons rushing to investigate, forbidden chamber or no forbidden chamber. They stood together in the Fissure, feeling the heat of the lava river which ran beneath the far wall, squinting into the brilliance of the Flame.

'Go on then,' said Brace hesitantly. 'Do your stuff.'

Ledra stepped forward and closed her eyes.

Ledra was not a charmed dragon. But during the great storm, ex-charmed dragon Hesper had seduced her with his flamboyant wielding of abandoned charm. This strange courtship had resulted in Ledra growing the extra forelegs of the Charmed and, for a while at least, enjoying limited power herself in the wielding of charm. As the basilisks' river of charm had dwindled so the magic had quickly faded, but its memory remained strong and even now Ledra's unnatural charm sense lingered. She set it to work on the Flame, probing, seeking, listening . . .

Brace watched anxiously as she trembled in the Flame's shimmering light. He had no clue as to its origin or purpose, he knew only that it was spoken of with reverence by the dragons of the Cult. And he knew it was the source of the power which had nearly destroyed the Fissures, and all the dragons within. One glance at his bright red scales was enough to convince him that the forces contained therein were not to be trifled with.

Ledra jumped, then stumbled backwards, shaking her head furiously. At once Brace went to her, gathering his wing about her and drawing her further away from the Flame.

'What is it?' he hissed urgently, keeping his voice low.

'Charm!' blurted Ledra. 'It's charm all right, a fantastic amount. It's incredible!'

'There's still magic in the world? Still so much of it?' Brace did not doubt it, but was there no end to the resourcefulness of charm? First the Turning, then the Gathering of the Deathless, and still it clung on.

Ledra swallowed hard before answering. 'Yes . . . I mean no, not really. This is new, Brace. This is totally new. And it's different, different to all the charm that has ever gone before. This charm is . . .'

'The future!'

Brace and Ledra whirled round at the sound of Scarn's voice. While Ledra backed away – towards the Flame again – Brace cast a quick glance left and right and then did the one thing he hoped Scarn would not expect: he lowered his head and charged.

A claw of charm lanced into his side, freezing him with

an agonizing pain. Ledra rushed towards him as he fell gasping to the floor but Scarn checked her advance with an invisible barrier which wrapped itself about her limbs and effectively pinned her to the spot. Had there been room in the narrow chamber he would undoubtedly have walked around his captives, gloating, but instead he simply stood and watched them writhe and squirm. Gradually he released Brace from his pain, expanding the magical skin which trapped Ledra so that it contained him too. The two dragons glowered at their captor through the sheer field of force, eventually giving up their struggles to wait sullenly for whatever fate he chose.

'What punishment befits the violation of a sacred place?' mused Scarn, twirling one long, red claw in the air before his eyes. 'Dismemberment, perhaps. Or some other kind of violation?' He eyed Ledra lasciviously as he said this.

'If you touch her . . . !' shouted Brace.

'I would not dirty my claws,' interrupted Scarn mildly, 'on such an unclean, unholy specimen. But let us leave aside the problem of punishment for a moment and consider instead the crime itself, for before justice can be served you must learn the true extent of your misdemeanour.

'You are trespassing in the most sacred place in existence on this or any other world. Quite simply, the Flame is the future, as I have already suggested to you. The future for dragons, the future for charm – indeed, the future for the world itself. Do you understand?'

'I would like to understand more,' said Ledra softly, and with a delicate roll of her shoulders. Brace gaped at her until she shut his mouth with a snap of her wing and hissed at him to stay silent.

'Oh, you shall, dragon, you shall,' murmured Scarn, leering at her through the invisible charm. 'You see, there is one question which has never been answered. Charm has left the world, as we all know – and I for one am tired of hearing about it – but what can possibly take its place? "Nature", you may reply, and you may be partly right. Or you may not.

'Because the charm left behind a tremendous hole in the world, a hole so big that mere nature is not enough to fill it. Something else is needed. And I promise you this, dragons – that something is coming. It's heading this way, it's coming fast, and there's nothing any of us can do to stop it.'

'The Flame, of course!' gushed Ledra, false enlightenment lighting her face. 'I knew it as soon as I saw it!'

'You did not,' replied Scarn matter-of-factly, 'and your pitiful attempts at seduction will not work on me, dragon. If I choose, I shall seduce you. I do not choose, however. So listen.'

'Why should we?' snapped Ledra, giving up her pretence. 'And why don't you just kill us now and be done with it?'

Scarn came very close to the cocoon he had woven around his prisoners. 'Oh, but you are too useful to me to be killed straight away,' he whispered. 'And in order for me to get the most out of you it is important that you know everything.

'So, let me tell you about the Flame.'

Smoke searched desperately for any sign of Vox in the rubble surrounding the fallen statue, but she found none. Soon she became hysterical, lunging out into the huge chamber, half-flying, casting around in the shadows and crying out his name. Her common sense told her that he had to be buried beneath the massive sculpture but she could not bring herself to believe it in her heart. Not her Vox, not like this, after all they had been through. All sense of time left her as she ranted and screamed, and during that time she had never felt so alone.

Later – it might have been a few breaths or half a day, she could not tell – she found herself slumped on the ledge next to the entwined bodies of Grell and Troo. Exhaustion had brought an end to her fruitless searching, but not to the speeding of her troubled thoughts. She nudged the black and white debris which surrounded her.

'Oh, Grell,' she whispered. 'He did it for you, or that was how it seemed. But I think . . . somehow he did it for himself.'

She could articulate her thoughts no more fully than this, but in talking to the giants' recumbent forms she felt a little of the panic subside. The terror was like a great crashing noise which would not go away, but little by little it dropped away to a background grumble over which she fancied she could hear her own name being called. She closed her eyes, imagining it was Vox calling to her.

'Smoke!' Her eyes snapped open and she rushed to the edge of the ledge.

'Vox!' she cried, searching the blue-limned chamber. Something was moving near the fallen dragon head. 'Vox?' she repeated in a whisper.

The shape emerged into the wavering light of the flame. It was dark and wingless – Wyrm. 'Come down, Smoke,' he called. 'Please – we have to talk.'

'I don't think I can,' wailed Smoke mournfully. It was true: her wings felt thick and useless, and she felt as though her spirit had altogether gone. 'I think I'll just stay here with Grell. I'll just wait for Vox.'

'He's not coming back,' shouted Wyrm, his voice booming in the huge space. Smoke made ready to weep anew until her tears were checked by Wyrm's additional words. 'Not yet, at least.'

Smoke glided swiftly down to where Wyrm awaited her. 'What do you mean?' she demanded. 'He *is* alive, isn't he? What's going on?'

'Ocher says . . .'

'I don't care what Ocher says, Wyrm, I want to hear what *you've* got to say. I want you to tell me everything, and I want you to tell me right now!' She was close to tears again but managed to repress them. Something in Wyrm's eyes told her that truths were waiting and ready to be revealed.

Wyrm coughed, then began to talk. In his inimitable way, he told a story . . .

Once the Nistri thrived, but this tale is less about their ways and more about their beliefs. In particular it is about their predictions.

They worshipped their Flame obsessively, sacrificing many of their kind to it and eating the unfortunate soul's remains. We should not be repelled by their rituals however, for they were honourably performed. Their belief in the Flame was strong, as strong as the integrity of their faith, and such strength cannot be denied.

They recorded their history along the walls of their tunnels, creating living panoramas of their discoveries, their knowledge. These memory walls breathed life into every corner of their dwellings; their colour, their movement, the emotion of the stories they told was without parallel.

The memory walls were a way of retaining the past, but what interested the Nistri more – especially Nistor himself – was the lure of the future. Was there not some way they could build a memory wall which trapped the future in the same way as the others trapped the past?

Nistor worked long and hard to this end, yet it was ultimately to no avail. He believed passionately that the power of the Flame was the key to the future of dragons in the world, and so he focused all his attention on moulding the Flame, shaping it, coaxing it into revealing its secrets. His final project involved encasing the mysterious source of the Flame in rock and carving that rock into the form of a dragon's head. Charm carried the sculpture up into the roof of the Tower Chamber and inverted it, so that the Flame burned upside-down. Thus, Nistor believed, would the flow of memory which the Flame commanded be reversed. Thus would the future be unveiled.

It was not to be. The Flame was mortally wounded by its unnatural inversion and even Nistor's ever-increasing flow of charm into its source could not sustain it for much longer. The Flame died and the Nistri dwindled.

And the future came like the stranger it had always been.

'An interesting story,' acknowledged Smoke impatiently. 'Now tell me what it means.'

Wyrm smiled. 'For once, my dear dragon,' he said, 'I shall do just that. Come with me.'

He led her to the sculpture and pointed up at the fire which was burning between the dragon's jaws. 'Nistor's Flame,' he explained. 'Once-dead, now reborn. And I think I know why.

'Nistor knew that the Turning would happen. That was one of the reasons why he poured so much magic into the Flame, in an effort to keep it alive through and after the Turning. In the event, of course, he and his race disappeared long before the fateful day when the magic finally departed.

187

'But Nistor predicted more than just the Turning. He accurately predicted the storm which followed, and I believe he knew more even than that.'

'How do you know all this?' interrupted Smoke.

'Ocher has been exploring. I have spoken with the basilisk at great length, both while you were looking for Vox and over the days we have been travelling. I have learned much from our once-deathless companion.'

'Oh, but Wyrm,' sighed Smoke. She flopped down and looked up at him with sad eyes. Eyes which pleaded, which wanted answers, now. 'How do you know so much of *everything*? Ever since you could talk you've told stories you couldn't possibly have heard. You're different – your knowledge goes far beyond what any normal dragon could learn in a lifetime. What *are* you, Wyrm?'

Again that smile. 'I am a dragon, just like you.' When Smoke began to protest Wyrm went on hurriedly, 'All right, I'll tell you.

'Some dragons tell of being aware when they hatched from the egg. I was aware long before that, Smoke. I remember the light of charm on the shell of the egg which carried me, the charm by which Archan was trying to make me immortal. I was to be her companion through eternity, a fact I'm sure you had not forgotten. That charm was basilisk charm, Smoke, the magic of the Deathless, and just like the Deathless it carried with it countless memories. Those memories became mine. Even before I opened my eyes on this world, Smoke, I knew everything the Deathless had ever known.

'The burden nearly destroyed my fragile dragon mind. Infinite memory is too much for a mortal creature to bear and so my mind quickly shed most of it. But it retained much of what it had learned about dragons. It remembered stories in particular, Smoke, stories about the past.

'Meeting Ocher has helped me to remember some of the things I thought I had forgotten, and helped me come to terms with the overpowering presence of the memories in my head. I do not sleep – but of course you know that. That is because my mind is never at rest; always some story is telling itself deep inside, and I cannot help but listen.'

Smoke shook her head slowly. 'It sounds terrible, Wyrm, but it sounds wonderful too.'

'It is all I have ever known,' shrugged Wyrm.

'Tell me about the Flame.'

'Very well. I will tell it simply, for in the end it is a simple enough thing. As I said, Nistor believed the Flame to be vital to the future of dragons in the world. With charm gone all dragons, even Naturals, would dwindle until finally the skies would be empty of our kind.'

'And empty altogether. What other creature is there that flies?'

'Indeed,' agreed Wyrm. 'Even though I do not sleep I dream of flight,' he added wistfully, indicating his wingless body with an elegant nod of his head. 'All the evidence we have seen confirms this belief of Nistor's: the madness among the Charmed which preceded the Turning, the sterility which has blighted us ever since, our declining numbers. Soon there will be no dragons left in the world.

'But Nistor believed something else too. He believed that charm would leave an empty space in the world, a space which brutish nature would be incapable of filling. This space, he claimed, would be filled by the Flame.' Wyrm's eyes were shining now as he warmed to his subject. Smoke was listening avidly, for the words seemed to flow from Wyrm's mouth like liquid truth; she did not doubt their veracity for a single breath. If Wyrm was convinced, so was she.

'Nistor's recordings, which Ocher has found and translated, predict a moment in the future which Nistor called the lighting of the sky. It is the Flame which is doing the lighting, of course, but that is not really important. What is important is this: the instant of the Lighting is the instant at which the world is created. Day one, if you like, the beginning of everything.

'Nistor believed that the day of creation was coming, and coming soon.'

Smoke looked confused. ' "The day of creation" – what do you mean? How can the world be created tomorrow, or next year? It's already here, or are we just dreaming all this?'

189

'Who knows?' laughed Wyrm. 'But that's a topic for another day. Listen, and listen hard. Let us assume that Nistor was right, and that at some time in the near future there will be an event – let us call it the Lighting – which will create our world. That sounds impossible, I know, but only if you assume that an act of creation affects only the future. Why should it not affect the past too?'

'I don't understand,' groaned Smoke.

'It's simple, it really is. Let's say I created you, a dragon, just now, but I created you in such a way that you already possessed twenty years' worth of memories. How would you know that you had only just been created, if your memories told you otherwise?'

'I wouldn't, I suppose.' The implications of what Wyrm was saying were beginning to dawn in Smoke's mind. Beginning to light it.

'Right. In the same way, an act of creation might form the world in such a way that an entirely new history of that world is formed at the same time. Creation can work both ways, Smoke, don't you see? It works backwards as well as forwards!'

'And you believe that such a moment is coming.'

'Coming soon, Smoke. Coming fast.'

'The Turning. The Gathering. The Lighting. It sounds right, somehow, don't you think?' mused Smoke.

'Absolutely right,' Wyrm agreed enthusiastically. Smoke had never seen him so animated.

'So if all this is designed to fill the gap left by charm, *what* exactly is it?'

'It's the Flame, Smoke.' And before she could complain that Wyrm's argument had brought them in a neat circle round to the very first question she had asked, he led her carefully up the sloping pile of rubble towards the blue fire.

Brace looked scornfully at Scarn.

'So what you're saying is that charm is simply going to be replaced by another kind of charm?' he growled. 'What difference does it make if you call it "charm" or "flame" – it's still magic, it seems to me.'

'Oh, but that's just where you're wrong, little red dragon,' leered Scarn, brushing his outstretched claws back and forth through the flickering blue fire. 'The Flame is much more than mere charm ever was. Charm was never really *alive*. I will grant you that many of the fire charms from the Realm were conscious to some small degree – but the Flame, oh, the Flame is very different.

'The Flame is *aware*, dragons. It sees, it learns, it knows. It is truly alive, this new magic, and it holds such power as the world has never before known!'

With a flourish Scarn whipped his claws clear of the fire, which immediately expanded into a fireball, a seething mass of flames which licked at the broken ceiling and splashed against the cocoon which Ledra and Brace were now thankful to have as protection. It flowed around Scarn's body leaving it quite untouched. The ends of his claws and the tips of his teeth glowed white-hot and tiny sparks busied themselves in the corners of his eyes. With a roar the flames subsided a little, although they remained high and violent, blue Flame-light overwhelming the orange of the lava in the long, narrow cave. Nature bowed to new charm.

'A day is coming, dragons,' Scarn went on. 'Coming soon, coming fast. A day of enlightenment will soon be upon us. We will enter a new age: the age of the Flame, when *I* shall be master!'

Scarn paused for dramatic effect, stretching the yellow sheets of fire which were his wings. Blue fire lunged at him, and his mood changed suddenly.

With a snarl he went on, 'But the Flame has an adversary. Victory is not assured. You, dragons, you were sent to help me achieve victory for the followers of the Flame.

'The ritual is simple. There is a place. There is a day. And there is a dragon. The place I have already located. The day is nearly upon us. But the dragon I have yet to locate.

'On the day of enlightenment, within the circumference of the Last Circle, one dragon must die if all dragons are to live. And the question you are here to answer is – where is that dragon?'

CHAPTER 14

Fires Joined

Smoke found it easier than she expected to climb the fallen head. Of course she could have flown, but keeping company with Wyrm had a way of making a dragon reluctant to take to the air: *sympathetic grounding*, as she had come to think of it.

Wyrm led the way up, using the rack of stone teeth as Grell had earlier. He was nimble, more agile than Smoke with her cumbersome wing membranes. Even so, the ascent was short and trouble-free, aided by the fact that the sculpture had landed at a slight angle: at least they did not have to tackle a sheer vertical face. Wyrm offered Smoke his tail when he reached the top, hauling her up the last stretch with a strength she did not expect. Together they clung to the curved plateau of the stone dragon's lower lip and surveyed what lay within its jaws.

The Flame burned brightly from a point about halfway down the cavernous mouth. It had no source – it simply sprang from the empty air as if by magic. *Of course*, Smoke scolded herself, *what else?* Shimmering blue light lit the interior of the mouth, which had been sculpted with as much care as the outside of the skull. A massive tongue curled down into the shadows beneath the Flame and tendons pressed behind the palates. Smoke shivered, uneasy.

'It's quite safe,' Wyrm reassured her. 'It really is just a statue. I found Ocher up here earlier, while you were up on the ledge. We explored for a while, then I came back to find you.'

'Is Ocher still in there?' Smoke peered apprehensively

into the dimly lit cavity. 'It shouldn't take long to explore a dragon's mouth, I wouldn't have thought.'

'That depends on the dragon,' replied Wyrm mischievously. 'Come on.'

With complete confidence he stepped over the edge of the precipitous stone lip and slithered down the folds of the tongue into the obscurity of shadows at the edge of the eerie light. 'Come on!' he repeated, his voice sounding too far away for Smoke's liking. Holding her breath, as though she were about to jump into water, she followed.

The Flame flashed across her vision like a ball of lightning and was gone. She braced herself, expecting to hit the bottom ... but she kept on sliding. One glance upwards confirmed that she was dropping away from the tooth-lined mouth at increasing speed, but before she could begin to guess what was happening a boulder thudded against her back, spinning her wildly around. Bouncing against a wall of rock she turned head over haunches and finally came to an undignified stop on a sloping stretch of dusty floor. Clouds of salt and rock dust settled around her as she shook her head and sneezed.

'I'm sorry,' came Wyrm's voice through the haze. 'I should have warned you about that.'

'Where are we?' stammered Smoke, looking around. Had they passed right through the recumbent head of the stone dragon?

It was another chamber, evidently some way beneath the main tower chamber. It was cool and, astonishingly, bright, a wedge-shaped cavern which flared outwards and upwards from this, its narrowest part. As the floor sloped away so the ceiling rose and the walls diverged; Smoke's overwhelming sensation was of looking into infinity. Then her eyes adjusted to the false perspective and she registered the far wall: a long, straight frieze of lines and shapes and patterns, all etched into pure white stone by some ancient and delicate claw.

She looked up sharply. There, several trees above their heads, was the blue glimmer of the Flame framed by dark stone teeth. 'I don't understand,' she faltered. 'Is this charm at work again? Did something allow us to pass through the floor, just like Grell let us pass into the tunnel?'

'Nothing so poetic, I'm afraid,' Wyrm confessed. 'The impact of the stone head seems to have simply opened up an old access passage. I imagine it was poor Troo who blocked it up in the first place, when he clambered up the altar. Hence the bumpy ride.'

Smoke searched for the basilisk but found it nowhere. 'No sign of Ocher,' she announced, stepping clear of the pile of dust in which she had landed. 'It does like to wander off, doesn't it?'

Wyrm shrugged. 'It will come back, if it wants to.'

Smoke moved cautiously out into the widening space. It was a strange sensation, an optical illusion which made her feel smaller the further she ventured. She felt the pain of gentle charm in her mind but for once it was strangely welcome, like an old friend. Halfway towards the far wall she stopped and beckoned Wyrm to join her.

'Beautiful, isn't it?' said Wyrm with relish as he caught up, indicating the wall. Smoke appraised the complex patterns and nodded silently. It was captivating, a magnificent feat of artistry which combined forms both realistic and abstract. Dragons swooped, charm boiled and weird, spiralling shapes swarmed and rolled; as Smoke looked she fancied she could almost see it move.

'Yes,' she whispered, 'it is.'

'Come on,' said Wyrm, his voice also hushed. 'Let's go closer.'

One pattern dominated all the others, and as they drew nearer it grew to immense proportions. Smoke squinted and cocked her head – it looked familiar. Three breaths later she recognized it and blinked in surprise.

'It's what we saw in the faery cave!' she cried. 'But how . . . did the faeries come down here, do you suppose?' Wyrm did not know; he seemed mesmerized by the pattern.

It was a set of simple shapes, etched large in the towering wall: a circle on the left and a long, vertical scratch on the right. Between the two was a series of wavering horizontal lines. Above the circle was a small star. If the other engravings had seemed alive then this central pattern seemed ready to leap clear of the wall and explode into the chamber. White, it was filled with colour; cut from raw stone, it glowed.

Then Smoke realized that it *was* glowing, that it was in fact the source of light in a chamber which by rights should have been as dark as night. It was a perfect, shadowless light, one which flowed through the space like liquid pouring forth. She could almost see the lines of force in the air, the aura which this thing emanated. She gasped and to her surprise felt tears stinging at the corners of her eyes.

'Vox thought it was a map,' she said, brushing at her face with her wing. 'Was he right?'

'Indeed yes,' confirmed Wyrm. 'It is the most important map ever to have been drawn in this world. It shows the location of the Last Circle. And that is where the day of creation will dawn.'

Aria led them across the great forest. At last food was plentiful, and the water in the rivers tasted fresh and pure. Large, shiny-scaled fish abounded in their waters, and the dragons could not help but rejoice in the bounty they had found in this new land.

All around them was evidence of the turned world, the natural world. The trees which made up the forest were taller than any they had known, huge conifers with thick, gnarled trunks strong enough to weather the fiercest storm.

'They would have looked clumsy in the days of charm,' said Cumber, a little wistfully. 'Once it was charm that held a tree upright while the dryads sported in its branches – now a tree is just wood.'

'But beautiful wood, my dear,' smiled Velvet. 'See how rich the colours are.'

'Tallow would have loved it here,' said Volley, and they all felt sad for a while.

New creatures peered at them from behind the trees. They had already found large rodents – many times bigger than the rabbits they were used to – that they could hunt and eat. But animals even bigger than these prowled the forest, heavy, lumbering creatures with thick pelts and soft, intelligent faces; they too fished. At first the dragons were wary, especially Cumber and Velvet.

'Remember those dreadful beasts we battled with on our way to the citadel?' said Velvet with a shudder when first they saw these big, black denizens of the forest. Cumber shivered too – he remembered the fight with the huge, primal wolves only too well.

But these beasts were different, and they left the dragons to themselves, indulging only in a few curious glances before continuing along their regular trails. Quickly they learned to tolerate each other. The dragons found it hard to adapt to the novelty of this situation: before the Turning there had been few predators in the world big enough to tackle a full-grown dragon. Now, it seemed, there were indeed beasts big enough.

For several days they flew and still the forest stretched below them. Aria's pace was slow but steady and they made progress. The weather stayed fine and the wind gusted gently at their backs, carrying them on into the west.

Then, one morning, shortly after they had begun their first stint of flying, Wist spotted a dark smudge just above the trees far away to their left. She was strangely agitated, but Gossamer could not determine why. As they tacked south-west towards the disturbance, Wist stayed close to Gossamer, but she would not speak.

The smudge was quickly revealed to be a huge pall of smoke, with towering flames visible beneath it. A deep roaring sound rolled up into the sky, a background noise to explosive cracks as trees ignited and tremendous concussions as they fell. It was a forest fire, nothing more, but one on such a scale as they had never seen.

A vast swathe of forest had caught alight, whether by natural or unnatural means it was impossible to tell. Lightning might start such a catastrophe, they knew – or charm, of course. Whatever spark had set it, the forest was ablaze!

Clouds of ash danced through the billowing smoke, lit from below by the fierce orange of the flames. The closer the dragons flew the more treacherous the sky became. Singed by embers, blackened by soot, choking in the smoke, they slowed to a hover . . . and none of them could make the decision to turn away. The sheer spectacle of unquenchable fire hypnotized them, despite the discomfort.

'I thought it was the Cloud you speak of, Gossamer,' murmured Wist, close to Gossamer's ear. Gossamer turned to

196

speak, expecting Wist to fall silent again, but instead the young dragon became increasingly excited, dancing in the air, her face aglow. 'When you mentioned the Cloud it made me think about what happened to me in the Fissures. I followed Scarn blindly, and at the time it seemed the right course of action. I loved him – we all did. And I believed in the Cult completely, Gossamer.

'It was Tallow who changed me. It was his wings, I think – they seemed so strong, so confident . . . so *real*. Up until then only Scarn had been real, him and his Last Circle. But Tallow changed all that. Poor Tallow.'

'Poor Tallow,' agreed Gossamer sadly.

'Whatever it was I sensed in Tallow I can sense in you too, Gossamer. And it's got something to do with this Cloud of yours. I want to know more, Gossamer. I want to know everything you know about it, because right now I think it's the most important thing in the world.'

Gossamer smiled, but beneath her benign expression her heart was thundering loud enough to drown the sound of the blazing forest in her ears. Until now no dragon had understood the depth of her feelings towards the mysterious Cloud – 'All right,' she said. 'I'll tell you everything I know.'

And she did. As they flew together high over the roaring flames, she told Wist about her strange encounter with the mysterious entity, she recited the Cloud's enigmatic words, tried to express the love she had felt projecting from it, described the promises it had made.

' "The answer lies within your wings," ' repeated Wist, her eyes wide and unfocused. 'What did it mean by that, I wonder?'

'I wonder too,' smiled Gossamer. 'I thought at first it meant Aria – she was lying in my embrace as the Cloud said those words – but now I'm not so sure. I have a feeling everything the Cloud said to me had many meanings.'

'And you haven't heard it speak since?' pressed Wist, still clearly excited. Gossamer shook her head.

'Not with my ears. In my mind, sometimes, I fancy I can hear that voice, but I can never really be sure. Of course, the Cloud actually intervened at the Gathering. It froze

Archan in place while Fortune rescued Aria's egg. It froze me and Scoff, too.'

'What did it feel like?' Again Gossamer shook her head.

'I don't remember,' she said regretfully.

'What about Fortune?'

Gossamer sighed. 'He saw it all, of course. He doesn't exactly disbelieve me, but he thinks it could just as easily have been some capricious charm at work. Who knows – perhaps it was.'

'You don't really believe that.'

Gossamer smiled. She liked Wist – she was intelligent and careful of speech, giving the impression that she said nothing without considering it well first. Given time, she felt sure they would become close friends. And the bond of the Cloud was strong . . .

'You love them all so much,' observed Wist.

'They are my family.'

They would have talked all day had not Scoff thrust his way between them and pointed excitedly into the cloud of smoke. A plume of dirty vapour was boiling towards them, its ragged edges in constant, unruly motion.

'Quick,' he urged, cycling his glorious wings so near to their faces that it seemed they had fallen into a rainbow. 'Backwards, now. Don't like the look of this.'

Other voices rang out, urging each other to pull away from the conflagration. Beneath the smoke the fire was licking higher, rising clear of the ruined canopy and arching up towards the sky. Individual flames were lost in a single torrent of light, a brilliant orange wall which spread itself across their vision. The heat crashed against them.

Then the flames turned blue and shapes began to seethe within.

Brace and Ledra, trapped within their invisible prison of charm, followed the line of Scarn's arrogant gaze and looked again into the Flame.

It was Brace who first noticed the shapes moving inside the fire. Ledra gasped as he pointed them out to her. They were clouds, moving towards them at dizzying speed.

The closer they looked the more they were drawn into the illusion – if illusion it was. The Flame cradled a view of the sky, tinted an unnaturally brilliant blue. Clouds raced past – it was as if they were flying at speed through the air. The effect was so realistic that they both squinted, expecting to feel the blast of wind against their faces. Ledra's wings twitched involuntarily.

'The Flame is searching,' said Scarn suddenly. 'And sooner or later it will chance upon what I am looking for. However, I would prefer it to be found sooner, which is where you come in.'

'I don't understand,' said Brace, unable to take his eyes off the rush of the clouds inside the fire. *If Scarn is talking to us*, he was thinking, *if he needs us, then we might yet survive this.*

'The Flame is an eye,' explained Scarn, waving his fiery wings extravagantly. 'A dragon looks into its depths and sees things that are happening on the other side of the world.' He paused for a moment to allow his words to sink in. 'There is more,' he went on, then he hesitated, smiling cruelly, 'but I will save that for later. Suffice it to say I am looking for a particular dragon . . . and with your help I can find that dragon quickly enough for my needs.'

'Why should we help you?' snarled Ledra.

'Oh, dragon,' sighed Scarn, coming close again. His teeth glistened blue. 'Do not imagine you have a choice.'

Without warning the net of charm tightened around the two captives, forcing them against each other. Ledra yelped as Brace's haunches ground against her flank and they both struggled to breathe.

'I want you to think about this dragon for me, think about her very hard,' snapped Scarn. His voice was savage now, bereft of patience. His every movement had become clipped, urgent. 'It should be easy for you both, for are you not closer to her than most?'

'Why do you want to find Aria?' blurted Brace, coughing and gasping for breath.

'Speak not the name of the temptress!' bellowed Scarn, whipping his tail around so that it lashed against the invisible cocoon. Sparks of charm splintered away from the inner skin, scalding Ledra and causing her to cry out in pain. 'She is not the one I want – I want her mother. I want the dragon called Gossamer! She is the sacrifice – she is the one who will feed the Last Circle when the day of creation finally comes!'

Charm pressed against Brace's head and leaked into his mind, damping his horror with an evil fog. Quite against his will he found his thoughts turned towards his sister, found his vision filled with her wings, his ears resounding with the echo of her voice, his heart thundering with the love they bore each other. Ledra too felt the onslaught, for though she had no sister herself, Gossamer she regarded now as family. Their stifling prison filled with the essence of Gossamer until she seemed to be with them inside it, a ghost-dragon unconfined by the barrier of charm which held them back.

Once this apparition had taken shape it slipped out into the chamber and circled Scarn's head. He watched it with undisguised wonder, and Brace noticed for the first time that he was not in control of events. The observation thrilled him – he nudged Ledra but she was still recovering from the grip of the charm. In that breath Scarn looked less like a leader than one of his own acolytes. *There is something beyond him, moving events*, realized Brace, at once excited and horrified. *But if Scarn is just a tool, who is his master?*

That question would have to wait, for the ghost-Gossamer was swooping towards the Flame and its surrounding sky-scape of moving cloud. The Flame shrank as the apparition approached, or else it receded far into some impossible distance – Brace could not tell which. At the instant ghostly wingtips touched the fire, blue light seemed to peel back, and suddenly the illusory clouds were not just speeding – they were *hurtling*. The ghost-dragon exploded into a thousand filaments of vapour, leaving the crashing clouds empty. But not for long. Weaving, accelerating still, Brace's line of sight dipped down and twisted to the side, revealing ocean where before there had been sky. Now the charm had been given its instructions it wasted no time. It sprinted across the tremendous belt of ocean in the blink of an eye and then there was a forest, a never-ending tract of green which was nothing but a blur to the three dragons watching transfixed.

Fire glowered on the horizon, orange light which hurled itself into view with an audible snap. With no warning the velocity dropped to nothing and the portal within the Flame was filled with this secondary fire. The tip of the Flame curled downwards, folding in upon itself to reach into its heart until blue heat was pumping into this vision of orange. To Brace it looked as though the Flame was turning itself inside-out.

The two colours merged to form a swelling, white aura which began to overwhelm the narrow Fissure. Scarn stepped back, eyes wide with ecstasy – and perhaps a little shock. His captives quite forgotten, he turned and rushed out of his secret cave.

Still gripped by the invisible charm, Brace and Ledra clung to each other as the new light of the Flame exploded towards them, to engulf them.

Scarn raced through the tunnels, his breath searing his throat. Fire bubbled all around him, spilling out from between his scales, filling his mouth and jostling his teeth. It felt like hot metal welling up inside his every pore.

Once I was a Natural, he thought blissfully. *Now I have achieved what was once thought impossible – I have truly become Charmed!*

The Flamehall was filled with red dragons. The entire Cult was massed here, defying the orders which had once been unbreakable – they flew. Some circled, some hovered; the hot air was busy with wings and lashing tails and loud with the thrill of conversation. Talk became a roar as Scarn burst in, trailing blue fire.

'The time has come, dragons!' he bellowed. 'Your days in the egg are over. When you joined me you were reborn – now prepare to be hatched afresh. Prepare to journey, dragons. We go now. We go on the greatest journey of all. We go to the Last Circle!'

The response was tumultuous. All the dragons began to circle until a living whirlwind had formed itself in the centre of the huge cavern. Their chanting redoubled, joining with the rumble of the fire to create a cacophony. Scarn arrowed into the still centre of the spinning mass and hovered there, surveying his work.

Dragons flashed past, individual faces blurred and lost. But that did not matter. Scarn cared little for names. Already he had forgotten the name of the dragon his prisoners had helped him to locate. In his mind she was simply the Sacrifice. That was enough.

Slowly the fire which Scarn had drawn from the Fissure congealed about his body, cloaking him in a skin of rippling, blue light. Then the light folded, opening a gaping hole in the air directly before his eyes. Though he was ablaze he felt no pain; his flesh did not burn, it *sang*. The rift widened, revealing a long tunnel of light stretching beyond. The whirlwind spun faster, sucking the fire into its dance.

Then Scarn entered the tunnel.

There was a resounding crash as some primary fabric was split open. Scarn vanished into the hole in the air, vanished from the Flamehall, from the Fissures – indeed from this part of the world altogether. Like some organic river the dragons of the Cult peeled one by one from their tornado and followed him into the tunnel, passing through into whatever reality lay beyond that threshold. Three blinks of a dragon's eye and they were all gone. The fire remained for a breath or two, boiling in the centre of the chamber, pouring its energies in pursuit of the escaping dragons, then it winked out. Silence came, and remained for a long time.

It was Wist who first saw the dragons moving within the fire. They looked like motes of dust with long, trailing wings, distorted both by distance and by the unnatural blue glare. They grew bigger with impossible speed, thundering into focus as though hurled from the other side of the cosmos. Transparent walls shimmered about their growing forms, a tunnel so sheer it could barely be seen. Perspective failed as Wist tried to determine the direction from which they flew: it was neither forward nor back, neither inside nor out – they simply *came*. Fast.

Something bumped against Wist from behind: it was Aria, her face contorted. She lunged towards the oncoming dragons then checked herself, turning to seek out her mother. Hanging in the air, she hesitated, swinging her head around wildly as the dragons of the Cult of the Last Circle erupted from the tunnel of fire and out into the sky.

Red motion surrounded the astonished onlookers, duplicated dragons powering their way across the tunnel's unnatural threshold to join the circle of wings which was growing around them. Behind the frenzy was the constant tower of the blue fire, a vertical river of light against which the dragons glowered, portentously dark. But no sooner had the last dragon emerged than the flames subsided, reverting to orange and cowering back into the trees which had fed them earlier, before this magic had been unleashed. Thick black smoke billowed up as the flames died down; soon even the roar of the forest fire had dropped to a barely audible crackle.

Wist flew in close to Gossamer and Fortune. As she did so the others of their band – Cumber and Velvet, Scoff and Volley and the trembling Aria – gathered too, cringing into the centre of the ring of dragons which had formed itself in the gloomy, ash-filled air over the decimated forest. Round and round the red dragons flew, slowing gradually now until each individual had reached a hovering position. Escape beckoned, up or down, but none of the band attempted it, for they knew such an effort would be in vain. Wist looked round the circle, seeking faces she knew, looking for hope. But all the dragons looked the same, from this distance at least, their Natural shapes dyed brilliant red by Scarn's new charm.

One dragon she would have known however, despite the camouflage, despite the distance: Lessen, her twin sister. One by one she picked her way round the ring until she had returned – more or less – to the start, but Lessen was not there. Wist would certainly have recognized the set of her wings, the tilt of her head – she would have *sensed* her. But Lessen was not there. Conflicting emotions tugged at her, for while there was much about her sister she despised (and she knew Lessen abhorred her) she could not contemplate the thought that she was dead.

If Scarn has killed you, she thought coldly, *then he will pay.*

Justice is building up against him – sooner or later judgement will fall.

As if in response to her thoughts, Scarn himself broke free of his place in the ring and flew into its centre. Trails of charm scattered behind his blazing wings. His eyes, dazzling in his shining red face, surveyed each member of the group in turn. They lingered on Velvet, and on Fortune, they passed over Aria and Wist with scarcely a pause . . . and they locked on Gossamer. A smile crawled over his face.

'At last we are together,' he whispered, the words seeming to glow as they fell from his mouth. The ash and smoke, already clearing of its own accord, fled swiftly from the passage of his voice until a globe of clear air had swelled around them all.

Then Scarn, who had once told stories to the infant dragons of Aether's Cross and who had now led his devoted followers across half the world to reach this point in space and time, opened his wings wide and balanced on an invisible cushion of charm.

'It is time for you to hear the truth about the Flame,' he intoned, as though it were those same infant dragons listening to him now. He closed his bright eyes and began to speak.

In the cavern beneath the Towers of Nistor, Wyrm had turned away from the map on the wall.

'The Last Circle,' he announced. 'That is where we have to go. That is where Scarn is going, if he has not reached it already. He has access to the Flame – all we have is each other. For now.'

'Where is this Last Circle?' said Smoke bravely. 'And what about Vox? Wyrm, if you know anything you must tell me.'

'Vox is gone.' Wyrm's answer was swift and cut Smoke like the sharpest claw. Then he said something which she did not hear at first. 'But do not fret, dragon, for you may see him again when his work is done.'

Fighting back tears, Smoke struggled to interpret his words. 'But you said he was dead,' she blurted.

'I said he was gone,' smiled Wyrm, enigmatic as ever.

'Now, since we came to the Towers of Nistor, I have learned a new story. Would you like to hear it?'

'Do I have any choice?' Smoke inquired weakly.

Wyrm chuckled. 'Then I'll begin.'

CHAPTER 15

The Story of the Flame

Once, the world was a place of charm.

Once, there was not just charm in the world. The charm was the world.

Everything – every creature, every river, every storm, every sunrise, every grain of sand on every beach – was ruled by charm. There was nothing else.

First-born in the world of charm were the troll lords. The thunder of their footsteps accompanied the birth cries of the new lands; their ponderous explorations opened up the valleys and canyons, made the mountains. Born of fire, they eventually retreated into the ice, and the world began to turn.

Dragons came too, and a host of others: the faeries and sprites, the long-lived erraps and the elegant zirafae, charmed all. But already the magic was leaking away and the forces of nature were beginning to assert themselves. Creatures of charm were starting to lose their powers, their colours. New and natural beasts invaded their lands – crude, muscular copies of their charmed cousins. For a time there was envy and conflict.

And then the world finally turned, and the magic was gone.

But there are places in the world so ancient, and so soaked in charm, that nothing, not even the power of a Turning, can liberate them of their energies. The charm in these reservoirs is old and hard, reluctant to yield itself up to the living world again. It lies far underground, aware, motionless, deep in thought, weaving plans. It remembers its origins in the fire of the trolls, and it considers its future. It does not fear death as mortals do, nor does it seek it as once the Deathless did – it simply wishes to regain the power it once lost. It refuses to live on as a cripple in the new world of nature. It yearns to break free, yet all the natural laws prevent it from doing so.

So it waits, and plans, and grows bitter, and wonders if there might not be a way for the magic of the fire to prevail once more.

Wyrm paused, frowning.

'What is it?' asked Smoke breathlessly.

'I don't know. It's as if . . . as if I'm not the only one telling this story.' He shrugged and went on.

Scarn stopped briefly, his expression confused. Then he continued.

The time the charm is waiting for is fast approaching. The last piece of the puzzle which is the Turning is about to lock into place, and the charm knows that this may be its only chance to survive.

On the day of the lighting of the sky, a new energy will enter the world. When its work is done, the history of this world will be one in which charm never existed. Fact will become legend, everything which was once true will be myth. Already we have seen the bones of the trolls bury themselves and turn grey and old – that was just the beginning.

What place then for the lingering charm in such a world? What place for its bitterness, its struggle for influence? How can it survive when it no longer has a past?

The answer is that it will change. The lighting of the sky will bring a new power to the world, but that same event will alter the charm irrevocably. No sooner will the Lighting have released its champion than it will have created an adversary. Two opponents will stride out across the world of nature, a world which will have become an arena.

On the day of the lighting of the sky, the new champion will confront the heir to all that charm has ever owned, has ever been. It will confront the brilliance of the Flame.

Scarn was ecstatic. 'And the Flame is already with us!' he concluded. 'Already the charm is gathering the strength it needs to face the new enemy. Magic is flowing deep underground, amassing at countless points around the world, making fire, building the future, building the Flame! There is a battle about to begin, and we shall be witness to it all!'

'So what is it that the charm is turning into?' asked Smoke. 'What *is* the Flame?'

'On the simplest level: fire,' replied Wyrm at once. 'Nistor's Flame represented the first efforts of charm to prepare for the Turning, before even the Seed, of Charm was formed. Nistor and his followers fed the Flame with constant prayer and sacrifice, without realizing its inherent evil. The Seed which Mantle took to the stars contained all that was good about charm, leaving behind something older, and much wilier.'

'I never liked stories about Nistor,' agreed Smoke with a shudder.

'Ah, but you don't understand the full truth of it,' Wyrm smiled. 'The Flame *is* evil – I know that for certain, now that I have spoken with Ocher, and now that I have seen and learned from these Nistri relics. I knew this story all along, I think, but it was buried in my head along with so many others. Now is the time for it to surface, for better or worse.

'But understand me, Smoke. Understand what I mean when I say that about the Flame. I do not mean simply that it is bad: the Flame is *Evil*. It is elemental Evil. Until now evil has existed simply as a concept, a way of behaving badly. Many dragons have been evil, or done evil things, but very soon all that is going to change. Evil itself will exist as a palpable force, a force with a life and a mind of its own, able to work mischief at a whim. On the day of creation, the potential for disaster in the world will increase to a catastrophic level.'

'But that's terrible!' blurted Smoke. 'Is the world after the Turning to be a place of evil then? Did we go through all this just to be consumed by the fire?' To her amazement Wyrm's smile broadened.

'Let me finish,' he chuckled. 'And forgive my humour, which is born less of amusement than amazement, for the solution to this puzzle is so elegant that it takes my breath away. I like stories, you see, and the new world will be a place of such tales, such wonderful tales . . .

'As I said, charm has become the Flame, and the Flame is evil personified. But evil is not the only force which will be at work in the new world, for we cannot forget the new champion which the lighting of the sky will bring. Remember how I spoke of adversaries? Of two opponents striding across the world? What opponent could be more fitting for Evil than . . .'

'Than Good,' breathed Smoke, nodding slowly. 'The day of creation – the lighting of the sky – will bring elemental Good into the world. That's it, isn't it, Wyrm? That's the answer!'

Wyrm too nodded, his smile broader than ever before.

'And just as Evil has a name, so too does Good,' he said.

'What is it?'

'Gossamer knows,' answered Wyrm quietly.

'On the day of creation,' Scarn boomed, 'the glory of the Flame will be pitted against the newcomer. The newcomer must be beaten back, have no doubt about that, dragons. Only within the circumference of the Last Circle can the Flame gather enough power to repel it. It is up to us to guide the Flame to this place of confrontation, and to focus its power against the invasion. If we succeed, the new world will be a paradise; if we fail, the conflict will never end.'

'He's right,' whispered Gossamer to Fortune, 'and yet he's so, so wrong. The newcomer is the Cloud, but it isn't evil. It's Scarn's damned Flame that's evil – can't these dragons see that? It's the Flame that must be cast down.'

'He wants me,' moaned Aria suddenly, twitching and dancing in the sky next to her parents. 'That's what he means when he says the power of the Flame must be focused. He wants a sacrifice: he wants me.' She lurched forwards, then pulled herself back, struggling in the air as though some rogue charm were in control of her limbs.

'One has been chosen,' announced Scarn, his voice like thunder. 'One alone is worthy of the journey ahead. One alone is ripe for the ritual which is to come.'

'It's me, it's me,' cried Aria, trembling all over. Both Fortune and Gossamer were horrified to see that she was smiling, that her tears were tears of joy as much as they were of fear.

But Scarn had other plans. His gaze bored through the group and fixed on the one dragon he really wanted, the dragon whom Brace and Ledra had helped him, however unwittingly, to locate across the immensity of the globe. The one dragon who really knew the power of the coming force, the Flame's adversary. The one dragon whose death at the moment of creation would ensure the death of that force even as it entered the world.

He looked through air and through dragon and found her.

Gossamer.

CHAPTER 16

The Killing Crystals

The forest fire erupted again like a predator gaining its
second wind. Flames lashed the air a mere wing's width
from where Fortune's group hovered, forcing them
upwards. Scarn and the dragons of the Cult remained at
their lower altitude, tracking the ascent of their quarry
through the smoke-filled sky and oblivious to the flames
that threatened to engulf them.

'Now's our chance,' suggested Scoff. 'Not much of one,
I'll admit. Could split up though. Meet later.'

'He'll find us,' answered Fortune at once. 'No, Scoff. We
have to settle this here and now. Scarn won't leave us alone
until he's got what he wants.'

He turned to Gossamer, and was unsurprised to see her
smiling. Aria was circling furiously behind her, but for the
moment he had eyes only for the dragon he loved most in
the world. 'Well?' he prompted.

'Let me look at you,' she responded, appraising him long
and hard. Finally she nodded, satisfied. 'You're beginning
to see it, aren't you?'

Fortune frowned. 'I see . . . something,' he agreed. 'Until
now I thought this Cloud of yours was . . . well, a dream
perhaps – or maybe a ghost. I still don't understand what it
was I saw at the crest of the world, and I still don't understand how you can be so sure. I don't have your faith yet,
my dear, but I do have . . . a suspicion?'

Gossamer laughed, a bright tinkling sound which carried
through the roar of the fire below. 'Oh, Fortune,' she
scolded. 'You don't make it easy for yourself, do you?'

'I need to see it for myself.'

'Oh, my dear, but that's just the point. It's the faith that matters, not the proof. Whether it spoke to me or not, that's not important – it's my belief that counts, can't you see that?'

Fortune sighed. 'Of course I can, but I'm much better at doing than believing.'

'You? A dragon who has seen the Maze of Covamere, who has helped the world to turn true?'

'But I didn't have to believe in anything to . . .'

'You believed in your father.' Gossamer's eyes bored into Fortune's, forcing him to look away. They hovered together, almost touching, wings matched in strength and rhythm, two dragons in harmony in the sky.

'You have to go with him, don't you?' murmured Fortune, still staring into the distance. After a long pause he looked back at Gossamer. 'Don't you?'

She nodded. 'Of course I do.'

'Do you know why?'

'Because it feels right.' It was Fortune's turn to nod. Tears gathered at the corners of his eyes.

'This is the last time,' he whispered. 'We will never be parted again.'

'It's not your place to save me,' said Gossamer bravely. 'There are greater things at stake than the life of one dragon. Scarn's strength lies in his faith, but that also makes him over-confident. We must submit to him until the last possible moment – only then can he be defeated. That is why I must go: if we try to destroy him now we will fail, and lose all hope of destroying the greater enemy.'

'The Flame,' breathed Fortune.

'The Cloud is coming,' Gossamer went on, urgently now for she had seen a flicker of movement in the corner of her eye. 'Coming fast. We must be there when it arrives. We must *all* be there, Fortune, or the future will be an endless fire.'

Hot air blasted their faces. A spiral of flame whipped between them, forcing them apart, and then Scarn was there, fiery yellow wings cycling hungrily. His smile was thin and cold.

'You might call this an abduction, I suppose,' he began, only to be interrupted by Gossamer.

'I come willingly,' she announced in a voice loud enough for all to hear, even those Cult dragons far away at the edge of the ring. 'But hear me, Scarn: I tell you, you cannot win. Justice will be done, and sooner than you think.'

Scarn laughed, his voice booming through the smoke and ash. 'Justice indeed,' he agreed. 'At last the world will be as it should be. Come, dragon, enter the fire with me.'

Splinters of flame jumped from beneath his body and the air crackled with fitful bursts of charm. He gathered Gossamer under his wing and escorted her down towards the centre of the circle of dragons. He passed very close to Volley as he descended, and Fortune thought later that the big mountain dragon had deliberately placed himself in his path. Words were spoken, but Fortune heard only Volley's voice say, '. . . justice for the dead . . .' before a whirlwind took his words into the sky.

Smoke massed itself around Scarn and Gossamer, and the whirlwind began to suck fire up from the forest. A spiral of red flame engulfed them both and then there was a series of detonations, like short, explosive claps of thunder. A tunnel opened horizontally through the smoke, which was so thick now that it was almost solid. The tunnel seemed to stretch across the horizon to infinity. One by one the dragons of the Cult entered, accelerating into its confines with unnatural speed and vanishing into the brilliant haze which concealed the distance within. As the last of them departed the smoke cleared a little, causing the tunnel to shimmer. Only Scarn and Gossamer remained. Both dragons stared at Fortune, then Scarn tipped on to his back and pulled them into the tunnel together.

There was a moment of confusion.

At first Fortune thought the tunnel was disintegrating, then he saw that it was stretching. It had led Scarn and the others west, as near as he could judge, but now it seemed to be extending eastwards, back across the forest towards the distant sea. Then he realized it was not stretching at all but *travelling* and with a flash of insight he saw that it was returning to its place of origin.

213

'Mahl!' he cried. 'The Fissures. That's where the Flame is, that's where Scarn has to draw all his power from. He's stranded here now!'

None of the others responded to his shout, perhaps failing to see any importance in the knowledge. Except Wist. Fortune saw a flash of light, which turned out to be the glint of the sun in her eye as she dived towards the speeding, shrinking tunnel. 'Wait!' he called as he realized what she planned to do, but it was too late.

With a scream Wist plunged into the side of the tunnel, piercing its tenuous wall with her lashing wings. Two breaths later the end of the tunnel whipped past and sprinted into the east, a long cylinder of smoke and air carrying Wist – if she was still alive – back across the Western Ocean to the very place they had laboured so hard to escape from.

Once more the flames from the forest fell back, this time for good. Before long the fire had died away completely, leaving a vast swathe of blackened land and a sky choked with ash. Slowly the smoke cleared, and the dragons found themselves facing each other in silence. Slowly they all turned to Fortune.

'I hope you know what you're doing, old fellow,' blurted Cumber suddenly. 'And Gossamer, of course.'

'They do,' rumbled Scoff. 'All have to believe now.'

'But how can we follow them?' moaned Velvet. 'And what about Wist – where in the world has she gone?'

'There's nothing we can do for Wist now,' said Fortune. 'She has made her choice, whatever her reasons. But we still have our pathfinder.' He soared across to where Aria was hovering, her expression unreadable. 'We need you, Aria,' he said gently.

'But he doesn't!' she snapped, her voice as hard as her face. 'Oh, I'll lead you all to the very middle of the Last Circle if that's what you want, but don't expect me to help you in whatever it is you plan to do there. All I want is to be there when the end comes. I won't raise a wing against Scarn but if he's going to suffer then I want to be there. Or if he really is to be the new lord of the world then perhaps . . . perhaps . . .' but she broke into silent, sobbing tears then

214

and would not be consoled. Shaking off Fortune's fatherly wing she struck out into the sky, turning over the smouldering remains of the forest belt and leading them all towards the west.

'Look at the map!' cried Smoke excitedly, tugging at Wyrm's foreleg. He had already seen the transformation, but he indulged her by adopting a suitably surprised expression.

'Remarkable,' he agreed.

Blue light bathed the wall now, casting long, hard shadows across the incredible detail of the sculpted patterns and pictures. It had redefined the map altogether, filling all the detail which had so far remained hidden.

The vertical scratch had become an embossed flame, a perfect facsimile of the fire by the magical light of which they were witnessing this transformation. To its left, the wavering lines were an ocean, its representation so exquisite they could almost see movement in its waves. Beyond the waves were the star and the circle. The star had elongated, losing its stylized points; the circle beneath it remained stubbornly geometric and featureless, but spread around it was the varied relief of scarps and mountains, a vast swathe of coloured desert and a long, deep scar of a canyon, an entire continent adjoining the sea.

'Ocea,' breathed Wyrm, tracing the contour of the coastline with his claw. 'Now I can be sure.'

'The continent to the west?' asked Smoke. 'How do you know? No dragon I know has ever been there.'

'Ocher described it to me,' shrugged Wyrm, turning away. Suddenly he seemed bored with the map. 'Come on, it's time to go.'

Smoke followed him, feeling more and more like a confused infant and not at all the confident pathfinder she once had been. Vox was gone (but not dead?) and she found herself wondering if she could really trust Wyrm.

He was odd, to be sure, and his motivations were impossible to fathom. Was he really on the side of the Cloud? *Am I to believe his story at all?* she wondered with a shiver. A glance back over her shoulder before she climbed back into the cavity within the fallen head did little to reassure her:

blue light now flooded the chamber, rippling down the walls like running water. Wyrm's shadow obscured fully one half of the beautiful wall, spreading darkness across the map and making the sculpting flat and drab.

They emerged into the Tower chamber to find that nothing had changed. Smoke was disappointed. Not normally prone to wishful thinking, she had been hoping to find some new exit tunnel – magically generated, of course. A glance up at the ledge confirmed that the bodies of the salt giants still lay where they had fallen, merged even more closely now with the binding rock. *No Grell, no way out*, she mourned.

'Where's Ocher?' she demanded. Surely the basilisk knew a way back to the outside world – after all, it seemed to know everything else about what was going on. 'Or is that something it didn't share with you?'

If Wyrm detected the sarcasm he did not respond. He was gazing across at the tall dragon sculptures, the Towers themselves. 'Ocher is with Vox,' he said casually. 'It cannot help us any longer.'

The will to speak left Smoke. Wyrm seemed intent on revealing things at his own pace and that she would have to accept. Mute, she followed him across to the nearest of the Towers. Slowly, but with increasing exasperation, Wyrm examined the base of each of the huge, elongated sculptures. Many times he scratched at them, releasing flakes of salt from the soft, binding charm which held them rigid, but he was clearly unsatisfied.

'All right,' sighed Smoke at last. 'Just what is it that you're looking for now?'

'Ocher said it would be obvious to a dragon,' answered Wyrm unhelpfully.

'Well, it isn't obvious to you!' retorted Smoke.

Wyrm stopped in his tracks and regarded her open-mouthed. 'By the Cloud, you're right!' he cried. To Smoke's amazement he ran over and embraced her. 'Why didn't I see it before? What Ocher meant was that it would be obvious to any normal dragon.'

'And you're not normal?' inquired Smoke sarcastically.

'And I can't fly!' Wyrm was triumphant. 'Quickly, there's

no time to lose. If you want to get out of this place and save the world, your friends and the dragon you love, then fly, dragon, fly!'

All doubt left Smoke then that Wyrm was anything other than good. Dazzling light seemed to surround him and his eyes were filled with such . . . *such beauty*, she thought with a rush of embarrassment. Suddenly she felt like an infant again, shy in the presence of an older male. Opening her wings she leaped into the air, unconsciously flicking her tail as though trying to impress some hoped-for love. Swiftly she made her way up the side of the sculpture beside which they had stopped, scooping the air downwards in great draughts. Soon she reached its shining, white face, where-upon she adopted a hovering position and called down to Wyrm.

'Its mouth is open. I think there's something inside.'

'We couldn't see it from the ground.' Wyrm's reply floated up like spider silk.

Vox would have seen it, before the fire took him, thought Smoke with a stab of pain. But she cast the thought aside. Vox was alive, Wyrm said so, and that was what she believed now. Had to believe.

'Bring it down, if you can!' called Wyrm.

Wedged between the dragon's open jaws was a small, sparkling crystal. Gently Smoke prised it free, sending a shower of salt down into Wyrm's upturned face. He splutt-ered in protest and Smoke grinned. By the time she reached the ground again he had recovered and was now hopping to and fro with excitement.

'Give it to me,' he cried, practically snatching the jewel from her as she swooped in to land.

'All right, all right,' she laughed. Her mood – both their moods – had changed again. Hope had infiltrated at last, bringing them new energy.

But no sooner had Wyrm taken the crystal than he placed it on the ground before him and stamped on it with both his forelegs together. He had already struck two blows before Smoke realized what he was doing and began to protest, but before she could intervene the third blow shattered it utterly. A thin wisp of charm whistled out from the remains,

217

its fleeting presence stabbing at Smoke's mind as it dissipated before her astonished gaze.

'What the . . .' she began, but Wyrm interrupted her, suddenly serious.

'It had to be destroyed,' he said quietly. Then, with an eloquent gesture he indicated the remaining statues. 'They must all be destroyed.'

'Why? What are they?'

'Each of these statues is the likeness of a dragon sacrificed by the Nistri. And held in each set of jaws is the remains of the charm by which that particular dragon was killed. A gruesome memento, if you will. The one I just destroyed was an especially nasty one, involving the liquefaction of the dragon's internal organs over the course of a whole day. The dragon would have remained conscious the entire time, of course.'

Smoke shuddered. Suddenly she felt sick. She rolled her tongue against her teeth, aware of an unpleasant taste where her mouth had touched the crystal charm. 'And the rest?' she quavered.

'This place,' Wyrm went on, 'this very chamber is the root of the Flame's power. Nistor was the first to discover the tendency of charm to transform itself into fire, and here it was that the Flame was born. Much of its original power – its evil power – was derived from the charms which Nistor used to kill his sacrificial victims. If we can destroy what is left of them we will go some way towards diminishing the power of the Flame now.'

'Only diminish?' asked Smoke. Wyrm nodded grimly.

'What good this act of ours will do I cannot say – perhaps very little. But every little helps. The Flame has spread across the world, Smoke. Everywhere there is fire there is Flame, or at least the chance for the Flame to take hold. The blue fire you see burning here is like a wound which has become infected: the time is long past when simply cleansing the wound will suffice. The poison is in the system, Smoke. There are many Flames now.'

'But cleansing the original wound is at least a start,' determined Smoke.

'Exactly.'

'Then let's get on with it.'

At first the work was easy. Smoke found herself settling into a kind of trance as she performed the repetitive sequence of tasks: fly vertically upwards, hover, take the crystal, descend, deliver it to Wyrm, move on to the next statue. She pulled herself out of this state of semi-awareness about one third of the way round the deep arc of sculptures and discovered that they were less than halfway round. Fatigue gripped her and from then on every wingbeat was agony. The crystals tasted like spoiled fruits and more than once she felt a trickle of charm across her tongue which caused her to drop them unceremoniously into Wyrm's waiting claws. Wyrm too grew tired, breathing hard and deep as he laboured between the statues, lifting himself up only with the greatest difficulty as he prepared himself for each new blow.

As an experiment, Smoke tried dropping one crystal out of Wyrm's reach, to see if it might shatter of its own accord on the ground and thus save her companion his task. But it simply bounced, rolling towards the pile of rubble in the centre of the chamber which was all that was left of Nistor's sacrificial altar. Wyrm scrambled after it, calling up to her, 'I appreciate what you were trying to do, but don't ever do that again. If even one of these charms were to be released from its place of rest and not destroyed the results could be catastrophic. Just give them to me, like you've been doing. There's only one way to do this job: slow and steady.'

So slow and steady it was, and by the time she reached the penultimate statue Smoke felt as though her wings were no longer part of her body. They ached down to the very roots, the long muscles which were anchored on to her breastbone throbbing with dull fire. Her jaws ached as though she had lifted a mountain; her mouth tasted foul, and she longed for water. *We have seen no water down here!* she thought with a stab of panic. *Nor food!*

It was this new fear of starvation which filled her mind as she made the final ascent, driving out all other concerns so that when she reached the top of the final Tower she did not at first register what she saw. She hovered dumbly, her eyes wide, unable to comprehend what was before her.

'Come on, Smoke,' urged Wyrm at length. 'This is the last one – just bring it down.'

The sound of his voice brought her to her senses and the world snapped back into focus. She twisted her neck, searching among the contours of the salt dragon's gaping mouth, trying to confirm the truth her eyes proclaimed. 'There's nothing there,' she called down weakly. 'This one's empty, Wyrm. There's no crystal.'

Wyrm cursed and made a half-hearted leap at the side of the sculpture. 'What I wouldn't give to fly!' he muttered under his breath. 'Are you sure?' he cried, knowing that it was true. Smoke swooped down, her eyes rimmed with red, her wings trembling and lending her flight an awkward, intoxicated air.

'I'm sure,' she sighed as she thumped on to the ground. 'Either there was never anything there, or someone has been here before us. Does it really matter? We dealt with the rest.'

Wyrm feverishly scanned the ground as though the missing crystal might magically appear there. 'I suppose it doesn't really make any difference,' he mumbled. 'One charm from so many – still, in the wrong claws.' He jumped, startled, as Smoke folded a shaking wing across his back.

'Come on,' she said kindly. 'We have to leave this now. We have to get out of here, Wyrm. Let's get back to somewhere we belong; let's find our friends.'

Wyrm held his breath for a very long time, his eyes still darting into the shadows at the periphery of the chamber. Then he exhaled, a long, slow whistle. 'Yes, you're right,' he said slowly, 'there is nothing more we can do here.' He lifted his snout and scented the air. 'We have finished our work here – you can smell it in the air. The salt giants are dead, our companions have already moved on and the Flame . . .' He glanced at the blue fire which flickered unchanged. 'Well, we may have damaged it, or we may not. Either way we can do no more. You're right, Smoke: it's time to go.'

'How?'

Vox indicated the ledge where the bodies of the salt giants lay blended with the rock.

'The same way we came in,' he announced to Smoke's surprise. 'But you'll have to carry me up there.'

Smoke had no idea how she managed to lift Wyrm up to the ledge. The first time she tried her wings buckled, devoid of all strength. Then she thought of the open sky, of clear air filled with dragon song and from some deep, inner place fresh energy jolted into her veins. Clamping her hind legs firmly about Wyrm's thin, dark body she lurched faltering into the air and, flight more a spasm than anything, dragged them both the comparatively short distance upwards. She practically dropped her cargo when she reached the ledge; she heard the breath burst from his lungs as he crashed down on to the rock, but he did not complain, just lay there recovering his breath while Smoke flopped beside him, massaging her throbbing wings.

'Th-thank you,' gasped Wyrm.

'You're welcome.'

They lay there, the two of them, nestled against the tremendous flanks of the giants, now transformed into lumpy black and white coils of rock and salt. Slowly their breathing returned to normal.

'Quite a view,' commented Wyrm, looking out over the arc of dragon heads. 'The Towers of Nistor. Were they what you expected, Smoke?'

She shook her head. 'I don't know. All I know is if I never see them again it will be too soon. Let's go, Wyrm, if you've got a way.'

Wyrm frowned and sniffed at the air. 'Does your head hurt?' he asked suddenly. Taken aback, it took Smoke a few breaths before she realized what he was asking. She consulted her lingering charm sense and found a dull ache at the base of her skull: a sure sign that charm was at work somewhere nearby.

'Grell cheated,' explained Wyrm, clambering to his claws and pacing the width of the ledge. 'She used Ocher's idea – the basilisk must have spoken to her in her sleep – of creating a dream-charm. That's a popular spell for wielders of earth charm, if you didn't already know. The faeries did it all the time; they needed to, mind you, being corporeal only once every hundred years.'

221

'She made a replica of herself, a ghost,' said Smoke.

'Exactly. So it follows that this is not really Grell's body before us. Her real body must still be forming the entrance just as it was when we came in.'

'It looks solid enough.'

'Probably because the rock it has merged with is real enough. The rock is taking them over now, Smoke. It's fascinating though, isn't it: dream joining reality, a ghost fusing with the land?'

'Perhaps, but if the ghost has fused then doesn't it follow that the original body has too?'

'Of course. Which is why there isn't much time. Somewhere nearby is the thread of charm which links this ghost-corpse to Grell's real body lying back at the entrance. And that's what we have to find.'

'But we can't get back through the tunnel,' protested Smoke. 'It was only by Grell helping us that we got across that chasm in the first place.'

'If the charm's still there, we don't need Grell,' answered Wyrm bluntly. He turned and started sniffing again, trailing his snout across the dusty surface of the ledge. Smoke watched him, shaking her head, wondering how he could be so infuriating . . . *and yet I do love him*, she realized with a jolt. At once an image of Vox sprang into her mind but it was hazy and distant – a ghost, in fact. Her love for him remained but . . . what was this new sensation? Scolding herself, yet unable to keep her eyes off Wyrm, she concentrated on the ache in her head, trying to locate its source.

They searched for what seemed an age, until Wyrm grew confused, scouting first near the heads of the fallen giants, then at their entwined and practically unrecognizable feet. Later Smoke realized what it was that so unsettled her about her companion's behaviour during this time: he was constantly yawning. In vain they looked for the thread of charm Wyrm was sure still existed, but they found nothing. The ache lingered in Smoke's mind but try as she might she could not focus on it sufficiently to identify its source. She became certain of one thing, however – it was not coming from the vicinity of the giants' bodies.

222

'I'm afraid you're wrong, Wyrm,' she sighed at last. 'It was a lovely idea, but I'm afraid we really are stuck down here.'

'Nonsense,' Wyrm replied, stifling a gigantic yawn. He touched a claw to his mouth as if surprised by its actions. 'Smoke . . . I do feel rather strange.'

'Come and sit with me for a moment.' Wyrm tottered over to join her at the back of the ledge. The giants loomed beside them as they both collapsed wearily against the rock wall.

'What's happening to me?' murmured Wyrm. His eyes looked red and sore. Another yawn cracked open his mouth. Worried though she was about him, Smoke could not help smiling.

'Oh, Wyrm. Just lean on me for a breath or two.' She nestled his head in her wings. Wyrm closed his eyes.

They lay together in the silence. Smoke listened to Wyrm's breathing grow slower, finally reducing itself to a shallow, steady whisper. His eyelids drooped and then closed. Charm fluttered at the limits of her perception as, for the first time in his life, dragon Wyrm slept.

When Aria looked back to where the smoke from the forest fire still smudged the pale blue of the sky she imagined the flames still prowled through the ruined trees. They were dead now, of course, but her mind wandered, playing tricks on her.

She remembered the love Scarn had shown for all the dragons of his harem, and how in many ways he had shown her the most love of all. Dragons such as Wist and her twin Lessen, and Dart and beautiful Riss, all those dragons he had taken to his inner chambers . . . but not her, not Aria.

I thought he was saving me for something special, she thought, unable to identify the emotion which ruled the idea. *But it was never really me he wanted. Archan took me and rejected me for my son. And now Scarn has rejected me for my mother. Where does that leave me? Who really wants Aria?*

A glance at Fortune, at his worried expression, provided a part of the answer, but it was Gossamer's face which dominated her inner vision. They wanted her, she knew that now. At that instant Aria finally recognized and embraced the unconditional love of her parents.

And what of Wyrm? He has no father, and he might as well have no mother, for all the good I have been to him.

She continued to look back, calling Wyrm's name in the silence of her thoughts, trying to summon his face against that of Gossamer. But to her distress she found herself unable to remember what he looked like. All she could remember was that he had no wings.

My wingless dear. Find the way back to me, back to us all.

Scarn's final rejection had cleared her heart. It was as though a whole cycle of seasons had swept through her, leaving her older and wiser by an entire year, if not an age. Was this what growing up was like? For the first time in her short life Aria began to believe that there might be such a thing as peace. She looked up.

In the sky above her the comet outshone the sun.

CHAPTER 17

Dreams of Flight

Vox assumed he was dead.

Out of darkness the stars gradually emerged, growing from minute points to brilliant lights, more brilliant than he had ever seen them in a terrestrial sky. All was silent, silent as death. The stars turned steadily. He was not aware of his body, of its normal functions, of breathing, of feeling hot or cold: all perception had left him except his sight. He felt calm, unafraid; and curious.

A new shape rose into view, sharing the slow spin of the stars. A black disc rimmed with a crescent of light. It traversed his vision until it had vanished and there were only stars again, and Vox did not understand what it was he had seen.

Then he saw something he did recognize. It followed the disc into his line of sight: a pure white nucleus tapering into a glorious trail of gossamer.

It was the comet.

The disc was creeping past again when its luminous crescent edge exploded with light. Vox discovered he could move his eyes and look away, and when he looked back he realized he was watching a sunrise. Colour poured over the disc, filling it with dimension as well as light until he saw that it was a sphere, a cloud-covered globe. Patterns were laid across its surface, patterns he knew in part from his many ordinary flights, in part from his one, extraordinary flight over the basilisk map, when the whole world had been unpeeled beneath him.

This is the world, he realized. *I am beyond the world*.

He flexed his wings before remembering that he no longer

had a body. But however imaginary the action was it slowed the rotation of the stars. A further motion stopped the spinning altogether so that he hovered stationary, watching the sun chase its shadow round the globe. Continents unravelled, seas unfurled, the long shadows of mountain ranges crept back towards their source as the world turned effortlessly into the sunlight. Vox looked to the side and saw twin shadows fluttering at his side: transparent dragon wings, beating against the background of stars.

I am a ghost, he thought calmly. Then he saw the basilisk.

Ocher drifted up to him, its face as unreadable as ever. It too was transparent, a spectral presence behind which the drama of the sunrise played itself out unconcerned. It appraised Vox, looking from one wingtip to the other. Then Vox heard its voice inside his mind.

. . . You are welcome here, dragon.

Vox tried to open his mouth, but he found no words emerged, nor even did any breath pass between his lips. Panic seized him unexpectedly and he began to thrash his insubstantial wings. The world tumbled out of view. The stars whirled.

Something shivered through his mind and his unruly motion steadied itself, finally slowing; it stopped so that the world was once more before him. The basilisk withdrew its ghostly claws, pulling them back beneath its belly, as though it were hiding something there.

. . . Do not be afraid, dragon.

. . . Am I dead?

Vox blurted the question without any knowledge of how he did it. It was like speaking . . . and yet not speaking. He tried to repeat it but found he could not. *Don't think about it,* he scolded himself. *Don't try to understand it – just do it!*

. . . Your presence here is real enough, dragon. As is mine. Our labour is required in places other than the normal world for a while.

. . . Required by whom?

. . . That may become clear, dragon.

. . . But if I'm not dead, then how can I be here? Every dragon knows the air grows thin as you fly higher. This high above the world it must be non-existent.

226

   . . . *That much is true, dragon. But you are not here in any true, physical sense. Just as the salt giant became a ghost in order to find her partner, so you have left your corporeal body to journey here.*

   . . . *Why? Is it the comet?*

   . . . *Of course. What it brings with it will complete this Turning.*

   . . . *What do you mean?*

   . . . *That too may become clear to you soon enough, dragon, but first there is work to be done.*

Vox shook his tenuous head. No wonder Wyrm had got on so well with the basilisk: neither of them made much sense.

But there was no time to dwell on such things. The basilisk was moving, speeding around the world. Already Vox could barely make out its transparent form against the busy stars.

   . . . *Follow Ocher.*

The command floated back and Vox considered his options. Should he return to the world he knew or follow the basilisk? If he did return, would it be as a falling star? *Am I a night dragon now?* he thought with a shiver. But he could not beat down his curiosity, nor could he ignore the feeling growing within him, the feeling that here, free of the confines of the world, he might at last find some answers. And some peace from the terror which had haunted him since . . . *Wraith killed my love.*

   . . . *I'm coming.*

Ocher called him towards the sunrise, and he followed.

The shock of entering the tunnel of smoke knocked all the breath from Wist's body. It had looked so flimsy from above, but what appeared to be a sheer and insubstantial boundary proved to be laced with energy. Penetration was like slipping through a layer of fire into ice water – no sooner did Wist's senses scream at the searing pain than they shrank back from the burning cold. The shock was transitory however, for no sooner had she entered this contradictory realm than she was through it into warm, calm air. Ahead and behind the tunnel vanished into infinity, a capsule of smoke which was bearing her eastwards. Back, she hoped, to Mahl.

She had little time to question her actions. Her reasoning

was sound, of that she was certain: the tunnel was the means Scarn used to travel across the world – some device of charm, no doubt – but its power was rooted in the Fissures of Mahl. Rooted in the Flame. Scarn had used it to travel first to the forest, then further across Ocea to his final destination. Now, its work done, the magical tunnel was speeding back to its point of origin. *And taking me with it!*

As she travelled she had the sensation that something else was moving in the opposite direction. Something hot, like an invisible fire. There was a smell too, the same sulphurous odour she knew from Scarn's private chamber. *As I travel east, something else is moving west, to meet with Scarn at the Last Circle!* A black disc appeared at the far end of the tunnel. It expanded before her at terrifying velocity until it was as big as the sky ... then it seemed to enfold her, pressing the smoke back with a sudden, gentle strength. Whirling round she just saw the last tendrils of smoke hissing into nothingness. The blackness acquired solidity with a soundless snap which jolted Wist's bones, and she saw that she was back in the Flamehall. Her wings failed her and she plummeted towards the broken cavern floor.

'Fly, dragon!' a voice called. Instinctively she opened her wings and clawed her way back up through the hot and dusty air to the nearest ledge. There she collapsed, wide-eyed and winded.

She looked around the chamber, moving her gaze from one ledge to the next, from tunnel opening to tunnel opening. A flood of daylight burst through from a tremendous break in the wall, casting glowing beams through the busy motes of dust which danced in the thermals and eddies of the Flamehall. On one ledge she thought she saw a hunched, dragon shape, but when a splinter of light fell across its red contours she saw that it was only a rock, some crystal formation bulging from the wall. Her eyes moved on and found dragons.

Two red-scaled dragons were huddled in the broad entrance to the tunnel which led to the Strokk geyser. At first she did not recognize them, then one of them shouted her name.

'Brace?' she called hesitantly, testing the name of the

dragon she had met only briefly before Scarn had filled the Flamehall with fire. And the other?

'Yes, and Ledra too.' Brace's voice echoed emptily in the deserted chamber, and Wist gave an involuntary shudder. She was used to the Fissures as a living place, a place filled with the steady bustle and chant of the Cult. But now it was dead and silent.

Wist flew gratefully down to where Brace and Ledra were hunched on the ledge. They regarded each other cautiously for a moment or two before Wist began haltingly to relate the story of what had happened to Fortune's band since their departure from Mahl. But as she spoke she found her eyes drifting continuously to the red scales and spines which now adorned the bodies of these two dragons.

'We're red like the others,' said Brace, interrupting her narrative. 'But we're still your friends – if you're still ours, that is.'

Again Wist sighed, and this time she felt a pressure lift from her back. Of course these dragons were her friends, and she found she needed them. She had come in search of her sister, anticipating solitude in her task, but now she was glad to have found some allies. 'I will never go back to Scarn,' she announced, and some small part of her was surprised at the assertion. 'I still hope to find the Last Circle, but on my own terms. It is my sister I need now – there is much we must repair before the day of creation.'

'So you've been listening to Scarn's babblings as well, have you?' grimaced Brace.

'Scarn is misguided,' answered Wist, 'and mistaken about many things. But a day is coming which will see the Turning finally at an end, of that I'm sure. It concerns charm and nature, the Flame and the Last Circle, and Gossamer's Cloud.'

Brace frowned. The mention of his sister's name brought with it a kind of peace and he found that he believed Wist. 'Go on,' he said quietly.

They all wept when Wist spoke of Tallow's death, and grew quiet when they heard about the great forest fire and Scarn's arrival in the middle of it.

'There's a pattern,' said Ledra slowly, as Wist described

229

the appearance of the Cult dragons from the flames. 'As if it's fire itself that draws the power of the Flame across the world. Perhaps the magic can only work where there is fire to feed it.'

'Perhaps,' shrugged Brace. 'Wist – we know it was Gossamer that Scarn wanted. We helped him to find her,' he added bitterly, 'though we could not help ourselves. Tell us: did he take her?'

'She seemed to go willingly,' replied Wist uncertainly.

'Good. Then she had the advantage over him.'

'What do you mean?' demanded Ledra, exchanging a puzzled glance with Wist; both dragons were surprised by Brace's response.

'Only this: Gossamer believes the Cloud will protect her, and her faith gives her more strength than Scarn has reckoned on.'

'And will it?' asked Ledra. 'Protect her, I mean.'

'It doesn't matter,' Wist answered, looking directly at Brace. 'Does it, Brace?' He shook his head.

'It's Gossamer's faith that matters,' he said. 'That's what will defeat Scarn in the end.' He took a step away from the others and looked up and around the huge chamber, squinting into the glare of the sunlight. 'One thing's for certain: this place is no longer a prison.'

'Scarn's used it up now,' agreed Wist. 'There's nothing left for him here.'

'What about the Flame?' put in Ledra sharply. 'Is that still here or did he take it with him somehow?'

Wist told them about the invisible fire she had felt inside the tunnel, but could not confirm whether it was indeed the Flame she had sensed – though she had her suspicions. The argument remained unresolved, and more pressing concerns began to make themselves felt: the light from outside was turning orange as the day drew towards a close. Would they stay here tonight?

'I for one don't want to spend another night in this forsaken place – I want to leave,' was Ledra's heartfelt proposition, and her companions agreed.

As they flew up towards the huge crack in the wall of the Flamehall, Wist glanced back. This would perhaps be her last sight of the Fissures, and despite the monstrous fate which had overtaken the dragons of the Cult, still she felt sadness at leaving. Here was where she had first glimpsed the possibility of a truth greater than any she had contemplated before. Scarn had offered her a dream, and though he had become a monster the dream remained vibrant in her heart.

Light flashed in the blackened depths of the chamber and again she saw the red jewel she had seen on emerging from the tunnel of smoke. *Where are you, Lessen?*

Eventually Vox caught up with Ocher. The basilisk still kept its claws cradled beneath its breast, the posture forcing it to gesture with its tail.

. . . We travel at the speed of night, dragon.

They were positioned high above the waist of the world. A great continent was spread below them, an arc of land divided into light and shade: the western tip of the land was still enjoying the last of the day, whereas the eastern flank was dark with night. The blurred boundary bisected the continent, and as Vox watched he began to appreciate the tremendous speed at which the onset of night was racing across the deserts and mountains of what he slowly recognized to be the southern part of the Heartland. *Or what used to be the Heartland*, he reminded himself.

. . . You have guessed, dragon?

. . . We're hovering directly above the place we started, aren't we? Directly below us, near the eastern edge of the Heartland where the sea cuts through the land like a claw – that's where the Towers of Nistor lie, isn't it?

. . . Your perception is impressive, dragon. What do you see that reveals this to you?

As soon as Ocher asked the question Vox saw the answer. His guess had been just that – a guess, based purely on instinct. But now he saw it: a blue spark set in the shadowy desert, a light in the darkness.

. . . There: the Flame.

It was then that Vox realized the enormity of what had happened to him. Here he was, floating high above the world, aware when he should have been dead, moving

231

through an airless void and able to see deep underground when he did not even have eyes.

. . . *Do not panic, dragon.* Ocher's words (thoughts?) slipped smoothly across Vox like a mother's caress. *You may taste the air again soon. You are needed here first, however.*

. . . *Why?*

. . . *A question burns at Ocher's mind: how long does a basilisk live? Once the question was meaningless, but now it has more meaning than even Ocher realized.*

Basilisks have been present at every Turning which has ever occurred, throughout the entire, infinite progression of Turnings this world and others have gone through. Through an eternity of change, the Deathless have been the one constant.

But no more. Thanks to the miracle of the Gathering, Ocher is the last of the basilisks. The time is fast approaching when this latest Turning completes itself, when the new world is finally created, and the question Ocher asks itself is this: can a basilisk live beyond this moment? Consider, dragon — Ocher is no longer the constant. Perhaps, at last, it is time to step down and admit another to the role.

. . . *You mean die? Is that what you mean when you say you want the measure of a basilisk's lifespan? You want to die?*

. . . *Ocher no longer seeks death as once it did, dragon. But perhaps death seeks Ocher, and there are some forces which even a basilisk cannot defeat. Ocher's task is no longer to prevail — it is to prepare.*

Vox shook his ghostly head, on the verge of understanding but ultimately confused. He gazed down upon the flicker of the Flame.

. . . *My friends are trapped down there. Is there anything we can do to help them?*

. . . *Dragon, that is exactly your task. Behold — see what Ocher has brought.*

Basilisk claws glinted in the last of the light as the edge of the atmosphere moved across the sun. The dying rays struck something sheer, a long, shimmering crystal — this was what Ocher had been concealing beneath its belly.

. . . *What is it?*

. . . *Your friends have been searching for this, but Ocher retrieved it shortly before you dragons reached the chamber of the Towers.*

232

It is a charm, or a ghost of one perhaps, just as you are a ghost. However it, like you, is not devoid of power.

Vox watched entranced as Ocher turned over the scintillating crystal in the low threads of sunlight. Dust seemed to spray from it, sparkling shards in the growing darkness. Below them the line of shadow raced across the curved horizon. Like the world, the crystal seemed divided, half in light and half in darkness. Ocher's claws contracted and the crystal split in two.

A shock wave burst from the divided crystal, a sphere of energy clearly visible to Vox's heightened senses. It pulsed over him like a wash of hot air and spread out into space, dissipating as it fled. Ocher reached out with its claws.

. . . Take this, dragon.

It thrust the light-filled half of the crystal into Vox's ghostly grasp. Fire flooded what passed for the bewildered dragon's senses. Then Ocher turned and cast the other, dark half of the crystal down towards the night-covered globe. Vox felt a wrench as it flipped over and over, a barely visible grain of shadow against the greater shadow which had claimed the Heartland. There was no doubt as to its target: the crystal eclipsed the Flame's spark over and over as it plummeted towards the ground. What it would do when it reached the Towers of Nistor Vox could not imagine. His half of the crystal burned in his grip, but he could not let it go.

It's coming, he called silently to Smoke and Wyrm.

Exhausted, Smoke had drifted into an uneasy slumber, but now she awoke with a start. Wyrm lay still beside her; the sight of his sleeping form should have been restful, but Smoke felt anything but calm.

'You've never slept before in your life, Wyrm,' she whispered. 'Why start now?'

The blue light of the Flame bathed the chamber and Smoke found herself listening hard. The flame itself was noiseless, but she thought she could hear something hissing at the very limit of audible sound. She thought of ghosts and long-dead dragons, of Nistor and the purple scales of the Nistri, and she shuddered, trying to close her ears. The hiss became a whistle, quite clear now and challenging her

233

to ignore it. She turned her head this way and that, seeking its source, but it was all around her.

'Wyrm,' she urged, prodding him with her wing. 'Wake up, Wyrm.' But he did not wake up. He did not even stir. She shoved him – harder than she had intended to – but even that had no effect. The whistling was loud now, very loud.

Smoke began to cast wildly around now, seeking shelter. The dragon sculptures watched silently as she scurried around the ledge, searching for some crevice, some tunnel which they had not noticed before, but the search was as vain as she had known it would be. Soon she had circum-navigated the chamber and was back where she had started, with Wyrm. The whistling pierced her ears like a bitter wind. She looked up.

. . . *There.*

Ocher gestured, a long, lazy sweep of its claw.

Light blossomed in the night. The moment was brief and far away, but its magnitude was not lost on Vox. He wondered what it might be like to be a night dragon, to fall to earth and burn a vivid trail through the sky. *Should I follow the crystal to the ground?* he thought, his mind whirling madly. Then the basilisk moved across his field of vision and the fading explosion was blocked.

. . . *Not yet, dragon.*

Vox looked deep into the basilisk's perfect, silver eyes. Within he saw the myriad stars, the incandescent thrust of the comet and his own, ghostly reflection. A ripple passed across the pale fans of his wings and he looked to each side. Now he was glad he was free of the sensations of touch and pain, for what he observed filled him with awe and horror.

His wings, even though still tinged with purple, were on the verge of invisibility, were burning away into space. A thousand tiny flames ate away at their gossamer fabric, busying their way back through the membranes towards his shoulders. He tried to pull away, seeking the impossible: a means of escape. But of course there was nowhere he could go.

Am I to be burned to nothing? his mind shrieked as the

flames grew huge at the roots of his wings. He could see nothing but fire now, darting and leaping and burying itself in his disappearing wings. Another breath and it would begin to work on his body, excavating a way through to his heart . . .

The whistling sound stopped an instant before the ceiling shattered. The broken outcrop of rock which had once supported the huge dragon head disintegrated into a million tiny pieces as something punched its way through from above. The cloud of debris and billowing dust crashed down on to the upturned head, covering the floor and – to Smoke's astonishment – extinguishing the Flame with a single puff. Several of the Towers were knocked sideways, striking the ledge's curved lip and breaking apart to add their own showers of white salt powder to the confusion.

Slowly Smoke realized that the entire event was taking place in utter silence.

The downward motion of the debris transformed itself into an outward one and finally a rising wave of broken rock and fine silt which loomed up over the ledge, falling across Smoke and Wyrm and the two – now all but unrecognizable – salt giants. This wave gradually subsided, revealing a gaping hole in the roof, the stars clearly visible beyond, twinkling through the dusty air.

Smoke looked down into the chamber. The head (*Vox's head*, she reminded herself) was quite gone, buried beneath the rubble. She half-expected blue fire to leap forth from between the fallen rocks but of the Flame there was no sign. She looked up at the sky again, confused, then she heard Wyrm's moan.

She rushed to his side. He was twitching violently, groaning and thrashing his tail against the floor. She bent over to embrace him but pulled away with a hiss: his flank was burning!

A sudden, searing pain doubled her up and she raised her wings to her head. At first she thought it was the whistling sound, returned and redoubled; then she recognized the sensation. It was charm, close by, and it was overloading her half-Charmed senses. She screamed, unable to blank it out, and between her partly closed eyes she saw tiny flames leap forth from Wyrm's back.

Abruptly the pain stopped. Opening her eyes again she stared dumbly at the flurry of charm which covered Wyrm's body. Hundreds of flames, each barely half the size of a dragon's claw, covered his dorsal scales. The glare was enough to make her squint once more, and in doing so she noticed a single thread of luminous charm leading back from the flames and up into the chamber behind her. She looked round, imagining that here was the way to Grell's body, revealed at last as Wyrm had predicted, but the truth was far stranger than that.

One of the stars she had seen was no star, but a sliver of crystal threaded on to a skein of magic. It floated in the void where the ceiling had once been, the axis about which the charm turned. At first Smoke imagined Wyrm was the source of the magic, then she wondered if something high above the world was transmitting the charm downwards; finally she understood. The crystal itself – and this was surely the one crystal they had failed to find in the chamber – was the origin, and Wyrm was merely the recipient of its power.

Who is up there? wondered Smoke. *Who is receiving the charm up there in the sky?*

Dark shapes were forming on Wyrm's back, twitching growths which began in the fire and reached out into the air. His scales snapped and stretched as these appendages grew and flexed and twisted into recognizable forms. Mouth agape, heart thundering loud enough to shake the stars which looked down on them, Smoke watched as Wyrm grew wings.

The stars blinked. Black space and bright stars and the steady swell of the planet. No flames. Vox looked cautiously around: the fire had gone out. He glanced at his wings, but of course they too were gone. Nothing was visible on the surface of the world where the crystal had fallen, neither fire nor shadow, just the secret shroud of night.

. . . You must rest now, dragon. Give me the other half of the crystal.

Vox did not argue as Ocher took the now-dark shard and

led him swiftly away from the world, towing his wingless form towards the crescent moon which lifted from behind the dark horizon. The comet dropped out of sight as they sped into sunlight once more. As warm light washed across his ghostly body, Vox imagined the pain he should have felt at such mutilation, but he discovered only a radiant calm, a feeling of triumph and a sense that great work had just begun.

Ocher's limbs moved against him and he looked round in time to see the broken crystal spinning lazily away into space. Some unidentified instinct made him lunge for it, but the basilisk restrained him.

. . . *Its work is done, dragon. It should rest unjoined now, for it is too dangerous to be left intact.*

. . . *What was it?*

. . . *It was, and is still, a dragon charm, one of the strongest ever forged by Nistor. Its cousins are easily destroyed – have been already – but it is different. Better that it should be wholly unmade, but that is beyond even Ocher's skill. It is a charm of exchange, dragon, similar in some ways to those used by the trolls and giants to infiltrate the land. But it is fire where they are earth, and it is many times their superior in both power and peril. And it has the ability to mend itself.*

. . . *Is it safe now?* If Vox had been able to yawn in this strange, ghostly state that is exactly what he would have done. He had lost interest in the magic which had robbed him of his – admittedly insubstantial – wings and wanted nothing more than rest.

. . . *It will never be safe, dragon. But it is, for the moment, neutralized. Had Ocher the time it would take this half far away from its twin, far beyond the stars where many Turnings might pass before the two were finally reunited. But this will suffice for some aeons at least. Ocher has used it well, and it is broken again, and that is all this basilisk can do. Time is short, dragon, as every mortal knows only too well, and there are more important things for dragon and basilisk to do. Come.*

So Vox came, entranced by the beauty of the stars, and that was the last any dragon saw of the crystal charm of exchange for a very long time.

* * *

The earthbound half of the crystal flashed once, a livid blue arc which momentarily blotted out the stars, then its light failed and it dropped on to the heap of rubble in the centre of the chamber. Simultaneously the flames which had covered Wyrm's back shrank away between his scales, leaving Smoke's friend and companion grunting and twitching on the dim, starlit ledge. His new wings lay draped across the flat rock, glistening with unspent charm. Then, slowly, his eyes opened.

'I had such a dream,' he began incredulously, then he stopped short, looking down at his newly acquired wings. Tears filled his eyes.

'How do you feel?' asked Smoke haltingly, cursing herself for asking what she considered a stupid question.

'I can't move them,' replied Wyrm with a mixture of awe and puzzlement. 'What's happened to me? Did I miss something?'

Smoke did not know what to say. She gestured at the hole in the ceiling. 'It looks like we can get out now,' she offered uncertainly. 'Do you think you can fly?'

Fly! The word flashed between them like fire charm and both dragons started to cry and laugh, a joyful hysteria which gripped them utterly for several breaths . . . and then left as soon as it had come.

'Fly? I don't know.' Wyrm clambered to his claws, a frown of concentration creasing his dark face. His shoulder muscles worked and his tail flexed, but the wings did nothing more than jerk erratically. 'I can feel they're there, but I don't know how to move them.'

'You will, soon enough,' Smoke said quietly. She had stepped back to give Wyrm room, and now she was struck by an eerie thought. His scales were dark, almost black in some lights, and now he sported equally dark wings – and they were *huge* wings, she was beginning to realize – he looked very much like a dragon she had once loved, and who had gone on to ravage the world. He looked very much like . . .

. . . *Wraith*.

'Come on, Wyrm,' she sighed. 'Let's go and get that crystal.'

238

Despite his new wings, Wyrm weighed little more than he had before and it was with relative ease that Smoke managed to carry him down to the floor. Those tremendous, lolling wing membranes caught in the air, spreading and falling back as the two dragons descended, one in the embrace of the other. Smoke could smell the charm on him, so close were they, and though it brought fresh pain to her head it was intoxicating.

What has happened to you, Wyrm? And what is happening to me?

They searched the pile of rubble but found nothing.

'It should be here somewhere,' cursed Smoke. 'I saw it fall, I know I did.'

Wyrm shrugged, clearly uninterested. 'Well, it's gone now. Its power will be spent, Smoke. I'm sure it's as harmless now as the ones we managed to destroy. Come on – the sight of that sky makes me hungry for the open air again. We've been underground for too long.'

Now it was Smoke's turn to frown. She felt uneasy about leaving the crystal here, but what could they do? Neither of them could wield charm – of which there was precious little to be found these days in any case – so there was no way they could penetrate whatever magic it undoubtedly had concealed itself with.

Maybe it dissolved away, Smoke reassured herself, unconvinced. *Maybe its work was done and it just melted away.*

'Smoke!' Wyrm was calling excitedly. 'Smoke! I can move them! They feel warmer now and I can really move them!'

His excitement was so like that of an infant dragon that Smoke could not help but smile as she turned back to face him. He was poised on top of the heaped debris, brow knotted, leaning forward as he worked new and unfamiliar muscles against the pull of gravity. As she watched she saw flickers of charm darting between his scales, she saw those muscles build themselves up beneath his dark hide. Tendons laced themselves under his soft belly, anchoring themselves on to his deepening breastbone. Wyrm's shape changed, but the transformation was somehow sensual. Smoke had seen charmed dragons alter their bodies like this, and the sight had always left her feeling mildly nauseated, but this . . . this was different. This was wonderful!

Wyrm's wings rose higher and higher as he gained the power and skill to lift them up. As they rose his breast filled out, partly because of the thickening of muscle and bone there, partly because his chest was swelling with pride. As the last of the charm faded from behind his scales he settled back into his new stance: the classic pose of the charmed dragon.

His scales were black. His body was long and supple, his four legs tucked low and strong to lift his deep breast clear of the ground. His tail rose a little above the line of his back before dipping slightly, a semi-rigid counterbalance to the elegant sweep of his neck. Massive wings were held up towards the sky, the edges of their membranes rippling in the gentle breeze which crept through the chamber. On his face a smile, a peace Smoke had never seen before.

'All my life I have dreamed of flight,' Wyrm said quietly. 'And now that dream has come true. All the stories are true, Smoke. Every story you have ever heard, and all those yet to be told – they are all true. Never forget that.'

Then, with a flicker of infant uncertainty which made Smoke's heart ache, Wyrm flexed his wings and pulled himself clear of the ground which had confined him all his life. Up into the open sky he flew, into the light of the watching stars, until he was a sheer, black shape against the twinkling constellations. His great wings beat a slow, steady rhythm against the immensity of space.

'Are you coming, Smoke?' he boomed, his voice larger now his body had changed.

'Where are we going?' she cried, weeping as she took to the air.

'To the other side of the world, to find our family, our friends, and see the lighting of the sky!'

They left behind the salt and the savannah, the mountains which were not really mountains and the quiet, satisfied graves of the salt giants, while above them in the welcoming sky the stars submitted to the brilliance of the comet which rose slowly into view, beckoning them on in their epic journey towards the Last Circle.

PART THREE

THE LAST CIRCLE

CHAPTER 18

The Bloodstained Rock

The great continent of Ocea slipped by with agonizing slowness. Gradually the belt of forest broke up. A wide land of river plains and tremendous deltas took its place. The ground was waterlogged, and the dragons stopped to rest only occasionally. Fortune saw more new creatures during these brief sojourns, of which the most memorable were the large waterborne rodents swimming lazily using their huge paddle tails; they pushed logs and sticks ahead of themselves and when he saw the dams they built across the river he found himself thinking of his home, of the wooden constructions of Tongue. Though they were good memories, they made him sad.

We fly and we fly and we fly . . . and still we are no nearer to finding our home.

'Clever little monsters,' commented Scoff, breaking Fortune's thought pattern. By far the oldest dragon of the group – apart from him they were all still youngsters – Scoff lent a certain authority to the expedition and Fortune was, as ever, glad of his company.

Fortune looked out across the river. It was a narrow tributary to a wider waterway flowing effortlessly over the mighty plain ahead. Such a big land! Everything here was sketched large, from the forest to the river to the very breadth of the continent itself. A dragon could lose himself forever in this wilderness . . . *and still never find his home.*

Unable to keep the sadness at bay, Fortune called the others into the air and struck out west once more. Aria flew close to him now that Gossamer was gone, saying little,

243

correcting him whenever he strayed from the course she preferred.

'I can't see what lies ahead,' she explained when Fortune asked how she could navigate through a land she had never seen. 'But each new region looks familiar as we approach it. I just have to trust to the visions.'

'Will we know the Last Circle when we see it?' Fortune could not help but think of faery rings and boulders. Even the mightiest stone circle could be lost in the immensity of Ocea. They might fly past it in the night, or in the middle of the day for that matter, missing it for the sake of a badly placed rock or mountain ridge.

'We'll know it all right,' answered Aria quietly.

Delta and flood plain gave way to rolling pasture on which grazed herds of large, black animals with shining horns and pelts matted into thick bunches at the shoulder. The dragons did not land here: the creatures looked peaceful enough but they were big and the herds in which they congregated defied belief: they blotted out the landscape with their proud, black forms. To land amid such a congregation would surely be taking an unnecessary risk; those horns, and the bulbous heads which they adorned, looked made for fighting.

So on they flew, chasing the dawn even as the night fled from them. Fortune lost count of the days and cursed himself for doing so. *Tallow would not lose track of such things*, he scolded himself and the thought of his friend's name was like a stabbing pain in his heart. Then Tallow's face seemed to float before him, smiling sympathetically, and Fortune felt a tremendous calmness descend. Tallow was surrounded by a swirling cloud, and though the vision lasted only a breath or two it remained with Fortune for a very long time.

Shortly after that he started counting his wingbeats again, and took to measuring the days and the distances with quiet precision.

The landscape hardened as they flew further into the west. Vegetation grew sparse until only scrub and thorn survived. Mountains forced them high; beyond them they descended into desert.

Red rock abounded, and though the ground was mostly

244

flat it was punctured by massive columns and slabs which thrust their way up through the thin soil. At first these strange formations – which were like teeth protruding from some unimaginable jaw, Fortune thought – were relatively small, but soon they encountered monsters, veritable mountains of stone which reached up effortlessly towards the broad, blue sky. Their tops were flat, their sides sheer and striated, full of colours. Hard-packed soil and rock leaned against them, buttressing the towers from which the stuff had fallen. In silence the dragons flew between them, fascinated by the patchwork of shadows they painted in the afternoon sun, dazzled by the brilliance of the pigments which adorned them.

'They're like icebergs in the sea,' cried Velvet at one point, so overwhelmed that she had to call out her astonishment.

'No danger of freezing here,' replied Scoff, glancing up at the sun which, though lowering now, had burned hard during the middle part of the day. 'Need water again soon.'

'I'm sure there are mountains ahead,' called Fortune from the head of the group. 'We can't see them yet but . . .'

'We're not going that far,' interrupted Aria. Her words halted them and they hovered in a loose line as she scanned the horizon. Slowly she turned her head, lashing her long tail so that her body swayed in the air. 'We're very close now, but I don't quite see the way.'

'The Last Circle?' blurted Velvet, rushing to Aria's side. 'Are we nearly there, are we really?'

'The Last Circle lies south of here and a little to the west. We might reach it tomorrow.'

The group drew in a sharp, collective breath.

'Close enough,' said Scoff, curling his rainbow wings in the low afternoon light. 'What's to be done?'

Aria shrugged, a curious motion which disrupted her hover and caused her body to dip slightly in the air. 'I await only the coming of the light.'

Then Cumber piped up, 'Look, Fortune, I know you don't like plans and all that, but I was wondering – well, what *are* we going to do when we get there? I mean, you seemed happy enough to let Scarn take Gossamer away – are you just going to fly in and take her straight back again?'

'That's not what Gossamer wanted,' murmured Velvet, her voice almost inaudible.

'Something is coming,' declared Fortune. 'Cloud, Light, call it what you will. If the Flame is not dealt with by the time it gets here then everything is lost. Everything we have achieved by helping the world to turn true will have all been in vain. Scarn is merely an agent of the Flame. It is not enough to destroy him; we must not lose sight of the greater enemy. There is only one thing we can do when we reach the Last Circle: watch and wait.'

'Watch and wait,' repeated Velvet, looking across at Cumber. Scoff nodded non-committally but Aria and Volley hovered stone-faced, betraying nothing of what they felt or thought.

'Probably best,' said Scoff as the silence stretched out uneasily. 'But still . . .'

Scoff pulled Fortune away from the others as Aria led them on into the dwindling light of the sunset. The sun burned fiercely on the horizon, throwing its fire against the towering rock formations; the landscape seemed to be glowing from within.

'You should be right,' Scoff ventured at last. 'But you're not.'

Fortune frowned. He had great respect for Scoff but could not see where his argument was heading.

'Don't ask why,' Scoff went on. 'Don't know. But you're wrong, Fortune. First time, as far as I recall,' he added with a feeble attempt at a grin. 'Right clues, wrong answers, maybe.'

Fortune flew steadily on at his side, unconsciously counting his wingbeats, measuring the speed of the wind against the sensitive skin of his throat, analysing, thinking, seeking the answers.

'I know,' he said eventually. 'But if I'm wrong then Gossamer's wrong too. And that means she could be dead already.'

'But she isn't.'

'No. I'd know if she was.'

Scoff sighed heavily. 'About the Cloud: she's right. About the Flame: she's right. About Scarn?' He let the dragon's name hang in the air between them like a spectre. 'Wrong.

246

Quite wrong, Fortune. And that's dangerous. *He's* dangerous. More dangerous than you imagine.'

That night Fortune dreamed.

They had landed in the lee of the tallest pinnacle yet, a
giant of a rock with striated sides and a flattened peak. While
the others had made themselves temporary scrapes in the
thin soil, Fortune had flown to the summit to sleep alone
beneath the stars. They had let him go readily enough,
despite the fact they were in a strange land; they seemed
to understand his need to be by himself.

The comet filled the heavens, or so it seemed to Fortune,
and it was the comet which flew with him into his dream.

*He rode on its back, his wings furled, his claws clasped tightly
about its flank, a burning mass of fire and water revolving about
a dimly pumping heart. He sensed something hard at its core,
something familiar . . . The stars flashed past at impossible speed
while ahead the orb of the world grew and grew until it filled his
vision and he closed his eyes against the coming impact.*

*It never came. When he opened his eyes he was flying above a
small group of dragons stationed on the ground. A ring of stones
closed in on the group, forming a prison from which the only
escape was up. But none of the dragons was looking up – they
were all looking to the side. Looking at Scarn.*

*Scarn's yellow wings were the primary source of light in the
scene. The dragons he was slowly approaching were trembling
with fear, or perhaps it was awe. Fortune decided it was probably
both. Before Scarn's approach the light had been dim, but now
he could make out faces and he saw that the group was his own
group: there was Scoff, there Cumber and Velvet, and there, over
to one side, was Volley, glowering at the approaching enemy. And
there, facing Scarn bravely, was Gossamer.*

*Fortune tried to call out to her but, as so often in dreams, no
sound came from his mouth. He tried to fly down into the ring, to
protect or warn his friends, but to his horror his wings had gone.
What force it was that kept him aloft he could not imagine, but
without his wings he was powerless to manoeuvre. All he could
do was look on with steadily mounting terror.*

Flames licked forth from Scarn's mouth. None of his friends

247

moved. Why don't they fly away? thought Fortune desperately.
Then he saw that they too were wingless. He tried to cry but there
were no tears.

Scarn came closer, a luminous dragon alive with fire. The flames
in his mouth were blue. He leaned towards Gossamer, grinning.

He will kill her first, then take the others! thought Fortune,
unable to close his eyes against the atrocity.

But Scarn stepped smoothly past Gossamer and closed in on
Cumber instead. Cumber bravely stood his ground, puffing his
breast out against the oncoming dragon. At the last breath Scarn
flicked his head to the side and belched fire not at Cumber but at
Velvet. She died screaming. None of the others moved.

Fortune awoke on the verge of screaming himself.

Velvet! he thought at once. *Why did he take Velvet, of all*
dragons. What has she ever done? Desperately he sought meaning in the dream, frantically seeking the answer to the riddle.
He slept no more that night; instead he watched the stars
turn in their course. The comet dropped below the horizon,
the sky lightened in the east. Then, as the darkness of the
sky faded towards purple and finally a clear, translucent
blue, so his mind cleared and something Scoff had said
turned his thoughts clear about.

'Right clues, wrong answers, maybe,' Scoff had said, and
Fortune thought about how, in his dream, Scarn had
ignored Gossamer for Velvet. *The right clue,* he thought, *but*
does it mean that's what Scarn would actually do?

'No!' he breathed, tasting the morning air as though it
were the sweetest spring water. 'But I know what it does
mean!'

'He's unpredictable,' he announced to the group over a
meagre breakfast of berries and tubers they had culled from
the sparse vegetation around the rock tower. 'That's what
we've been missing all along.' His excitement was born
partly of relief, partly of terror, because if this was true it
could mean only one thing.

'That makes him dangerous,' said Cumber, echoing
Scoff's words of the previous night. 'Very dangerous,
Fortune.'

'Do you mean he could kill Gossamer at any time?' asked Velvet, her young voice trembling. 'But isn't he obsessed with his damned Cult? Isn't she supposed to be a sacrifice – I mean, surely he'll wait until the proper time?' Her voice shook as she held back her tears; Cumber consoled her.

'My father is right!' Aria's voice broke in unexpectedly. She had been loitering some distance away, but now she rushed in to join them. Her eyes were blazing. 'I could not have predicted what he did to me, and none of us guessed he would find us on the other side of the world. He is the servant of the Flame, but he wants to be its master, don't you see?'

Fortune and Scoff both nodded enthusiastically but Cumber and Velvet merely looked puzzled. Volley, as ever, remained unmoved.

'It's very simple,' Fortune explained. 'Frighteningly so. Scarn believes that he controls the power of the Flame, but in reality it is the Flame that is controlling him. And all the dragons of the Cult, for that matter. Don't you see what that means?'

Cumber and Velvet both shook their heads dumbly.

'It means they're not dragons any more,' said Aria softly. 'It means that Scarn and all the others died a long time ago. All that's left now is the Flame. And we can no more predict its actions than we could predict the course of a forest fire.'

'So I have sent Gossamer into the jaws of death,' concluded Fortune with simple, dreadful certainty. 'She has no idea of the peril she is in, because she thinks she is with dragons. And I don't know if even her faith in her Cloud can protect her there.' He gave a huge sigh, heavy with the weight of the world. 'That means there's only one thing we can do.'

'And that is?' prompted Scoff, though he knew the answer, as they all did.

'Get her back *now*!'

It was still early morning when they saw the first body.

Fortune led again, stroking the air calmly and efficiently, his calmness disguising his inner turmoil. With every beat of his wings he cursed himself for being so foolish, for letting Gossamer go so easily.

'You couldn't have stopped her, old fellow,' Cumber reassured him when he caught up with his old friend after Fortune's initial burst of speed. 'She knows her own mind well enough, you know that. And it seemed right at the time.'

Fortune could find nothing to say in reply and so they flew on in silence while the sun wound its way up into the sky, beginning once more to bake the moisture from the towering rock slabs which were at last thinning out. Ahead was a vast, grey plain, its far reaches hidden by the early haze. Then, suddenly, Volley cried out.

He led them in a slow spiral down towards the flat peak of one of the huge slabs of red rock. A dark, metallic shape was spread across it, its contours strange at first but becoming all too familiar as they drew near. It was a dragon, ex-Charmed, dead, its wings splayed out, its neck and tail stretched taut in a perfect line. Its body was coated with a layer of dried blood, almost concealing the highly reflective scales. Beneath its prostrate form the red rock was stained an even darker brown, the deepest markings occurring at its head and the tip of its tail, and the tips of its wings.

Volley landed near its head and paced the length of the corpse, sucking air pensively between his teeth. He did not glance up when Fortune alighted at his side. His face was grim.

'Scarn?' suggested Fortune, for Volley seemed particularly sensitive to the gruesome sight. The big dragon was grimacing, casting his gaze first up and then down the length of the unfortunate dragon. The others hovered a tree's height above, reluctant to join them.

'See?' said Volley at length. He pointed to the dragon's tail with one, large wing. 'Most blood here.' He marched up to the tip of its left wing and indicated another bloodstain. The biggest stain lay beneath the dragon's head, a ragged brown blot which straggled away down a slight decline in the surface of the rock. Volley sniffed the air. 'I can't smell anything rotting, Fortune. This poor soul's been here less than a day.'

Fortune nodded agreement.

'Look here,' continued Volley, leading Fortune back to the nearest wingtip. 'See this hole in the membrane? It's burned through – the edges are charred.'

'They look blue,' said Fortune cautiously and he looked up into Volley's troubled eyes.

'Scarn did this,' blurted Volley, his normally smooth voice cracking. 'He kills, Fortune. *It* kills.'

Looking up, Fortune saw his friends circling close above their heads. *I have never led any dragon to battle*, he thought, fearful of where his emotions were leading him. *Can I start now?*

His thoughts were interrupted by a tiny flash of light in the distance. Blue light.

It flared low in the sky to the southwest. There the rock slabs were sparse, but a few still pierced the dull grey of the stony desert which was beginning to dominate. The light seemed to emanate from just above the summit of one such slab. Fortune looked back into Volley's eyes and the thought they shared spurred them both into immediate action.

'Come on!' bellowed Volley, throwing his wings wide against the air. Fortune was barely half a breath behind him. Their combined urgency rallied the others and almost as one they struck out towards the source of the light, Volley and Fortune vying to maintain the lead.

The rock slab was nearer than it seemed and soon they had halved the distance to it. Instinctively Scoff and Cumber moved ahead of Velvet and Aria, squeezing them to the back of the group. With a disgruntled yelp Velvet barged through them again and regained her position near the leaders.

'I've seen as much action as you two,' she protested. 'And don't you forget it!'

Aria appeared content to bring up the rear, and it was in this tight formation that the five dragons sped towards the flickering blue light.

As they approached they saw that the light was indeed coming from a point maybe three trees above the centre of the slab's summit. It was too bright to look at directly and so its source was impossible to determine. Not so its target.

A dragon was pinned to the rock, writhing in agony. As they watched, as they doubled their speed in horror, a thin lance of fire sliced down from the light and punctured the tip of the dragon's tail. The wretched creature screamed, a dreadful, boiling sound which echoed across the desert. Desperate to prevent this atrocity, their wings pumped harder and harder, but the light and its unfortunate victim drew near with agonizing slowness.

Two more lines of fire speared each of the dragon's wing-tips. Blood filled the air like rain; already the dragon was coated in it. Its head lashed about, and Fortune fancied he could detect the source of the light moving too, tracking from side to side as it followed the frenzied movement of its prey. The light expanded suddenly, increasing its luminous circumference as though it had taken a breath. Then they were upon it!

Volley was first to reach it. Heedless of his own safety he crashed straight into the heart of the glowing orb of blue light, lashing his claws in every direction in the hope of finding a target. The instant he made contact the light winked out, leaving orange after-images trailing across the eyes of the approaching dragons. There was a flurry in the air and then Volley was wrestling with a slippery red shape, a dragon shape which writhed first into and then out of his grip. Several blue sparks cascaded down on to the surface of the rock and then there was a tremendous crack. The air opened up and the dragons found themselves staring into a miniature version of the tunnel which had brought Scarn to Ocea in the first place. The red dragon turned on to its back and vanished into the smoke-lined orifice, which snapped shut as though it had never been there.

Volley continued to thrash for several breaths before he realized that his opponent had gone. As he slowed, controlling himself until he was hovering, breathing hard, Fortune saw that he was weeping.

'Was it him?' Volley demanded. 'Was it?'

Fortune shook his head. 'I don't think so,' he answered. 'I don't think they have much identity of their own any more, Volley.'

'Help me!' Velvet's voice wailed up from the flat peak of

the pinnacle of rock and their thoughts turned back to the hapless victim of the elusive dragon-monster. They all joined her beside the head of the prostrate dragon. Fortune winced as he noted the blood soaking his hide was already flooding the rock beneath his wingtips and tail, and he knew that there was nothing they could do to help him.

'Who are you?' he asked gently, trying to attract the dragon's attention. He was moaning gently, motionless now but for a slight tremor in his jaw. Fortune watched a pulse in his neck with morbid fascination. The dragon was old, his once shining scales deeply etched, his hide wrinkled and worn. The four legs which were splayed across his flanks indicated that he, like the other unfortunate victim, was ex-Charmed.

'What is your name, dragon?' echoed Velvet. The dragon responded to her soft voice, turning milky-white eyes up towards her face. Blood covered his features, but where his eyelids moved she saw the brilliant, mirror-like surface of his skin.

'Are you alone?' he whispered.

'My friends are here.'

The dying dragon closed its eyes, apparently satisfied. 'Are you all so young?' he asked after an ominously long pause.

'More or less,' replied Velvet, fighting to keep her voice steady.

At this the dragon smiled. Again the interminable pause. 'Then you might help us,' he murmured, his voice as fragile as a thread of smoke.

'Are there more of you?' urged Fortune. Velvet pulled a face at him but Fortune just looked pleadingly back: *We have to know.*

All fell silent as they listened to the old dragon's hoarse, barely audible breathing. Then the breathing stopped and Velvet had to stifle a choke. 'Oh no,' she blurted, then the old dragon spoke for one, last time.

'The Rift,' he hissed, his voice now a mere wisp, an eddy in the hot morning air. 'They found us there. West. They took the Circle . . .'

The pulse in his neck stopped.

253

It fell eventually to Fortune to break the silence. 'Well,' he ventured, 'what should we do?'

'It doesn't seem right just to leave him here,' answered Velvet sadly.

Fortune felt ashamed. He had not even considered what should be done with the poor dragon's body – nor that of the other unfortunate they had left on the other rock. His indecision was more concerned with whether they should journey on to the Last Circle or . . . or what? *Or try to interpret what this dragon was trying to tell us.*

'Rift,' mused Scoff, his own thoughts obviously tracking close to Fortune's. He looked to the west.

'Is that where this Rift is?' wondered Fortune. 'Or is that where Scarn's dragons came from?' He held up his wing as Velvet began to protest. 'I know, Velvet, it seems harsh to talk of such things now, but I don't see what we can do for this dragon.'

'Fortune's right, my dear,' interjected Cumber, flapping his white wings nervously as he hopped about on the rock. 'We can't bury the body, not in terrain such as this – not that we could even lift it from the rock, not with all that charm around.' He indicated the wounds at the dragon's extremities: the flesh was still taut, as though some hidden force were pinning the corpse to the rock even now, despite the fact its attacker had fled. 'There is still magic here, Velvet,' he concluded softly, 'and I don't believe we can break its hold yet.'

'He will be safe from harm here,' said Fortune, and he actually began to believe that this might in fact be a fitting place for the body to lie. 'Look – he is high above the ground, where every dragon should be. He is safe from any scavengers, for no animal could scale these sheer walls. Here he is at least at peace.'

Velvet looked about to argue, but Fortune's expression was so sincere that she relented and expelled a long breath. After a brief pause she turned to Volley. 'Perhaps you would sing him a lament?' she asked shyly.

To their surprise Volley, grown introverted since Tallow's death, needed no encouragement. His voice lifted them into the sky and they circled above the dead dragon whom they had never known, wondering what dark secrets this mighty land yet had in store for them. As Volley's words died away, Aria pulled away from the group and lifted her head towards the west.

'If we continue on our way we will reach the Last Circle tonight,' she announced with absolute certainty. 'But it does not feel right.' She turned her head. 'Does it, father?'

Fortune shook his head. 'No, it doesn't. We cannot afford simply to descend upon Scarn and his dragons – or what used to be his dragons. First we have to find out exactly what it is he's doing here. Then we might find a weakness we can exploit.'

'If he's got one,' grumbled Scoff under his breath.

'South of here lies the Last Circle and that is where Scarn is, of that I'm certain,' Fortune went on, looking to Aria for confirmation, which she supplied with a single nod of her head. 'We will go west; we will try to find the Rift, whatever that may be.'

They flew through the afternoon towards the thunderheads which were stacking themselves on the horizon. The sky was aglow behind the angry black of the clouds and the air was rich with moisture, heavy and ready to burst around them. The land beneath them was dark in the shadow of the approaching storm, and although it began to rise again and spawn trees and vegetation, it grew less and less inviting the further they travelled.

'My guess is that it's a gorge of some kind, perhaps a bit like Aether's Cross,' suggested Cumber as they flew lower and lower, reluctant to venture high as the clouds rolled past overhead. Now they were completely enclosed by the vast, black body of the storm; the air was ripe and humid. At any breath it would strike.

They could see only a short distance ahead, so dark had it become. It was less like night and more like a dense, grey fog which swallowed the middle distance and rendered the horizon quite invisible. Treetops clutched at their bellies as they sank further and further towards the ground. Only Fortune's Tallow-taught confidence gave him the strength to continue flying, and even he was almost ready to call a halt and bring them in to land. Something held him back however, a feeling that they were not far from their goal, that something was looming close by.

A rumble of thunder sounded far away to their left. The air grew suddenly cold as a vicious wind swept through the group, then the hot blanket descended once more and the sky exploded.

All the heat of the day had sucked itself into the clouds and now it was unleashed in a torrent of lightning. They saw nothing of individual streaks: the entire sky was alive with light, great swathes of brilliant white fire opening above them, in front of them, inside them it seemed. Thunder tumbled over itself, inseparable from the flashing of the lightning, wave after wave falling so fast that the dragons were practically knocked from the air beneath its onslaught. Only the unkind spikes of the spruce and pine canopy prevented them from taking immediate shelter.

'The trees drop away just ahead!' bellowed Fortune, not knowing if he could be heard. 'There may be shelter there. Just a little further.'

Whether they heard him or not they followed all the same. The sky had become an angry monster, a gnashing, snarling thing which displaced all their instinctive, dragon trust in the sky at a single stroke. They wanted nothing more now than a deep cave, a refuge from the angry elements, the safety of the ground, and they all trusted Fortune to find them such a sanctuary.

So it was that, in the claws of the late afternoon storm, Fortune led his band of weary dragons up over the rising forest which opened on to the single, greatest flaw in the continent of Ocea. Spruce and pine thinned then stopped abruptly. The ground hesitated ... then *plunged*. The dark fog was banished completely as the lightning accelerated to a monotonous, strobing whiteness expanding around them. Over the precipice they flew, momentarily blinded by the ferocity of the storm and only gradually comprehending what it was they had flown into.

It was the Rift; it was, as Cumber had predicted, a canyon. But if Fortune had thought this a mighty land then nothing could have prepared him for the scale of this.

The ground plummeted. Layer after layer of canyon wall revealed itself as they flew out over the great divide, unveiling progressively deeper gullies until the layers merged into a single, yawning emptiness. There was a bottom to the gulf, but it was so far below that it seemed to belong to another world, another time. Ahead was the same. The lightning might have flattened distance, making things seem nearer than they really were: not so the Rift. The far wall was far enough away to seem as remote as a foreign land; they could make out neither form nor feature on the opposite side, it was merely a pale brown line sketched beneath the glowering storm.

And as if the depth and breadth were not enough, the canyon expanded to either side, boasting a winding, complex length. White haze swallowed the furthest reaches, where the crags and contours seemed even bigger than they were here. At that moment, as they soared out over the precipice in the clutches of the storm, it seemed to go on forever.

CHAPTER 19

Rift

Contrary to what Fortune believed, there was a shred of Scarn that could still be called dragon.

It was this part of Scarn which looked out across the expanse of the Last Circle, not the new, fiery core which had all but consumed the essential spirit of the dragon. The afternoon light entered what passed for dragon eyes and registered in a mind which, for the time being at least, believed itself still to be what it was born to be. And the predominant idea in that mind was that Scarn – *dragon* Scarn – was triumphant.

The symmetry of the moment was what stood out: the pure, unblemished circumference of the Circle itself – no faery ring this but something much stranger – the knot of red at its heart, and the speck of white at the centre of that knot. Circle, dragons, sacrifice, the perfect representation of the focus of his ambition. Looking up he saw the comet prowling high in the clear, electric sky. Storm clouds loitered to the northwest but they would not venture this far. They would not dare disturb his peace.

The red scales of the dragons of the Cult – or what Scarn believed still to be the dragons of the Cult – glistened with charm. They crowded round the sleeping Gossamer, perhaps curious as Scarn was curious about how she could rest when she was in such peril. Above them, below the comet, hung the final piece in the puzzle: the Flame.

It burned ferociously from empty air. Like the Flame which had once illuminated Nistor's chamber it was inverted, sending tongues of fire licking not up into the sky but down towards the ground. Like all the other forms of the Flame it was a searing blue colour. Scarn could feel its heat from here, baking his scales; down there, in the centre of the Circle, the temperature was almost unbearable.

He turned away, wondering briefly what was left behind on Mahl. Nothing, he supposed, since the Flame which had burned there had followed him here through the tunnel of charm. In fact, Scarn believed *all* the world's Flames were here now, their powers gathered into a single, all-powerful Flame, burning at the centre of the Last Circle.

Scarn was well aware that such a concerted focusing of its energies made the Flame as vulnerable as it made it strong, but then the day of creation was nothing if not a day of risk. *All or nothing*, the dragon part of him thought, while the rest of him, the hidden bulk of the blazing iceberg he had become, remained silent. *The Flame will prevail, and when the day of creation has come and gone, only it will remain. It will own the world, and Scarn will be a glorious part of it.*

Symmetry again, a great arc of an idea which curled round upon itself until it devoured its own tail. The ultimate turning, with Scarn in triumph at its heart. Scarn in ultimate communion with the new god.

The storm waned silently on the horizon and Scarn watched as another of his flock rose from the group and flew directly upwards into the Flame. Two breaths later a near-invisible line of smoke exploded from the fire, arrowing north and turning slightly west as it receded. A red blur accompanied it on its lightning journey towards what remained of the storm. Another raid on the old and helpless dragons of the Rift had begun.

The storm was as brief as it was violent, an angry purging of the afternoon's humidity. It passed swiftly overhead, evaporating into a radiant sky which shone its cool light down into the Rift. The sun dropped low, sculpting the elaborate contours of the canyon with ever-lengthening shadows, some of them pale cloud-shadows which rolled loosely down the precipices and through the gullies, their ordered motion describing the majesty of the place more eloquently than any song. A cool breeze blew in from the south and the air felt cleansed. Behind them the last vestiges of the storm grumbled, but they too would soon be gone. Although night was near, it felt like a new day.

The dragons looked at the view and still could not believe their eyes. Cumber had been right when he predicted a canyon, but so wrong when he'd guessed it might be like Aether's Cross. The gorge which led to the Cross had been formidable indeed, and so deep in places that a dragon felt dwarfed, but it was a mountain pass, and in the mountains such scenery was to be expected. It was narrow too for almost its entire length, a meandering, high-sided slit which progressed through the Low Mountains with simple authority. Impressive though it was, the canyon of the Cross had held few surprises. But the Rift . . .

This was no mountain pass. This was a gaping wound in the skin of the world. The land was high to be sure, but the dragons sensed they were simply atop a plateau of considerable breadth but only moderate height – there were no peaks, and no hint of snow. The Rift cut its way through this plateau, carved the land with mighty strokes. It was complex beyond belief. Here the ground dropped, turned into a sliding mass of red gravel; there a sheer cliff displayed a fine grid of horizontal lines, rock strata revealed in myriad colours; further down a series of blunt crags erupted from a dark and sombre trench; lower still, a maze of scrub and wiry trees wound its way around a spiky, volcanic hillside. Every rock form the dragons had ever seen was on display here, or so it seemed, and the horizon up to and beyond which the Rift still yawned promised more wonders beyond the limits of their vision.

Fortune sensed immediately that dragons had once lived here. Rock and dragon were inseparable; never had he known such a dragon place. Or was the Rift merely haunted as so many places in the world seemed to be these days? Fortune himself had seen many of the truths at the heart of the Turning, including the dreadful revelation that most of the dragons left in the world had been gathered at the Plated Mountain when it finally erupted. All those who survived the cataclysm – to his knowledge at least – came with him to Haven. He shuddered when he realized that most of those were now dead, prey to the world-storm

260

which had decimated their island sanctuary. The dragons freed from Aether's Cross had swollen the dwindling dragon population considerably, but Scarn had soon claimed most of them for his own.

And they are no longer dragons, thought Fortune bitterly.

The breeze strengthened and then he heard a rhythmic sound which pushed the thunder away with gentle strength. For a breath or two he could not place it – he thought in fact it was the beating of his own, over-anxious heart – then he recognized it for what it was: dragon wingbeats, drawing near.

None of them could locate its source at first, so weird was the play of sound against the elaborately sculpted canyon side. The noise seemed at first to be all but upon them, but then it retreated to a point far below in the dark haze which evening was sucking into the depths. Fortune thought again about ghosts. Then, just as excitement was beginning the short journey towards fear, Cumber saw them.

'My goodness!' he exclaimed, drawing the attention of his friends to a glittering patch of air below an outreaching cliff. The glittering solidified into a patchwork of motion and out of the shadows emerged a slow-moving group of dragons. They flew close, their wings almost touching; for an instant it was as though they were not a collection of individuals but a single organism.

As the dragons drew near the travellers identified them as ex-Charmed. Their wings were as large as those of Naturals – though clumsily made, as though grown in a hurry – but beneath their bellies were tucked the characteristic four legs of the magic-wielding dragon. But the thing that really betrayed their origins was their scales. Fortune had seen metallized scales many times before, but nothing like this. Each dragon (and there were forty at a rough count) bore scales which had been polished to an incredible shine. Their scintillating colours were less a result of pigment than reflectivity: they were virtual mirrors, flexible mercury dragons whose bodies, as they moved in flight, captured, enhanced and then threw back the magnificence of their sunlit canyon environment. Something else struck Fortune as they approached, something which their perfect, dazzling scales belied, something to do with the stiff set of their wings, the ragged motion of their tails: they were old, all of them, very old.

'Greetings,' boomed a loud, but undeniably wavering voice from the head of the group. 'It is a long time since travellers have come to us in peace. Show us quickly why we should trust you.'

Fortune looked at Scoff querulously. 'They certainly get to the point, don't they?' he murmured. The dragons were close now, hovering in a close-knit formation, regarding the newcomers with open suspicion. Fortune opened his mouth to speak, but a keen whistling sound cut him off. Every dragon there looked towards the cliff-top.

A line of smoke raced into view with audacious speed, slithering to a trembling halt scant wingspans before the leader of the old, mirrored dragons. The dragons recoiled in a single, co-ordinated move when, with frightening suddenness, the smoke peeled back to reveal one of Scarn's red dragons floating and snapping, glowing eyes searching the air for prey. Fire surrounded it, belched from between its jaws; a guttural snarling sound issued from somewhere deep within its breast; its tail was a whiplash of unrestrained motion. It cruised towards the retreating dragons, picking out its target, while somewhere in the vicinity of its heart, a rich, blue glow began to expand.

Fortune understood instantly what had been happening here, even if he did not yet understand why. Scarn's dragons were picking off these elderly souls one by one, spiriting them away into the desert of the red rocks and killing them horribly. Using the power of the Flame to generate these tunnels of smoke, these devices of almost instantaneous transport, they were slowly decimating the population of what had to be one of the last dragon colonies left in the world. If not the last.

Fortune looked at the invader and saw red – red that had more to do with his own perception than the colour of the once-dragon's scales. Without regard for his own safety Fortune plunged towards it, screaming against the injustice of Scarn's hideous actions in this new land.

Belatedly Cumber and Scoff followed, swiftly overtaken

262

by Velvet, who was faster in flight than either of them and nearly as fast as Fortune. Aria loitered behind them, her face a crumple of misery. Even so, Fortune was on the monster first.

As soon as his claws met its scales he knew that he was right: this was no dragon. A great swathe of its hide tore away as he slashed at its flank, revealing not flesh and bone but a glowing, liquid interior that pulsed with a slow, sick heartbeat. He slashed out, and two red horns splintered, tumbling down into the canyon depths. The thing screamed, and the sound was like nothing made by a dragon throat. It fought viciously, striping Fortune's underbelly with his own blood, but the one-on-one battle did not last for long. A few breaths after Fortune struck his companions were with him, dragging the writhing beast free of their injured friend and hurling it bodily against the nearby cliff wall. It struck with a wet, heavy sound and stayed there, jerking feebly against whatever hideous glue had emerged from its guts to hold it on to the rock.

Abruptly the smoke tunnel retreated, slamming back over the cliff-top in silence. The twitching creature broke the silence by screaming its agony. The four friends hovered warily, Cumber and Velvet eyeing it with unguarded suspicion, Scoff checking Fortune's wounds, which luckily seemed slight. A shadow fell across them as the group of mirror-dragons (as Fortune had named them in his head) came close. Their formation remained as tight as ever and again that slightly shaky voice boomed out.

'You have done well, dragon. Do you wish to finish the task, or shall we assist?'

Before Fortune could reply, the injured red dragon – it still had the shape of a dragon, if not the heart – pulled itself free of the rock with a hideous sucking noise, shot clear upwards over the cliff-top and was gone.

'After it?' suggested Scoff uncertainly, but Fortune shook his head.

'No, it might give Scarn something to think about if he sees one of his minions in that state.'

There was a murmur from the mirror-dragons and suddenly one of them pulled away from the rest. He was old, of course, but with a long, elegant body still discernible beneath the wattles and loops of loose flesh which hung from his flanks and throat. The travellers watched with fascination the way the evening sky was reflected in those shining scales, how their own faces peered back a thousand times from those countless, tiny mirrors.

'Your sympathies you have demonstrated well enough,' he announced, his booming voice gentler now. 'But tell me, what is this name you use – "Scarn"? You sound like dragons who might know more about our predicament than we ourselves do.'

'First things first, Oster,' called a second voice. 'Where's your hospitality, eh?'

'Limner's right, Oster,' a third agreed. 'Food and water first, then talk.'

'Yes, yes,' tutted the dragon called Oster impatiently. Then he addressed the visitors with his previous charm. 'If you would care to join us, we should be most interested to hear your news. We have little enough to offer you, but what there is we will gladly share.'

It seemed rude to debate, so Fortune restricted himself to a quick glance around his friends. They were all tired, clearly, but none of them seemed in any fear of these dragons. He consulted his own heart and found it settled – they would join these dragons if only for tonight, if only to find out what evil Scarn had been hurling upon them.

And tomorrow? he wondered.

Tomorrow he would go to the Last Circle and rescue Gossamer from Scarn's clutches, whatever promise he had made her not to interfere.

He was nearly hypnotized by the smooth, fluid motion of the mirror-dragons' wings as he followed them down into the cool canyon depths – they were confident in flight, especially in so tight a group. He wondered if they had always flown like this or if their formation-flying were a precaution against the recent attacks. It looked efficient and well-trained, although there was no air of the military about them. Perhaps age had softened them.

Whatever their reasons, they fly beautifully, thought Fortune, and for no reason he could identify a series of ringing sounds chimed in his head. *They fly beautifully*, he reiterated, staring at their flowing backs, the dorsal spines which rippled in harmony with the slow flapping of their wings like rushes in a windblown pool. The thought was important somehow, but why? He could not hold on to it; it slipped aside and became simply: *They fly*. Then he tired, and as they swooped in towards a broad, open cave about halfway down the canyon wall that single thought had become simply this: *Dragons fly*.

Of course they do, he scolded himself wearily, but the thought would not go away. *Dragons fly, Fortune, they fly . . .*

The mirror-dragons were good hosts, cheerful and easy. They made the five travellers feel at home straight away, and soon news was being exchanged at astonishing speed over a supper of fruit, fish and fresh water. Far from asking about Scarn and the red dragons, Oster and his shining cohorts were initially more curious about the Turning, especially when they discovered that their guests had actually been present at the heart of that great event.

'We experienced the loss of charm, of course,' explained a dragon with the unusual name of Wemp, 'but we could only guess at what was going on.'

'Hence the clumsy wings,' commented another dragon, lifting one scrawny membrane sadly.

'You fly superbly,' said Fortune, gulping down a draught of the cold spring water.

'We retaught ourselves,' Oster agreed. He seemed the closest these dragons had to a leader. Even on the ground they stayed close together, as perfect in their formation here as they had been in the air. Before long, it became clear to the visiting dragons that all thirty-eight of them were males. 'It was our duty,' he added, as though it explained something.

Oster's closest neighbour nudged his leader. 'Sun's getting low,' he prompted.

'Off you go, then, Limner,' replied Oster, keeping on eye on the visitors and allowing himself a small smile. 'Are you warm enough?' he asked Fortune.

Fortune looked round at the other members of his party

and shrugged. 'I've been warmer, but it's not uncomfortable.'

'I think your friend is feeling it though,' answered Oster,
nodding at a pair of trembling white wings. 'You are feeling
cold . . . Cumber, is it?'

Cumber lifted his head with a snap. He had been day-
dreaming, rubbing his flanks with his wings. 'Oh, er, sorry.
Well, yes, I am in a way. I was just thinking that in the old
days we would have struck up a fire, roasted a few rabbits,
you know. I *have* managed it once since the Turning,
though,' he added proudly, then his expression turned to
one of dejection, 'but it was rather a fluke, I'm afraid.'

'If it's fire you want, Cumber . . .' replied Oster, his smile
even broader.

'Without charm?' countered Cumber. 'Don't be absurd.'

But Oster continued to smile and drew Cumber's attention to a large pile of sticks and brushwood which one of
his companions had dragged into the cave entrance on a
wide tray of woven branches. 'Watch Limner,' he said, and
they did.

Limner was hovering a short distance from the entrance,
his wide, metallic wings beating a remarkably slow rhythm
against the haze which now concealed the far side of the
canyon. His scales glittered in the low, orange sunlight. He
was moving his head, judging distance and glancing frequently to the west, where the sun itself was still just visible
over the lip of the Rift. Then he gained height, opened his
wings to their furthest extent and glided slowly in towards
the cave.

As he drifted down (Fortune decided he must either be
as light as air or using some shred of flight charm to control
his altitude without wingbeats) he cupped his wings into a
smooth arc. They caught the sun and now they did not
merely glitter – they dazzled. The rest of the mirror-dragons
looked away but Fortune, Cumber and the others continued
to watch in fascination. Fortune thought he knew what
Limner was about to do, but he wanted to see it for himself.

A broad disc of light flashed into existence on the ground
just short of the entrance and sped up the crags towards
them, shrinking as it approached. It fell across the firewood

and halted there, continuing to shrink until it was focused into a blinding point of brilliance. There was a pause, then the brushwood began to smoke. Another of the mirror-dragons was crouched low and began to puff gently until the smoking became a smouldering and suddenly a tongue of fire leaped up.

Fortune looked from the fire to Limner, then back to the fire again, marvelling at the precision in flight it had taken for this dragon not only to curl its wings into a perfect lens in the first place, but also to retain enough control to direct the light so accurately. Limner was beating those shining wings again now, slowing his lazy descent and returning to the gathering. Cumber lifted one of his own, pale wings in salute as he landed.

'Most impressive,' he cried. 'Was there any charm in that, any at all?'

Limner shook his head emphatically. 'Absolutely not. Once I would have used charm to stop my descent altogether, but I am flier enough to manage it without magic if I must.'

Cumber exchanged a glance with Fortune. *This dragon's flying is a match for yours, Fortune, even Tallow's*, the look seemed to say. Fortune nodded almost imperceptibly.

Oster watched the silent exchange with interest while behind him the fire took proper hold and sent ribbons of flame up into the darkening sky. Thousands of orange beads were scattered by the mirrored scales of the dragons of the Rift, drawing the magic of the charmless fire deep into the cave and casting long, scintillating reflections into its darkest recesses.

Between them, Fortune and his friends recounted most of the events of the Turning and the world-storm which followed it. By the time they had introduced Scarn and the Cult it was dark outside, but the fire kept the cave bright and warm and they felt comfortable here, more comfortable than they had felt for some considerable time. Then, their story over, it was time to hear that of the mirror-dragons. Inevitably it was Oster who told it.

The dragon population of Ocea had always been small. Despite the immensity of the continent it had always been

267

a colony remote from the densely populated Heartland.

'Halcyon had his contacts here, of course,' Oster explained, 'but travel between them and Halcyon was usually made by the mind, not the body. We kept ourselves to ourselves for the most part.'

Several years before the Turning infant dragons had begun to grow sick. The cases were isolated at first, then they escalated at terrifying speed. Soon, at the same time as a plague of madness was decimating the charmed dragons of the Heartland and its environs, an infant-killing epidemic was destroying both the inheritance and the will to live of the dragons of Ocea. Tiny bones littered the ground, the dreadful product of the flesh-wasting disease. Not a single adult appeared to be infected; every infant below the age of five years died. When they were all gone, no more fertile eggs were laid on the continent of Ocea.

'Here too,' grunted Scoff, and his friends nodded sadly. They had already told the mirror-dragons about their fears of permanent sterility – now it seemed those fears were justified.

'Many parents killed themselves,' said Oster, his voice tight, restraining his emotion. 'Many others retreated into grief and never returned. A few got on with life.'

'We got on with life,' interjected Wemp.

'We grew old fast,' continued Oster. 'All the dragons of Ocea grew old fast – too fast. We believe now that the disease *was* passed on to adults, but in a different form. How old do we look to you, Fortune?'

Fortune pondered for a moment, weighing up politeness against honesty and deciding upon the latter. 'Very old,' he concluded. 'Ninety at the youngest – probably over one hundred?'

Oster nodded. 'Not one of us is over thirty-five,' he sighed. He appraised his guests. 'There is little surprise on your faces.'

Cumber gave him a humourless smile. 'Well, Oster, we have encountered quite a few twists of time in our time, if you'll forgive the expression. So, you see, this isn't really all that remarkable.'

Oster looked unsure of himself for several breaths, cast a

worried glance back into his crowd of allies, then his face cracked and he laughed. So unrestrained was his laughter that very soon they were all laughing, mirror-dragons and travellers alike, laughing longer and louder than any of them had laughed for a very long time. The rocking of their bodies sent a million shards of firelight showering out into the night, perfect reflections of the natural flame which was guarding them here in the depths of the Rift.

Conversation moved to more recent times, and Fortune asked cautiously about the two dragons they had found murdered on the rocks. Oster listened grimly as he described what they had seen.

'Race and Darten,' he sighed as Fortune concluded. 'We feared the worst, of course, but to hear of it is . . . terrible. Five of us are gone now, and were it not for your intervention today it would be six.'

'But can't you repel the attacks yourselves?' blurted Cumber suddenly. Velvet dug him in the ribs but Oster waved her apology aside.

'They come so swiftly,' he answered. 'Even if we see the smoke coming we do not know exactly where it will strike. Today was the first time it stopped short of actually entering our formation – perhaps because it sensed your presence too. It is usually towards the end of the day, when we are flying together. Suddenly there is a flurry in our midst and the tunnel of smoke is there, piercing us like some dreadful claw. Then one of us is gone. That is all; there is no time to respond, none at all.'

'Why would this Scarn of yours do such a thing?' asked Wemp.

'He's not ours!' blurted Aria, and all eyes swivelled to her. This was her first contribution to the proceedings, and the way her eyes were blazing it did not look to be her last. 'But if we sit around talking then *we* will soon become *his*.'

'Discussion may point to the way to the truth,' replied Oster smoothly.

'The truth is that Scarn is a monster and will stop at nothing to get his way. Carry on like this and he'll pick us all off, one by one.'

'What does he want?' Limner interjected, but Aria fell silent. As one the mirror-dragons looked back at Fortune.

'I don't know for certain,' sighed Fortune, 'because I'm not sure he's really a dragon any more. And if that's true, then none of us can hope to get inside his head.'

'This place,' announced Scoff suddenly. 'Last Circle. It's near, we know. What is it to you?'

Oster chuckled. Fortune realized that he liked this prematurely old dragon immensely – he was honest and direct, and appreciated such qualities in others. *I bet he's as good a flier as Limner*, he thought. *If it comes to that, I bet they all are.*

'The Last Circle,' Oster mused. 'Yes, you could say that we know it.'

'What is it then?' asked Cumber excitedly. 'Is it important to you, a place of worship, I'm wondering?'

'No, not worship.' Now Oster's expression had become sad. 'The Last Circle – for we know it by that name too, though for different reasons than your Scarn, I suspect – is a local landmark. It's something under a day's flight from here, more or less to the south.

'Once this area held the highest concentration of dragons in Ocea. The Rift attracted dragons from all over the continent for many years until it was a thriving centre. Then came the infant plague, of course, and the ageing disease. The ground was littered with bones, you know – you cannot imagine it . . . Anyway, it was decided that all the remains should be gathered and burned in one, single ceremony. An offering, if you like, to whatever spirit might be willing to accept those wretched little ones.

'We took the bones to the Last Circle and built a great pyre. Then one of our number, a mighty charmed dragon called Woredel, created an all-consuming flame in the heart of the pyre, and we all stood and watched our future burn. As those tiny bones cracked and melted into vapour, a huge cloud of smoke rose above the Circle. I imagined it was a cloud which had come from far away to claim the lives of those we had lost. To rescue them and take them somewhere safe. But the wind swept it away, and when the fire had done its work nothing remained – no ashes, nothing.'

The cave was silent now but for the steady crackling of

the fire. Cumber shuffled nervously. It was Velvet who broke the silence.

'Your infants were on that fire, weren't they, Oster?'

Oster shook his head and smiled sadly. 'You forget that we are much younger than we seem. No, I have no infants. But I had two young brothers.'

At first it seemed that the gloom which had descended upon them would not be broken, until Aria lifted her head and spoke again.

'It's not a faery circle like my father and Cumber think. It isn't that at all, is it?'

Oster looked surprised. 'Indeed no, Aria,' he answered. 'That would be a reasonable assumption, of course, given Scarn's obsession with what he believes to be its power. Have you seen it?'

Aria frowned. 'I have seen its place,' she said, forming the words with difficulty. 'I mean, I could find my way to it – I have done so many times in my dreams – but what it looks like . . . I cannot say.' She opened her eyes, which she had closed in concentration. 'But I think we're all going to find out quite soon, aren't we?'

'Now that we know what we did not know, yes,' came Oster's curious reply. He elaborated by explaining that he and the mirror-dragons were ready to make war against their attackers, but that up to now they had no idea whence the attacks came, nor even the true nature of their foe. 'Now, however, we know the location of the enemy camp,' he proclaimed, 'and something of what we are up against.'

'That "something" could be "very little",' murmured Cumber to Fortune, who nodded his agreement.

But Fortune was distracted. Listening to Oster speak, he found himself carried back to a time before the Turning, when dragon was set against dragon and war was imminent. Then he had turned away from violence, rejecting the leadership others had offered him and pleading for peace. Yet now, in similar circumstances, he found an anger inside himself which would not be denied. At first he did not hear Oster's question, coming to only when Cumber jabbed him sharply with his wing.

'I'm sorry,' he apologized. 'What were you saying?'

'Will you join us?' Oster repeated. 'Tomorrow we go to the Last Circle, though none of us may return.'

No! cried an inner voice. *There must be another way!* But try as he might Fortune could find no other way. They had defeated today's attacker, certainly, but that had been only one. What could they possibly do against the whole of Scarn's force, against his charm? *If we do nothing, what will Scarn do to us?*

Gossamer's face came to him, white and sad. Silently he asked if he should break his word to her, if he should break the word he had kept his whole life. The vision said nothing, merely turned away with a gentle, knowing smile. Then her whisper caressed the edges of his heart: *You have never turned from anything, my darling.*

'They are not dragons,' he said, startled by the sound of his voice in the stillness. 'And there is no way we can know what they will do next. They plan to subvert the new order, and they have my Gossamer. There is no choice for us. They must be wiped from the skin of the world.'

Oster grunted approvingly, and even Fortune's companions, though surprised by the venom in his words, nodded their agreement.

'Something has just struck me,' said Cumber urgently, even before the import of what Fortune had said could really sink in. 'Scarn's power is in the Flame, and the Flame gives him access to fire – perhaps *all* fire.' He stared significantly at the blaze which now half-filled the entrance to the cave.

'Douse it,' commanded Oster peremptorily, and several of his comrades set to work dumping water from a nearby cache and scattering the smouldering embers. Presently all that remained of the glorious bonfire was a damp and flattened heap of cinders. The flurry of activity seemed to have circumvented any need for debate. The decision was made; all that was left was to discuss the means by which victory might be achieved. Long into the night they talked, protected now by the absence of the fire where once they had trusted its presence, and when the sun rose Fortune was in possession of something he had never bothered with in all his life.

He had a plan.

CHAPTER 20

Dreams of Escape

Wist was surprised to find herself glad to be back on Mahl. It was like coming home, for she could not deny that she had once been happy in the family of the Cult. And there had of course been genuine family here – her twin sister, Lessen. What had become of her?

What do I care? We never got on.

That was largely true. Identical in appearance, the two dragons had shared little else. During their youth in the dramatic surroundings of Aether's Cross, Wist had been unusual in that she had wanted to become a fisher dragon, a role usually reserved for the males. She was skilled in flight however and her sharp wit and precise speech made her more than a match for the boisterous males who considered dragons like her better suited for roles as nest-makers and teachers. Many times over she proved her ability, challenging her male rivals in dramatic diving contests to snatch fish from the fast-flowing canyon river. She did not always win, but she never failed to impress. And she loved to race.

Lessen was not interested in flying, nor in the more traditional roles Wist's male colleagues might have tried to impose upon her. In fact she seemed to be interested in very little at all. She would sit for hours contemplating the forbidden charmed cavern entrances on the opposite wall of the gorge – 'hole-watching' as Gossamer and Brace would have called it – or soaring in the easy air near the top of the cliffs. She drifted, enjoying the occasional bout of flirting with some hungry young male but never committing herself to anything like a relationship. And she was jealous of her sister.

Wist knew about the jealousy, of course, and resented it. She felt guilty whenever she saw Lessen, and that made her angry, just as Lessen was angered by her own jealousy. So their increasingly rare encounters resembled nothing less than snarling competitions; few words were spoken, and when they were Lessen would mock Wist's more cultured accent, her richer vocabulary, and Wist would resent what she perceived as Lessen's arrogant superficiality. Alike, and yet unalike.

Yet the hatred was there in both of us, mused Wist now as she wandered sleeplessly through the night beneath the Kull Wall. The sheer white of the cliff shone in the combined light of moon and comet, and the steaming lake in the broad valley below hissed and glistened as it lapped against the landslides which hugged its shore. *Were we really so different after all?*

Their time together in Scarn's harem had served only to increase their antagonism towards each other (each kept a private tally of the number of times Scarn had invited them into his private chamber), but at the same time their proximity had awakened – in Wist at least – an odd feeling of empathy. Occasionally, during their early life at Aether's Cross, Wist had felt as if she were reading her sister's mind, and from Lessen's expression at the time she knew the feeling was reciprocated. She had heard of twins sharing such experiences, but only occasionally had she felt it herself.

On Mahl, in the confines of the Fissures, that feeling had grown. As Wist and Lessen had grown more hateful towards each other, so they had begun to share more and more in each other's thoughts and emotions. It was a gnawing sensation Wist had largely blocked out, so distasteful did she find it, but now she was keen to open herself fully to it. She was parted from her sister, and despite her hatred, her anger, she was astonished to find that she did not like it one bit.

Lessen, where are you? she called silently, and she reached out with her heart.

She turned first to the west, where she knew Scarn had

taken the Cult. Why she did this she did not know – she was sure Lessen had not gone with them; after all, that was precisely why she was here now. It was with a kind of mourning that she looked out across the lake and wondered what might have been. Tallow was the one whose promise she had followed across the ocean, but now Tallow was gone. Had she not fled, might she have been Scarn's chosen one? Might he not have taken her to the Last Circle, to the glory awaiting them there?

Wist shook herself, telling herself not to be absurd. She was well rid of Scarn and all he had preached. The image of the Last Circle – her own, private vision of a perfectly round lake surrounded by towering trees, with a dome-shaped island at its centre like the pupil of some vast eye – filled her mind as it often did. *That* was what she believed in, not Scarn's lies. All she really regretted was that she had passed up the chance to travel there and meet . . . whatever it was that was coming.

But I chose my sister instead. I pray it was the right choice.

She looked up at the entrance to the Fissures and staggered back in shock, a terrible, droning wail filling the spaces in her head. To her amazement her nose began to bleed. When she looked away she found the sensation diminished, but it did not altogether depart. Biting down with her mind, trying to regain some kind of control, she looked cautiously up again.

This time it was better, although the sound was not gone completely. It rang in her head like a singing infant, bearable now but eerie, ghostly. Then, a revelation: *I have been hearing it all along!*

This very sound, Wist realized, had been present ever since she had returned to Mahl – no, before even then. *Since the time Tallow brought Aria from the geyser. Since Scarn sent his fire through the Fissures and turned the dragons of the Cult red.* A thin, wailing cry which she had not heard because her mind had long been desensitized to its source.

The cry which came from the mind of her twin sister.

If Wist felt close to home, Brace had never felt further from his. However far he travelled across the world – and sometimes it felt as though he had circled it a hundred times – he never seemed to get any nearer to his ultimate goal.

Whatever that may be, he thought wearily.

His recent history, since the Turning at least, seemed made of tasks, none of which had very much to do with his own ambition, his own destiny. First he had resolved to free the dragons of Aether's Cross from their imprisonment – that, with the help of his friends, he had achieved. Now he had set himself the problem of freeing his own parents – his father in particular – from the less tangible prison into which Scarn had placed them. With Rarch and Jevell on the other side of the world he seemed further now than he had ever been from completing this latest mission.

And even if I do succeed, what then? What does the future hold for Brace?

Brace eased himself away from Ledra's sleeping form and ambled down towards the lakeside. He kept his eyes on the ground; the comet seemed to press down on him with an unwelcome weight. His gloom only increased however, for adding to the turmoil in his mind was an overwhelming feeling of detachment. Time was moving, fast. And Brace was remote, useless, unnecessary.

Just when it seemed his mood would become as dark as the waters of the lake beside which he loitered, he heard wings and felt a rush of air as Wist landed next to him. Her scales glinted in the eerie light of the moon and comet combined, looking reassuringly normal. He glanced down at his own, red scales and found that when he raised his eyes again he was smiling.

'You'll get used to it,' said Wist. 'And I always liked red.' She hopped from one leg to the other, dabbing at the broken rock of the shore with her wingtips to maintain her balance; clearly she was agitated.

'Is something wrong?' inquired Brace. 'Should we wake Ledra?'

'No. Yes. Oh, now you're confusing me. What I mean is, something might be wrong, or rather I think I've finally worked out where Lessen is, which could very well amount to the same thing. And yes, I think we should wake Ledra right now. We have to go back into the Fissures, Brace.

She's there, I'm sure of it. But I'm not sure if we're going to like what we find.'

Intrigued, and a little unnerved, Brace led her back up the shore to where Ledra lay. Shortly afterwards they were climbing towards the top of the Kull Wall, heading for the deep crevasse which led through the newly-formed cracks to the Flamehall within. The twin lights of moon and comet tracked silently above them in the still, silent night.

In the Flamehall, Wist led them straight across the black, sculpted rock to the ledge on which she had seen the crystal formation. She landed lightly while her companions hovered a short distance away, watching for anything out of the ordinary. Wist circled the crystalline deposit, dipping her head close then drawing it away. Each time she backed off she let out a hiss as the whine in her head stabbed at her, then she drew near once more.

The translucent rock was brilliant red, brighter now than any of them remembered it. It glowed with a subtle light so that although it was much brighter than it had any right to be, they could not detect the source of the illumination. *Some inner fire*, Brace guessed. *Charm, no doubt.*

Now that they inspected it properly they could see that it was shaped roughly like a dragon. Its rear half was buried in the melted rock of the wall, but its forequarters lunged clear, lumpy and disfigured but still recognizable. A coil of neck was folded round upon itself, almost completely concealing a long, elegant head. Its proportions were similar to those of Wist, who was now sniffing at it, although the crystal was so distorted that no clear comparison was possible. Flat facets of red approximated the curves of dragon flank and dragon back, while splinters of the strange crystal sprang up in place of spine and flight-controlling cartilage. The wings were absent, though two stumps seemed welded to the thing's shoulders, their ends ragged with short spikes. Neither Brace nor Ledra felt any urge to approach it: it was just too weird.

For Wist the experience was akin to being in the claws of a gale, except the gale was in her mind. It took all her self-control to keep her body steady as she prowled – she did not want to scare her companions. Nevertheless she knew that this was her task, her moment, and she was glad they seemed to sense that too.

After what seemed an eternity the indiscriminate screaming in her mind began to separate into different strands of sound (she still thought of them as sounds, even though she knew the others could hear nothing). The first was the unmistakable sound of her sister's voice, chanting low prayers whose words she could not make out. The second was a bland, roaring noise, like the sound of a waterfall heard from a distance. But the third noise was scary: it too was a voice, but unlike that of Lessen this was deep and guttural, a crackling bass which surged loud and then quiet, its words indistinct but tinged with threat. Wist decided on the spot that this voice was unutterably evil.

No sooner had this third voice become distinct in her mind than it exploded with such fury, such venom, that she snapped her entire mind shut against it in an instant. She staggered backwards until she nearly slipped from the ledge. Ledra swooped in to gather her up but Wist held fast with her claws and clambered back to safety, trembling uncontrollably and weeping. Her companions ushered her carefully down to another ledge several wingspans away from the crystal dragon. By and by her breathing slowed and, though she cast frequent terrified glances at the red shape which loomed, just visible, over the edge of the outcrop, she gradually calmed herself again.

'She's in there,' she gasped. 'Lessen, my sister, is in there somewhere. But something else is in there with her!'

'What did you see?' demanded Brace.

'I can't see it, I can hear it.'

'Do you know what it is?' asked Ledra gently, cupping her wing around Wist's shaking flank.

Wist thought about the sound of that voice, heard the edges of its indistinguishable words searing the corners of her mind, felt it explode again, burning into her, crackling, leaping . . . and she knew. She nodded dully.

'It's a voice,' she said, her eyes glazed now. 'It is the voice of the Flame. It's here, now, with us, and it's got my sister.'

It was some time before Wist felt strong enough to approach the crystallized body of her sister again. So clear

278

was the evidence of the statue's origin that the dragons were amazed they had failed to identify it before.

'But who would have thought it?' said Ledra as they landed gingerly on the ledge once more. 'I mean, it's just so horrible.'

'Is it?' Brace asked Wist. 'Is it horrible for her?'

Wist nodded her head vigorously. 'Oh yes, I think it is. She was a troubled soul – there's so much anger in her – but she didn't deserve this.' She sniffed the air cautiously, then slumped down on the rock and cast her gaze about the deserted Flamehall. 'Look at this place,' she sighed. 'It's dead. However bad the Cult may have been it made the Fissures live. There was an atmosphere, a sound, a sense of purpose.'

'But was there a heart?' asked Ledra gently.

Wist thought hard for a moment and then answered, 'No, I don't think there was. And I think maybe we all knew that, deep down. But there were dreams, Ledra – that's what Scarn gave us, and that's what I still carry with me, even now. My dreams.'

'Well, there's certainly no life here now,' announced Brace, opening his wings and stretching them briskly. 'Apart from us, of course. Scarn's gone, the Cult's gone.' He frowned. 'Even the Flame has gone.'

Wist nodded, a little sadly, Brace thought. 'Yes, the main body of the Flame has gone, I'm sure of it. If we went to the Fissure where Scarn once fed on it, we would find it extinguished, I'm sure of it. And yet . . . and yet poor Lessen has somehow kept a tiny part of it alive here.'

'Or it has kept her alive,' suggested Brace darkly.

Feeling the need to confirm Wist's suspicion, Brace went off in search of the Fissure, leaving the two females together on the ledge. The Fissure was, as Wist had predicted, quite cold and dark; even the stream of lava which had illumi- nated the far end of the long, narrow space had stopped flowing. The Flame was gone, and with it all sense of charm, all sense of life. Brace did not linger any longer than he had to – the place felt haunted.

Upon his return he found his companions huddled over the crystal dragon, peering into its depths. Wist informed him briskly that she had managed to control the screaming in her head and was looking closer in the hope of finding some clue as to what, if anything, they could do to help Lessen.

'Look,' she said eagerly, pointing at the translucent material. 'There's a crack of some kind, there, just behind the head.'

Brace looked and sure enough there was a long, ragged streak buried deep inside the crystal. It ran back along the spine from the base of the skull, a spinal flaw which seemed to vibrate before his straining eyes. It was barely visible at all and it was some time before he could convince himself of what he was seeing: a thread of blue fire, burning away inside the statue.

'You were right, Wist – it's a little piece of the Flame,' whispered Ledra, startling him into jumping away from the crystal. 'Can't you feel it?'

Brace nodded. He knew the flavour of that magical fire only too well after his encounter with it in the Fissure. Curiously, it made his mouth water. 'Why has it been left behind?' he wondered out loud. 'And what has it to do with your sister, Wist?'

But Wist did not know, and it was in a dejected mood that they eventually left the Flamehall in search of food.

'It – she will still be there when we get back,' said Ledra, trying to reassure Wist. 'She's not going anywhere.'

'I know,' replied Wist mournfully. 'But that's just the trouble, isn't it?'

That night, Wist had a dream. She was flying through the Flamehall, only the Flamehall was different: now it extended both up and down into infinite space, an endless chimney with neither floor nor ceiling to define its boundaries. The air was pure and brilliantly lit, with no trace of atmospheric haze to mask the distances. Perspective simply shrank the converging verticals until they lost all dimension. It seemed, quite simply, to go on forever.

Lessen was there, released from her prison. She was still made of crystal, but now she could move and fly and speak. As she flew at Wist's side, the blinding light of the changed

Flamehall coruscating through her hard, translucent flesh, Wist wept at her beauty. Her tears flowed even more freely when she recognized something which made her sister yet more beautiful: she was smiling the most perfect, dazzling smile.

'I can be like this in my dreams,' announced Lessen, her voice flowing through Wist like the scent of some exotic flower. 'I can be like this *only* in my dreams, sister; that is why you have never seen me as I truly am. Only the Flame has seen me thus. Only the Flame understands.'

Wist inhaled her words and found them intoxicating. She was amazed to think that behind Lessen's frown and acid temper there had always been this beauty, this eloquence, this . . . contentment. 'Why have you never shown this to any other dragon?' she asked, her tears still flowing. 'Why have you never shown yourself to me, Lessen?'

They continued to fly and Wist realized that they were flying not horizontally as she had thought but upwards, up into the infinite reaches of what had ceased to be the Flamehall and was now a channel cut through some brilliant, glowing substance. Sparks chased round and round its circumference, fine disorientating streaks which dizzied Wist. With an effort she focused her eyes on the glittering red of her sister.

'The Flame has been in me for a very long time, Wist,' Lessen replied solemnly. 'It is a part of me. That is why it has chosen me now.' She gave a small, perfect smile. 'Do you know when the Flame was lit inside me, Wist? It was the day we both learned to fly. You went first, of course, as you always did. I didn't mind. I was your match in all but speed, and competition was not on my mind. I remember the sound of the river was loud that day – snow was melting high in the mountains and the gorge was full. I remember its roar.

'Do you remember it, Wist, do you?'

Wist shook her head. She remembered the day well enough – the roar of the river, the rush of the wind against her face, the terrifying ecstasy of flying free for the very first time. But she had no idea what Lessen was building towards.

'Until then we had shared everything, Wist, and that

comforted me. Then we flew together,' Lessen continued, 'much as we fly now, in our dreams. And there was a moment when our wings touched in the narrow canyon. If I had just tipped a little to the left, Wist, I could have dashed you against the cliffs with a single flick of my wing. You would have died instantly, I am sure of it even now.'

'It never occurred to me,' blurted Wist, still mesmerized by the light, sparkling rings of light flowing past her speeding body . . . or were they stationary and the tunnel itself was moving, accelerating past them? It was narrowing up ahead, and she instinctively drew closer to her sister.

'I know,' answered Lessen, and something about the way she spoke made Wist alert. 'But it occurred to *me*, Wist.'

Wist shivered, unable to respond. She could see almost completely through the sheer crystal of her sister's skull. Complex facets glimmered in the elaborate facsimile of flesh and bone, while behind it – *through* it – raced the background of the wall. The tunnel was closing in still.

'That was the moment the Flame came to me,' Lessen continued. 'And from from that day, I hated you.'

Wist was shocked. The sides of the chimney were upon them now, their outstretched wings skimmed them. 'The Flame is evil, sister . . .' she began.

But Lessen's crystal gaze had softened. 'I know that as well as you,' she said, 'but I am powerless in its influence – except in my dreams, my dear, dear Wist. In my dreams I have always loved you, as once I did in the world we like to call real.'

Then they were out of the closing walls, flying free in a vast, open space which Wist took at first to be the sky she loved so much. Only gradually did she comprehend that they had entered a tremendous cavern, white and fluorescent. Far to one side was drawn the only feature she could make out in this blank and brilliant void: a line of fire, blue, scratched into the distant wall as though by the claw of some rampant dragon god.

'Now you will see,' said Lessen softly. 'Now you will know what it is you must know, and what it is you must do.'

As they drew nearer to the fire, which dwarfed them as the mighty canyon of Aether's Cross had once dwarfed them in their youth, Wist saw that, like the canyon, this was a wound. It was a slit, rimmed with blazing fire, through which she might exit the glowing cavern and enter ... what? Another world? Or was there simply a succession of chambers, each larger than the preceding one, on and on in eternal progression?

Her mind shrank back but her wings drove her on, on into the fire, until it engulfed her and she was passing through the crack, out into whatever lay beyond. She had the briefest glimpse of a great vertical drop, a succession of rough grey slabs rising into infinity ...

Wist's cries woke Brace and Ledra instantly. They rushed to where she lay at the back of the shallow cave they had chosen as their temporary home and tried to rouse her from what they assumed to be a nightmare. Her eyes flew open and she lunged forward, battering at Ledra with her wings. She was halfway into the air before she realized where she was, whereupon she sank unceremoniously to the ground, panting and shaking. Slowly she came round, and as the dawn rolled its soft light across her troubled features, she turned away from the promise of the sun to face her two worried companions.

Her voice, calm and confident, belied her trembling form. 'I have spoken to my sister,' she announced, quietly and firmly. 'And she has told me what we must do.'

Brace looked quizzically at Ledra, uncertain whether or not to humour Wist, whom he assumed to be delirious. But Ledra's face was intent, her body pressed forward as she awaited Wist's next words. Brace looked back at Wist and all suspicion drained from him: her eyes alone told him that everything she said then was true.

'Lessen has been possessed by the power of the Flame,' Wist went on. 'And although it has drawn itself across the world to the Last Circle it has, as we guessed, left a tiny part of itself here, buried deep inside my sister's heart. It is scared, you see, the Flame.

'It knows it might yet be defeated by what is coming to challenge it, so it has opened an escape route for its twisted soul. Lessen is the way through to the freedom which lies beyond. If it wins, it inherits the world; if it is cast down then it will flee, like the coward it is, into some other world where perhaps the sky is not so bright, where it can once again work its evil in other hearts than those of dragons.

'Lessen cannot bear the thought that she will be responsible for the unleashing of the Flame upon another world. It cannot be allowed to escape. It must suffer the knowledge of its defeat for as long as it survives – which may be a very long time indeed.'

Brace shook his head. 'I'm following some of this, Wist, but . . . Ledra?' He looked to his lover for support but she was watching Wist, a small smile playing at the corners of her mouth. Brace got the impression that she was following all of it closely, very closely indeed.

Wist smiled too, a chilling, humourless smile. 'Just trust me, Brace, that's all I ask, and help me. Very soon – a day or two from now – the sky will be alight and the day of days will be here. If, as we pray, the evil Flame is vanquished then it is sure to return here, seeking the crack it has made in the skin of the world.

'But we will be here too, and we shall stand in its way.'

CHAPTER 21

The Last Circle

They flew at dawn.

The light was hard and yellow, and the flowing wings of the mirror-dragons splintered it into a dazzling rain of fire. Fortune felt as though he were flying inside the sun itself.

Swiftly they left behind the gaping wound of the Rift. The landscape turned to dull brown, virtual desert, broken only by the threads of dry stream beds and the occasional clump of cactus. Balls of weed tumbled past like lost spirits; dust lifted like a fog.

Fortune's apprehension grew the further they went. Oster had indicated that the flight to the Last Circle would take less than a day and as the morning brightened around them he began to imagine that at any moment he would see their destination loitering on the horizon, staring back at him like some vast eye. In fact, an eye was all he could imagine – Oster had quashed his theory that the Circle was a ring of stones made either by faery or troll, but although he now knew what the Last Circle truly was, Fortune found he could still visualize only the eye of a monster. By now it had taken on unearthly proportions, until it threatened to become the world itself, a slowly blinking orb floating in the blackness between the stars . . .

Fortune shook himself, keen to divert himself from the fear which was beginning to grip his heart. 'You are such fliers!' he cried, suddenly and loudly, directing his cry at Oster. 'Tell us, how do you all keep together so well?'

As one, the mirror-dragons halted in the air, their shining wings beating slowly to maintain their perfect hover. Oster, who was stationed near the front of the formation, just

285

behind Limner, smiled broadly and glanced around at his comrades.

'Shall we show them, dragons?' he asked. When they all nodded, he cried, 'Line of Light!' and they moved like mercury.

With a powerful, fluid motion Oster slipped to the head of the troupe and dived towards the ground. One by one the mirror-dragons tipped forward to follow him, each one touching his predecessor's tail with the tip of his snout; one by one they fell until all thirty-eight were swooping down in a lance of silver light. Then, without a word, Oster pulled out of his dive, flinging his tail downwards so as to flip the upper part of his body round and into the climb. Silent but for the rush of wind across their metallic wings, the others followed.

Desert dust parted, swirling away into countless eddies and whirlwinds as the line of dragons curled up and away from the ground again. Only now Oster was on his back, continuing the curve until the line had become a circle. Teeth bared, he advanced on the last dragon in the formation, stretching his neck out just as his opposite number pulled out of his own dive and entered the circle. His snout met the tail of the thirty-eighth dragon and there in the sky turned a flawless ring of silver, showering sunlight across the astonished faces of the onlookers.

Barely had the spinning pattern been created than it broke apart and, by some unspoken choreography which left Fortune baffled, the mirror-dragons folded themselves back into their original, close-knit formation. Without needing to check, Fortune knew that each was in exactly the same place as when they had commenced. He breathed out slowly, his breath shuddering slightly.

'Wow!' was the best he could muster.

'That was how we used to start the display,' explained Oster proudly. 'Things got more elaborate after that, but we don't get the practice with an audience these days.' He smiled, his face looking suddenly very young despite the wrinkles which creased it. 'We're a bit nervous.'

Fortune shook his head disbelievingly. 'You did this all the time?' he asked. Most dragon settlements supported one or two individuals so adept at flying that they performed for others, but never had he come across such a group as this.

'Of course, we're a little depleted,' called Wemp from somewhere near the centre of the hovering formation. 'At our height we numbered eighty-six.'

Fortune turned to Cumber and smiled sadly, knowing that they shared a thought: *If only Tallow could have seen them!* But the memory of his friend gave way to an inexpressibly exciting hope. Given the dangers inherent in the plan by which they hoped to defeat Scarn, what better allies could they have than these mirror-dragons of Ocea? The previous night, when Oster had outlined potential battle plans, Fortune had been doubtful, querying many of the mirror-dragon's suggested formations and arguing always for simplicity, agreeing to much of the scheme only with the greatest reluctance.

'Tomorrow we will show you what we can do,' Oster had repeated several times, quietly and knowingly. Now he had honoured his word and vindicated his approach. Fortune felt ashamed ever to have doubted him.

'With you at our sides,' he proclaimed, 'we can take on the world.'

'Might have to,' muttered Scoff gloomily in his ear. 'Nice show,' he called to the mirror-dragons. They bowed in unison, sending a ripple of sunlight glancing off a sea of horns.

The dust lingered through the middle of the day until a sudden shower of rain damped it down. Oster looked around doubtfully.

'Unseasonal weather,' he proclaimed uneasily. He scented the air sharply. 'Storm or charm, but it's hard to tell which.'

'Charm, I should guess,' offered Cumber, who was also alert, scanning the distant line of hills with a keen gaze. Far from releasing the increasing humidity the rain seemed only to intensify it. The sky pressed down on them, heavy with moisture, thick and unyielding.

'The storm season's a whole moon away,' commented Wemp. 'Something's forcing the sky.'

'How far are we from the Last Circle?' demanded Aria,

flicking her wings against the damp air in an agitated fashion.

Oster indicated a distant ridge, a ragged line on the horizon which curved away to either side. 'Very near,' he answered. 'Just beyond that ridge the land dips and there . . .'

'. . . there it lies,' Aria breathed, her eyes wide.

Fortune scanned the sky, noting the approach of a tower of white cloud from the west. It swelled as he watched, its base darkening noticeably. Now he could see its shadow racing towards them, stroking the undulating ground in its eagerness. The first breath of wind touched his wings.

'Storm season?' he queried.

'Every afternoon for the space of three moons there are storms over the Vale of the Circle,' explained Limner. ' "When the heat of the day has done its worst and the air is full, the sky breaks free and is full of light." That is what my mother taught me, and her mother before her. Most dragons of southern Ocea learn this before they grow foolish and try to fly in a storm.'

'We should ground ourselves,' agreed Oster. 'Even we do not challenge the thunder.'

In counterpoint to his concern, a rumbling sound broke free of the approaching bank of cloud. Light flickered within, lightning seeding itself in the heart of the storm. It was clearly travelling southeast – the same direction as they were travelling.

'You may not have flown in a storm,' responded Fortune grimly. 'But I have. My friend Tallow led me through blizzard and fog, and worse. No weather ever deterred him; nor shall it deter me. Trust me, dragons, and I will show you how it may be done. This storm may be the ally we have sought.'

By now the wind was buffeting them insistently. Fortune was not sure if the mirror-dragons would follow him, so he looked first to his friends. Cumber and Velvet looked back at him with determination – they would not leave his side! Scoff's reaction to Fortune's inquiring glance was a rude gesture with an outstretched wing . . . and a broad smile. Volley's face was set like stone but his eyes were aflame.

He was nearly as good a flier as Tallow had been, which made him more or less Fortune's match; he would not be outflown by a mere youngster.

'This is where we begin,' shouted Fortune over the wind and the thunder. 'This is where we fight back.'

Any doubts that the mirror-dragons would join them were cast aside as the wall of cloud broke across them like a tidal wave. Their formation as tight and controlled as it had ever been, they turned into the climb Fortune described and pursued him into the light-torn heavens.

Fortune took one last look at the ridge which squatted on the horizon. 'Well, Scarn,' he murmured, 'it looks like we're coming your way.'

Water surrounded them, fat droplets tossed on speedy and erratic eddies. No sooner did they break free of one current than they were snatched away by another, thrown into cloud upon cloud of hot, wet air. Deep inside the clouds a ribbon of light ripped skywards from hidden depths. The sound was sudden and catastrophic, and both Cumber and Velvet cried out in unison.

'It's all right!' bellowed Fortune, his voice a thin thread of reason in a sky full of turmoil. 'We must climb, then it will be easier!'

'But what if one of those lightning bolts hits us?' yelled Cumber. 'I mean, will it hurt?'

'Not for long!' called Scoff.

'Think of something else, Cumber dear,' suggested Velvet as they struggled upwards through the treacherous air.

It grew darker as they ascended, and the humidity increased. An ever-changing lacework of light surrounded them now, crackling claws of lightning slicing through from one part of the cloud to another, occasionally stabbing the ground below, charging and discharging as the energy of the storm transferred itself in massive concussions. Ice shards mingled with the water now, sucked down from the storm's peak and whipped into the melee. Giant hailstones bombarded the dragons; sharp bangs signalled their impact with dragon-scales.

Then came a region of cooler air. The transition was so sudden that several of the dragons looked around for evidence of some visible junction between the layers. The air was no less turbulent but for a while at least it seemed that the lightning had abated.

'There are areas of relative calm even in the most violent storm,' explained Fortune, his voice still raised against the ever-present thunder but not quite a shout now. 'Tallow taught me to track those areas as best a dragon can.'

'And how well is that, Fortune?' inquired Oster, his smile respectful of this young dragon who seemed to have seen so much.

'Not very well,' confessed Fortune, his grin radiant. 'Storms are unpredictable.' He thought for a moment, riding the eddies. 'But then so is our enemy,' he added thoughtfully, 'so perhaps this weighs the odds back in our favour.'

He managed to keep them inside the calm centre of the storm for some considerable time; finally he decided that the time had come for an exploratory foray back into the outside world. Without hesitation he chose Volley for the task. 'Be quick,' he said, his voice pitched for Volley's ears only. 'And be careful. Just see where we are and come straight back.'

Volley nodded once and vanished silently into the depths.

A beam of light accompanied his return some fifty breaths later, a loose streak of lightning on its way to the top of the cloud. Volley's first words confirmed Fortune's suspicion.

'The storm is dying,' he proclaimed. But there was better news than that. 'I have seen the Last Circle. We are thirty, perhaps forty trees short of its eastern perimeter. There may be a better place from which to strike, but I cannot think of it.'

Fortune listened both to his words and to his voice. The words brought the message he had hoped for; the voice? Did he dare to believe that something of the old Volley was there again, something of the old song, at last? Unspoken, understanding passed between them.

Fortune said, 'Justice for all of us, Volley. Tallow included.'

Volley nodded once and rejoined the huddle. Lightning painted their backs but it was weaker now, reaching up through the colder air only with reluctance. Already the air felt thinner, drier; soon the late sun would break through and the long, cool evening would begin.

It did not take them long to decide upon the plan of action. The storm had provided them with the cover their scenario had previously lacked, but other than that the strategy remained unchanged: the mirror-dragons would distract the Cult while Fortune led a smaller, direct assault to seek out where it was Gossamer was being held. As soon as she was rescued, the battle could begin in earnest.

Shreds of vapour swirled through their midst and the wall of cloud immediately behind them began to brighten.

'Now is the time!' cried Fortune, and then he bellowed words he had never thought he would say: 'We attack, dragons!'

Most places have at least one history; most places of worth have many, and sometimes more than one of these is true. Places, like lives, begin and end. There are exceptions, of course, but the central truth of history is story.

The faery circles – the rings of tiny stones which filled the ancient forests and marked the crossing places of capillaries of charm – have their stories. And their larger cousins, the rings of the giants, and even the early, crude versions built in lazy fashion by the trolls, they too were made, and were, and were unmade. Stories for every one, each one a life, each one a living place. Even the charm by which such places were constructed has a story, though its telling in full is too great a task for any mortal.

Stories: beginnings and endings, and between them lives. And sometimes, woven through and commanding all . . . turnings.

And what of the exceptions? What of the places without history? What of the stories which have not yet been written, and what of the places which they *describe?*

What of the Last Circle?

First to break clear of the belly of the storm, weak crackles of light chasing him down through the cloud and into the clear air below, was Fortune. And though Oster had described to him in great detail the nature of the place which was the Last Circle, still it took his breath entirely away.

Grey vapour peeled away to reveal sheer, clear air. He

291

was diving as fast as he had ever flown towards a broad landscape of brown and grey, a flat vale marked with ragged lines and clumps of boulders. A drab place, cracked and bland.

At first, crazy though the idea seemed to him later, it was as though he did not notice the Circle at all. It was just another part of the drabness, flat and unremarkable. But then, as the wind whispered its warnings in his ears and the cool air folded its way around his speeding body, he opened his mind fully to what was spread out beneath him.

It was a depression, a crater. A colossal, circular scoop taken out of the flesh of the world. Its near edge was a mountainous arc of broken rock; its far perimeter was so distant it was almost lost in the low afternoon glare. Long shadows swooped into the curve of its bowl. No eye this but a socket, an expectant cavity waiting to be filled. Lines – whether ridge or gouge he could not judge – descended along with the shadows, describing the perfect concavity with a precision he could not believe. It was a crater as wide as a mountain, a bowl-shaped arena in which his love was held prisoner.

It was the Last Circle.

What made this place? he wondered, wondering too why he had not asked Oster that question the previous night, when the mirror-scaled dragon had described it to him. *Did a giant night dragon fall to earth? Or did a troll lord scrape himself a grave, only to move on before dying?*

But there was no time for speculation. Already he could see the flaws in the structure of this prodigious cavity. He could see the specks of red which were Scarn's warriors busying themselves around its circumference, the tighter knot of red at its centre. And above that knot he could see the source of Scarn's power: he could see the Flame.

Brilliant blue, it burned inverted over the heart of the Last Circle. Suspended at what Fortune judged to be ground level, it hovered fully twenty trees above the shallow dome of rock which marked the centre of the crater. Its livid light flickered across the striations in the rock, making patterns which swarmed like living things up the sides of the crater, jabbing at the raised perimeter before slipping back into the

292

depths again, probing, testing, seeking ways to escape, ways to defend. At once he knew where Gossamer was: she was there, at the heart of things. *Where else?* he thought wryly and increased his speed.

It was Volley who cried the warning. Volley, whom Fortune had feared would be impulsive, liable to throw away his own life and the lives of others as soon as he caught sight of Scarn. 'Pull up, Fortune!' he thundered, his voice carrying like a song through the sky.

An instant before he saw the Flame expand Fortune was responding instinctively to Volley's cry. Flattening his wing membranes against the rushing air he crashed into an agonizing stall. The pressure of the air ripped a blade of cartilage from his left wing and sent it spinning down towards the crater; blood spattered his flank and a dark film began to spread behind his eyes. Painfully he beat against his own momentum, nearly blacking out before he managed to recover himself and turn his dive into a slow, turning climb. His heart crashed like the thunder which was still powering the storm overhead.

Did I consider him reckless? he wondered dreamily. *What was I thinking?*

A single breath later he saw the reason for Volley's shout: the Flame spewed forth a circular sheet of blinding blue fire which expanded across the top of the crater faster than Fortune's eyes could track it. Before he could blink it had reached the edge, where it halted, biting into the roughly hewn ridge, the boundary of the Last Circle. And there it stayed, a scintillating membrane which shielded the interior of the crater from view and sealed it against attack. Had Fortune continued his dive he would have been directly in its path as it appeared; he had no doubt that it would have cut him in two.

The thought made his wings shake with delayed shock. Then he saw something odd: a blur of red, tumbling through the air to strike the lip of the crater. It was the head, neck and torso of one of Scarn's dragons, but even a cursory inspection was enough to remind him that this was no dragon. Glowing liquid – not blood but some pulsing, steaming ichor – was splattered all around the gruesome remains, the same liquid he had seen released from the dragon which had attacked Oster and the mirror-dragons the day before. As he watched the mutilated corpse twitched, turned over and lay still.

Memory chased shock through his racing mind and he reviewed what he had seen of the explosion. Not one but two streaks of red had cheated its leading edge. Two dragons, one in pursuit of the other. The trailing dragon had been too slow. The fire had sliced through it, separating its body into neat halves. He had seen the result. But what of the fugitive?

Suddenly all Fortune could see was rock, seemingly flying towards him. He blinked, startled, and saw that it was the mirror-dragons swooping down in front of him, their polished scales throwing back at him a reflection of the landscape below. They levelled out and turned blue, the blue of the skin of fire which had sealed the Last Circle. Oster opened his mouth to speak but Cumber, tucking himself tight against Fortune's side, beat him to it.

'Can you feel the charm, Fortune?' he demanded, and without giving his friend a chance to respond, he carried on, 'I mean to say, it *feels* like charm, and to some extent it is, I suppose. But it tastes different, very different – like meat that's been overcooked, I should say. Rotten meat at that. It's not good, Fortune, not good at all.'

'Cumber's right,' agreed Scoff gruffly. He was hovering between Fortune and the listening mirror-dragons. Aria and Velvet were waiting a little to one side, both scanning the surface of the fire-skin as though searching for something. 'Charm's been taken, then changed. Turned, if you like. It's the Flame now. Can still do what charm did. But isn't the same. Evil now. Destructive. Epitome of fire. Very bad, Fortune.'

Fortune listened to this, which amounted to a major speech from Scoff, with great concentration. He could taste a little of the scent of charm in the air, but had to trust his ex-Charmed friends when it came to measuring its strength.

'Powerful?' he hazarded.

'Immensely,' confirmed Scoff.

'And unpredictable.'

'Of course.'

Fortune's first impression that they could no longer see into the crater was contradicted as he looked more closely at the layer of fire. Streamers of light chased across its surface, followed by darker patches where the gossamer-thin structure of the membrane became translucent, revealing glimpses of what lay beneath. He saw dark rock, eerie in the blue glow, and the vague, scurrying shapes of the dragons of the Cult, their livid red hides turned purple and indigo. Clouds and ribbons and strange, spiralling patterns pulsed outwards constantly from the source, the Flame itself, which was visible now only as a brighter glow at the centre.

'Well?' demanded Cumber eagerly, just as Oster opened his mouth. 'What should we do now?'

The storm had passed overhead and was dwindling into the east, its clouds dissipating as a light wind blew in. The sun was revealed once more, lowering and turning orange behind a veil of dust lifting on the breeze.

Oster made to speak again, and was again interrupted, this time by Velvet. He turned, sharing a brief smile with Fortune who, he saw, understood his humour. For his part, Fortune found himself liking Oster more and more – this dragon who looked so old yet was so young. He liked his straightforward manner, his honesty and his ready smile.

'Down there!' Velvet was shouting, gesticulating wildly with one white wing. 'It's one of them. I knew I'd seen one.'

'It needs our help,' said Aria, so quietly that her words were hard to catch.

Sure enough, on the ground, near the partial corpse of the unfortunate victim of the fire-skin, the second dragon – the fugitive – was prowling, red scales glinting in the low sunlight. Fortune thought it looked familiar, although from this distance it was difficult to be sure.

It was Aria who dived first, and Fortune who followed her most closely. He registered two things as they flew down together, their wings tucked close in identical fashion, so alike. The first was that both she and Velvet had referred to the creature as 'it' – already they were beginning to accept that these were *not* dragons, whatever their outward appearance. The second was the change which had come over Aria since Gossamer had been taken.

If he could have defined it as any one thing, Fortune might have settled for *peace*. It showed in everything: in the set of her wings, the way she carried her head, the strong, regular pulse of her breathing, the calmness in her voice. It was a new thing for Aria, for this dragon who, like Oster and his companions, had aged prematurely, though for entirely different reasons; this new peace embraced her and, Fortune sensed, *defined* her.

What has created this revolution? he marvelled. *What has brought her certainty where before she had none?*

He saw that the last of the clouds had peeled apart. There, directly above them, shone the comet. It was bigger than the moon and almost as bright as the sun, and its tail stretched over the horizon. Its light fell across Aria's dark back, seeming to pierce it with a magical beam. She stared up at it as she swooped down, her eyes wide and filled with tears, and Fortune knew the answer to his question.

They landed at the foot of the ridge while their friends hovered above them, cutting off all possible lines of escape for the cornered dragon. Halfway up the crater's mountainous lip the dragon (for Fortune could think of no other word to use for these creatures, whatever their nature) squatted, showing no signs of nervousness nor any apparent desire to flee. It simply sat and waited.

Fortune motioned Aria to wait but she ignored him, following him up the slope as soon as he had turned his back. They ascended together, slipping a little on the loose rock but making swift progress. Soon they were close enough to discern its features, and here they stopped.

The dragon's red scales made it difficult to recognize its face, and Fortune noted how much a dragon learned to rely on colour in identifying others. *Once Gossamer was not white*, he thought, *yet I know her still, and Cumber and Velvet too. The dragon lives on the inside.*

Still, there was something familiar about this face. For what seemed like an age he stood there, his head tilted, trying to place those eyes, those low horns, that smooth brow. It was in many ways a bland face, a face any dragon

296

might pass a hundred times yet never notice, never remember . . .

Then he had it! The dragon's very blandness was what triggered his memory and it was with something close to hope that he breathed the name which sprang into his mind: 'Anchre.'

The dragon – if dragon it was – nodded slowly, then looked around on the ground. Fortune heard Cumber's warning cry from above him as Anchre's claws closed around a sharply pointed stone, but he waved his friend silent. Slowly the red dragon approached, his eyes never leaving Fortune's.

A wing's width away he stopped, then looked pointedly at the corpse which lay a short distance downslope. Fortune followed his gaze to the pool of steaming fluid which had gathered in a cleft; he could smell it from here – a curiously sweet aroma, like rotting flowers. He looked back at Anchre, who had brought the stone close to his breast. Without warning, Anchre slashed it down through the soft hide of his own underbelly, and then he reclined so that all could see the wound.

Every dragon watching gasped: rich, dragon blood flowed out from between the fractured scales and torn skin.

'Hello, Fortune,' said Anchre, his voice as bland as his face. 'I think the time has come to tell you who I really am.'

CHAPTER 22

In the Path of the Comet

The sky was filled with brilliant dust. Vox closed his ghost-eyes against the glare but it made no difference; his eyelids were scarcely more substantial than the void through which he sped. He turned to look at Ocher and saw that the basilisk had become solid, seemingly more solid even than the planet which rolled lazily behind them. What this meant he did not care to imagine. Sheer dragon, opaque basilisk, both approached the cascade of light which was the comet.

The sight of it was overwhelming. Vox was assaulted by a barrage of information, a reminder that he was not seeing at all in the traditional sense but sensing, absorbing: he saw individual crystals of ice surrounding the comet's core; he saw ring-shaped shock waves spreading backwards through the long fan of its tail; he studied the metallic grains of dust the tail was made from; he measured its static; he tasted its air.

At its heart was an incandescent sphere, a mirror-perfect reflector which threw the light of the distant sun back like a lens. Surrounding this core was a cloud of dust which was perhaps half the diameter of the world which turned at their backs, and which sprawled across the star-flecked sky, reaching far beyond the region known to the basilisk as the Place of Rocks. It loomed, a tangible, on-rushing force before which Vox felt not only transparent but insignificant. Together they crossed the tenuous boundary of the cloud and entered the realm of the comet.

The shadow Wyrm cast across the sea was great. Smoke soared in the cool air it made, her body exhausted, her mind free.

They flew low, only a few trees above the water. Wyrm's

huge, black wings dragged vapour into long, white streams; the soundless rush of his body lifted lines of foam clear of the waves. Behind them, reaching almost to the horizon, a trail was drawn across the surface of the ocean. Ahead, there was only more water.

They had come together just once, a gentle coupling in the air. Wyrm's claws had held her tight as his wings had pumped them up into a bank of low cloud. The cloud had enveloped them, turning the world white, taking them briefly into their own realm. Smoke had closed her eyes, letting her mind fly free, imagining first that it was Wraith with whom she flew, then Vox. Then she remembered her partner's true identity and was pulled back to the real world with an uncomfortable wrench.

Afterwards she withdrew from Wyrm's side, wary for a while but soon rediscovering the trust he demanded. Their intimacy already seemed like a dream, a half-remembered moment which might not have happened at all. Then it was that she took her place beneath his shadow, flying straight and true, sure of her heart and the song it sang.

The days flowed like water. Once they found a remote island, a nugget of green in the desert of the ocean. Only Smoke stopped to rest, while Wyrm prowled impatiently in the sky like a tremendous black cloud. Despite his unspoken urging she made time to sleep before they continued on their endless journey into the east.

Wyrm's mood darkened still further as they flew on. Silent during the day, he took to telling stories through the long, windless nights. His tales merged together in Smoke's head so that she could not remember where one ended and the next began . . .

'. . . hundred years there was a change in the colour of the sunlight, and it was then that the faery council was drawn together. The charm of the rings ran deep beneath the stones, drawing chains of life together from around the world, joining them to the places beyond the world, converging, meeting, fusing. Only then could their history move on. Only then could mortal concerns be brought to bear and weapons be wielded. The colour of their blood . . .'

* * *

*'. . . and the time of the silver waves was over. Lands rose, van-
quishing the oceans of mercury and dulling their shine forever.
What became of the denizens of those deeps of metal no-one
knows . . .'*

'. . . the voice in the dark . . .'
  '. . . the lighting of the sky . . .'
  '. . . the comet's tail . . .'

The comet was the only thing that could match Wyrm in
the sky; between them they dominated the space between
the horizons. The comet outshone the sun now, a glorious
trail of cloud against which Wyrm was a fluid silhouette, a
moving flaw in its perfect, shining skin. Smoke thought it
was beautiful; they were both beautiful.

Then, one day, a ripple of grey cloud appeared low above
the eastern horizon, a distant stack of storm which Smoke's
pathfinder instinct told her could mean only one thing: land.

Wyrm's voice, loud and strange in the daylight, thundered
out.

'Not far now, dragon!'

The words sounded remote, despite the volume at which
they were bellowed. Smoke found herself missing Vox desperately.

For some time now Vox had been convinced that the comet
was destined to strike the world, but now he saw that this
was not the case, that it would slip easily between the world
and its moon, passing harmlessly into the darkness of space.

Why is it here? he wondered as he slipped through the veil
of dust.

They floated together for some time, dragon and basilisk,
stroked by the comet's cloud as it sped towards the gap
between the spinning planet and its infant satellite. Vox was
awed by its colossal speed, and the momentum that implied
– the irresistibility of the force behind it.

Nothing could ever stand in its way.

The planet slipped in front of the sun. All else grew dark save
for the comet; the stars were dim in its presence. Vox realized
that, far from floating, they were speeding like the comet itself.

He saw that one of Ocher's long, mobile claws was hooked into the tenuous mesh of his wraith-like body and knew that it was the basilisk alone that was propelling them both.

. . . *What are we doing here?* he demanded suddenly, the words thin inside his mind.

But the basilisk did not reply. Though its deep, silver eyes remained unreadable, there was something urgent in the set of its muscular shoulders. Vox's sensation of speed increased; he could almost feel the blast of the dust pellets against his skin – or what passed for his skin – almost feel the wind from the comet's tail.

Then he saw that Ocher was measuring something, holding out its free claws against the background of stars and shifting worlds, judging their angles against the swell of the comet. Those silver eyes flicked to and fro, scintillating in the reflected glow of the dust cloud. There was a sharp tug, a yanking sensation which pulled at his mind as though reclaiming it from some insistent dream, and they were accelerating ahead of the comet again. The dark orb of the world grew in Vox's vision; the comet chased them, a clean rush of light in the blackness.

Vox's heightened senses tasted the pull of the two opposing spheres: world and moon. They felt equal; Ocher had located a point in space where neither held sway. Their motion ceased utterly. Vox turned and barely held himself back from screaming as he saw the comet head-on.

It glared back at him like an eye, an on-rushing eye bared wide and eager. The cloud of dust no longer looked thin but hard and impenetrable.

. . . *Be steady, dragon.*

Ocher's words surrounded Vox like a shroud; he could almost see them.

. . . *You need only bear witness to Ocher's last stand.*

With a gentle push, the touch of a mother sending her infant from the nest for the very first time, Ocher nudged Vox away, sending him spiralling down towards the night-side of the world. Vox watched helplessly as the light of the approaching comet expanded across Ocher's pale flesh. The basilisk's silver eyes shone, reflecting their fate.

*   *   *

301

Nothing goes.

The thought filled Ocher's mind as it watched the comet open its one, white eye. Its light was clean and charmless, quite free of magic in a way Ocher had never known before. Ocher thought of charm and nature, and the junction between the two, and it knew that here at last was the beginning of the end of the Turning.

The basilisk had never been able to guess what form the final transformation might take. That vague phrase – *the lighting of the sky* – drifted occasionally through its mind as it did through the minds of others but its meaning had never been clear. Until now, of course. Now Ocher knew exactly what its role was, and now too it knew the lifespan of the basilisk.

The basilisk lives until it meets its maker, Ocher thought joyously. *But even then it can never be fully destroyed. Nothing goes. There is more even than this small life, even for the Deathless. That is the miracle of the world which is to be.*

Nothing goes.

Though there was no sound propagated in the emptiness, Vox imagined he could hear the crashing of the comet against the weave of space. Perhaps he could at that – his marvellous senses were attuned to this alien environment. He knew for certain that the comet was his whole world now, that the limits of his vision, of his entire sensory net, were dominated by the disc of perfect light. He could not have looked away even if he had tried.

He glanced at Ocher, just one more mote in the cloud of dust, and remembered the clearing in the trees.

Then he had stood in the path of the basilisk, claws dug into the soil, trying to block its approach towards the injured Wyrm. Ocher had not even slowed.

He thought of the citadel of the basilisks, which he had once visited with his friends; of the way it clung to the face of a waterfall, a rock immovable in the flow.

Silver eyes reflecting perfect light.

The 'sound' of the comet was a scream now, but a scream of joy, of ecstasy even. Vox could not tell from where the sound issued, nor even if it were a sound at all – it was all around him, inside him, like his own birth-cry, the shout of life. The comet looked suddenly like an egg.

A narrow shock wave preceded the comet, a faint bulge in the dust cloud. Now that bulge approached Ocher, now it enveloped the basilisk, melting its contours. Ocher sparkled, stretched by distortions in the cloud, refracted, twisted out of true. But not moved, not at all.

The comet came. Fast.

It struck Ocher, or perhaps Ocher struck it, Vox was never entirely sure, even at the end. The basilisk's body hit the spherical core about two-thirds of the way across its diameter and vanished. At first Vox thought it had been obliterated, vaporized perhaps, but then he saw that the comet was peeling apart.

It was like watching a fruit being pressed against a stone. Somewhere inside the comet's howling, freezing heart Ocher remained immovable, as stubborn in the face of death as it had ever been. The comet's flesh opened up, spread by the basilisk's unearthly solidity, its dense and ancient *thereness*. Bellowing in celebration, screeching in agony, the comet dashed itself against the rock of the basilisk and broke into two distinct pieces. The tail trembled as new shock waves cascaded down its length. Gyres and whirlpools disrupted the tail's once perfect form and it too split apart. Dust splintered and the sun burst free from behind the world, illuminating not one comet but two.

By far the greater mass of the comet was proceeding on much the same course as it had before, roughly towards the sun, some distance from the curve of the world. But now it had spawned a son, a ragged infant dragging a rough-hewn fragment of tail behind it. This new comet tipped and tumbled, its core as bright as that of its parent but coarser, less uniform. And one thing was very clear to Vox as he watched it roll further away from the larger piece: its journey would be short indeed.

Had he thought the world safe from impact? Now he saw how wrong he had been.

The comet fragment was falling towards the sunlit rim of the world. Soon it would brush the uppermost limit of the air shrouding the planet. What would happen then Vox could not imagine, but he prayed that he might be far, far away when it hit.

He looked back at the place where Ocher had been.

There was very little left of the basilisk. Both its arms had been torn off, and its tail was a mess of raw meat and broken bone. Its remaining eye was a dull, tarnished orb.

. . . What . . . Vox began, but trailed off, feeling hopelessly lost. What could he possibly say to this creature who had lived forever, whose motivations were so alien to him?

Ocher swivelled its one good eye to regard the dragon ghost which floated before it.

. . . You are alone now, dragon. Basilisk charm – what shreds remain – will sustain you for a while. It closed its eye briefly then and a spasm of what could only be pain tugged at its blunt and wrinkled face. *Seek only your final destination, and the one who calls to you.*

. . . What do you mean, 'basilisk charm will sustain me'? What happens when I want to return to my body? A sudden terror seized Vox: a question had risen which he had never thought to ask. How could he have been so stupid? *Where is my body, Ocher?*

The basilisk's one good eye swivelled erratically before locking on to Vox again.

. . . The dragon body you once inhabited lies where you left it.

. . . And where is that?

. . . Beneath the rubble of the fallen sculpture, in the chamber of the Towers of Nistor. It is crushed, dragon. It is dead.

Vox beat back an urge to rush at the creature.

. . . But you told me I was not dead! he screamed, his imaginary voice a mere whisper in the vacuum of space. Slowly, in agony, the basilisk shook its torn head.

. . . Ocher never said that.

. . . But I might as well be – is that what Ocher is saying now? Vox turned away, his ghostly body shaking with rage and fear.

Ocher's voice, Ocher's thoughts, pressed insistently into Vox's awareness despite all his efforts to blank them out.

. . . What you once were is no more, dragon. Soon the world

*will be made anew. The same may be true for you, if you will it
to be so.* The thoughts were faint and croaking now. Vox
tried hard not to listen but they slid into his mind like slivers
of metal. *Deathless no more. There are many constants in the
world – no longer is Ocher one of them. Constants remain, however.
Vengeance is one, dragon. Remember that, and you may be whole
once more.*

. . . I don't underst . . . Vox started to say, but a fresh cloud
of shimmering blood, this time coughed from the basilisk's
broken mouth, silenced him.

*. . . Nothing goes, Vox. Change comes, as it has come for Ocher.
There is more to come, more of everything, and it begins now. It
begins in the light. Move fast, Vox, or you may lose what you
dream of.*

. . . What is that?

But Ocher did not reply.

The retreating comet seemed to swell in Vox's vision. He
wondered how that could be when it had already passed
them by. The basilisk floated before its dazzling light, a
broken husk spilling shining fluid. Then Vox understood
that the comet had not grown but slowed, the checking of
its forward motion creating the illusion that it had reared
back towards them.

In fact, everything seemed to have slowed. On the world
below them, Vox could no longer make out the solidity of
continents, the depth of clouds: the planet had flattened,
and instinct told him that it had paused in its rotation, its
stillness turning it to a mere portrait of itself. The light from
the sun had frozen and turned flat; the eddies in the comet's
trailing dust cloud were motionless. Vox floated alone in a
single moment stolen from the heartbeat of the cosmos.

All was still but for the basilisk. It rotated slowly, an aura
of peace descending over its tortured body. Silver liquid
sizzled on the ragged remains of its scales.

. . . Take this moment, dragon.

It was a whisper, almost inaudible. It carried through the
timeless gap between basilisk and dragon and Vox understood its meaning. Though faint, the thought struck with all
the power of eternity and at last Vox knew what it was he
had to do. Alone with the dying basilisk in the immensity

of the heavens, he turned his head to look at the comet, still so near.

But it would not be near for long.

Vox looked back. Ocher drew in a long, rasping breath, then remained still for so long that he thought it was all over.

Then it exhaled for the last time, its breath lethal no more, simply mortal. If there were words on that breath then Vox did not hear them.

He found that he was weeping clear, ghostly tears as before him Ocher the basilisk, first-born of the Deathless, ancient immortal who had given up eternity to discover the perilous wonder of life, died.

There, in the missed heartbeat by which the river of time bowed its head to the last of the Deathless, Vox abandoned Ocher's tattered body. Already the river was straining again, preparing to tip the comet forward on its inexorable orbit. Vox prayed that he was fast enough. He prayed, and for the first time in his life he knew what it was to which he prayed. He *saw* it: it filled his vision.

In this way the last remains of dragon Vox accelerated into the light.

CHAPTER 23

Battle Plans

The sun was low. The prodigious crater should have been almost entirely in shadow by now, but the magical skin lent a fearsome blue glow to its interior. The indigo shapes of Scarn's minions continued to bustle beneath this eerie shroud, their intentions quite impenetrable to the watching dragons.

The air had freshened considerably after the storm, and as the afternoon cooled towards evening Fortune took a small group of dragons out to a long ribbon of canyon he had spied some way off to the west. Anchre was among them. The rest he had stationed at regular intervals around the entire perimeter of the Last Circle, with strict instructions to call alarm should there be any sign of activity. Every dragon, even those nominally under the command of Oster, obeyed him without question.

'Does the power taste good, father?' whispered Aria as they flew swiftly through the air. She asked this without hostility; her voice was as different now as everything else about her, mellow and untroubled.

He pondered her question, then replied, 'Not particularly. But I think it can *do* good, my dear.'

She nodded, a simple, candid gesture of agreement which reminded him achingly of Gossamer. 'I think so too.'

'Something has changed you, Aria,' he said after a moment's reflection.

She smiled demurely. 'Do you like what you see, father?' He nodded, his eyes moist. 'For a long time I did not know the meaning of peace,' she went on. 'My whole life has been a storm, father. I thought Scarn would bring me the answers I sought but he was a false prophet. I have one thing to thank him for, however: he has brought me here, and this is where I should be. This is where I shall be called upon to take my place. Do you see how important that is to me – to know my place?'

'We thought you were to be Scarn's sacrifice,' said Fortune cautiously. Aria laughed, a delightful tinkling sound which caused the other dragons to turn their heads.

'Once I wanted that. That was when I was living in the dark, father. Now I have flown into the light.'

'What are we doing out here, Fortune?' demanded Volley, breaking into their private exchange.

'See something?' suggested Scoff.

'Yes and no,' answered Fortune. Aria smiled warmly at him as his attention was dragged away from her. 'I just want to check something, that's all, and I don't want to do it alone.' He glanced sideways at Anchre. 'And I want to take you up on your word, Anchre. I want you to tell me who you are, and what you really want.'

'I could have done that back there,' Anchre said.

'But you like your privacy, don't you Anchre, when all's said and done?' Anchre thought about this for a moment, then nodded.

'I appreciate your consideration, Fortune, I really do. But I no longer think I need to protect myself.' He smiled to himself, as though considering a secret joke. 'No, even I don't need to worry about that any more.'

Fortune looked ahead. 'The canyon is about three hundred wingbeats away, Anchre. Do you think you can tell your story in that time?'

Anchre had not always lived at Aether's Cross, any more than he had always been a Natural.

'I arrived there when I was twenty years old,' he explained, his voice sounding freer now. His words were no longer flattened and remote; at last it seemed that the real Anchre was talking. 'By that time the shape-changing was virtually complete. Though I was born charmed, I had changed myself to look entirely natural, and so I fitted in just fine. That was my job at the Cross, you see, to fit in, to watch, to take note. Then to report back.'

'Report back?' interrupted Scoff suspiciously. 'To whom?'

Anchre chuckled. 'Not to Halcyon, if that's what you're thinking. No, Scoff, Halcyon did not send me to spy on you. He trusted his ambassadors. In any case, do you not think I would have been better placed in the caverns of the Charmed, just as you were, if that were my role?'

Scoff harrumphed uncertainly, but seemed at least a little mollified.

'Let him go on,' said Fortune, smiling reassuringly at his rainbow-winged friend.

'I joined the ranks of the fisher dragons on the lower west wall,' Anchre continued. 'I was reasonably good at it: good enough not to be noticed, not so good that I became well-known. Average, if you like.

'I came from a small settlement far to the south of Cova-mere, did I tell you that? It used to be savannah land, but I suppose it's all changed now. I didn't fit in, even there. I was considered . . . strange.'

'Why?' blurted Aria with sudden passion.

Anchre looked hard at her before saying, 'I saw things no other dragon could see.'

'What kind of things?' Her voice was a whisper.

Anchre shrugged. 'Visions, you might say. Most days I used to wander into the foothills and bask there – it was a hot land. I used to lie back and watch the clouds moving across the sky, imagining them into shapes. This one would look like a flying dragon, that one like a river, snaking through the air . . .'

'But you are a charmed dragon,' said Volley, appraising Anchre's undeniably natural shape. 'You like the open air? I thought your kind preferred caves.'

Again came the shrug, and the disarming smile. 'I told you I was considered odd. Anyway, the more time I spent staring at the clouds the more elaborate became the patterns I could make with them, until one day I saw . . .' Here he hesitated, uncertainty creeping into his voice for the first time.

'Saw what?' asked Aria kindly.

'I didn't know at first,' said Anchre slowly, his eyes narrowed. 'It was . . . it was just an oval light, like a hole in

309

the sky. Its edges were blurred, hard to make out, and they seemed to pour into themselves somehow, like the edge of a waterfall. It was mostly dark, except somewhere near the middle there was a light, a dim, orange light.'

Aria's eyes burned into those of her father. A similar vision had come to Gossamer, shortly before Archan had worked her evil in the basilisk citadel. But there was more, Fortune realized. Then it struck him, the reason his daughter was changed. *Aria has seen the Cloud too. That is what has changed her!*

Holding her father's gaze, her eyes like beacons, she nodded once, slowly.

'And I heard a voice,' Anchre was going on. 'It was deep, like my father's voice, but somehow like my mother's too – yet . . . not really like either. It was not a dragon voice, though it seemed to be trying to sound like one. It said many things I did not understand, about time being like a river, and about a future which was not yet made. But what I really remember was the way it described a place, a pass through the mountains. Aether's Cross, as I was soon to discover. The voice made it sound like a paradise, a place filled with light and life. A place where I might fit in. I wanted so much to go there.

'Then it asked me a question, a simple question but one which shaped my entire life thereafter. The voice said, "If you wish to see the lighting of the sky, you must live there as a Natural and watch the dragon called Scarn. I will need him at the end. All you dragons will. Do you wish to go?"'

They paused in the air. By now the canyon was close, but Anchre was just as close to the end of his story and they all sensed this. They would go no further until he had told the rest.

'That was inspiring?' Scoff growled, unimpressed.

'The way the voice in the cloud said it,' replied Anchre firmly, 'yes. Yes, it was. Because there was so much more to it than the words. When it said "lighting" I saw a vision of the sky ablaze with beautiful fire. When it said "Scarn" I saw more flames, but dark and ugly. And when it said "All you dragons" . . .' He broke off, stifling a sob. Aria brushed a wingtip against his and prompted him to go on. 'When it said that . . .' he hitched in a choking breath '. . . I saw all the dragons in the world. They were flying in the light, all of them, flying in the cloud, and their wings were like fire in the sky, and they were all colours, more beautiful than anything I'd ever seen before, or have seen since. I knew then that I would give anything to see that day, when all the dragons of the world might join together to celebrate the lighting of the sky.'

He exhaled slowly, eyes closed, considering what he had said for a moment, then concluding, 'So I did exactly what the voice said. During the journey to the Cross I changed my shape so that by the time I got there I had lost my forelegs and my silver scales were the same, dull brown you see now. As the voice had promised I fitted in perfectly. Do you see? At last I had a home! I watched Scarn and each time the moon grew full I went to the lonely rock I had chosen for my task, turned my head up into the sky and spoke to the Cloud.'

'You saw it again?' demanded Aria excitedly. 'It spoke to you again?'

But Anchre shook his head. 'Not once since that first time.' He beamed. 'But it doesn't matter. I know it was there, listening, waiting. All the time, I knew it was coming.'

'Coming fast,' breathed Fortune, his voice practically inaudible over the wing-rush of air.

Though they probed him for more detail it seemed that Anchre's story was more or less told. He had observed Scarn consolidate his role as storyteller to the Cross infants, and had noted more subtle changes which no other dragons had been aware of. Physical changes like the red tinge which had begun to creep through the cracks between Scarn's scales shortly before Wraith had arrived and taken all the natural dragons – including both Anchre and Scarn – prisoner. Like the fire he had seen glinting occasionally in the depths of his eyes. The way Scarn would stare fixedly at the ground for intervals of a hundred breaths or more, his spirit apparently absent from his body.

All these changes and more he had sent into the heavens in the form of whispered prayers, faithful reports despatched skywards beneath the light of the swollen moon. And though he had received no reply he had kept his faith

311

through the years, even up to this day, when he knew his reward was drawing near.

'There's a dragon you should talk with,' said Fortune. Anchre nodded.

'Your Gossamer. I already have. We used to speak secretly on Mahl, during the time Scarn was recruiting for his wretched Cult. She saw and heard the Cloud too, much as I did. I think Tallow would have seen it too, had he lived. And Gossamer has kept her faith.'

Fortune gaped. Aria, flying close at his side, simply smiled and murmured, 'Don't be offended, father. She just knew you would take your own time to catch up.'

'I'm catching up fast,' he stammered, looking up into the transparent blue sky.

The comet was a long, white bulge. It was as though something were pressing it through the sky from behind, as if the sky were merely a membrane and beyond it lay some greater, more glorious realm. Suddenly he saw that the comet had split in two, that while the greater part of its bulk continued to splay itself across the sky, a smaller fragment had detached. It seemed to have no tail, this strange offspring, and all of a sudden Fortune thought he knew why.

'That's what's coming!' he announced decisively, indicating the broken comet. It appeared to slice the sky in two, so huge had it grown. He looked back at the foreshortened disc of the Last Circle. 'And I think I know where it's going to come to earth!'

'Don't fancy being around when it hits,' said Scoff, eyeing the onrushing object. 'Other side of the world won't be far enough.'

I wonder, mused Fortune.

No dragon except Fortune saw anything of interest in the canyon. It was considerably shorter than it had appeared from a distance, shallow and uninspiring over much of its length. The rock from which it was carved was dark, almost black, making it look deeper than it really was. Only at the far end did it open out into a broad cutting, down the sides of which trickled a few dismal streams of water, vanishing almost unnoticed into some hidden, subterranean river.

312

'I'm afraid we may be wasting our time here,' announced Oster as they circled over the canyon's head. From above it really did look like a head, trailing a long, sinuous tail – a giant tadpole swimming through the barren landscape in search of water.

'No,' responded Fortune. 'Wait. I want to look closer.'

'There's nothing but rocks down there, Fortune,' sighed Volley, loitering in the sky with Oster and Scoff.

'Exactly,' replied the young Natural.

Aria and Anchre followed him down, exchanging a wondering glance as he prowled through the air over the bed of the canyon. The shadows were thick down here – night was almost upon them – but they could just make out a great fan of boulders spreading out from the sheer wall that closed off the canyon: debris left by some ancient collapse. After inspecting the rocks Fortune climbed again, leaping into the grey air above as though surfacing for breath from the ocean. From above he could see the canyon's tail snaking away towards the crater, its lip glowing brilliant orange in the rays of the dying sun. A strange thought occurred to him: that the canyon was somehow aimed at the crater.

'Anchre, Oster, Scoff,' he said, his voice urgent and clipped. 'Between you, you should know pretty much everything there is to know about charm. How strong do you think that shield of fire is?'

Anchre frowned while Scoff blustered about how it was impossible to judge, and anyway it wasn't the sort of charm he was used to dealing with. Oster thought for a while, then said cautiously,

'Why? What do you have in mind?'

It was cold in the Flamehall. Only now did they realize the warming effect the Flame – and the underground fire that had run beneath the Fissures – had had on the cave system. Only in the early afternoon, when sunlight pierced the huge chamber, did the temperature rise to anything approaching comfortable.

Wist sat next to her sister's crystallized body, her teeth chattering, watching the sky brighten beyond the broken wall, anticipating the first strike of its rays against her scales.

313

She knew what she had to do – the first part of it at least – but had no idea how she was going to achieve it. If this morning's effort was anything to go by, the task she had set herself (or rather that Lessen had set for her) was impossible.

'We must move her outside,' she had announced, and Brace and Ledra had exchanged a dubious glance. To their credit however they had accompanied Wist uncomplaining into the Flamehall and turned their minds to the problem. After an initial bout of heaving and levering proved in vain, they settled down to think the problem through.

'The crystal has fused with the surrounding rock,' sighed Brace. 'I just don't see what we can do.'

And although Wist tried to keep her spirits high, it was with mounting gloom that she watched her two friends fly off at noon to forage for food.

'We have to eat,' explained Ledra, but it sounded more like an apology than an explanation. Wist knew that what she was really saying was, 'We have to keep ourselves busy.'

So here she sat, her heart low, driven by an onrushing imperative which warned of imminent danger, the danger of the Flame, but with no real idea of when that danger would come, or what it would comprise. She only knew that when it came it would come fast.

She gazed into a thin sheet of ice which had solidified in a dip in the rock shelf. A runnel of water had found its way to the edge of the shelf and frozen there; already a tiny icicle had started to form, dangling from the precipice like an infant dragon's claw. As she watched, the first rays of the afternoon sun slipped through the air and struck the tip of the icicle. Before long a bead of water had gathered there. Wist watched it stretch, quivering, and finally break free, falling into the darkness.

A slow smile broke across her face, and as Brace and Ledra flew in with their meagre cargo of fish she turned to welcome them with wide-stretched wings.

'My friends,' she proclaimed. 'I think I have it!'

'Now is the perfect time for the first strike!' cried Fortune, throwing his voice through the darkness to reach every one of the dragons awaiting his word. 'We will be practically invisible in the night sky, if they can see anything at all through that cursed wall of fire.'

'But it's so simple,' protested Wemp from the ranks of the mirror-dragons, his wings reflecting the stars, the last shreds of the comet's tail and the dark line of the canyon above which they had all gathered.

'The simpler the better,' interjected Velvet. Like most of her companions, she was glad that they were doing something positive at last. Until now all their talk of plans and strategies had seemed like dreams, but now they were here, within striking distance of the Last Circle itself, everything had become real. 'The sooner we can get Gossamer out of the clutches of that evil dragon the better, don't you agree, Cumber, my dear?'

'If Scarn still *is* a dragon,' Cumber warned.

'Rescuing my mother is only part of the challenge,' said Aria, her voice calm and reasonable. Though it was quiet, it carried as far as Fortune's shout. Her eyes were alight and full of passion. 'Let us not forget that greater wills than our own are being brought to bear here.'

There were grunts through the ranks, most of agreement, some of confusion. Aria knew as well as Fortune that Gossamer was a useful focus for the attack, but she knew better than any dragon there – except perhaps Anchre – what was really at stake.

'We are agents of the Cloud now,' she announced, steel entering her tone. 'And as such we have but one enemy. Call it Scarn, call it Flame, call it what you will. It must be sent from here so that the day may come when all is made right again in the world.'

'Remember this,' said Fortune, continuing smoothly from where his daughter had left off. 'They have killed dragons, yet they are not dragons themselves. They are all of the Flame now, and they must all be put down.' *Do I mean 'killed'?* he wondered as he said this. *Can I kill another, however much evil there is in its heart?*

An image of another dragon rose before him, a pale spectre with long, white wings and a serpentine, eyeless visage. Archan, who had stolen his daughter from him, and stolen her infancy from her. Yes, had he had the chance,

315

he would have killed Archan, he had no doubt about that.

He looked to the horizon, where the comet had just vanished behind the distant, low hills. Then he looked at his army.

'Listen to my daughter!' he cried. 'And fight, for the day of creation is near!'

He led them down the canyon to the site of the landslide. Hovering there, he cast his eyes across the sea of wings and finally picked out Volley.

'Many of us have reason to despise Scarn,' he said, his voice as quiet now as Aria's had been earlier. 'But you deserve the first strike, my friend. Do it for Tallow.'

In silence, Volley swooped down to the pile of boulders and selected a massive chunk of rock. He hefted it in his claws, groaning at the weight as he regained the sky with long, heavy thumps of his wings. The first wave, already chosen from Oster's troupe, followed him down. Fortune himself brought up the rear. He picked out a sharp-edged rock and joined his friend at the head of the flight.

'One hundred breaths,' he called, 'then the second wave will follow.'

Oster acknowledged this with a flick of his wing, then together Fortune and Volley led ten mirror-dragons back towards the Last Circle.

At first, Wist thought it was not going to work. Her claws blunted and two of them actually splintered as she tried to gouge away at the base of the red, crystal sculpture which was the trapped remains of her twin sister. Then Ledra pushed her gently aside and set to work. Her own claws, hardened by the charm which had pumped if only briefly through her Natural veins, proved much more efficient and soon she had cut a deep furrow in the rock.

'It's softer than it looks,' she panted, rocking back on her haunches as she took a break. 'We'd never cut our way through altogether though.'

'We won't have to,' responded Wist with a tentative smile.

Brace took over while Ledra rested, but without much success. Like Wist's, his claws were not up to the job of cutting rock, however friable it had become.

316

'Do you want me to go on?' asked Ledra, leaning forward once more. Wist frowned, looking out at the sun which was rapidly dropping out of sight beyond the hole in the wall. Soon the temperature would begin to drop too, and there was more work to be done before then.

'Let me see,' she said, narrowing her eyes as she inspected the work. A deep crack ran two thirds of the way round the seam between the red crystal and the black rock of the ledge. She glanced back. The sun was almost gone. It would have to do. 'No, let's get the water. There's not much time, and if we don't do it tonight . . .' She let her voice trail off, because she was not sure what lay beyond the 'if', she only knew that it was bad.

In fact, Ledra managed to do a little more carving while Brace and Wist flew out to the cataract which tumbled from the cliff-top above the exit from the Flamehall. They returned carefully, carrying between them a deep, woven basket lined with waxy leaves. Mahl was a bleak place, and it had taken Brace most of the morning to gather enough branches and leaves to create this container. It leaked furiously but they did not have to carry it far; it would have to suffice.

'Out of the way, Ledra,' Brace called as they swooped in. She jumped back just as they touched down, a heavy landing, spilling the water clumsily across the ledge. Some of it drained into the crack which Ledra had made; most of it splashed across the ledge and poured into the depths of the chamber.

'Damnation!' cursed Wist, swivelling and lunging back towards the exit. Brace followed, and before long they were returning with a second load of the precious water. This time they came in more smoothly, taking their time. At the last moment Wist allowed Brace to take most of the weight and drop the basket softly in front of the crystal dragon. Its front edge folded down into a crude lip and delivered the water neatly into the crack, which filled up almost instantaneously. The overflow spilled out in pursuit of the first load but they were unconcerned: they had done the job they set out to do.

'Now we wait,' sighed Brace, glad to be working, frustrated that he did not fully understand what was going on.

317

He watched the flow of water draining over the ledge and disappearing into the gloom. *Into the gloom*, he thought dejectedly. *Is that where we're all headed too?*

Fortune almost laughed as they approached the Last Circle again. Had he really thought it bland the first time he had set eyes on it? Had he really almost passed it by in the immensity of the landscape?

By night the Last Circle was ablaze. The sheet of fire crackled and frothed like an angry, electric sea, illuminating both the upraised lip of the crater and its barely-seen interior. The indigo dragon-shapes were now lavender, bright and sharp when visible between the waves of light which oscillated to and fro between the central Flame and the crater's edge. Above, the stars were gone, dissolved by the brilliant blue aura crowding upwards into the sky.

'Volley will go first!' barked Fortune. 'He's already picked his spot. Follow him close, but not so close that you can't watch for the effect of the previous strike. I need all of you to observe. I don't expect to break through yet, but I do expect some clues. Volley?'

'Yes, Fortune?' Volley's voice was deep and rich and, Fortune thought, nearly at peace.

'You know who it's for.'

Volley pulled in his wings and dived straight down towards the light-filled crater. He was aiming for a point near the perimeter, well away from the main centre of activity around the Flame itself. When he was perhaps three trees above the membrane of fire he began to flatten out, at the same time releasing the giant boulder he had carried all the way from the canyon. The boulder spun slowly, dreamily in the air as it plunged towards the fire. Then it struck.

Ripples burst from the point of impact, shock waves. Splinters of charm were sent oscillating through the protective shield, and the rock exploded, the fragments launched back upwards, vaporizing before they had even begun to fall again. Purplish bubbles swelled and popped, firing sparks up towards Volley's wings. But already he was clear, climbing high again as the next dragon flew down. Rock after rock struck the membrane, all of them within a few wingspans of

318

Volley's hit. With each run the fire jostled like a sea in a storm, and each time it healed itself again, spitting angrily at its attackers. Soon only Fortune was left. He too tucked in his wings and dived.

The descent was terrifying. The fire – or charm, or whatever it was – loomed and for a moment he was not sure in what direction he was flying: for a dizzying moment it was as though he were travelling upwards and the fire was a net cast across the sky to stop his ascent. Then the ripples caused by the previous dragon's boulder expanded before him and he unlocked his claws. His own weapon, a jagged black silhouette spinning lazily against the glare of the flames, shrinking as it dropped away, hit hard, cutting a swathe of light through the membrane and generating the now familiar skein of waves and bubbles. But unlike the others, Fortune's *sank in* before exploding.

He pulled out of his dive just as the air became filled with vicious chunks of rock, and it was with a narrow smile on his face that he rejoined his comrades in the sky.

'That's one lesson learned,' suggested Volley. 'Sharp rocks from now on.'

'No,' replied Fortune. 'That wasn't it. It still didn't get through. It wasn't the sharpness, Volley, it was the cumulative effect of all the rocks together that weakened the shield. Most of them hit close to where yours did, but mine was in exactly the same place. There's a dark shape, an angular crack, on the crater floor precisely below where you dropped your boulder – I saw it as you pulled up. I was lucky enough to hit the very same spot. That's what did it. Accuracy is what we need, Volley, not sharp rocks!'

'Second wave's coming,' called Wemp from the ranks of the mirror-dragons.

'I'll pass on what we've learned,' said Fortune. 'The rest of you: you know what to do. As soon as you've gathered more ammunition make your way back here. Use Volley's mark. We've got a proper target now!'

Eleven more dragons emerged from the darkness into the glow of the crater, their metallic scales shining blue, rocks clutched tight beneath their bellies.

*   *   *

319

Wist flew impatiently in the dark Flamehall, her wings sending the cold air wafting across the crystal dragon. Now the sun had gone the temperature was dropping rapidly. Down on the ledge, shivering, Brace was talking to Ledra.

'You know that I love you, don't you?' he asked tentatively. Her expression he could not see, but the gentle touch of her snout against his face was enough. 'It's just – all my life I've been either searching for something or running away. And what I really miss, more than anything else, is a place to call home.'

'That goes for most dragons now, Brace,' replied Ledra, her voice soft. 'Where is there left for us?'

Where indeed? thought Brace sadly.

From behind him came a thin cracking sound. He turned carefully, calling to Wist, and as he did so the ledge itself trembled.

'We should take off,' barked Ledra, opening her wings.

'No,' answered Wist. Her body was a dark sketch of a dragon as she alighted before them. 'It's all right, look.'

By the dim evening light which just managed to filter into this subterranean realm they could make out the faceted curve of Lessen's crystallized flank. Beneath it the surface of the ledge was hard and smooth, covered now by a thin sheet of ice; the slot which Ledra had cut was now filled with freezing water. More cracking sounds emerged from the junction between rock and crystal and a splinter of ice flew sideways into the air. The dragons held their breath.

Suddenly the cracking was interrupted by a tremendous, tearing noise, a virtual explosion. The ledge shook again and a shower of crystal shards and ice fragments rained across the dragons' legs and claws. Expanding as it froze, the water had finally levered the crystal free. The explosion elongated into a groaning, ripping shriek and in amazement they watched as the crystal dragon lurched to one side, tipping ominously towards the precipice.

'Hold it!' yelled Wist, frantically throwing her wings about what had become of her sister. Her hold was true, but she had not reckoned on the weight of the edifice; she too began to slide towards the sheer drop, her claws scrabbling uselessly on the ice-slick floor.

To the surprise of both her and Ledra, Brace abandoned them, launching himself away into the air.

'Brace!' shouted Ledra. 'Come back! We need you!' Unable to believe that he had abandoned them both to save himself, she threw herself at Wist and the great slab of crystal. Her plan was not to stop their sliding but to divert them sideways, so that they fetched up against the cavern wall before reaching the edge of the ledge. But she too slipped and succeeded only in propelling them more swiftly to their approaching doom.

'Jump free!' she called hopelessly. 'Get clear and save yourself, Wist!'

'The crystal will shatter!' came Wist's reply, a desperate moan. 'All will be . . .'

'Hold tight!' Brace shouted just as Wist's claws slipped out into thin air. The crystal – a boulder now, dead weight – pressed into her breast, forcing her out into space. Brace flew in fast and low, claws outstretched. In them he held a large chunk of ice.

He struck the crystal at the exact moment when Wist found herself unsupported by the ledge. Her wings opened instinctively as her claws flailed in emptiness, relinquishing her death-grip on her treacherous burden. Brace's makeshift ram disintegrated instantly, but not before it had done its work. Its momentum checked, the crystal dragon slewed to the side, riding up on to a low crest of rock near the back wall of the ledge. Brace drove in further, following up the impact of the ice with the weight of his own body, grabbing with his claws and pumping with his wings as he rolled the crystal on to its side. It crashed against the wall with a sharp, ringing sound; flakes of ice scattered around like hail.

The ringing sound seemed to go on for an eternity. When it finally faded all that was left was the rhythmic hiss of Wist's wings against the cold air. Brace and Ledra lay panting silently in the darkness beside the toppled sculpture, the ice which had levered it free surrounding them like a sea of gems.

'Well,' gasped Wist. 'All that's left is to see if we can lift it.'

CHAPTER 24

The First Assault

It was only when he was flying back from the canyon for the second time that Fortune realized the absurdity of his plan. By now the separate waves of dragons had merged into a single, steady stream of individuals picking up rocks from the landslide, then returning for more ammunition after unleashing their load. This dragon chain looped to and fro through the cold, night air, intent on its crazy, hopeless task.

Here is one of the most intense manifestations of charm I've ever seen, he thought, half-mad with fatigue. *And we're throwing rocks at it!*

Yet somehow, despite the madness, on some level it seemed to be working.

'Look at it, Fortune!' That was Cumber, close behind him, having slipped up through the formation to be near his old friend. And Fortune looked.

They were perhaps fifty wingbeats short of the Last Circle, close enough to see over its lip and into the maelstrom which the skin of fire had become. Many of the rocks were still missing the target – it was hard even to see the target most of the time – but enough were striking the fire above the mark Volley had chosen, creating a clearly defined area of stress. The glowing skin was depressed over the dark, angular blemish in the same way that the surface of the sea might be depressed by a whirlpool; there was no hint of rotation, however, only a concavity which steadfastly refused to go away.

The blue fire around the depression was brighter than anywhere else, almost white, in fact, and painful to look at.

It looked stretched, *injured*. Immediately around this glowing wound the skin had turned virtually transparent, and as Fortune and Cumber approached they could clearly see Scarn's forces massing beneath it. The red of their scales seemed . . . *icy*, simultaneously hot and cold. They swarmed like insects, climbing over each other, stretching up with hideously distorted claws to touch the fire which pressed down on them. Where they made contact it pulsed and thickened, renewed itself.

The creatures were much altered from their original dragon forms. Though their unnatural colour lingered, their bodies seemed fluid, shifting before Fortune's astonished eyes. Shape-changing was something he had seen before, but this was something new. There was a horrific kind of order to the transformations, a repetitive quality which gradually became apparent. Necks and tails narrowed and lengthened, then shortened and grew fat, cycling endlessly back and forth as though whatever forces were implementing these changes in some way lacked imagination, were trapped somehow. The liquid, distorting fire through which these patterns of flesh were viewed lent additional horror to the scene.

'What are they turning into, Cumber?' he murmured. His claws dug into the rock which he held against his breast, pressing it against his ribs.

Cumber did not reply at first, choosing instead to pull close beside Fortune as they began their dive towards the crater. 'Tell me this cannot be our destiny, Fortune, please tell me it isn't true,' he said nervously. Ahead and below, the once-dragons of the Cult scurried like beetles.

'I can't tell you that,' Fortune replied. 'Only the Cloud knows what may or may not be. But I think Gossamer may know, and perhaps Aria. Yes, I think Aria may know the truth.'

Cumber shook his head as though to dislodge an unwelcome thought. 'I always know when magic's been at work on you, Fortune,' he grumbled. 'You make even less sense than you normally do.'

They flew low, side by side, wings almost touching. They dropped their rocks simultaneously and they fell as a single boulder, their paths converging until they struck both the sheet of fire and each other at exactly the same instant. Sparks etched their way skywards as hard-edged pebbles battered the underbellies of the two speeding dragons. Underneath, the scuttling, mutating monstrosities of the Cult busied themselves with their ongoing repair work.

'Do you believe the comet will fall?' blurted Cumber as they turned, wings aching, ready to begin the return journey yet again.

'Is that what's bothering you?' Fortune laughed. 'Do you think I know something you don't?'

'Isn't that usually the case?'

'Oh, Cumber! Look, all I know is that the Cloud – whatever it may be – will soon enter the world. And I think the coming of the comet is wrapped up with the coming of the Cloud somehow. But that's all I know, I'm afraid. If you want to know what I really think – yes, I believe the comet will fall to earth. But what that means for us mere dragons I couldn't say.'

'Is the Cloud good?'

'As the Flame is evil.'

Aria joined them then, dark wings whistling in the night air, her face grim.

'It isn't working,' she said.

Gossamer watched as the fire-shield trembled under the attack. It was Fortune, she knew, come to prevent Scarn from making his sacrifice.

I should be angry, she thought. *He should not have interfered. It was not the will of the Cloud.* But she could not be angry. Indeed, she felt nothing but relief that he had come at last.

Her time as a prisoner in the Last Circle had passed in a kind of daze. The only dragon faces which seemed whole to her were those of her mother and strange Anchre, the dragon to whom she had talked about the Cloud on Mahl. She had not seen Anchre for some time now, and her mother would not be separated from the catatonic shell of her father. The Flame itself kept Gossamer trapped at the centre of the crater by means of an invisible wall of charm. Not even Scarn entered her prison; he had not even spoken to her since her abduction. She slept a lot, and prayed. Still the Cloud did not answer her. She cried too.

So now, as she looked up at the disturbance in the shield, she rejoiced as she opened her heart to the possibility that she would be rescued.

The Cult was in pandemonium, dragon-shapes hurrying away from the light of the Flame, distracted both by the weight of the storm and the explosions caused by the falling rocks. She could not see Scarn. One shape moved more slowly however, moved towards her while all others raced to the perimeter, raced to various stations around the crater. It was still some distance away when she identified it.

'Jevell!' she called, using her mother's name. She found herself thinking of Wyrm, and how he had always used names in preference to titles. Her mother was dragging another dragon behind her. It could only be . . . 'Father,' she breathed.

Jevell hauled the limp body up the shallow slope of the central rock dome. Rarch's head lolled, dragging against the rough stone of the crater floor. A shower of pebbles fell away as one of his horns caught on a protruding outcrop. At last Jevell reached the invisible barrier – its position was betrayed by a circular indentation in the dust – and stopped, her breast heaving, challenging Gossamer with dark eyes. All other activity in the Last Circle seemed to recede; it was only the three of them, a tiny family alone at the heart of the crater.

'Is he dead?' asked Gossamer, her voice low.

'No,' replied her mother. 'But he is dying. Only your Cloud can help him now.'

'I don't believe . . .' Gossamer began. Then she looked at Jevell, looked deep, and what she saw filled her with hope. The despair she'd felt at seeing the wretched state of her father was overwhelmed.

Gossamer reached out a wingtip, ignoring the stab of pain as it glanced against the barrier. In Jevell's eyes she had seen the light of revelation.

Where the others had succumbed to the disease of the Cult, Jevell had remained steadfast. Outwardly conformist she had retained her own, strong will, her own identity, just as Anchre had done. Now, while the other members of Scarn's Cult swarmed and stretched, their bodies beginning to swell obscenely with the changes the Flame was wreaking upon them, Jevell had stepped free of the evil which had tainted her scales, but not her heart.

'Your Cloud can help,' Jevell repeated. Then, seeing Gossamer's eyes widen, she added, 'Yes, I too have heard its call.'

Gossamer felt her mother's certainty wash over her like a cleansing flood of water. Had she really doubted the existence of the Cloud, its ability to touch her heart? How could she have been so foolish? The Flame seemed to shrink above her as her head filled with images: the oval light which had spoken to her in the basilisk tower; the radiance of her mother's smile; Anchre's account of his mission at Aether's Cross; Fortune's love, which had brought him back to her; the Cloud, its light and beauty. The goodness it would soon bring to the world.

'It's true, isn't it?' she wept, and her mother nodded ecstatically, over and over again. Their tears flowed freely; their wings reached out and pulled back, desperate to embrace but prevented from doing so by the barrier charm.

'Just now,' blurted Jevell, the words tumbling from her mouth like water from a spring, 'I saw it just now. Just as the attack began – or just before, perhaps – I was looking upwards. It was all over in an instant. The storm was overhead, the thunder was so loud. I saw beyond the fire, beyond the storm, right up into the sky. I saw the comet, Gossamer, split in two. It blurred and became a great oval of cloud. The Cloud.'

'Did it speak to you?' Gossamer felt a brief stab of envy, for her mother had heard the call which she had long wished to hear again for herself. Then relief took over: *my mother has heard the voice of the Cloud. All that I have believed is true!*

'It did!' Jevell's eyes shone like the comet itself. 'It said that tomorrow the sky would grow lighter than it had ever been before and all evil would be cast into its rightful place. It's really coming, Gossamer! It's nearly here!'

'Tomorrow.' Gossamer nodded. 'And Rarch?'

Here her mother faltered. 'He is not well, Gossamer. I

thought . . . I thought between us we might . . .' Her face crumpled. 'Oh, my dear, I'm afraid he's gone from us already. Do you think, I mean, perhaps the Cloud . . .'

Gossamer looked past her mother and across to where her father lay. Tears welled in her eyes once more as she gazed on his prostrate body, a thin, red replica of the dragon she had loved as an infant. The tears came but she felt nothing; she prayed.

Sweet Cloud, if it is your will, bring him back to us. Please don't let him suffer, don't let him be taken by the Flame. Set him free, in whatever way you see fit. And . . . I'm sorry I doubted you.

Then Gossamer smiled. 'They're one and the same, aren't they? The comet and the Cloud.'

'My darling, the comet *is* the Cloud!'

'What do you mean, it isn't working?' spluttered Cumber. 'I would have said it's working pretty well, if the state of that fire-thing is anything to go by. Wouldn't you say so, Fortune?'

Fortune waved his friend silent and asked Aria to elaborate.

'Scarn's dragons are altering the charm every time we strike a blow against it,' she explained. 'Oh, we're weakening it all right, but we'll never punch through it, not like this.'

'How can you be sure?' Fortune demanded.

Aria shrugged. 'It feels true.'

Fortune nodded curtly. 'I believe you, my daughter, but we will continue with the bombardment until morning. All it needs is for one of them to make a mistake. There's still a chance we might get through.'

'I don't think they're acting as individuals any more, father,' commented Aria. She rejoined the line of dragons leading back to the canyon and took up her next rock with the others, obviously content to follow Fortune's orders despite her feelings.

They did indeed continue the onslaught until sunrise, and for some considerable time after that. There was a moment shortly before dawn when five of Oster's dragons tried a simultaneous attack, each of them dropping two rocks directly on to the target. Six of the rocks were pulverized; four actually broke through the barrier and fell to the crater floor below, crushing one of Scarn's minions beneath them. The hapless creature must have died instantly, for a veritable flood of black, sticky fluid poured from its fractured body the instant the boulders struck. If there was any doubt that these were no longer dragons it was dispelled at that moment, as the twitching remains were drawn up from the ground by a thick strand of charm which extruded itself from the fire-skin. Boneless, bloodless but for the sticky ichor which dripped from its fleshy corpse, the creature was returned to the fire which now owned it.

By now Fortune was operating a shift system, using only half the available dragons at any one time, but upon seeing this first successful penetration he stepped up the pace again. Unfortunately, no other dragons came close to repeating the success of their colleagues, and by mid-morning Fortune called a halt to the operation. Dragons were tired, some close to exhaustion, and they seemed to have achieved very little. They gathered in the shelter of the canyon, where the shadow of the steep walls kept the hot sun off their backs.

'Kept them busy,' grunted Scoff philosophically.

'What do you suggest we do now, Fortune?' asked Velvet, huddling herself close to Cumber. Fortune looked at his friends and noticed how young they seemed against the shining yet time-worn dragons of Oster's troupe. He was struck by their loyalty.

'Lay low through the middle of the day,' he answered promptly, before his feelings could fly ahead of him. 'They might think we've given up – though I doubt it – and come out of their own accord. In any case, we need time to think and it's getting too hot out there to fly for any length of time.'

As he said this the sun crept over the rim of the canyon and sent its light chasing down the rock walls to meet them. It was more than hot – it was searing, and the dragons flinched at its touch. With it came the light of the comet, rising once more into view. The secondary glare of the piece which had broken away now overwhelmed its parent, glowing nearly as bright as the sun itself.

Oster came to Fortune soon after they had stopped to rest. At his side was Limner, the dragon who had so artfully ignited the bonfire at the entrance to the cave in the Rift wall.

'Limner has an idea,' Oster announced perfunctorily.

Fortune nodded. The sun was baking the dry ground, and baking him too, or so it felt. His head felt thick and muzzy.

'Go on,' he said, waggling his wing lazily.

'I pride myself on the condition of my scales,' began Limner enthusiastically. To one side sat Cumber and Velvet, both listening intently. 'Of all the mirrors we own, mine are the most highly polished. Hence my role as fire-starter.' He glanced at Oster then went on. 'Our scales act as mirrors not only to light, however. They are also mirrors to charm.'

'Were,' cautioned Oster. 'In the old days that was certainly true, but what chance do we get now to test our old skills?'

'This might be just that chance, Oster,' countered Limner, his eyes shining. 'Listen, Fortune – part of our display used to involve one of our number ejecting a fireball at another. The target dragon would catch the fire charm in his wings and bounce it back into the sky, usually transforming it into some harmless show of light, or a shower of sparks.'

Limner took a deep breath. 'I think I can get through that sheet of fire,' he said rapidly, as though the speed of his words might somehow assure success. 'I think I can slip through at the weak point we've already created, and if I can do it quickly my scales will reflect the fire just long enough for me to make it all the way before . . .'

'Before you are cut in half!' interjected Velvet. 'Fortune, tell him what a fool he's being. I don't want to see any dragon throw his life away. Besides, what would you do when you got in there?'

Limner shrugged. 'Some damage, I suppose,' he offered with a disarming grin.

Cumber hissed at Velvet, pulling her close. 'It's not such a stupid idea, if you think about it, my dear. It *is* possible to reflect charm like that, it really is. I used to do it all the time.' Velvet gave him a withering look. 'Well, perhaps not all the time – but you know what I mean.'

A few others had gathered around now, having overheard

Limner's suggestion. Several of the mirror-dragons were nodding in agreement with their comrade, and a few even raised their wings as though volunteering to join him in the attempt. Scoff and Volley both looked sceptical, as did Anchre. In the end it was Aria who broke the awkward silence.

'Let me tell you the way of the Flame,' she proclaimed. 'Because it owns no real power in the world, because it cannot touch the world in the way you or I can touch it, it relies upon others to do its work. It is using Scarn and the once-dragons of the Cult to do its work, and to feed it information, to touch things. But everything it touches turns to evil – or most things, at least,' she added with a shy smile. She added, more softly, 'Some of us manage to escape.'

'My dear,' interrupted Fortune hesitantly, 'this is all very well, but . . .'

'But nothing, father!' snapped Aria, her eyes blazing suddenly. Fortune took a step backwards, shocked and confused. 'Velvet asked what one dragon could possibly do inside the Last Circle. Well, the answer is *everything*. If we are to stand any chance of vanquishing the Flame, its disciples must be destroyed, altogether or one by one, it does not matter. If Limner can penetrate the shield and kill a few of those creatures we shall be a long way towards achieving our goal. If more want to follow him, so much the better.'

'What about Gossamer?' said Velvet quietly. A hush descended over the gathering.

'Her fate lies in the light of the Cloud,' replied Aria, her face stiff.

It was a sombre group that accompanied Limner out to the perimeter of the Last Circle. They flew low and fast, skimming close to the dry and dusty ground to remain always below the level of the rim. They landed at the base of the incline and Oster led them up, halting just short of the summit. The noon sun shone with merciless heat, turning the two-headed comet into a smeared blister of light.

'Are you sure you want to go through with this?' asked Fortune. In all, four other mirror-dragons had elected to join Limner on his perilous mission. Fortune and Oster had followed them out here, along with Aria and Cumber.

Cumber in particular was keen to observe the proceedings.

'I have had experience of charm's use in battle,' he had tried to explain to Velvet before he left. 'First at Aether's Cross, later in Covamere and on the Plated Mountain. These mirror-dragons have seen nothing compared to what I have seen, despite their undoubted skills.'

'That won't help them when they get in there,' responded Velvet petulantly. '*If* they get in there.'

He kissed her gently and made for the crater with the others.

To his surprise, Fortune noted what an effective camouflage the mirror-dragons' highly polished scales created. In the air they were easy to see, but on the ground, with their wings flattened and necks tucked in, all he could really make out was a series of distorted reflections of the brown and grey rock.

'Do you remember when Scoff and I made you invisible?' whispered Cumber. 'I wish I'd thought of just changing your scales like this – it would have been much easier!'

Oster lifted his head gingerly over the top of the rim and scanned the sea of fire. They were so close that they could hear its crackle and see the occasional spark which leaped clear of the rim. After a moment's observation he drew back his neck and turned to the others.

'There are several of them gathered around our target,' he said softly, 'but most seem to have moved away. We may not get a better chance than this.'

At once Limner began to advance up-slope, but Oster held him back with one trembling wing.

'What's the matter?' hissed Fortune.

Oster shook his head and gave Fortune a sad smile. 'Nothing,' he said. 'Fortune, the time has come to say goodbye.'

Fortune blinked stupidly, not understanding. but Limner understood only too well. 'You're not going instead of me, Oster!' he blustered. 'Fortune, tell him. Whatever he says I'm . . .'

'Calm down, Limner,' Oster interrupted, still smiling. 'Who said anything about taking your place? I'm going with you, that's all.'

Limner and the other mirror-dragons began to protest but it was Fortune who articulated their concern.

331

'But . . . if you weren't to return, Oster. The others all look up to you. You claim to be a leaderless group, but you know the truth as well as any dragon.'

Oster smiled and nodded and said, 'They look up to you now, Fortune. I was never a leader, not as you are.'

'You don't have to do it, Oster,' maintained Limner. 'And stop smiling – it's infuriating!'

Oster's smile disappeared then, and the expression which replaced it was one of sorrow and anger. 'Yes, I do.' He gestured over the top of the crater rim with one metallic wing. 'Here, in the bowl of the Last Circle, I laid my brothers' bones to rest. Here I watched the cleansing fire of charm take those bones and deliver them into whatever world lies beyond our own. Here I wept for their tiny lives and wished the plague had taken me instead.

'Time *has* taken me instead, and here I am again, older than my years. The Last Circle has been violated by an evil presence no dragon can tolerate. The Flame has killed, it has taken possession of dragon minds and dragon hearts, and if what Fortune and his daughter say is true then it threatens to take possession of the world we love. All I want now is to see this place purified of the evil that taints it, and if it means I go to join my brothers in their graves then so be it.'

Fortune looked hard at Oster, then across at Cumber. He was not surprised to see tears in his young friend's eyes. Suddenly he felt out of place here, an intruder in another dragon's grief. *In the grief of a whole community*, he reminded himself as Oster and Limner embraced clumsily. The other four mirror-dragons touched their comrades with nervous wingtips, their eyes closed against the pain Oster's words had brought back to them. Fortune had heard more stirring speeches in his time – indeed he had made a few of his own – but none compared to this for its open honesty, and its devastating awareness of loss.

'Good luck to you all,' he gulped as he and Cumber stood back, allowing their new friends to climb the last wing's breadth to the top of the rim. They paused there, a line of five shining dragons framed against a burning sky, then they were gone.

Fortune stared into the glare of the comet for several

breaths as though in a trance, then suddenly Cumber's wing dug him in the ribs.

'It's started!' his friend hissed.

Above the rim summit, a flicker of wings marked the ascent of Oster's squad into the air above the target spot. The wings cycled twice, then curled round and vanished from sight. They were going in.

Gossamer's heart leaped when she saw the flash of light from the far side of the crater. An opening had appeared in the skin of charm which was her sky. Its edges were clean and shone with a brilliant, white glow. There was movement there, just as there was movement all around. Fragments of silver slipped through the opening while a tide of red, flowing bodies marked the progress of Scarn's disciples towards the breach in the shield.

Someone – or something – had broken through!

Fortune, she thought, but she knew it was not him. From behind, her mother called, but she ignored her. She was counting the streaks of light cutting through the air beneath the breach; she thought there were five individuals, but she could not be sure. Five dragons, against Scarn's army. *And where exactly is Scarn*, she wondered, *while all this is going on?*

Her heart was thundering now. The slivers of silver became circles marking the course of agile dragons looping through the searing air. The red tide rose towards them, made contact, swallowed them. Angry motion defined the interface. A tremendous cloud of dust exploded from the crater floor, obscuring her view of the battle.

Fortune took one look at Cumber and opened his wings. By unspoken agreement they launched themselves into the air and hurried over the rise into the glare of the shield of charm. They emerged from behind the rim just in time to see the first mirror-dragon (all Fortune could see from this distance was that it was neither Oster nor Limner) strike the fire.

The dragon's body was a smooth, clean line of metal. Its wings seemed altogether gone; in fact they were tucked so close that they were quite invisible. The tip of its snout slid smoothly into the fire and for a fraction of a breath it seemed that it would get through safely. Then a circle of blinding white light expanded from around the point of entry, a shock wave which lifted the surface of the fire into a bubbling ring.

The dragon's body followed his head through the fire, but it was already clear to both Fortune and Cumber that all was not well. The shield was translucent and they could see something of what lay beyond, and what they saw emerging on the other side was not clean and metallic but . . . pulped. Cumber groaned and looked away.

'Wait,' murmured Fortune, for the shock wave from the impact had reached the centre of the crater. Had reached the Flame itself.

There was an infinitesimal pause, then the Flame seemed to *shrink* briefly. For a drunken instant Fortune thought that was it, that they had defeated it, that it would continue to shrink until it collapsed into itself and vanished from the world, taking all its evil with it. Then it recovered, but not before the shock wave had been reflected back, stronger now. The Flame continued to waver for several breaths.

Scales like mirrors, thought Fortune excitedly. *The Flame has stared into its own face!*

By the time the shock wave returned to its point of origin it was much weakened, almost non-existent in fact. Then, at the very moment it passed back over the disintegrating body of the unfortunate pathfinder, Limner fell from the sky.

He hit the flaw in the fire as the shock wave contracted to nothing. His scales glowed unbearably bright as his body, blurred by the tremendous speed he had attained in his dive, slithered neatly through the shield. One by one the others followed. Explosions shattered the integrity of the fire charm; for this short, critical time it was in disarray.

'I see!' exclaimed Cumber excitedly. He had turned back almost as soon as he had looked away. 'Fortune – it took that initial reflection to set up the reaction. That poor soul didn't know what he was doing, but it was the only way they were ever going to get through, I can see that now. His scales *did* counter the charm, you see, but not enough to offer him the protection he needed. But what it did do was to send a . . . a bolt of pure charm back into the heart of the Flame. Something like that anyway. That in turn set up a weakness at the focus of that bolt . . . and so the others got through.'

'Not without sacrifice,' noted Fortune. 'Cumber, if I didn't know better, I would say you just made all that up.'

Cumber began to smile, but the expression was wiped from his face as he peered down through the trembling shield. The information they received was distorted as though by water, made remote by the rippling blue fire which now concealed, now revealed the battle raging below.

They could just make out the forms of Oster and the other mirror-dragons as they burst free into the clear air inside the crater. A wave of red bodies was breaking across them already, and where the two forces met there were great flashes of light. Dust rose to envelop the fighting, but not before they saw two of the silver shapes broken apart by a busy red knot of motion.

'There!' cried Cumber indicating a clearer area to one side of the melee. A single arrow of silver was cutting through a swathe of red, scattering bodies in its wake. Fortune counted three of Scarn's troops thrown back into the dust.

The remaining mirror-dragons (were Oster and Limner among them? – there was no way of knowing) gathered beneath the flaw through which they had gained entry to the Last Circle. A sea of red surrounded them; it seemed solid, as though the individual bodies which made it up had fused together. Fortune shuddered – perhaps that was just what had happened.

A silver streak. Part of the advancing red line fractured, then remade itself. Blue fire licked down from the protective skin, breaking one of the mirror-dragons in two. More activity, this time descending into the dust: some unseen skirmish. Then the advancing army closed its pincers and the colour of blood was everywhere. The dust rose further, obscuring all.

Unmindful of their vulnerability, Fortune and Cumber continued to hover there, straining their eyes, waiting for the dust to settle.

CHAPTER 25

Light and Dark

Nothing moved except Vox. The dazzling wall of the comet expanded before him as he accelerated into its embrace, then the world started to turn once more.

As the whiteness expanded so did his perception. He was aware of a series of veils falling across his consciousness. The sensation of falling was overwhelming and he gave himself over to the experience. A lone spirit tumbling far from home, Vox fell into the comet's heart.

Streamers of light punctured him with strange feelings, feelings of hope and despair, of fear and exhilaration. The dominant feeling was hope, however, hope and . . . faith? Vox had no idea what senses he was using to absorb these feelings; at times it seemed that he was seeing emotions with his eyes, at others he appeared to be scenting light, tasting shadow. All sense of time had left him by now; he was aware only of the comet.

Gradually this play of emotions transformed into a flood of information. Vox touched the gases which were boiling from the comet, was caressed by the silicates unravelling around him, tugged by the electric charges which sculpted the trail of dust. All these things he heard, he tasted, all these things he *knew* in an intimate way he could never have imagined when he had been a slave to his earthly body. That body seemed remote now, irrelevant even, in this wondrous halo of light.

He emerged into the glow of the comet's nucleus. The light was cool and soothing, free of glare and soft as an infant's caress. Its source turned slowly beneath him – an irregular ball of frost as big as a mountain. Its crystalline surface glistened with beads of frozen dew; tiny plumes of vapour chased themselves across its curved horizon; cracks scurried around its equator, revealing deep pools of brilliantly glowing liquids which seeped out and solidified, repairing the damage almost instantaneously. An icy moon in constant motion, the heart of the comet was laid bare below him.

The proximity of the nucleus brought a sudden tension: was he going to strike it? He had no body to speak of but the prospect of impact with this crystal moon was not something Vox relished. His fears died however as he realized that his forward (or was it downward?) motion had all but stopped: now he was drifting lazily over the comet's light-filled contours, bathed in its glow.

This in itself seemed odd. Vox's impression when circling the world with Ocher had been that the comet, though brilliant in the sky, possessed no light of its own but was rather illuminated by the sun. This was certainly true of its tail, part of which Vox had clearly seen eclipsed by the world's shadow. It was a reflector, not an illuminator.

Yet here, at the comet's heart, was a light like none he had seen before, a cloudy, aethereal glow which billowed out from the rolling, crystal skin as if welcoming him as an old friend.

Or a new ally . . .

Aware that he was again in control of his own movements, Vox tipped forward and slowly approached the nucleus, staring in wonder at the myriad reflections of his own, ghostly form which the crystals threw back. A single dragon spirit made into a thousand copies of itself, one giving birth to many.

Another crack churned its way around the nucleus, unleashing yet more of the inner light. This time the crack did not heal at once; this time the light reached out for Vox, drawing him in. The light was like a cloud. It enveloped him, swallowed him. Dancing within, moving like a dark ember, was a fragment of solid material; it looked like a piece of an eggshell. Or part of the husk of a seed. It drifted out of sight and Vox knew where the comet had come from.

Vox entered the light and the crack closed over.

*   *   *

Clouds were beginning to stack themselves on the western horizon when Fortune and Cumber returned to the canyon. Dragons awaited their news, their impatient wings churning the sultry air. Velvet flew down to Cumber as he alighted on the edge of the canyon, touching him nervously as though to make sure he was all right. He said nothing, simply nuzzled her.

'Several of Scarn's creatures have been killed,' announced Fortune without ceremony. He paused. 'No dragon survived the fight.'

A quiet groan spread through the group, more of a whisper. Metal wings shone grey in the hazy light which had invaded the afternoon. Of Fortune's original group, only Aria and Anchre looked unsurprised. Then Wemp pushed through the ranks of the mirror-dragons and spoke up.

'Oster was not our leader,' he began, 'but he should have been. It is you we need now, Fortune. You are the one who must lead us into battle.' There was a chorus of 'ayes' from the ranks; a field of dragon horns nodded agreement. Fortune echoed the gesture, tipping his own horns forward in acknowledgement.

'I have always turned from such things,' he said, his voice broad and strong, 'but I know you speak the truth, Wemp. I will lead you forward, dragons, though I do not yet know the course I must take.' He felt a draught of warm air as Aria coasted up to his side. 'Our hopes here are many – you dragons of Ocea seek vengeance for those of your number Scarn has killed, and for the way he has defiled your most sacred place. Volley: you seek vengeance too, but of a different sort. Anchre, and you, my dear Aria . . . your goals are different again, and perhaps less certain than those I have mentioned.

'As for me – all I wish for now is to see my Gossamer freed from the trap into which she flew with such willingness – and which I allowed her to enter.

'We have different goals, then, but a common purpose. Scarn and his acolytes must be cast down. The Flame must be extinguished. We must prevail.'

The sky had grown steadily darker through Fortune's speech, and as he concluded he was forced to raise his voice

338

above the strengthening wind. The clouds were racing in from the west with prodigious speed, wiping all light from the sky, erasing both the sun and the twin trails of the comet. Beneath the clouds, still far distant but looming, hung a translucent sheet of rain; soon it would reach them.

'Fire and water,' muttered Fortune, glancing at Aria. She nodded, her brow creased.

'We can use the weather,' she replied, 'can't we?'

'Yes.'

But the storm proved far worse than even Fortune had been expecting. Wemp protested that it had closed in far too early in the day.

'Storm season isn't due,' he shouted over the howl of the wind and the lash of the rain, echoing what Oster had told Fortune the previous day. 'And this isn't the right kind of storm.'

'What kind do you prefer?' Scoff grunted.

Fortune had led them once more to the rim of the crater and here they were gathered, the mirror-dragons of Ocea and the remains of Fortune's motley band. Wings were hunched. Heads were raised bravely against the gale but spirits were low. Dragons had died today, and nothing tangible had been achieved. Wars of attrition could be won but no dragon, given a choice, would elect to be on the side of the besieging army.

'They could stay in there for many days, Fortune,' Cumber warned. 'For many moons, come to that. I doubt they need to eat any more, or drink for that matter. I suspect the Flame gives them all the sustenance they need.'

'We don't have moons, Cumber,' said Aria, answering for her father. 'And neither do they.'

Fortune was looking up into the sky, scanning the black underbelly of the storm as though seeking its heart. Thunder came, but it was distant and muted, reluctant to join them here on the ground. Slivers of lightning chased across the surface of the fire, their serpentine trails of light just visible over the crater's rim, but whether they were products of the storm or of charm no dragon could tell.

'What are you looking for, Fortune?' asked Anchre

quietly, his calm, bland voice startling the young Natural more than any shout.

'I don't know,' Fortune replied. 'But I was thinking about times past, about the turning of the world, about how all things turn.'

He looked to the west – and saw it.

It started low on the horizon, a bulge in the base of the cloud bank. Everything was rendered flat and formless by the driving rain, but the movement in the cloud was dramatic enough to be visible even from this great distance.

'What is it?' asked Velvet, sensing Fortune's sudden alertness.

All his friends gathered round him, a protective knot surrounded in turn by a ring of mirror-dragons. Together they formed a single edifice, a mass of scales even the storm could not penetrate. As one they searched the sky. Some abstract part of Fortune's mind noted that his claws were no longer touching the ground, that he was raised aloft by the closeness of his companions, the press of their bodies.

'I don't know what it is,' he said slowly, 'but it's coming this way.'

By the time the thing took on a definite shape the sky had become completely black. Now the primary source of light was the Flame and its shield of fire charm; though both were hidden from view by the rim of the ridge they cast a livid blue glare up through the rain. Lit eerily from below, the bulge in the cloud grew markedly bigger as it approached, until it formed a cone of darkness, its pointed end reaching towards the ground. A low fog of scattered hail obscured the ground itself. Soon it became apparent that the cone was spinning.

'Tornado,' interjected Scoff brusquely. 'A turning wind. No help for any dragon in its path.'

Still tightly bunched, the dragons watched in awe as the whirling black cone crawled across the rain-lashed plain. Larger it grew, and longer, until its tip touched the ground and a tremendous cloud of dust was lifted into its clutches. Thus fed, it expanded still further until it seemed as wide across as the Last Circle itself. *Surely that cannot be so*, wondered Fortune doubtfully.

He shouldered his way to the edge of the group – dragons parted before him, glancing uncertainly at his eyes – where he turned and took off in a single movement, so that he was looking down on his comrades.

'Wemp!' he bellowed. Behind him the whirlwind was a shrieking monster. 'Seek the shelter of the Flame! Watch for our signal!' He sought Aria and found her, her head high and proud above all the others. 'All of you who love me, come now!'

They came, Aria and Anchre, Cumber and Velvet, Scoff and Volley, Fortune's companions through many a storm before this day. Wemp and the mirror-dragons looked on in confusion as one by one these strangers from beyond the sea lifted into the air to join their friend and leader.

'What do you mean?' Wemp cried, but the wind carried his voice away. Dragon wings thumped dark against a darker sky and then they were gone. 'What is the "shelter of the Flame", Fortune? What do you want us to do? Fortune!' But it was too late. They were gone into the belly of the storm.

Wemp found faces turned towards him and suddenly felt the void which Oster had left. Had they believed themselves leaderless? How wrong they had been!

The shelter of the Flame, Wemp thought frantically. *Can it be as obvious as it sounds, insane though it seems?*

'This way, dragons!' he barked, his voice hoarse with fear. 'Follow me!'

A spark of static crackled across his wingtip as he took to the air. Ignoring the tumult of the storm he led Oster's dragons up over the rise and into the glare of the Flame.

Again Fortune was inside a storm. Surrounding him was chaos, a lightless, orderless world where direction had no meaning, where speed was impossible to assess, where no two wingbeats measured the same. *Would Tallow have found sense in this nightmare?* he wondered. A massive wing crossed his vision and for an instant he thought his old friend had returned from the dead, but when he jerked his head round to look he saw that it was Volley, lunging past him on a

341

treacherous current of air. Their eyes met briefly; Fortune saw determination, and love.

We are within the cloud. With this thought he closed his eyes and offered his prayers up into the heavens.

> *Show me the way through the chaos.*
> *Bring your light to the world.*
> *Come now, for all is prepared.*
> *Let our fight not be in vain.*
> *Hear me, for I believe you can.*

These words Fortune spoke in his mind, and as he spoke them he heard not just his own voice but many voices, some of which he recognized, some unfamiliar.

Show me the way through chaos, whispered Smoke. Black wings cycled between her words while before her rose the flank of a mighty storm. Hearing her voice, Fortune realized it was the same storm she witnessed as the one through which he now flew. It looked different though, the light was wrong in some way he could not identify.

Bring your light to the world. That was Vox. His voice sounded thin and distant, the words broken. Smoke and Vox – what had become of them? Fortune prayed they were still alive, and that the voices he heard were as real as they seemed.

Come now, for all is prepared. Shockingly, these words were Scarn's. They even took on a colour in Fortune's mind – the red of blood. Each syllable stabbed like a tiny claw, yet buried at the heart of this prayer Fortune fancied he detected . . . what? Hope? Remorse? Could it be that some shred of Scarn remained, trapped within the monster of the Cult? This was a prospect Fortune had not anticipated, and he did not welcome it – it complicated matters. *Does Scarn need to be redeemed?* he wondered. *Does he deserve it?*

Let our fight not be in vain, shouted not one voice but many. In the cacophony Fortune heard Cumber and Volley, heard

342

the myriad voices of the mirror-dragons, heard the terrible, liquid growlings of the creatures Scarn's dragons had become. These latter were truly dreadful to hear, all the more so because Fortune knew very well that it was not the Cloud to which their pleas were aimed.

And finally.

Hear me, for I believe you can.

These words were reserved for himself and Gossamer alone. Her voice entwined itself with his own, wrapping itself intimately between breath and utterance. Hearing her made him cry, his tears joining the flood of the rain through which his body carried his wandering spirit.

There was something else, a whisper behind all the voices. He struggled to hear it, and when he first managed to make out its words he thought he was hearing the Cloud itself.

I'm coming. Coming fast.

But then he realized it was not the Cloud at all.

It was Wyrm.

There was little light in the heart of the storm. Vicious winds pummelled the dragons first this way then that. At first it was all too familiar – as wild and unpredictable as the storm they had ridden the previous day, but soon they understood that this was quite different. Despite the darkness, despite the randomness of the squall, there was a direction: not up, not down, but *round*.

The spinning was subtle at first, a gradual drawing of the dragons into a deep spiral of air. Then, all too swiftly, the spiral began to tighten. All around them, beneath the sound of the thunder, was an insistent hissing – the voice of the whirlwind. The tighter the spiral the deeper the hiss, until it had become a roar.

They flew entirely on trust. Glimpses of wings and lashing tails gave hope that the group remained together, but there was no way to be sure. Curiously however, the more the tornado wound itself up the easier it became to keep track of fellow dragons; they were literally forced together by the pressure of the air.

Fortune saw with relief that they had lost none of their number. Lighter clouds beckoned high above, and a colossal draught was pressing them up towards the sanctuary they offered. The darkness had started to fold around them now, turning itself into a vast, open funnel filled with dust and debris. Rocks tumbled past blown like seeds on the wind; every gust pushed them higher; with every wingbeat they strove to force themselves back down.

Fortune saw Volley's mouth moving but heard nothing. The big Natural was making better progress than any of them, battling his way down against the updraught. Signalling to the others as best he could Fortune tacked across to where Volley was, ducking into his slipstream and tucking his wings close, halving their surface area. Volley, he saw, was almost vertical in the rising air, shaped to present the least resistance to the gale. As he followed suit so did the others, until they had formed a tower of dragons, each stood on the tail of the next. Thus they descended, and whether it was by using some trick of the eddies that Volley succeeded in punching through, or by sheer brute strength, they never knew.

The roar filled their heads as the funnel tightened around them. If anything the air grew slightly clearer and the pressure lowered as they dropped, make progress a little easier. Still, every wingbeat was torture, and the upward rain of dust and rocks was even more lethal than before. A sizeable boulder struck Velvet on the flank and she cried out in pain, a shriek rendered silent by the monstrous voice of the tornado. Cumber bumped clumsily against her as she gritted her teeth and forged ahead once more. Blood stained her side, flecking her tail, but the wound was slight.

In the throat of the funnel its rotation was all too apparent. Fortune grew dizzy and eventually shut his eyes against the relentless spinning, opening them only occasionally to assess his position relative to Volley, who continued to carve his way heroically through the whirling debris. Closing his eyes brought Fortune a strange peace in which he heard echoes of the prayers which had carried him this far.

A glance back, a brief concession to vision, revealed a brightening in the clouds overhead. The light seemed to be pursuing them into the depths. Ahead, all was black. Yet Fortune knew where they were – he knew *exactly*.

A shower of pebbles flailed against his breast; then, suddenly, the air cleared. Everything else – the spinning, the roaring – continued unabated but suddenly there was no more debris. There was something in the blackness too, far below them: a round dot like a bright pupil in a vast, dark eye. It shone blue, staring up at them, challenging them to approach. The funnel gave a lurch to the side as though some mighty paw had swiped it from its path, then it shuddered and settled again, spinning yet faster.

The eye grew wide, its edge a blurred halo of residual dust, trapped between the base of the tornado and the surface over which it now skated. The surface of the fire charm, the shield which until now had protected the Last Circle.

Until now.

From his vantage point at the rim of the crater Wemp could see everything. He was still astonished that the mirror-dragons obeyed his command, that the close-knit group of which he had once been a tiny part was now turned to him, eager to obey. He felt at once whole and alone, integrated yet possessed of a terrible solitude. *Is this how Oster felt?* he wondered.

But there was no time for such reflection. Already the whirlwind was biting into the rock scarp to their right, cresting the rim and plunging into the crater itself. At any breath it would strike the shield and then . . . but Wemp could not imagine what might happen then.

'The shelter of the Flame!' he cried, his voice hoarse and weak against the roar of the tornado. If he doubted the power of Fortune's words then the rest of the mirror-dragons did not, and it was with an awesome confidence that they struck out as one across the plain of blue fire.

Never before had their formation been held so tight. Wingtips slipped past each other with intricate grace. The steady surge and ebb of each dragon's body through the air was perfectly matched against that of his neighbour so that not a single wing's width of airspace was wasted; no sooner did this dragon's neck coil backwards ready for the next thrust than the vacuum it left was filled by a folding tail, a flattened membrane, an eager limb. Working like a single organism, the mirror-dragons of Ocea cut their way through the turbulence towards the centre of the crater, towards the Flame itself.

Their course took them perilously close to the tornado. At one point Wemp was convinced that they would be pulled apart by the brutal currents lashing about its base. But at the last breath it held back, allowing them to pass safely through a narrow cleft of relatively still air. It fell behind them; now they moved smoothly between cloud and fire, while ahead was the blue-white fountain of the Flame. Positioned at the exact centre of the crater, on a level with the peak of the outer rim, it protruded from the flat sheet of fire like a swollen, infected wound. Here, near its point of origin, the shield was dull and malformed, pulsing with a steady throb which sent random waves of energy across its bloated skin. It looked as though dark shapes were trapped within it, struggling to release themselves.

Fire charm, thought Wemp. He was reminded of the Realm, that distant other-world which had once been the source of all fire charm. The thinnest of membranes had separated this world from the Realm; to see it a charmed dragon had only to know where to look. *Yet this is like no charm I ever saw. It has . . . evolved.*

Indeed, everything about the Flame and its skirt of fire tasted evil, from its livid colour to the hideous lurching of its outer surface. Behind the brilliant light which was its mask, Wemp saw that there was nothing but total, over-whelming darkness.

And this is supposed to be a shelter?

Behind them there was a crash and a thin scratching sound, like a dragon scraping his claws across ice. Afraid that the tornado had turned in pursuit, Wemp looked back.

Far from following them, the tornado had in fact stopped dead. Its upper part still coiled and twisted but its root was now firmly embedded in the fire. Dust and smoke and a weird, insubstantial vapour lashed around the junction between storm and shield. The dark funnel lashed impatiently, trapped.

346

Energy began to be drawn from the Flame in a series of resounding booms. Each pulse was like a thunderclap made visible, a swelling of the fire-shield which raced from the flame towards the tornado, a thumping sound like the footstep of a troll. Wemp realized that the tornado was in some way attacking the shield, that the Flame was focusing all its power on beating back the intruder. The plain of fire beneath them was now an ocean in torment, a storm-lashed sea of light and snapping, crackling charm. Yet at its centre the Flame itself seemed relatively calm and untroubled, the eye of the hurricane. The shelter.

As they raced for the clear air above the incandescent Flame, it occurred to Wemp that there might be one other place where the sky was safe enough for dragons to survive. He glanced back once more, this time looking up into the wider part of the tornado's funnel. Were there shapes moving in there, descending where all else was being ripped skywards? He could not be sure.

Good luck to you, Fortune, he mouthed soundlessly. *Wherever you may be.*

The tornado punched through the fire-shield. A dreadful wailing rose from the ranks of Scarn's once-dragons. Gossamer saw several of them ripped to pieces by a huge swathe of fire which burst outwards from the point of impact. Their bodies fragmented, spilling dark liquid, then the fragments melted surrounded by a cloud of black, hissing vapour. Neighbouring creatures fled the source of the explosion, their bodies elongating and merging to form two flowing rivers of crimson flesh. The unnatural speed which these monstrous gestalts were able to achieve pulled them clear of the danger area, whereupon they fell apart again into individual entities – if that indeed was what they were and not simply mindless claws on the arm of the Flame.

Creatures crawled clear of the maelstrom. They looked even less like dragons now. Their wings were limp and ragged and their eyes glowed a horrible blue. Most of their scales had peeled away to reveal sagging flesh and jutting bones. Claws had fused into horny stumps, useless for grasping.

The worst of it for Gossamer was the fact that despite these escalating deformities, most of the creatures still had faces, some of them recognizable. Many of them she had known all her life. But the very worst moment of all came when one of the monstrosities flailed through the air a mere wing's width from her side. It looked at her with a blank, uncaring gaze. It was Quill, who had once stood next to Fortune on the council dais of Haven, and who had helped lead the rescue of the dragons of Aether's Cross.

'Why did you save them?!' Gossamer shrieked as what was left of Quill swooped past without even acknowledging her presence. 'Why did you bother, if this is what was to become of them all?' Tears came, floods of them, and she buried her head in her wings.

'Save your tears, dragon,' came a warm, comforting voice from immediately behind her. Her first thought, an electrifying one, was that it was her father, so kind and knowing was its tone. But as she turned she heard the metal in it and knew it was not. 'There is much to come which will grieve you more than what you have seen today.'

She turned away from the sight of the tornado's funnel tearing through the sheet of fire. She did not see the line of dragons which descended through the whirling column of air and spread out into the crater. She was quite unaware that Fortune was now with her in the Last Circle.

All she knew, as she looked around, was that her world had filled up with dazzling blue light, and that she was looking directly into the burning gaze of Scarn.

All this and more was seen by the one dragon who owned the view to surpass them all. Vox, riding the light of the comet, looked down upon the face of the world and saw the opening of the Last Circle. He saw the black back of the storm, saw inside its heart, saw the whirlwind strike its blow against the fiery shield, saw the dragons swept along by the gale. He saw it all, near and far: the thrust of the storm against the land; the reflection of the Flame in Fortune's eye.

As soon as he had entered the comet's nucleus he had known he was in the presence of Gossamer's Cloud. It was like . . . like entering the mind of another dragon, but a dragon whose senses spanned the cosmos. He found no memories here, only perception, but such a perception as he had never known before.

The world was opened to him in all its glory. Vox knew about maps – indeed, he had been the one to operate the basilisk's intricate, living map of the world – but this was to the basilisk's map as that was to the scratchings they had seen on the wall of the faery cave. He saw everything, for this was no map – this was *real*.

He saw the curve of the continents across the planet's skin, saw their tracks through history, saw the myriad futures which might direct them here, or there. He saw the trollveins which pierced the flesh of the world, identified the foci where they bunched thick, spilling their residual charm into the land. He saw the mesh which lay beneath them, the old layers of exotic power which had survived through many Turnings. He saw cracks in that mesh, cracks which led away into darkness. He saw bands of light at the end of that darkness.

He saw stars born and stars grown old and cold; he saw the wheels they made, spinning across the aeons as the worlds they nurtured turned and Turned. Each of these worlds he saw possessed the complexity of his own, and each of them he viewed in a single burst of awareness which left him tumbling in the Cloud's warm, safe light.

All this he saw in the first blink of his ghostly eyes, but then he realized he could see the tiny as clearly as he could see the vast, and he knew where it was he wanted to look.

Vox's eyes roamed the desert of the southern Heartland and found the Towers of Nistor. It was deserted but for the bodies of the two giants, and at first he thought the air over the salt caverns was empty too. Then he saw the tracks which no ordinary dragon could see: wing-tracks, left in the air by flying creatures.

And it is only dragons that fly!

Swiftly he followed their course, understanding in the next eye-blink that what his mind interpreted as tracks was in fact a complex combination of a thousand tiny pertur-bations in the air: scale-dust, residual heat, exhaled breath and, remarkably, the steady shedding of charm. All this dragon spoor must already have been scattered many thousands of wingspans from the line of the course he was now tracking, but the infinite perception of the Cloud – which Vox realized he was *borrowing* – reassembled the puzzle to create this trail of light in the sky.

The trail led to two dragons flying together over the sea. Smoke he recognized at once, but the other . . .

Wraith!

The thought chased through his phantom body like a winter flood, and for an instant he was back with his first love, Choliel. Back on the remote rock tower, watching the Black Dragon take Choliel's head from her body. The promise of revenge he had made then rang clear in his head, all the more loudly when he saw that Wraith appeared to have claimed Smoke – *my Smoke!* – back for his own. The knot tightened, for Wraith had already taken Smoke once before, back in the past which she alone had owned before she had met Vox.

Black wings, huge and indomitable, stroked the air, casting their tremendous shadow across Smoke's back.

Wraith!

Then he faltered. He looked again, for it was *not* Wraith. Strangely, he found it harder to believe the truth than to believe that the Black Dragon had somehow come back from the dead. But the truth was there for him to see and slowly he accepted it. With mounting joy he realized that the mighty black dragon who flew with the one he loved was none other than Wyrm. Wingless Wyrm, flightless dragon, strange companion. Now he had wings wide enough to cast a shadow across the world.

Vox pulled his awareness (*the Cloud's awareness*, he reminded himself) back from the tight focus he had achieved. Instead he found himself focusing on himself, seeking the knot which had bound itself around his heart. *Wraith, Choliel, Smoke, Wyrm, Ocher.* The names whirled round and round like a captive wind, tearing at his soul. *Nistor!*

He looked out from his heart and saw that his new body had no colour, none at all. No hint of pigment marred the clean translucency of his ghostly form. For almost as long as he could remember his scales had borne the purple of the outcast – now that had gone he felt naked . . . yet liberated.

Wraith . . . Choliel.

The knot snapped. Its coils dissolved leaving not nothing but *everything*. Everything was still there – the memory of the murder, the shame of his trial, the terror that Smoke did not truly love him, the jealousy of Wyrm – but now . . .

'Now it's all right,' murmured Vox, retaining sufficient sense of wonder to marvel that his aethereal form had spoken real words.

He looked down again on the two dragons. As he watched they crossed the coast of Western Ocea, approaching high mountains. He closed in on Wyrm again. Those great, black wings. He felt love.

Then the Cloud spoke to him.

'There is a place for vengeance,' it said, its voice soft yet strong, as warm and fearful as a father's. 'But I do not think you need it any more, dragon.'

'No,' whispered Vox. 'No, I don't think I do.'

He found that, as well as being able to speak, he could also cry.

'Listen to me well, dragon,' the voice went on, 'for you are valuable to me. Every one of your kind is valuable to me, though some may doubt it before this day is over. Listen to me well and you will learn of your place in the day of creation. It is more special than most . . . except perhaps one.'

Vox found that he was crying again, but he had no idea why. He did not stop for a very long time.

CHAPTER 26

Under Fire

Fortune was hovering beneath the shield. Directly above him was a circular tear in the fire, the wound inflicted by the tornado. His friends drifted a wingspan or two beneath him, scanning the terrain as he was doing, occasionally glancing back up towards him, awaiting his instructions.

Before them, Scarn's army re-formed itself – literally. Two great strands of squirming flesh crashed together, then separated into individual creatures. They still looked like dragons, but only just. Huge and red, they lumbered into the air, their jagged wings spitting fire, their eyes burning, greasy fluids dripping from their flanks. Each beast was fully twice the size of an average dragon, bigger even than mighty Volley, and it seemed to Fortune that they were growing bigger still. They numbered far too many to count, but it was obvious there were more individuals here than there had been dragons in the Cult.

'Two hundred?' Scoff hazarded, his thoughts clearly mirroring Fortune's.

'Where have they all come from?' wondered Velvet, the tremor in her voice all too apparent.

'I don't know,' answered Fortune tersely. 'But we cannot defeat so many. All of you – come with me!'

So saying he dived to the side, heading for the gap between the bustling monsters and the crater wall. Scoff and Aria followed him immediately, but Volley lunged forwards, straight towards the army.

'What are you doing?' shrieked Velvet. To her horror, Cumber moved after Volley, but the bigger dragon moved with a speed which belied his size and Cumber's claws

352

slipped through clean air. Flipping his white wings out in a passable imitation of Volley's skilful manoeuvre, Cumber followed him down towards the once-dragons. Her face a mask of terror, Velvet turned and pursued Cumber.

'Where's Anchre?' barked Fortune, desperately trying to keep track of the rest of the group, but their red-scaled companion was nowhere to be seen.

'What's to do?' demanded Scoff, his voice cutting through the fog in Fortune's head.

'Look there!' cried Aria simultaneously, her words vying with Scoff's for attention. Her wing picked out four dragons near the far-off glow of the Flame.

'Gossamer!' breathed Fortune.

He looked around again in anguish. Volley was a clean, brown arrow cutting through the air towards the front ranks of the once-dragons. Close behind him were the white lines of Cumber and Velvet. They seemed very far away. 'May the Cloud forgive me,' he howled and surged down towards the gap and away from his friends.

Cumber saw at once what was happening. Volley no more wanted to mount a head-on attack than the rest of them: what he sought was the shortest route to Scarn. Blinded by his desire for revenge he had failed to see the gap which Fortune had located, choosing instead to risk his life in a frontal assault against the army. The reward was a clear line through to the centre of the crater, the Flame – and Scarn.

He'll kill himself trying to avenge Tallow, Cumber thought as he accelerated in his pursuit. Then he cursed as he realized that Velvet was a mere breath behind him.

'Go back!' he bellowed.

'Make me!'

But the opportunity to change their minds had already gone. Their momentum was too great for them to consider retreat. Ahead loomed a veritable wall of red claws and bent horns. Volley was just out of reach; his wide wings sliced sparks out of the air, scattering a trail of tiny explosions in his wake. Cumber and Velvet were forced to squint against this unexpected onslaught.

'What is it?' blurted Velvet, at the same time wondering

why she cared what it was, when only a few wingspans away was a slavering mass of distorted dragon bodies reaching up with hideous, dripping claws.

But Cumber did not reply. He was reaching urgently into his past.

Once, before the turning of the world, Cumber had been a charmed dragon. He had experienced the strange otherworld known as the Realm, the remote place from which fire charm came. He had learned how to pierce the membrane between this world and that, to draw out its magic, to wield it against his enemies.

He looked up at the fire-shield and was reminded of the Realm's translucent membrane. Enough of his charm-sense remained to detect the flow of magic through the shield from its source: the central Flame. He stretched out with his mind, seeking weaknesses, seeking power. He imagined a claw, the claw he had once used to penetrate the Realm, except now he used it to cut a swathe through the shield.

A scream blotted out all sound. Time around him slowed: the wingbeats of both Velvet and Volley juddered and the air grew dark. Even the shield became dull. The Flame itself, however, visible behind the monstrous once-dragons, glowed brighter. It was the Flame that was screaming.

As he touched the shield in his imagination – and therefore touched the Flame – a flow of events became apparent to Cumber, a story. It was a simple story but one which only now did he fully understand . . .

The turning of the world . . . the loss of charm and the abandonment of its seed to the stars . . . the gathering and destruction of the abandoned charm . . . the coalescing of the residue into a hard nugget of light, a burning flame, the Flame.

Charm becomes Flame, but in doing so it changes its essential character.

Hearing it scream, Cumber understood how it had changed.

The Flame has gained awareness. It is sentient now, it wishes to increase its powers, to advance itself. To prevail.

But though it is aware, it is not substantial. Lacking physical form, it cannot manipulate the physical world in the way it wants to. Therefore it relies on others to do its work. It finds agents. It finds dragons, and makes them into something else.

It knows ways to shape minds, and the more it practises the more skilled it becomes. It finds the weak spots, it finds the dark corners. Soon it discovers the power of mind to do evil and it knows it has finally found the key. Working evil, it becomes evil . . . and more.

It becomes Evil.

Cumber blinked his eyes open, surprised to find that he had closed them. The Flame blazed against his widened pupils. In his mind, his imaginary claw maintained contact with the fire-shield and the Flame continued to scream.

'You cannot prevail in this world!' shouted Cumber over the persistent wailing. Around him time continued to stutter forwards in random bursts. His companions' wings moved erratically, flicking from one position to the next without seeming to cross the space between. 'Good will always triumph over evil.'

'But my adversary has not arrived yet!' The voice of the Flame was raw. Cumber's mind felt as though it were being peeled by the sound. 'Do you not think the battle will be rather one-sided?'

Cumber ignored it. He was all too aware of the small distance separating Velvet and Volley and the wall of once-dragons. While the Flame screamed in his head he carried on scratching away at the protective shield.

There was charm there all right, he could sense it, but it was distorted so far beyond what he remembered that it was like tasting badly burned food. *Not burned*, he corrected himself. *Poisoned*. Magic swirled, a bitter blend of ancient spells and the evil ambition of the Flame. He felt it leaching into the claw, infiltrating his mind.

There must be something here I can use! A coil of light closed around his claw and tried to drag him bodily up into the shield. He pulled away, nearly breaking contact before realizing that was what the Flame wanted him to do. *It's still screaming*, he reminded himself. *I'm hurting it*. He plunged back in again, heedless of the clamouring which only he could hear. Something slipped into his thoughts and, against his will, swivelled his head towards his companions.

'They can't both survive,' it whispered. 'Which one would you save?'

He saw Velvet's slender, white body torn apart by snapping red jaws. He blinked and she was whole again.

'She doesn't love you.'

Velvet leaped hungrily on Volley, lashing her tail around his and sliding her body underneath his belly. Volley's back arched and he bit down upon her neck as she opened her mouth in a long, silent scream. Again Cumber blinked and again the vision was banished.

'Or would you rather see the truth?'

Cumber was looking out through Velvet's eyes, looking up at his own body hovering overhead. His scales were white like hers, but they were splattered with red. Hundreds of tiny legs twitched below his flanks, each bearing a single, elongated, venom-dripping claw. His head was golden; he had no eyes.

'This is how a natural dragon sees one touched by charm! Do you really believe her when she tells you she loves you?'

This time Cumber ripped a great chunk of fire out of the shield, sending a shower of tiny flames down upon the waiting army. The volume of the Flame's scream doubled.

'Now!' Cumber's voice boomed. 'Now you will know the power of charm!'

At his command the imaginary claw grew barbs. It reached deep into the shield, located a thousand shreds of charm and hauled them bleeding into the clear air of the crater. The screaming abruptly stopped, but Cumber barely noticed. He looked up and for an instant he actually *saw* the claw, a huge, phantom spike soaked in magic; a massive pulse caused it to swell and then contract with shocking speed. It vanished as swiftly as it had appeared. He dragged the shards of charm into his grasp and held them there as they struggled for freedom. Smoke billowed from his breast and sharp splintering sounds reached his ears – scales cracking, his own.

His contact with the Flame's treacherous mind had stopped the instant he had withdrawn the claw, along with the screaming. He did not regret this. One impression lingered: *it's scared!*

356

Everything about the charm he gripped in his claw felt wrong. In fact, Cumber could scarcely bring himself to think of it as charm at all, so random was its energy, so disruptive were its urges. It was trying hard to rip him in half. Partly by the strength of his will, partly by sheer brute force, he squeezed it together and hurled it down into the ranks of the once-dragons.

Time flung itself forwards again. Velvet chased Volley into the army's closing pincers and was lost from sight. Two breaths later Cumber followed them in and the world around him turned red.

'You've seen it, haven't you, father?'

Aria's words echoed off the rock of the crater wall. They flew fast through deep blue shadow, hugging the contours of the terrain, trying to make themselves invisible to the once-dragons.

'The Cloud? It's all around us now. Up there especially.' Fortune nodded back towards the breach in the shield. The fire was beginning to rotate there, dragged into motion by the tornado.

'Never mind that,' Scoff interrupted. 'Getting tight here.'

And it was. To their left the crater wall reached out with rough outcrops and scarps; to their right the squirming flesh of the once-dragons gave a sudden bulge, spilling a horde of red dragon shapes across their path. They separated, Fortune soaring high while Scoff and Aria ducked below the tumbling bodies. Angry mouths spat fire but they were too fast. Fortune glanced back as they met up again on the other side: the gap through which they had flown had closed up and the newly-formed conscripts to Scarn's army were opening their ragged wings to strike out in pursuit.

'Faster!' he grunted.

Now there was a clear way through to the centre of the crater. Fortune could see beams of light cutting through the dusty air. Tracing them back to their source he saw to his horror that they emanated from the eyes of a red dragon with bright, burning wings: Scarn. They reached first up to the injured shield then swept groundwards again. Where they touched the ground a huge pall of smoke lifted, flecked with tiny sparks. Fortune had no idea what Scarn was doing, but the sight of the smoke terrified him. *Unpredictable*, he remembered with a shudder. They increased their speed.

Cumber's charm struck the once-dragons an instant before he and Velvet did. He had not wanted to create a destructive charm, but the magic's fiery origin had precluded any other form. The charm detonated on impact, sending sharp splinters of flame through the ranks, opening a passage through which they were able to weave their way. All around them writhed the red-scaled bodies of the once-dragons, massed so tightly that they were quite incapable of flight. It was like flying down the throat of a monster.

'There's Volley!' shouted Velvet, spinning on a wingtip and ducking into another corridor of flesh.

Volley was deep inside the monster, near its heart. He confronted a gigantic, many-winged serpent which looked very little like a dragon. Three heads sprouted from a single, sinuous neck. Each head lunged and snapped at Volley, a solitary eye glowing dull blue in the centre of each brow. Volley's jaws opened wide and bit down on the beast's common throat. Black fluid splashed across his face, but he did not pull away even though it made him choke. The monster slumped backwards, melting into the composite structure which had spawned it.

Another monstrosity – this one squat and boasting a huge mouth filled with thousands of minute fangs – erupted from the mountain of flesh and bore down on Volley. He lashed his tail across its broad face and knocked at least half of those vicious tiny teeth from their sockets. They rained across a sea of scales and were absorbed. Partly defanged, the monster grew a tongue studded with barbs which it lashed across Volley's back, drawing a line of blood down as far as his tail. Lowering his horns, Volley struck its bottom jaw, driving it shut and severing the tongue neatly at its root. Again the creature was reconstituted, this time as a virtual copy of the original, three-headed serpent.

Volley backed away, pulling himself into the air. Cumber swooped in behind him, crying, 'How can we defeat such an adversary?'

This time it was Velvet who put down the foe, piercing two of its three eyes with well-placed blows from her claws. It gave a hideous squeal – horribly like that of an infant dragon – and retreated yet again. The three dragons hurried clear of the pulsing body of the army. A flurry of tentacles exploded beneath them but somehow they pulled themselves clear.

Walls of flesh rose around them. Looking down, Cumber saw that the army had swelled even further. Hundreds of bodies writhed against one another, each individual surfacing only briefly before being absorbed back into the underlying mass.

Systematically the mass moved to seal off all lines of escape. Soon the three dragons were isolated in a bowl-shape formed in red flesh and scale. Cumber looked around hopelessly. Velvet and Volley were both bleeding, Volley quite badly. The upper surface of the homogenous army was rising as its mass increased, forcing the dragons up towards the fire-shield. Above them the shield was spinning faster and faster as the tornado ripped into it. Poisoned charm showered across their backs, melting into their scales and filling their minds with evil thoughts.

'Sing, Volley!' shouted Cumber. 'It wants us to fight each other. We must distract ourselves somehow.'

So Volley sang, and his voice thundered through the roar of the fire and the shriek of the gale. Gradually the rain of charm subsided and the dragons shook free the images of violence which had filled their minds.

'I wanted to kill you!' blurted Velvet, rolling her tail across Cumber's back. Her eyes were red and filled with tears.

'I know, my dear. But it wasn't really you.'

It's scared of us, Cumber thought as he reassured Velvet. *And it's weaker than it seems. Why else would it try to trick us when it's got a whole army to simply wipe us out?*

Despite these hopes the army continued to rise towards them. Spine-backed dragons emerged from its upper surface and opened wings covered with claws. Pairs of these mutations blended together to form monstrous hybrids, tooth-winged abominations which took to the air and accelerated towards Cumber and his companions as they hovered trapped just beneath the turmoil of the shield. Velvet screamed.

Anchre appeared from nowhere, startling Fortune so that he nearly struck out at him.

'Where did you come from?' he demanded.

Anchre jerked his head up at the spinning shield. 'I wanted a closer look at what's going on up there.'

'And?' put in Scoff.

'You were right to send Wemp and the mirror-dragons to the Flame, Fortune,' said Anchre. 'They'll be perfectly positioned there.'

'For what?' Scoff asked.

'The counter-attack.'

'And the shield?'

'Look.'

They looked, and what they saw caused them to slew to the side, taking temporary shelter beneath an overhanging canopy of rock.

The entire underside of the shield was in motion. The wound made by the tornado was a ragged bolt behind the mountain of Scarn's army: this was the centre towards which countless streams of fire charm were being sucked. The Flame itself was distorted by the force – indeed, it seemed as though it would shortly be pulled from whatever roots were holding it at the crater's centre. The rotation of the fire was at its greatest immediately around the base of the tornado. As they watched it increased its speed tenfold.

The Flame glowed unbearably bright. Before Fortune looked away he actually saw shreds of fire peeled from its outer surface to join the whirling shield. He heard a tremendous ripping sound, almost a scream, and fancied it was the voice of the Flame . . .

Then the Flame simply gave up.

The ripping sound ended with an ear-splitting shriek as the last filaments of charm were cast free and the Flame was stripped of its shroud of fire. At once the true power of the tornado was revealed. With dizzying speed the great sheet of fire charm was sucked across the crater and gathered into the jaws of the gale. Revealed behind its trailing edge was the dull grey of the storm-clouds, perforated by occasional flashes of lightning. Into the whirlwind the shield was dragged, spitting fire as its bulk was compressed into the narrow spout. Then it flowed up the funnel, which shone brilliant blue as it consumed the magic, and disappeared into the giant cloud which filled the sky from horizon to horizon. One final bead of charm chased fitfully up into the sky and then it was gone. All that remained was the Flame and the shining tower of flesh.

The storm gave one last crash of thunder then the tornado withdrew into its belly. A breath or two later the clouds began to rise with unnatural speed. A dry wind beat them to the side as they ascended and the first hints of sunlight started to bore through the disintegrating fabric.

No longer trapped against the shield, Cumber led Velvet and Volley high in pursuit of the storm as the squirming army fell back in confusion. From behind the Flame there rose a wall of glittering wings – the mirror-dragons, led by Wemp, ready to pitch themselves against their unpredictable foe. Beneath the Flame Scarn and his prisoners waited.

Satisfied that his friends were safe for the moment, Fortune led Aria, Scoff and Anchre towards the centre of the Last Circle. A shallow dome of land rose there, at the top of which stood Gossamer, her white scales brilliantly lit by the Flame which hovered perhaps ten trees above her. He could see no visible means by which she was being held, but assumed that Scarn had in some way restrained her. To her side crouched Jevell and a slumped body which instinct told him had to be Rarch. Scarn himself was prowling around them, those unearthly beams of light marking the direction of his gaze.

A glance upwards showed him that Cumber and the others had rejoined the mirror-dragons. For the moment Scarn's grotesque army – or was it the Flame's? – was quiet. Fortune wondered why.

Then he slowed his speed and observed his enemy. Scarn had paused and was scanning the ground before him, sweeping his luminous gaze back and forth over a seemingly unremarkable patch of dust. Fortune alighted a

361

short distance from the dome. Scarn continued to sweep his head from side to side, paying his adversaries no heed. He was perhaps fifteen wingspans from where Fortune stood.

'Wait here,' Fortune muttered.

'He won't listen,' warned Scoff, knowing what Fortune was about to do. But Fortune ignored the advice and stepped slowly forwards until he had halved the distance to Scarn. Still the fire-winged dragon did not look up.

Fortune looked beyond Scarn to Gossamer. She and her mother were watching intently. Gossamer stretched out a wing and deliberately struck a tiny splinter of charm from the cylindrical wall which held her captive. A ghostly ring of light chased around its circumference and Fortune nodded to show that he understood both the power and the dimension of her prison. He returned his attention to Scarn and found himself staring straight into blue fire. Scarn had looked up. The touch of his eyes was like the sun on a summer's day – warm and soothing. At any other time Fortune might have considered it pleasant.

'You know what I have come for, Scarn,' said Fortune, striving to keep his voice calm.

'A dragon!' exclaimed Scarn, runnels of fire dripping from his tongue as he spoke. Fortune squinted into the glare of his eyes, barely able to make out his features. 'We are becoming a rarity, you and I.'

'Speak for yourself!' retorted Fortune.

Scarn leaned forward conspiratorially. The intensity of the light in his eyes lessened somewhat, allowing Fortune a clearer view of his face. His smile was chilling. 'Between you and me, dragon, I don't believe the Flame is quite sure what to make of our sort.' He nodded at the unnatural contours of the army. 'A dreadful mess, if you ask me.'

Fortune said nothing. He had not expected this. Was this some ruse or was Scarn daring to defy the power which floated above him? Who was the master, dragon or fire?

Scarn went on. 'You see, dragon, what we come to is this: our kind belongs to the old world. There is no place for dragons in a world of nature, that much has been clear to me for many years. Surely it is clear to you. So we have a choice.'

362

'And what choice is that, Scarn?'

'We can watch ourselves die. Or we can escape.'

'Escape? Where to?'

Scarn cackled. 'Wouldn't you like to know, dragon?' Above him the Flame flashed angry tongues of fire up into the sky. The cloud was thinning rapidly and presently the sun broke through, casting a swathe of gold across the crater. Beside the sun loomed the resplendent disc of the broken comet. A white halo surrounded it – all that was visible of its tail as it plunged directly towards the waiting world. A faint streak of light high in the sky showed the path of its parent body; already it was distancing itself from the events it had initiated.

'If it is escape you crave, why take prisoners?' demanded Fortune. 'Where is the need for sacrifice now, Scarn, if you have rejected the Flame which brought you here? Let them go, Scarn, and go yourself if that is what you desire.'

'Foolish! No dragon can reject the power of the Flame.' Amazingly, Scarn lowered one eyelid in an exaggerated wink. The corresponding beam of light blinked out then reappeared as he opened both eyes again. He lowered his voice to a whisper. 'Mind you, I don't think it's as prepared as I would have been in its position.'

Fortune shook his head, unable to track Scarn's thoughts. Surely the Flame was aware of what he was saying – was he deliberately goading it? Again the question occurred to him: *who is in control here?*

Something brushed his flank and he jumped. Then Aria's voice rang out next to him, clear and composed.

'I will gladly take my mother's place, Scarn, if you will have me back.'

Scarn's eyes narrowed; the beams became flattened rays jostling their way through the dusty air. 'I am content with my choice, dragon.'

'I have a name!'

Scarn waved one of his fiery wings nonchalantly. 'Names have little use. Could you find names in the middle of that throng?' Again he indicated the army. 'They will defeat your pathetic band, you know.'

'And the Flame?'

Scarn laughed uproariously. 'Its failure will be glorious! In its failure lies my future, dragon. When all are blinded by the lighting of the sky, none will think to look in the shadows. But that is where I will be, dragon, making my way through to what lies beyond this world: making my escape!'

'He's mad,' muttered Fortune, but Aria shook her head.

'No, what he says may be true – why is the Flame tolerating all this? Why doesn't it strike him down where he stands?'

'Where does he hope to escape to, Aria? Where *is* there to go?'

She shook her head. 'I don't know. But I think Wyrm does.'

'*Wyrm?* How can he possibly . . . ? Is he *here*?'

Aria smiled radiantly. 'Not yet, father. But he's coming!'

The beams of light vanished from Scarn's eyes. The sudden absence of heat was like a gust of cold wind blowing across Fortune's body. Scarn turned and marched up the dome towards Gossamer.

Unpredictable, thought Fortune suddenly.

'The time has come to make up your mind!' roared Scarn. Fire cascaded from between his teeth, sizzling where it struck the ground. 'Will you stay and face your fate . . . or will you turn and flee?'

'Who is he talking to?' whispered Fortune.

'The day of creation is upon us!' Scarn went on. 'There can be only one survivor. Who shall it be?'

He looked directly upwards into the sky. Light and fire boiled from his eyes and his mouth, illuminating the dissipating clouds and punching up into the face of the descending comet. The Last Circle was filled with light now: the light of the Flame, of Scarn, of sun and comet, all combined to create a massive, all-pervading luminescence which banished shadow. Everything seemed flat and clean, ready to be moulded anew.

Ready for the lighting of the sky.

PART FOUR

THE LIGHTING OF THE SKY

CHAPTER 27

Battle

Scarn's gaze locked on to the Flame. At last it was clear in which direction his words had been aimed. His challenge to fight or flee had been directed at the Flame itself, and if any dragon doubted that the huge, floating pyre possessed consciousness then it was in the very next instant that those doubts were dispelled.

'Back, little dragon!'

The voice was like a detonation. A ring of vapour sped outwards across the crater, a fragmentary band of fog created by the sudden shock wave. It evaporated swiftly, leaving silence.

'So you don't need dragons to speak for you any more,' came Scarn's taunt.

'Silence!' The voice of the Flame launched more fog rings through the air, each syllable creating its own, unique code of vapour. *'The Flame needs nothing!'*

Scoff sidled up to Fortune. 'Not true,' he murmured.

'It needs Scarn,' affirmed Aria.

'No,' said Fortune. 'It just needs a dragon – any dragon. Scarn is playing a dangerous game.'

The Flame was changing its appearance. Where once it had been simply fire, a random dance of fiery tendrils emanating from empty air some distance above the centre of the crater, now it took on a more defined shape. Two long arms of flame reached up from behind it, curving forwards to make a pair of horns. Cavities opened around its circumference, snapping mouths which constantly formed and re-formed, never resting. A brighter patch appeared high up, a rotating bulge which roamed across its fiery skin like a hurricane; it might have been an eye.

'Tell me why I should not kill you, dragon.'

At once Scarn pointed skywards with one blazing wing. Fire dripped from its yellow tip. 'You can see for yourself. Your adversary is nearly here. You will need me when you are finally defeated.'

Another shock wave, this one made not of fog but of fire – brilliant blue fire – pulsed across the crater. *'The Flame does not know the meaning of defeat!'*

The clouds were gone now. The sky was totally clear. The comet drowned the sun, a blinding, onrushing disc poised in the brilliant blue.

Fortune became suddenly aware of a network of lines in the air. They crystallized before him like a spider's web materializing beneath the dew. Somehow he understood that this network had been present all along, but only now was he able to perceive it: it was the tangle of charm that joined the Flame to its army, the magical mesh by which it controlled the rogue once-dragons of the Cult. But no sooner did the mesh become visible than it began to fall apart.

One by one the lines of force pulled tight until they snapped. One by one the connections between the Flame and its minions broke into streamers of glittering dust. The Flame grew more luminous; as it withdrew what was left of the mesh back into its fiery body, tiny holes appeared in the mountain of flesh pulsing sluggishly on the far side of the crater. Then the mountain began to slide, and the composite army spilled across the ground. The seething flesh lost its mutability and individual forms started to lock themselves together. Mutant dragons and long-limbed, wide-eyed monstrosities limped forth; all manner of ghastly creatures condensed from the greater mass – the final manifestation of what the Flame had once controlled, and which it now rejected.

Soon the flesh-mountain had broken apart completely. In its place there crawled a more conventional – if hideous – army: rank upon rank of armoured beasts ready to do battle against the dragons who had invaded the Flame's sacred place. Rejected they may have been, but still they were loyal to their former master. Wings were gathered and those creatures that could fly took to the air. A tremendous hissing rose with them, and from their mouths burst livid blue fire.

'The Flame is cutting its links with this world,' said Anchre, grabbing Fortune's wing to attract his attention. 'It still needs its servants to do its work, but it will abandon every last one of them if it finds itself unable to win against the Cloud.'

Flame against Cloud, thought Fortune. He realized that no dragon had yet put the conflict in such simple terms. *Evil against good – only one can prevail.*

Splinters of fire were jetting out from the underside of the Flame, scorching the thin soil of the central dome. They landed dangerously near the dragons sheltering there. Jevell retreated downslope, trying to drag Rarch with her. Gossamer was still trapped.

'Scoff, Anchre!' barked Fortune. 'Help Jevell. Aria – let's save your mother!'

Above and to one side of the seething Flame hovered Cumber, Velvet, Volley and the mirror-dragons. The air was hot and bright; the comet was like a hole burnt into the sky, and it grew larger with every breath they took.

'Get away now if you want to!' shouted Cumber over the roar of the Flame. 'There's still time.'

'This is our fight as much as it is yours,' snapped Wemp by way of reply.

'This is a fight for all dragons!' added Velvet, her eyes fixed on the tide of distorted, red bodies rising beneath them. 'This is the battle for our place in the world. We fight for ourselves and our friends.'

'Our friends,' agreed Volley.

The air was full of red bodies now, a veritable tidal wave of fire-spitting dragons, their ranks confused with other, stranger creatures. There flew a copy of the three-headed serpent which had so nearly claimed Volley's life; there a squat, many-winged beast which seemed all spike and spine, with no discernible head at all. The few monsters remaining on the ground joined in a headlong rush across the crater floor to attack Fortune and the others. Cumber faltered, an urge to warn his friend pulling his wings close in anticipation of a dive. Then red wings punctured the air before his face and he was dragged into the heart of the battle.

At once a set of claws raked down Cumber's flank, drawing blood. He spun round and bit hard into the neck of his attacker, flesh spongy and loose in his mouth; black fluid spilled into the air and the beast dropped like a boulder. Cumber lashed his tail against another and was heartened to see that it too plummeted towards the ground. Would they all be this easy to kill?

A yelp from Velvet brought him forging through a line of bodies to butt away a large creature with long, spine-covered wings and a single, bloodshot eye. It shrieked and fell upon him. Recovering quickly, Velvet bore down on the monster, jabbing at its throat with her claws and battering it with her tail until it dropped back, nursing its wounds. She touched Cumber briefly before another wave of the once-dragons closed in, snapping at them with fire-soaked jaws.

Volley was faring rather worse. Nightmarish creatures surrounded him, taunting him with narrow tongues of fire. Already badly wounded, flames licked at his flanks and belly, burning him. He lashed out with his tail, but weakly.

One of the creatures – an enormous once-dragon with yellow teeth and great plates of bone jutting from its back – came closer. Flames sprouted from its nostrils as it tilted its head down to appraise its victim. Volley glared back, ready to die.

The once-dragon inhaled, paused, then hurled its fire at Volley. Suddenly a mirrored wing was thrust into the path of the fire, and the fire was reflected back upon itself so that it consumed its creator. An unearthly scream split the air and the once-dragon turned over, blackened and misshapen. Its wings fluttered uselessly as it fell, blundering against its comrades in its short journey to the ground. Volley had just enough time to register that a mirror-dragon had saved his life before Wemp was gathering him up and herding him out of the circle of torturers.

'We must regroup!' Wemp shouted, circling behind

Cumber and Velvet and bullying them backwards out of the mêlée. A wave of silver-scaled dragons dropped down and created a wall of wings in the air. Dazzled by the reflections, the front ranks of the army blundered sideways and for a breath or too all was confusion. Wemp and Cumber seized the opportunity to gain still more height and distance themselves from the battle.

After a hurried consultation with two of his comrades, Wemp turned to Cumber and announced, 'Leave this to us!' Both Cumber and Velvet began to protest but Wemp waved them silent. 'I'm not being heroic. We're heavily outnumbered and it'll take some fancy flying to outwit these monsters. But fancy flying's what we do best, and we'll do it better without you three messing up the formation.'

'But . . .' Cumber blurted.

'No time for "buts". Get down there where you can do more good.'

Velvet gasped as they all looked towards the ground. The group of earthbound once-dragons – wingless every one of them – had virtually encircled the dome. Fortune and the others were trapped between the advance and a canopy of fire which the Flame had thrown over their heads.

Cumber looked at Volley and saw that he was about to dive. He looked at Velvet and saw her nod once, briskly. He looked at Wemp and saw the determination in his face.

'Very well, Wemp. But I won't say goodbye.'

'See you soon,' called the mirror-dragon as the three dragons rolled sideways and began to accelerate towards the ground. Then he looked back across the faces he had known for most of his life. 'Well, dragons. Let's put on a show they'll sing about for years to come!'

Cumber had little hope that they would make much of a difference. Fortune's band – like their own – was greatly outnumbered; what could they possibly do against such odds?

'There!' he cried, indicating a thin place in the ranks of the once-dragons. They had died easily enough in the air; perhaps they would die as easily on the ground. Velvet turned with him but Volley flew straight on. His eyes were wide and horribly empty.

'Volley!' Velvet shouted, but already he was a long way off course. They could see his target – it was Scarn, naturally.

Rage had restored his strength. He bellowed, 'Murderer!' as he pulled his wings in tight. Scarn looked up curiously, flapping his own burning wings casually at his sides. Fire flickered where flight membranes should have been stretched taut, creating a ghostly yellow aura.

Volley opened his mouth and bared his teeth. His dive flattened out; vapour streamed from his outstretched claws, dyed red with the blood leaking from countless wounds in his body. He looked ready to embrace the dragon he had marked as his enemy. Scarn closed his eyes and spread his wings. Abruptly they doubled in size, spraying sparks across the dusty arena. He opened his eyes and two beams of solid blue light punched a hole in each of Volley's wings. Volley screamed but did not slow down.

It was Anchre who saved Scarn, though Fortune was only a breath behind him. Anchre leaped up and hooked claws with Volley, a colossal momentum wrenching him clear into the air. Fortune dropped square in front of them both and wrestled them, spinning, to the ground. They landed with a great thud a mere wingspan from where Scarn stood growling quietly. The blue light which streamed from Scarn's eyes mingled with the canopy which the Flame had unfurled, connecting and disconnecting with the evil charm therein. He closed his eyes once more and the light was extinguished.

'This is not the time, Volley,' panted Fortune as his friend struggled to free himself.

'Let me go!'

'Not until I know your intentions.'

'You know them. I want that monster dead!' Volley had at last pulled himself free and was standing before Fortune, his breast heaving like Scarn's.

'Trust me, Volley,' Fortune replied, looking deep into the big dragon's eyes. 'Trust me as Tallow always trusted me.'

The mention of Tallow's name seemed to pacify Volley a little. He drew in a long, deep breath and let it out slowly, the air hissing through his teeth. Then he stretched out his neck and spat in the dust before Scarn's claws.

Scarn smiled, and for a moment Fortune half-expected Volley to go for him again. But the big mountain dragon stood his ground and waited, his eyes reddened but reassuringly clear. Then Scarn spoke.

'Soon none of this will matter. Soon the Last Circle will be a place of ashes, as it deserves to be.'

The Flame will rise from those ashes, dragon! The voice thundered out again, crackling with the noise of the canopy of fire through which it was heard. *'Can you say the same of yourself?'*

Scarn waved one elongated wing dismissively. 'Take no notice of it,' he said, as though the Flame were some unruly infant. 'Your choice is simple: stay and die, or flee and live . . . for a time, at least.'

'We will go,' answered Fortune. 'All of us, together. *All* of us.'

'She stays,' said Scarn mildly. He indicated Gossamer.

The comet was all-consuming now. The sun had vanished, eclipsed by the greater light of the falling star.

Fortune felt a great tension leave him. He bunched his limbs and made ready to leap upon Scarn.

'Look out!' cried Anchre.

The army fell upon them, knocking Volley and Anchre to the ground and lifting Aria into the air on a wave of busy limbs. Scarn turned his back and walked slowly up the incline towards Gossamer's prison. A single beam projected from one of his eyes pierced the invisible wall and he was inside the cylinder of charm. The shield closed behind him with a faint crackle. He opened his blazing wings, obscuring Gossamer from view. Fortune felt hot breath on his back and turned to face a river of fire.

Wemp had the advantage of altitude, but that was all. He planned to use it to its full extent, however.

The mirror-dragons were outnumbered perhaps ten to one. The bank of flying creatures rising towards them seemed huge and impenetrable, but therein lay its weakness – or so Wemp judged. Where once the mutants had existed as unstable elements within a greater body, now they were clearly defined as individuals, and each of them was vulnerable. That made them afraid. So they clung together still; that made them clumsy.

The mirror-dragons too were afraid, but they were anything but clumsy.

'They die easily!' shouted Wemp as he led half his troupe into a shallow dive. 'We do not!'

By splitting his forces Wemp immediately confused his enemies. The leading edge of the army of once-dragons began to bunch and stumble in the air, and a series of scuffles broke out as they blundered into each other. Amazingly, several bodies fell away towards the ground; even Wemp had not imagined they would be this disordered.

His attack was a feint. Having covered only half the distance to the army Wemp led his dragons away in a wide curve to rejoin the others high up above the crater.

'They've lost ten already!' cried a dragon from behind him. 'And we didn't do anything!'

'We were lucky,' warned Wemp. 'I doubt we'll manage it twice.'

In fact they managed it three more times before some intelligence began to filter through the ranks of the once-dragons. The series of feints and swoops drew the army first this way then that, and each time the bewilderment thus caused set off any amount of minor skirmishes. Bodies fell, many of them ripped horribly, some still twitching in agony, dreadful evidence that loyalty to the Flame did not translate into loyalty for comrades. The final attempt resulted in little more than a scuffle and Wemp decided that they had played this unexpected advantage as many times as they were able.

Still, simply by taunting their enemy, the mirror-dragons of Ocea had removed perhaps fifty of their opponents from the battle arena. And all without striking a single blow. Blows would be needed soon, however, Wemp knew that for certain.

Something was happening in the heart of the red army. It seemed that they were capable of making decisions after all. A spire formed itself – like an inverted facsimile of the tornado – as a line of once-dragons rose from the ranks. For the most part they were small and long-winged, bearing curved, dangling claws. Their heads were stretched horribly, so that their jaws met in a point at the end. Their eyes were black slits, utterly without expression.

Wemp considered this new development briefly, then barked, 'Light and Shade!'

At once the mirror-dragons leaped into action, their wings moving in perfect synchronization as they adopted the formation they had practised so often. For a long time they had performed without an audience; now they had an adversary instead. Wemp glanced up at the dazzling circle of the onrushing comet and smiled grimly. Normally they just used the sun for this manoeuvre – the comet should make it work like a dream.

They had already confused the once-dragons with the dazzling trick, but it worked just as well the second time. Ten mirror-dragons set up a fan of wings carefully positioned to reflect the light of the comet (much brighter than that of the sun) into the eyes of their attackers. Wemp led a second team into the shadowy air on the opposite side of the rising force while the rest hovered behind the reflective wall, out of sight.

As a showpiece, 'Light and Shade' was designed to surprise an audience by hiding one group of dragons behind the reflected light and another in the dark region of contrasting shadow. At the crucial moment both would leap forth, raising gasps of wonder.

The moment came, marked not by any spoken signal but by the patient practising of the skill at which great Tallow had excelled: counting wingbeats. Each of the groups had a leader, and at the critical moment he fell away, prompting his fellows to begin their own part in the choreography.

The wall of wings collapsed; the reflected light blinked out, leaving the once-dragons virtually blind. From behind the collapsing wall sped half of Wemp's force, while from the air behind the once-dragons surged Wemp himself and his band from the shadows. They met with a tremendous crash of claw and thunder of voice, crushing the rising army between them.

In this way, the great battle of the Last Circle truly began.

*　　　*　　　*

On the ground too the fighting had started in earnest. As in the sky, the odds were stacked in favour of the once-dragons, but on the ground they lumbered with even less co-ordination than their airborne allies, and they were slow enough for the more agile dragons to dodge. But there were so many of them!

The first task Fortune set himself was to lure them away from the dome. Scoff, having reached the place where Jevell was watching over Rarch, had been joined by Velvet; between them they were fending off a small contingent of the once-dragons. Several red bodies lay in the dust and Fortune was confident they would win through.

He leaped over the river of fire which threatened to burn him where he stood and flew over the ground army. Suddenly Cumber was at his side.

'You see that mark on the far side of the crater?' panted Cumber.

'Yes. What of it?'

'We want to go there. Draw the enemy there.'

Without further explanation Cumber swooped low, lashing out with his claws and drawing rich, black blood from the head of one of the writhing monsters. Anchre and Volley joined them then, and together they buzzed the once-dragons, taunting and jeering, slashing and striking, leading them down the slope and away from the vicinity of the Flame.

'We have the advantage of flight,' gasped Cumber. 'But we cannot win using that alone. There are too many of them.'

'You have a plan?' demanded Anchre.

'We'll see.'

They made swift progress across the dry bowl of the Last Circle; though clumsy, the earthbound once-dragons were fast. Once Anchre was nearly dragged down by a out-stretched tentacle attached to a spitting, spinning ball of flesh, but his friends grabbed him and hauled him clear. The monster dangled from his tail briefly before falling back into the throng.

The dark blemish which Cumber had pointed to turned out to be a long crack running along the ground and halfway up the crater wall. It was black, a deep crevasse just wide enough for a dragon to fly into, should he choose to do so.

'Shelter?' asked Fortune, surprised.

'No. Get *them* down there,' cried Cumber as they drew near. 'And keep them there!'

So saying he turned on his tail and accelerated back towards the Flame.

Fortune increased his speed and reached the perimeter of the army. Volley and Anchre followed. They dived low before the front ranks and led them over the edge of the crevasse. Though the sides were steep, the entrance was a shallow ramp. Sheer walls rose around them and it grew dark. Outcrops of rock bumped against the wings of the flying dragons and they faltered.

'If we land we're dead!' warned Anchre.

'Then we fly!' answered Fortune. Then, under his breath, he added. 'Well, Cumber, I hope you know what you're doing!'

Teeth clashed a claw's-width beneath his belly. The monsters were climbing over each other, trying to reach up to their adversaries. Already a few were beginning to drift back towards the ramp.

Cumber felt a certain calmness descend as he flew back. The crater floor was deserted, and he could almost imagine the Last Circle as it must once have been – a tranquil place, a sanctuary from the troubles of the world.

Now we've brought the troubles of the world here.

He looked into the light of the comet and tried to judge how close it was to falling to earth. He could not even begin to guess.

Today, though, oh yes – today.

He looked back at the knot in the sky – the battle between Wemp's forces and those of the Flame. Mirrors glittered and wave upon wave of brilliant red wings moved first forwards then fell back. He could no more tell who was winning than he knew when the new star would fall.

The Flame loomed before him, unchanged from when he had last seen it. Horns of fire still curved around its crest; dark mouths still roved its flanks; its approximation of an eye still floated high above the ground, seeing all. It was awesome – only now did Cumber fully appreciate the depth of power, of history even, which had gone into its creation.

The Flame turned its eye towards him.

'*You mean me ill, dragon!*' The voice came unexpectedly, a physical blast which knocked Cumber back in the air.

Good. It still has a temper.

'Naturally,' he replied.

There was a pause, during which time Cumber slowed his approach until he was hovering before the Flame. He could feel its tremendous heat. Half his world now was a curve of blue fire. He was dimly aware of Scoff and Velvet looking up at him from below; Gossamer and Scarn he could not see, for they were obscured by the fire.

'You see,' Cumber went on, struggling to keep his voice steady, 'I don't believe you have any real power in this world.'

Another ominous pause.

'The power of charm – especially fire charm – has always been inextricably linked with the power of dragons. Without dragons to do your work, you are nothing. Without their belief in your power, you are nothing. In short, you yourself are nothing.'

The fire boiled and Cumber retreated from a pulse of superheated air which exploded across his body.

'*You dare to taunt me? Do you believe yourself invulnerable as your pathetic brother does? Then you are as misguided as he!*'

'Prove it then!' retorted Cumber. 'If you are not nothing, show me your power.'

For an instant he thought it was going to work exactly as he had planned. The eye of the Flame expanded and grew white-hot. It bulged, and Cumber prepared to duck away from the blast of fire which would inevitably ensue. But it did not come. The eye darkened again and the Flame chuckled, a dreadful, barren rumble.

'*The Flame has no need of proof. Not if faith is all, as you suggest.*'

Cumber glanced behind him. The bolt of energy he had been anticipating would have struck the crevasse dead-centre. Even if he had not managed to dodge it his burning body would scarcely have dampened its power: nothing would have survived the Flame's tantrum. But would Fortune have known it was coming? Would he have got out in time?

'Of course he would,' he muttered. 'That dragon's instinct defies belief.'

He weighed the various risks he was taking and began to shake uncontrollably.

'Scared, dragon?' mused the Flame. 'You have good reason to be. For you there will be no escape.'

Then, at last, Cumber saw it. He saw *everything*. And he saw what he had to do.

'No escape,' he repeated, trying to disguise the trembling of his voice. 'Then there is after all something you don't know.'

'What?' Suspicion, naked and hungry.

Cumber had no desire to waste time. Fortune and the others could be dead already.

'Just this. Scarn seeks a way off the skin of this world, just as you will when you are beaten down by the Cloud. But he has found a way that is a lot easier than yours.'

He turned, closed his wings and opened his throat into the loudest shout he had ever uttered.

'FORTUNE!'

Cumber fell like a rock. Behind him the Flame turned pure white. Its outer edges swelled and fragmented, then a beam of light parted the air. It smashed into the ground and ripped a swathe of disruption across the entire radius of the Last Circle until it struck the crevasse into which Fortune had led the army. There was a sound like an earthquake, then the earthquake came.

Fortune saw the Flame turn white and knew that Cumber's plan had worked. He thumped his wings against the still air of the crevasse and forced Anchre and Volley clear of the lip of the narrow gorge. The air around them was white now. In fact, it seemed the whole world had turned white and for an instant Fortune thought the comet had fallen. He hesitated.

Then he heard his name on the scalding wind and knew it was not that time, not yet.

'FORTUNE . . .'

Cumber's voice was thrown across the crater by the blast of charm from the Flame. It fired his wings again and he climbed with the others into the radiance above the beam of charmed light.

The Flame's wrath reached the crevasse and the ground shook. In the space of time it took Fortune to blink the crevasse closed, crushing the entire ground-army in its jaws. The light flickered then vanished. A low shroud of dust scurried over the new scar. The trembling of the ground died away. An eerie silence descended.

CHAPTER 28

Escape Routes

The white scales on his back were scorched almost black where the Flame's beam of energy had seared them. One of his wing membranes was perforated, the ragged holes cauterized by the fire charm which had made them. Velvet tried to tend to his wounds but Cumber shrugged her off, telling her not to fuss.

'It's very simple,' he explained to Fortune and the others. 'Scarn wants to leave our world – quite why I don't know but that's neither here nor there – not yet anyway. The Flame has also decided to leave, but only if it is defeated by the Cloud. Good defeats Evil: Evil flees, do you see? Now, the Flame has hidden *its* escape route far away where it hopes the Cloud will not find it until it is too late. All I did was to suggest to it that *Scarn's* escape route is right here.'

'The crevasse!' exclaimed Fortune.

'Yes! I had hoped just to anger the Flame into firing a bolt of charm into the crevasse to destroy the army. Unfortunately it proved more a master of its temper than I had anticipated. But then it started talking about escape and suddenly I had it! I suddenly knew where the Flame's escape route actually was, and I knew that the last thing it would tolerate was a second route right where the Cloud could make use of it. Right here, in the Last Circle. As soon as I suggested it, the Flame was so angry and so *afraid* that it closed up the crevasse without even investigating it properly – which I'm glad it didn't, of course. After all, it was only a hole in the ground!'

'So where does the Flame really plan to make its escape?' demanded Velvet impatiently.

'Mahl,' breathed Fortune, suddenly understanding.

'Yes,' agreed Cumber. 'Mahl indeed. That's where the Flame originally came from – or a part of it at least – and that's *exactly* where that tunnel of smoke was heading back to when Wist flew into it. I'm sure of it: Mahl is where it will go if the Cloud is victorious.'

'And where will it go from Mahl?'

Cumber shrugged. 'I don't know. That's the surprise.'

'Need an escape route ourselves before long,' interrupted Scoff suddenly. He poked his wing at the sky. 'Falling comets. Best stay out of their way. Old dragon lore.'

'Scoff's right,' agreed Fortune. 'But there's still work to do here before we can leave.'

They gathered around the invisible cylinder of Gossamer's prison. Scarn stood motionless beside her, his head lifted into the light of the Flame. Trails of blue light drifted to and from his eyes, linking with tendrils of fire which the Flame extended down towards him. He seemed in a trance, absorbed in some unholy communion.

'You must leave me,' said Gossamer sadly. 'It is a day of sacrifice.'

'Then let it be Scarn,' insisted Fortune.

Gossamer shook her head. 'A dragon of the Cloud must die, if the evil of the Flame is to be cast down.'

Fortune scratched his claws against the transparent charm of Gossamer's prison. 'This prison was made by the Flame, not by the Cloud,' he said.

A pattern was beginning to form itself in his head.

He turned to his friend. 'Cumber, do you think Wemp can win against those monstrosities?'

The sky was alive still with the clamour of battle. Bodies fell to the ground. Most of them were red, stained with black ichor; some were metallic, shining like mirrors. Cumber shook his head. 'The odds are too great, despite what Wemp said.'

'Then help him. No more dragons should die in this world. Aria, stay with me and Jevell. The rest of you – go to war!'

Fortune astonished himself as he said this, yet he was even more astonished when his companions obeyed without question. It was Cumber who led them into the sky, barking orders and refining their formation. A cramp of terror seized Fortune as he wondered if he had sent them to their deaths.

Yet he believed he had not.

There was a way. A pattern. He could not see it properly, not yet, but it was there and he knew that this was the first stroke of the wing on the way to discovering its true nature. He appraised the dragons who remained with him on the dome of dusty rock: Jevell . . . her daughter, Gossamer . . . her daughter, Aria. Himself and the catatonic Rarch.

He discounted the male presence. It was the three females – each a mother, each a daughter – who had gripped his imagination. *Family* was what was here in the Last Circle, family and . . . *continuity*.

Suddenly Jevell gasped. She had been bending over Rarch, holding her face close against his mouth. Now she bolted upright, her eyes wide.

'He isn't breathing. Someone help me!'

Gossamer rushed to the barrier, glancing against it and smearing luminous charm across its skin. Aria held Jevell while Fortune lifted old Rarch's head gently clear of the ground. Contrary to what Jevell had said Fortune could in fact detect the faintest murmur of breath from between those cracked, red lips. Then, slowly, Rarch's eyes, which had been wide open all the time they had been here, closed. They opened again, slowly.

Gossamer sobbed as she saw the glint of new light in her father's eyes. Even from here she could see the change. She looked up into the face of the comet, then back down at Rarch. His eyes were dark and ancient, yet in them she saw light and life and the movement of his soul.

'Father!' she sobbed. He did not move, but his eyes moistened and she knew that he had returned to them.

'I saw . . . many things,' Rarch croaked. Jevell stood trembling in her grand-daughter's embrace, not daring to believe.

'Hush,' whispered Fortune, but Rarch shook his head, imperceptibly.

'Many things . . . your friend . . . is in the light. He is coming. I saw such beautiful things, such beautiful wings . . . I saw . . .'

Fortune glanced at Gossamer and saw her agony. No

longer was she content in her prison: now she was thumping the invisible wall with her wings, not caring that each blow scraped skin from their membranes. Fortune remembered how Scoff had once been imprisoned by Wraith in a similar cell . . . and the thought brought with it a shred of an idea.

'You must go . . . all of you,' Rarch was saying. 'None of you are needed here now . . . escape . . . that is what . . . escape . . .'

'He's right!' screamed Gossamer. 'Just go, Fortune. All of you . . . Aria, mother! Leave me here and save yourselves. It is the will of the Cloud!' She was quite beside herself now, tearing at the ground as though she might dig her way out through the rock. Scarn sat silently behind her, oblivious to all that was going on around him.

'No . . .' breathed Rarch. A thin line of blood traced a path between the scales beneath his jaw. 'Not you, dear Gossamer . . . the end of your line . . . you are a part . . . not the end . . .'

'What does he mean?' quavered Jevell.

Fortune found his gaze locked with that of Aria.

Rarch's last words were for his mate.

'Be strong . . . my dear Jevell . . . free our family . . . and mourn him for me . . .'

There, in the heart of the Last Circle, filled with the light of the comet and the presence of the Cloud, Rarch died.

'What did he mean?' echoed Gossamer. It would be a long time before she understood that her father was really dead. Until then she focused on his final words. 'What did he mean: "not you"?'

'Just that,' replied Fortune. 'It's not you, my dear. Now, stand back. I think I've a way to get you out of there.'

The sky was filled with blood.

Scales floated on blasts of air and fire; dragons tumbled and strange, deformed creatures dealt blows upon their enemies and allies alike. All sense of order had left the battle. Even the tight formations of the mirror-dragons had disintegrated into the mêlée.

'Those monsters are killing as many of their own kind as

they are of ours,' exclaimed Velvet as they neared the edge of the conflict.

'Then let's help them out!' shouted Volley.

A tight unit, they plunged into the nearest bank of red bodies and fought their way through, relying on surprise to take them clear before the enemy knew what was happening. In this way they knocked nine once-dragons from the sky almost immediately without taking a single blow themselves.

'They're weak!' observed Scoff as they circled back. 'Flimsy!'

'Remember, the Cult was only about a hundred strong,' cried Cumber. 'The Flame stretched them to more than double that number. There's bound to be a penalty.'

Together they pulled a group of three mirror-dragons clear of a particularly fierce skirmish and quizzed them breathlessly on Wemp's whereabouts. None of them knew, but suddenly Velvet spotted a familiar face high above them.

'There he is!'

Wemp was trying to maintain order by bellowing instructions down to his comrades as he fended off blow after blow from the red-scaled horde. But the mirror-dragons were not performing their neatly choreographed routines now – they were fighting for their lives.

'We have halved their number,' he gasped as he caught sight of Cumber and the others. 'But they come back for more. We cannot win!'

'We must not lose!' responded Cumber.

A shower of light exploded beneath them and they looked down just in time to see a swathe of fire tear through a line of five mirror-dragons. Wings were blown apart and scattered into the dust-filled sky.

'We cannot win,' moaned Wemp.

'Never give up!' snapped Velvet.

The winged monsters rose steadily beneath them, forcing them higher and higher into thinner air.

'What are you doing, Fortune?' Gossamer paced impatiently back and forth, ignoring Scarn just as he was ignoring her.

Fortune did not reply, simply continued to drag Rarch's

body up the slope towards her. His heart revolted at the notion that he was somehow abusing the memory of this poor, dead dragon, but his mind urged him on. When he reached the line in the dust which marked the boundary of Gossamer's prison, he stopped. Aria and Jevell remained near the base of the dome, watching his every move.

'Do you remember . . .' Fortune panted, '. . . that when Scoff was imprisoned like this . . . he said that inanimate things could pass through the fire charm easily enough? Food and waste, that sort of thing.'

'I don't know,' answered Gossamer. 'I suppose so.'

'Well, I'm hoping this charm works the same way. You couldn't have done what I'm about to do with Scoff's cell because that charm really *was* fire charm: it would have burned through anything which lingered in its way for too long. But I think this is different – not so dangerous. I hope, anyway. Stand back.'

Carefully, Fortune pushed Rarch's tail up to the line in the dust . . . and across it. The dead flesh passed cleanly through the shield of charm without raising so much as a spark. Fortune sat back and nodded, satisfied.

'So? Are you going to kill me to get me out?' Gossamer stared blankly at the tail which lay motionless before her. *That was my father*, she thought, but the thought seemed to have no meaning.

Fortune leaned forward and pulled Rarch's tail clear again. Then he braced his claws into the ground and lifted the tail – dead weight, of course – up and over so that it curled round upon itself. Now Rarch's tail had formed an almost perfect circle through which Fortune found himself staring into Gossamer's eyes.

Forgive me, my darling, he thought, only too aware of the macabre nature of his actions. *Trust me*.

He panicked a little as he tried to lodge the flared bone at the end of Rarch's tail between two of the scales which sprang from the base of his spine, but at last he managed it. Now the tail formed a closed, vertical loop. Gingerly, Fortune began to push Rarch's hindquarters over the line in the dust.

This time there was a faint crackling as the shield sensed

386

this greater violation. But the sound was the only evidence of its disapproval; Fortune prayed it would not find some hidden fire to unleash as well.

Scale by scale he manoeuvred Rarch into the path of the charm until the coiled tail formed an upright ring which exactly intersected the space occupied by the shield. The crackling continued for a breath or two, and the air between Fortune and Gossamer shimmered, then all was quiet again. Fortune stepped back and looked at what he had made: a circular portal through which, he hoped, Gossamer could step to freedom.

He closed his eyes and prayed that Rarch would forgive him.

Hesitantly, Gossamer held out a wingtip. There was no way to see if the charm still held in the void inside the coil of the tail, or if Fortune had indeed managed to create an area of isolation. There was only one way to find out.

Gossamer's wing slipped smoothly through the hole.

She ducked her head and stepped across Rarch's back, kissing her father's tail as she did so. Scarn made no move to stop her. Once on the other side, she turned and gently dislodged the tip of Rarch's tail from the scales on his back and laid it to rest on the ground. Then she went to his head and embraced it.

'Thank you,' she whispered.

Then she went to Fortune and held him so tight that he could not breathe. Not that he wanted to breathe, so overjoyed was he that his love was at his side again. He looked at poor Rarch and the joy was matched with grief, and then all emotion mingled into a great weight of feeling and he wept.

'Thank you,' sobbed Gossamer, hugging him even tighter.

He could think of nothing to say.

She unlatched her wings and stumbled down the slope to join her mother and daughter. Fortune watched their strong embrace and was reminded of his earlier intuition. *Mother ... daughter ... continuity.* He looked at Rarch and remembered what the dying dragon had said.

'Not you, dear Gossamer ... the end of your line ... mourn him for me ...'

387

He looked up into the sky, saw the fury of the battle which raged still and knew that only a miracle could save his friends from annihilation.

He bent his head and sent a silent prayer into the light of the Cloud.

Good must prevail today. Send us the miracle we need, to make this so.

He opened his eyes and found them turning to the west.

Low in the sky, two pairs of wings were cycling against the haze. Fortune recognized Smoke at once, but the other dragon he did not know. Its body looked dark, black perhaps.

Jevell saw him looking and sought out the objects of his gaze. She nudged Gossamer and they watched open-mouthed as the two dragons drew nearer. Aria was the last to look and the first to recognize the strange, dark dragon.

'It is you,' she breathed, detaching herself from her mother's embrace. She took a single, faltering step forward. 'Wyrm!'

'It can't be . . .' began Fortune but as soon as the words left his mouth he knew that it was true. That this huge, black dragon with wings like night was the son of his daughter, the end-point of the continuity he had sensed here at the centre of the Last Circle.

The missing piece which Rarch had predicted would complete the puzzle, the pattern.

Wyrm came – flying! – and his wings were mightier even than those of Wraith, whom he greatly resembled.

Wyrm came, filling the emptiness between land and sky, and Fortune saw his face. Where Wraith's eyes had burned with the light of evil ambition and jealous revenge, Wyrm's were afire with the light of the comet, the light of the Cloud, the light of the day of creation.

The missing piece, thought Fortune, a swell of emotion blurring his eyes. Then his heart turned over and cried out in agony. *And the sacrifice!*

Then everything turned blue. The air glowed. Every grain of dust on the ground grew a long, tapering shadow as a fireball rose from the centre of the dome where, moments before, Gossamer had been held captive by the Flame's charm. Fortune whirled round, hoping to see Scarn consumed by some treachery of the Flame. What he saw filled him with horror.

The Flame had grown tall and thin so that now it reached down to pierce the thin soil of the dome. Scarn was there still, only now he was bathed in blinding blue light, a faint dragon silhouette cut from fire. His wings thrashed slowly. Fortune realized he was moving upwards; he saw Scarn's claws leave the ground, sprinkling a trail of dust; the dust ignited, sending sparks rolling down the slope towards the watching dragons. Scarn's body seemed to stretch gradually until it was fully twice its normal length. Had he seen them, Fortune would have been reminded of the strange, elongated sculptures in Nistor's chamber.

The Flame pulsed like a great heart, throwing beams of light out across the crater. One such beam strayed into the sky, slicing several low-flying once-dragons from the air.

Scarn continued to rise, and Fortune began to believe that the Flame had claimed this dragon as its sacrifice after all, that it was in some way absorbing Scarn into itself, consuming him.

He was wrong, of course.

With a single, silent flash of light, the Flame sucked Scarn all the way into its belly and hurled him up into the sky. Scarn had become transparent now, a stretched dragon ghost accelerating skywards. His distorted form entered the pure white glow of the comet and was lost to view.

'Is that the end of him?' quavered Jevell.

Fortune shook his head gravely.

'It's just a beginning,' he answered.

Shadows crossed in front of the Flame which seemed to have settled into yet another level of stasis. It flickered and rumbled but otherwise remained stable. The shadows flexed their wings and then the dragons who made them descended majestically from the sky.

It was Smoke who landed first. It looked initially as though she would maintain the dignity of her graceful approach to the end, but the final half-tree of her descent saw her wings fold and her tail slump. She dropped heavily to the ground, raising a cloud of dust. Fortune and Gossamer

389

rushed to her side, shocked by her emaciated appearance.

'Where did you come from?' was all Fortune could think of to say.

Smoke smiled wearily. 'Other side of the world.'

'Non-stop?' asked Gossamer, returning the smile. Smoke nodded.

'Of course.'

'Where's Vox?'

But the question was lost for it was then that Wyrm alighted.

Fortune stood back to take in the sight of his daughter's son.

Wyrm had four legs like the Charmed. From his back a pair of massive wings burst forth, their night-black membranes glistening in the harsh light of the Flame. His neck was long and elegant. His eyes glowed from the darkness of his face. *Here are eyes into which you could fall,* thought Fortune dizzily.

He was the most beautiful dragon Fortune had ever seen.

'We have come,' said Wyrm. His voice was as deep as that of the Flame, yet smooth. At his side, dwarfed by his magisterial presence, Smoke nodded impatiently.

'We haven't flown all this way to tell them the obvious, Wyrm.'

Wyrm did not react. He inclined his head towards Aria.

'I am sorry, mother.'

Aria stepped forward, leaving Jevell to gape at this giant dragon who had flown in from nowhere. 'Forgive you, my son? There is nothing to forgive.'

Gossamer began to cry quietly, though she did not understand why, and Fortune clasped her tight.

Wyrm coiled his neck back and stared into the sky. The battle raged unabated, although numbers were reduced, and the fighting seemed fiercer than ever.

'There is work to be done. All is yet dark.' Dark wings lifted from his flanks and he appraised them wryly. 'Moving fast, isn't it?'

Before any dragon could ask what he meant, he spread his wings and bunched his muscles, preparing to take off.

'What about Scarn?' demanded Jevell from behind the others. 'Has everybody forgotten about him?'

Wyrm's head swivelled to face her. He regarded her as he might an insect, then he seemed to recognize her and his features softened.

'He is not forgotten, Jevell. But we cannot influence his actions. Scarn has gone . . . elsewhere.'

'Escaped? As he desired?'

Wyrm shook his head firmly. 'No. He is not far away, but he is beyond even my reach now. Come, we have no time to waste.'

Abruptly he launched himself into the air. One by one the others followed, even the exhausted Smoke. Gossamer flew close to her as they ascended.

'What happened to Vox? Is he . . . ?'

'Dead? No, but he isn't with us any more. I don't know if I'll ever see him again. Wyrm tells me I will, but even he isn't really sure.'

'Are you all right?'

'No, not really.'

Led by Wyrm's mighty wings, Fortune, his family and his companions joined the battle.

The mirror-dragons had retreated into high, clear air where they had re-formed in a single line, a dazzling strand of dragons, for a final stand. At its centre the duller bodies of Cumber, Velvet and Volley stood out in sharp contrast; even the white scales of Cumber and Velvet could not compete with the metallic sheen of their comrades. But the line wavered, breaking and re-creating itself. They were tired and, despite the closeness of their formation, disorder threatened.

Altogether they numbered just fifteen.

Approaching them at high speed were three separate squads of once-dragons, each one equal in number to the entire mirror-dragon force. A wave of fire breached the air at the head of their loose formation: their mouths were agape and they clearly hoped to sear these defiant dragons from the sky at a single stroke. It looked unlikely they would fail.

Then Velvet spotted Wyrm, and her cry carried down to his party.

'Oh my . . . it can't be . . . !'

She broke clear, dragging Cumber and two mirror-dragons with her. Volley remained with the rest; his wing-beats were laboured and erratic.

At the same instant the nearest of the three groups of once-dragons caught sight of the newcomers and turned to charge them. Fortune was once again faced with a wall of blistering fire. He flew on, knowing that there was no way to turn, that here he would live or die.

What happened next was unclear to Fortune. Wyrm seemed to gather himself in some way, then he was accelerating ahead of his companions at a speed Fortune considered impossible; it was almost as though he and the rest of the world had slowed down to allow Wyrm to move with the speed he desired. However it was achieved, the next thing he knew the fire belching out from the onrushing army had struck Wyrm's wing membranes. Fortune had a vivid impression of those great, black wings illuminated from behind by brilliant flames, networks of veins thrown into elaborate silhouette. Then the wings folded. When they opened the army was gone.

Wyrm pivoted and moved again with that same, unnatural speed. His extraordinary flight was utterly silent. He neared the next battalion and again Fortune saw his wings gape and close . . .

A shower of red scales was all that remained of the once-dragons.

Which left just one of the three groups of red-scaled monstrosities. The remaining mirror-dragons, inspired by Wyrm's sudden arrival and extraordinary show of strength, dived into the fire exploding all around them and dealt a series of deadly blows to the enemy. Again, Fortune's perception of events was confused by the steady cycling of Wyrm's wings against the tableau: he saw a severed neck fall, reflexes still twisting its lifeless coils; he saw a spine-backed creature devour its own tail as a mirror-dragon's claw sliced through its spine; he saw Wemp bite down on the throat of the very last once-dragon, a wretched beast which looked almost ordinary, close to the form of the dragon it had originally been, before the Flame had made it a monster.

It fell soundlessly.

There was a brief rain of black fluid as mirror-dragons unlocked themselves from death grips and the last bodies found their way to the crater floor.

Wyrm's coming had turned the tide. The battle was over.

The victors flew high. But beneath them the Last Circle was a bright disc. At its centre the Flame burned triumphantly.

Above them the sky had gone. Only the comet remained.

CHAPTER 29

The Lighting of the Sky

Mahl, which Fortune had always thought of as a land of fire and ice, a land of contrasts, was living up to that vision. In the bitter cold of night, while the last great battle of the dragon world raged on the far side of the globe, the freezing air was suddenly pierced by a line of fire. The subterranean fire which had once run through the Flamehall, and through Scarn's private chamber, at last found its way above ground and erupted through the thin crust of the lake bed.

It was a strangely undramatic event. A line of lava breached the waters, sending tendrils of steam hissing into the air. The line reached the shore, tumbling over itself with slow, easy grace, then a crack opened in the stone of the shore itself. From this crack fresh lava was pushed forth in the same serene way. And there it settled, pulsing and bubbling, darkening as it cooled, glowing as it revived itself, a thin trail of molten rock oozing down into the lake, content beneath its aura of steam. The flow of the lava was calm and unhurried, though insistent. The line it carved down the shore defined a boundary between the approaches to the Fissures and the wider land beyond.

Nearby, three dragons stood and watched.

'I don't think there's any danger,' commented Brace, edging nearer to the lava then drawing back nervously.

'You two can leave now, if you like,' said Wist. 'Now she's out of there.'

She huddled close to the crystal statue which encased the soul of her sister. They had managed to heft the weighty object out of the Flamehall by a combination of skilful flying and sheer strength. Wist and Ledra had been able to support most of the weight with their claws, but the crystal was slippery. Several times Brace had intervened – by flying beneath the statue and supporting it on his back – to save it from plummeting into the depths. Several times Ledra and Wist blundered into each other, caught out by some unexpected shift in the crystal's mass as they wove their way through the tricky air currents. But they managed, and when they finally deposited the statue on the lake shore they stared at each other in surprise – the operation had gone more smoothly than any of them had anticipated.

Now, late in the night, they kept their vigil by the statue of Lessen, waiting for some sign that, far away, the day of creation had dawned.

Brace was just beginning to drop off to sleep when the lava started to flow. They watched entranced as the night was lit up by its baleful orange glow.

'Go,' repeated Wist. 'It could get dangerous around here.'

'But we know that already,' replied Ledra, unable to take her eyes from the flowing, glowing rock.

'Besides,' yawned Brace. 'Where would we go?'

Soon the darkness began to fade. The comet rolled into view. It was immense.

'New dawn,' whispered Ledra.

'Look!' exclaimed Brace, pointing to the statue.

Blue fire was clearly visible beneath its slick, crystal skin. It leaped outwards, striking against the internal facets. Looking for a way out.

Scarn was transformed. He felt the tremendous heat of the Flame percolate through his veins. He resisted at first, suspecting treachery, but soon relented. The feeling was one of such ecstasy . . .

As the Flame flowed through him, he felt his senses expand. Now he saw with the Flame's many eyes, heard with its many ears. In a single eye-blink he visited numerous sites around the world, sites where once the Flame had burned fiercely: the familiar Fissures of Mahl, the coastal mountains of the Hook, the Towers of Nistor, the deep core of the world. He saw the patchwork of forces that made up the light of the comet, saw the hard nugget of energy at its heart. Turned all his attention up towards it. Launched himself towards it. Sucked the power of the Flame with him. Directed it even as he was directed by it. Entered its light. Passed through.

Inside the comet, Vox had grown used to the light. It surrounded him as the egg surrounds the unborn infant, warm and protective.

Yet something was breaking through.

Something rose from the world, from the complex pattern of land and sea and heart and mind which Vox had been studying with fanatical intensity.

Don't let me forget this, he had been thinking. *What other dragon has seen such sights?*

One other, it seemed.

Scarn looked across the sea of light at Vox and smiled confidently. Scarn, like Vox, was translucent. His virtual wings rippled like sheets of fire. Behind them the curve of the planet was huge and near. Very near.

Scarn spoke.

'Are you the best it could come up with?'

Vox considered carefully before replying.

'I am not the best. But then neither are you, Scarn.'

Scarn dipped his head in salute.

'A clever reply, dragon. But meek.'

'What do you want here?'

Scarn looked around, appraising his surroundings.

White light was everywhere, bound together by an overwhelming sense of circularity. It was as though these ghostly, almost transparent dragons were both inside and outside a great, incandescent sphere whose perimeter was soft and diffuse. Light pulsed lazily through their sheer forms. They were inside the comet. They were inside the Cloud.

'I want to take all this apart, dragon. And I think I'll start with you.'

Vox waited as Scarn charged him, watching as his attacker grew to prodigious size, feeling the swell of energy inside his own, transparent pores, feeling the weight of the comet pushing him forward.

Trust in me, whispered a voice in his mind.

Then they were upon each other.

'Behold,' intoned Wyrm, gesturing skywards with his wing but keeping his head lowered. 'The real battle begins.'

They had landed, all of them, on the lip of the crater. Twenty-one dragons in all. They, together with their friends on Mahl, were the only dragons left in the world.

Fortune and Cumber were trying to tend Volley's appalling injuries. Blood leaked from almost every part of his body; but worse, he seemed to have no will to live.

'Leave me,' he moaned. 'Let me find Tallow. Let me go.'

'Don't talk nonsense,' hissed Velvet, shouldering Cumber aside. Then she, like the others, looked to where Wyrm was pointing and her words left her.

Two dragons had appeared in the sky. They were immense, like dragon gods, each as big as a mountain and as transparent as mist. At first they seemed to waver in and out of existence, but they grew more substantial. The light of the comet burned through them. They moved in front of its light like two tremendous clouds; they filled the sky. They were familiar.

'Vox!' screamed Smoke, unable to believe her eyes.

'Scarn,' muttered Fortune.

Vox's outline glowed with beads of pure white light while that of Scarn oscillated between orange and blue, a fiery spectrum betraying the source of his power. Like two young males they lowered their horns and charged each other.

They met and their forms interlocked, exchanging wisps of vapour. These cloud-dragons slipped through each other, tearing shreds from flank and wing. They crossed half the sky in this first exchange. Then they reared up and clamped their claws together, turning over and over until the strands of cloud and flame from which they were made were whirling like the tornado. No recognizable dragon-form was left, just a spinning mass of energy, a flickering shadow over the land most of the way to the horizon.

'What's happening, Wyrm?' whispered Gossamer. The others were struck dumb by the incredible display in the sky.

They even seemed to have forgotten the imminent threat of the falling comet.

'Today is the day of creation,' replied Wyrm as if it explained everything. He turned to Wemp. 'Tell me, dragon-with-shining-scales, what is the history of this place?'

'I don't know what you . . .' stammered Wemp.

'How was it made?'

'I don't know. There are no stories . . .'

'Stories!' Wyrm pounced on the word. 'No stories. Exactly! The Last Circle has never had a history of its own. Until now. Today its history begins. Today it will be created. Today everything will be created!'

In the sky, the phantom gods drew apart, resumed their misty shapes. Scarn pulled away from his opponent, then twisted his neck . . . and suddenly his face was looming large before the grounded dragons, a mass of intricate cloud forms and darting flames, an abstract representation of a dragon floating in the sky above the astonished onlookers. From the tip of his snout to the end of his horns his head was as long as the crater was wide.

'*Aria – will you join me at last?*' It was Scarn's face but the voice was that of the Flame. Ordinary dragon faces turned to her but she did not respond either to them or to the monstrous ghost which hung suspended above her. The Flame-voice answered itself. '*Of course not. You were never an object of desire for any dragon, least of all me.*'

'That isn't true,' answered Aria quietly. 'Go, Scarn. Go now.'

Vox's face appeared then, pressing Scarn's out of the way, but a series of fireballs exploded from Scarn's eyes. They ripped through the crater's lip near to where the dragons were clustered. Several of them took to the air in fright.

'*I'm coming back for you!*' So saying, Scarn seized his opponent and the unearthly conflict returned to the heavens once more.

'Vox!' cried Smoke, but it was in vain. Fortune thought he had never seen a dragon look more distraught.

The sky was beginning to take on a warped appearance. The two giants crashed back and forth before the blazing comet. With each blow that was struck a shard of phantom flesh was torn free. These translucent trophies fell towards the ground, blistering the air as they descended. Where they hit the ground they bored deep holes from which great gouts of steam exploded. Some fell close to the dragons.

'We must take to the air,' urged Fortune, pulling at Volley's wing.

'Leave me,' Volley grumbled, his eyelids drooping.

'You're coming with us!' shouted Velvet. 'Whether you like it or not!'

Somehow they got him into the air. His wings flapped automatically; his eyes were glazed over.

Fortune flew across to where Wyrm was hovering with long, languid strokes of his immense wings.

'You know what's happening up there, don't you?' he demanded. Wyrm nodded.

'This is the test,' he explained, suddenly eager to please. 'The Flame is afraid to face the Cloud directly, so it is pitting its champion instead. It reminds me of a story about . . .'

'Wyrm! There's no time for stories! What can we do to help Vox?'

'Nothing!'

In the centre of the crater the Flame burned brighter than ever.

The comet was even more brilliant.

Vox and Scarn were gone again. They had withdrawn into another spiral of energy. There was no way to know who was winning the contest. The whirlwind revolved frantically, then the shapes of the god-dragons seemed to explode again from its midst, locking themselves into a sudden, frozen tableau.

Scarn was underneath, his head twisted round upon itself in a manner which would have broken the neck of any normal dragon. His wings were spread wide as though for balance; they stretched from the western horizon all the way to the clouds stacked in the east. His lake-sized eyes were stricken with a single, naked emotion: fear.

Vox loomed over him. His wings hung like a shroud over Scarn. His jaws were gaping, ready to strike. In his eyes there was nothing but love.

There they remained for what seemed an eternity, though

it was surely only a breath or two. Then Scarn flexed his neck still further until he was looking directly down upon the crater. He opened his mouth and emitted a strangled, watery cry. If that cry contained words they were no words ever uttered by a dragon before, yet it was quite clear what he was saying. It was a cry for help.

The Flame responded instantly. Light bubbled along its upper edge and a lance of fire shot straight up into Scarn's breast. At once a coil of smoke wove itself from the empty air beside Scarn's massive, diaphanous head. It spun, then elongated until it had formed something which was all too familiar to the watching dragons: a cylinder of smoke which raced across the sky to meet the eastern horizon – the same device by which the Flame had transported itself halfway around the world.

'He's going to get away!' shouted Cumber. 'Stop him, Vox!'

But Vox – or whatever it was Vox had become – did not move.

The end of the smoke tube flared open and Scarn's head began to contract. Slowly, but with increasing speed, it was literally sucked into the tube. Scarn's vast wings drew forwards from the distant haze, diminishing until they vanished along with the rest of his unearthly body. Soon only the tip of his tail remained; then that too was gone.

The smoke tube glowed as it launched itself across the sky, speeding away into the east until it could no longer be seen. Taking Scarn towards Mahl. Escaping.

Vox started to move again.

'Vox!' screamed Smoke. 'Don't go!'

But if he heard he did not respond. Vox too shrank away as Scarn had done, except he was drawn upwards into the comet's light. The sky was empty again, but for the watching dragons and the colossal presence of the comet.

An almighty roar rose from the centre of the crater. The Flame had flattened as though something were pressing it down into the dirt. Then a second line of smoke erupted, this time from the heart of the Flame. It changed colour from dirty grey to rich, glowing blue, and suddenly the Flame itself was travelling along its length, pursuing the first smoke trail east along the escape route it had laid for itself. Pursuing Scarn.

There was a rumble like distant thunder then the smoke cylinder, the Flame and the blue light were gone.

All that remained was the corpse-littered crater of the Last Circle, twenty-one dragons and the glorious light of the comet.

The world fell into silence.

'Does this mean the Cloud has won?' inquired Velvet tentatively.

The air began to rattle. The comet came, fast.

'GO!'

Wyrm's voice split the air. Every dragon obeyed his call instantly, for every dragon there knew that this was truly their last chance. Every dragon moved . . . except Volley.

'Come on!' screamed Fortune and Velvet simultaneously, but in the end it was Gossamer who persuaded him.

'Tallow would not stay,' she whispered.

'But I'm not Tallow!' Volley answered, weeping. His wounds were awful but somehow he managed to keep hovering. With a dreadful wail he fell into her slipstream.

They flew then, these last dragons, flew faster and harder than ever they had flown before. The rattling in the air behind them was growing louder, its insistent sound threatening to overtake them at any moment. None of them dared to look back.

It was a headlong dash, simply. They had witnessed more than they could comprehend both in and above the Last Circle. The enemy's army had been defeated, but what of the enemy itself? What of Scarn, and what of the Flame? And what strange part had Vox played at the end?

Too many questions, none of which mattered in the agonizing moments during which they fled the crater. The comet finally was falling to earth, and whether it was bringing the Cloud with it or not, whether its arrival signalled some mysterious creative act or not, no dragon wanted to be there when it came. Good or evil, neither mattered now – all that mattered was survival.

The rattling deepened, vibrating their tortured lungs in their breasts.

401

Ahead rose a series of towers, red pinnacles of rock. They offered sanctuary, though no dragon could be sure that anywhere was safe on this day. They made for them all the same. Hope remained.

It was no longer a rattle but a voice.

The land rolled by like time.

A thousand trees, thought Fortune. *We'll never make it!*

The flight was a torment beyond imagining. Every single dragon was exhausted already, and emotionally they had taken more punishment than any of them could have thought it possible to bear. All that remained was the desire to live. And even Volley still possessed that. They flew – all else was stripped from them, for the litany was simple: fly or die.

The voice was calling to them, but they could not make out its words.

Five hundred trees! Never!

'Never give up!' cried a voice. No dragon seemed to know whose it was.

The voice sang.

Two hundred. One hundred . . .

A blur of red rock, a spray of dust which marked their wake.

Fifty . . .

Something overtook them, flying faster than anything they had known. It was a solid wall of light.

Ten . . . now!

The comet struck.

This day, this place.

The Last Circle, which until this day had owned no story of its own, suddenly acquired a history.

On this day, a piece of a great comet broke through into the world and came to earth, creating a mighty crater. The crater had always been there; but until this day, nothing had created it.

Nothing had created anything.

Now the creator had come.

This day. The Day of Creation.

* * *

Twenty-one dragons huddled together behind a tower of red rock. On the horizon a flash of light too bright to look at illuminated the darkest recesses of the darkest shadows.

For the briefest of instants, the light was everywhere.

Then a cloud of dust and smoke and rock and debris rose high into the air. The column rose and rose until it began to billow out into a shape like a mushroom. Fires blazed at its root. Winds tugged at its upper reaches, sculpting it. Lightning laced its underbelly, crashes of static as cloud rubbed against cloud.

Then came the sound.

The sound of creation was the sound of thunder. The shock waves lifted soil and small boulders as a series of pressure ridges radiated outwards from the crater. Fortune felt the blast transferred from ground up into his body via his claws. As his body vibrated he felt something move deep inside him, and sensed its echoes moving through the deep rock of the world, far below where he stood clinging to his family.

He felt his flesh being sorted, his heart being pumped against its will, his blood being cleaned and strained. Strange forces tugged at his muscles, stretching them, working them, organizing them. And, in a series of infinitesimal jerks, *changing* them.

The force leached into his mind and worked there too; then, abruptly, it left altogether. It had more work to do, all the world over. Fortune cautiously reviewed the way he felt. Nothing really seemed to have changed – he still felt like Fortune . . . yet . . .

Yet my place in this new world has changed.

He probed his memory and found that at least was unaltered.

But would I know if it were altered?

Once the initial, explosive sound had moved past them, all they could hear was the dull and distant rumbling of the column and its mushroom cap. One by one the dragons began to emerge from behind the tower which had protected them. They blinked and gasped and touched each other to reassure themselves they were still alive. Above them the sky had darkened ominously. The sun reappeared briefly before it was dimmed by the dust cloud rising higher and higher into the air.

Fortune looked around, suddenly alert. Something was wrong.

Then came Aria's howl.

'Where's Wyrm?!'

He was nowhere to be seen.

It was as much as Fortune and Gossamer could do to hold her back. She struggled in their combined grip until gradually she relented.

'Why did it have to be this way?' She wailed, hurled red dirt at the sky.

'He might have survived,' interjected Cumber. 'I mean, perhaps he flew off another way, or maybe he was hit by the blast but didn't actually . . .' He broke off as Velvet jabbed him in the ribs.

A hot breeze was blowing from the crater now. The mushroom was widening, overwhelming the sky. A premature night was falling. In the Last Circle the fires continued to burn, their brilliant orange flames clean and somehow reassuring after the unnatural blue of the Flame. Ash tumbled from the underside of the cloud, falling across the dragons' backs. The air was growing thick and uncomfortable.

'Fortune,' whispered Anchre. 'We should think about moving. It may not be safe to stay here.'

'Ought to go,' agreed Scoff. 'Getting stuffy.'

The others were looking at Fortune expectantly, awaiting his decision.

'Aria?' he asked.

But she was not looking at him. She was staring intently at the distant fire, her head cocked curiously to one side.

'Listen,' she said.

At first Fortune could hear only the whisper of the wind. It had strengthened considerably, and as it whipped through the elaborately weathered contours of the rock pinnacle he fancied he heard words carried on its currents.

Listening harder, he realized there *were* words in there, faint but growing stronger. They rolled across the landscape, deepening, becoming enriched by the thickness of the atmosphere, feeding off the rain of ash, sorting themselves . . . making sense.

The words coalesced into a voice. Fortune believed it was Wyrm's voice, although he could not be certain. It told a story . . .

This is the story of creation.

All creatures have their legends, and dragons are no exception. Dragons tell stories of the first of their kind, of the first trolls, of the first workings of charm. Of many firsts . . . except the most significant of all: the first breaths of the world itself.

Dragons have no stories which tell of the creation.

There is a good reason for this.

The world of dragons existed, like all other worlds, between Turnings. Many other worlds preceded it, just as many other worlds will follow it. Throughout its existence the world of dragons was ruled by charm, yet at the moment of the most recent Turning that power fled. There followed a brief period of storm and doubt. The world was waiting; the world was between.

But now a new power has come, and it has brought with it something which the world of dragons never had: a first cause.

The new world of nature lives by the laws of nature where the old world of charm had only magic and the boast of an infinite past. But a world with a beginning needs a day of creation.

This is that day.

Creation works on the past as well as the future. Already the world of dragons is gone. Not only does it no longer exist . . . but now it never existed. All trace of it has gone, except the memories which linger in the minds of those creatures who survived the Turning. Those memories, handed down through generations, may live on as legends long into the future, at least among those creatures who have a future in the new world.

Dragons have no future in it.

But there is hope. The Cloud loves this world and all this world's progeny, even those it has inherited from different times. There are ways that dragons may find their way into a future where there is a place for them. There are ways to escape, and there may even be ways for dragons to become a part of the new, natural world.

But there is not much time.
Seek the ways, dragons, if you wish them.

Fresh fire exploded from the crater, sending jets of orange flame up into the expanding ash column. It looked at first like natural – beautifully natural – fire, but soon the random flames began to take on a more definite form. They joined together and grew in a series of gentle pulses, like a flower opening. A slow spinning drew them into a wide oval of light, a shape which Gossamer recognized at once.

'The Cloud,' she whispered, for she had seen it in this form before.

'Is it coming for us?' asked Velvet, her voice trembling.

'No. I think it wants to show us something.'

The oval dimmed a little, then rushed towards the dragons. Fortune flinched along with the others but stood his ground. When it stopped Fortune did not know whether it was huge and distant or small and close. A ripple passed across its surface, then it *opened*.

Petals of light unfurled, revealing a landscape wavering beyond the oval. It was blurred, but Fortune knew it even before it began to slip into focus. Rough grey scarps, a lake emitting wisps of vapour, a line of glowing lava breaking through a rocky shore. It was night. The scene became sharp with a sudden snap and he was looking across the world to Mahl.

Three dragons were huddled on the shore, their backs to the watchers. They were gathered round a strange, crystalline form. Blue light was pumping inside it.

'Brace!' cried Gossamer, rushing forward.

The largest of the dragons turned. His jaw dropped comically and he took several hesitant steps towards his sister. Fortune wondered what he was seeing, there on the other side of the world. Perhaps a vision not so different to what he himself was looking at: the twin of this oval aperture, giving Brace a clear view of the red rocks of Ocea.

'G-Gossamer? Is that you?' He reached out a wingtip towards the oval, then withdrew it quickly.

'Are you all right?' wept Gossamer, mimicking his gesture. They seemed so close, almost able to touch.

'We're waiting . . .' began Brace, then Aria interrupted.

'They're coming! You must take care!'

A second dragon detached herself from the vigil by the steaming lake and approached the oval. Fortune recognized her as Wist, and in the same instant saw that the third dragon was Ledra.

'I told you!' Wist was shouting. 'The Flame is nearly here. Come on, Brace – there's no time!'

Brace looked round at her, then back at Gossamer. His face was contorted with agony. 'All right, I'm coming!' he called to Wist. Then he spoke again to his sister. 'You could come with us. If you wanted to.'

Fortune looked at the blurred edge of this luminous oval aperture and knew that it was true – dragon bodies would slip through this world-crossing membrane as easily as dragon voices. Mahl was only a step away. But . . . 'Come with us'? *Come where?*

'Where are you going?' demanded Gossamer.

'Mahl is the place where the Flame plans to abandon our world. You see the crystal dragon on the shore? That is what is left of Lessen, Wist's twin sister. In some way I don't understand, she is the gateway to another world. And if the Flame can go there, we can go there, Gossamer.' Brace looked pleadingly at the row of faces watching him from the other side of the world. 'We can all go. There may be a place for dragons there.'

Gossamer looked at Fortune through tear-filled eyes. Then Aria pushed her way between them and barked, 'Brace! You are in grave danger!'

'Wist has planned a surprise for the Flame,' Brace reassured her. 'Come with us, please. It's the only way.'

'But Wist didn't listen to what I said!' snapped Aria. 'She thinks it's just the Flame that's coming, but it's not – *Scarn* is coming. The Flame is pursuing *him*. It is furious. You will have to deal with *both* of them before you can find your way through to this other world! There is more peril than you can possibly know!'

Brace's eyes darted between those of Aria and Gossamer, then flicked back to the scene on the shore.

'Wist . . .' he began uncertainly.

Then there was a great rush of wind and the lake was whipped into angry motion, turbulent water and steam. The blue light which was glowing inside Lessen's crystallized body flared brighter than the sun. Wist and Ledra staggered back, shielding their eyes.

A point of light appeared low in the night sky of Mahl, widening as it drew near. It took on dimension, lengthened. It was a huge cylinder of smoke, pulsing rapidly between grey and red. It was Scarn, coming.

Close behind, a second smoke trail.

CHAPTER 30

Continuity

Scarn felt the hot breath of the Flame on his tail and pressed forward. There were two forms of motion operating here: his own movement through the smoke tube, and the movement of the tube itself through the air. The former was severely limited by his physical bulk within the narrow cylinder; the latter worked at the speed of charm. Between them they conspired to transport Scarn from one side of the world to the other very quickly indeed.

But the Flame was even quicker.

Though events around him were unfolding at stupendous speed, Scarn found his thoughts lucid and unhurried. He *would* beat the Flame: this *was* his destiny.

To begin with it had been enough to be simply the storyteller of Aether's Cross. Then the Flame had opened his mind to greater pleasures by providing him with the narratives far grander than any he had told before. Stories of Good and Evil, of Light and Dark, of the Last Circle and the Day of Creation.

But now Scarn understood something he had never before heeded: *stories end*. Even the epic tales the Flame wove into his thoughts had conclusions and that, Scarn considered, was just small-minded.

The basilisks fought against immortality, he thought as the searing heat of the Flame licked at the tip of his tail, *but . . . immortality . . . eternity . . . both hold out false promise. Neither has any real power of its own.*

Neither did the Flame. It was nothing but a coward skulking in the shadows. Its evil could shape the minds of dragons, to be sure, but without them and their weaknesses it was nothing.

When dragons are gone, what creatures will it seek to mould then?

The true power had brought new light into the world, had remade the past as well as the future.

The Cloud had refashioned all the stories which had ever been told, and for that reason Scarn could not countenance sharing the world with it.

First and last, I am a storyteller. I am the storyteller. The Cloud will not usurp my place – because I will escape. I will be listened to again.

So Scarn fled, not asking himself who there would be, where he escaped to, to listen to him, believing that he had finally shaken free the grip the Flame held upon his mind. Believing he could beat the Flame to Mahl, and hence cheat it of what it believed to be its rightful destiny.

So he believed. On both counts he was quite wrong.

The two smoke tubes materialized over the lake a mere breath apart. Scarn was first to emerge, his wings beating in a deep, orderly fashion. Immediately apparent was the fact that they had returned to normal: no longer were they made from livid yellow fire but simple, red skin. He seemed shrunken, exceptionally *ordinary*. But his eyes blazed with desire.

A single breath after Scarn burst from his tube of smoke, the second tube arrived and the Flame erupted into the night sky of Mahl. It expanded from a tiny blue point into an electric arc of light which crackled from one side of the lake to the other. The whole valley was lit up; crazy shadows danced vigorously down the scarps and over the shores; even the glow of the lava seemed dull by comparison to the brilliance of the Flame.

But Lessen's crystallized body outshone even that.

Until now no dragon, not even Wist, had known exactly what seed it was that the Flame had planted inside Lessen. The twin dragons had shared many dreams over the past day and night, but they had been strange and abstract. Wist had described the shared dreams, unearthly sights, to Brace and Ledra: tunnels barred by thousands of brightly-lit rods, weird lands where the horizon was tipped on its side, crowds of scuttling, shelled creatures which bled resin and chattered in a sophisticated tongue she could not understand. A blur of fantasy and half-seen fact at the heart of which, unseen, throbbed a nugget of truth.

Now, at last, it was revealed.

The blue glow inside Lessen fled the interior of the crystal to become a thin, vertical shaft of light punching up into the sky. Its edges were sharp, perfectly defined. It was too bright to look at, more brilliant than the sun. Where the Flame was jagged and random, it was sleek and perfectly ordered. It was beautiful.

Scarn made straight for the shaft. He might have made it all the way across the lake had he not succumbed to the urge to look behind him. Many of the watching dragons wondered what might have happened had he chosen simply to fly on. Would he have made it through? There was no way of knowing.

Scarn looked back, and fire sprang free of the gyrating Flame, piercing his eyes and forcing its way into his mouth. His head was suddenly locked motionless in the air. Momentum carried the rest of his body on, slewing it round until his neck extended and snatched at his trapped head. The sound of snapping bones was loud enough for all to hear.

You dare to defy me here?' The voice of the Flame came from *everywhere*: from the sky, the rocks, the lava stream, even from the waves lashing across the surface of the lake, whipped up by the frenzied movement of the fire above.

Scarn's body dropped limp towards the water, hanging from his broken neck. His tail cut through the highest peaks of the waves; his tongue lolled.

The fire which held him curled round and like the tail of an angry dragon threw Scarn's body across the lake. It landed with a tremendous splash between two distant rocks, and sank.

The Flame gathered itself then, bunching all its energy tight into a knot of furious light. The glowing shaft widened slightly. Everything began to turn white.

*   *   *

411

Fortune watched as these events played themselves out. Before he knew what was happening Scarn's broken body had disappeared into the water and the Flame was readying itself for what looked likely to be some final blow against the world.

The coming of the whiteness took him quite by surprise. Everything, even the Flame, froze as the air began to turn milky. It was like a liquid mist falling across the valley. The rocks flattened, their rough surfaces smoothing over until they were featureless echoes of their former selves. The water turned to ice and its wave-ruptured surface solidified into peaks and troughs, strangely rounded. The flowing lava lost all colour and hardened into a serpentine trail of lime.

The softening continued further. For Fortune, watching through the oval aperture, it was like seeing Mahl simply melt away. Soon the milky mist had infiltrated everything, blended together the individual elements . . .

But no. Certain things did not change. The Flame stood out against the new blandness with startling clarity, as did the dark shapes of the three dragons and the brilliant blue column of light. And the crystal dragon! It had started to move.

Lessen lifted herself from the ground, uncoiling her neck and tail and stretching her crystal wings wide. Her body glowed from within, red facets burning with blue-white heat, a column of light reaching out from between her wings. She paced slowly across to where her twin sister was watching with mouth agape and nuzzled her, just once. The shaft of light which sprang from her back followed her every move. Then she turned to the Flame.

The Flame spoke first.

'Did you think to deceive me with such a ruse? Did you believe that simply by moving the crystal into the open air you could prevent me from finding it? How pitiful you are, tiny ones!'

Lessen's mouth opened. Fortune was surprised to hear that her voice, when it emerged, was soft and fluid, not hard and glassy as he had expected.

'Sometimes the simpler a plan the more chance it has of success.'

Wist recovered herself and pressed close against her sister's shining flank.

412

'Do it now!' she hissed. Fortune wondered what it was they had planned. He looked again at the aperture through which he and his friends were perceiving this drama and remembered that a mere stroke of his wings might carry him round the world from Ocea to Mahl.

Not yet, he cautioned himself. *Understand before you act.*

The Flame was talking again.

'There is no way to hinder me. Though I wonder – should there be an addition to the day's sacrifice?'

Fortune felt Cumber nudge him in the ribs. 'I say, shouldn't we just let it go? After all, a world without Evil seems like quite a good idea to me.'

Fortune shook his head. It was Aria who replied.

'Cumber, even if the Flame does escape there will still be Evil in the world. Remember the abandoned charm? Nothing ever really goes, not completely. There are always echoes left behind, memories.'

'And what of the world it is going to?' added Gossamer. 'Does that world deserve its evil any more than ours?'

'There's something else,' put in Fortune.

'What's that?' asked Cumber petulantly.

'Volley knows.'

All eyes turned to the big mountain dragon.

'Well?' urged Cumber. 'Why can't we let the Flame get away?'

Volley thought hard for a moment, then sighed heavily. 'Justice, Cumber. That's why.'

On the other side of the oval the Flame had started to move, but before it could reach the edge of the lake something exploded from the water directly beneath it, something red-scaled and full of wrath. It was Scarn.

His body was deformed, its joints twisted violently out of true. His head drooped sickeningly, and as he brought his neck up it swung seemingly unsupported at an alarming angle. Bones jutted out through his flanks and both his wings were bent and perforated. Black fluid coated his scales. He looked like a dragon who had fallen from the sky into the jaws of a troll. Given his injuries, he could not possibly have been alive. Yet he lived still.

Bringing his tail up he flailed at the underbelly of the

Flame, but the crackling ball of fire withdrew to a safe distance, cruising high above the frozen waves on its way towards Lessen. Scarn followed it, snapping and cursing in a thin, gargling voice which Fortune found utterly chilling.

Something was connecting in Fortune's mind. He concentrated hard, narrowing his eyes as though it might help the flow of his thoughts. *The Flame could have killed Scarn many times over. Yet, even here, even now, it cannot bring itself to do it. Why does it let him live?*

He looked at Aria and Gossamer, and found them both staring back at him.

'It cannot escape without Scarn,' the three of them said simultaneously.

'Come on,' barked Gossamer, surging forward.

Fortune was close on her tail as he slipped across the threshold between Ocea and Mahl. It was an unsettling sensation, a feeling that his body had been shut down then suddenly revivified. In this way he travelled from one side of the world to the other in the blink of an eye. He looked back and saw his friends, Volley and Cumber at the front, pressing close against the face of the oval. They paused, perhaps unsure whether by following they might ruin whatever plan it was their companions had in mind. Then Volley leaped.

He struck an invisible wall and was thrown back unhurt. He tried once more, rubbing his snout with a strangely infant-like gesture. He looked at the others and shook his head; clearly the Cloud had its own ideas about who might and might not cross the barrier.

It's up to us then, resolved Fortune as he entered the weird, milky world which Mahl had become.

Scarn knew about justice. He did not know which was the greater indignity: that the Flame had dealt with him so easily or that, having dealt with him, it had kept him alive simply as a means of achieving its own end.

As soon as it has broken through it will cast me aside, Scarn thought. *And that is unjust.*

He watched with interest as the three dragons emerged on Mahl from Ocea. If this was to be a showdown it was a pitiful one, he considered. The Flame would burn them to ash and blow their remains to oblivion.

Is that where I am headed, too?

Perhaps they would be a useful distraction though. Perhaps he could slip through the portal while the Flame was occupied with these interlopers. He looked into the column of light which rose from the crystal dragon's back, seeking detail in its glare. He saw nothing, although there was a strong sense of movement inside its brilliant light, of a wind blowing not across but *down*.

Scarn looked up into the Flame again and saw that it had hesitated. It did indeed seem preoccupied with the dragons. He coiled ripped muscles, readying himself for his leap for freedom.

Fortune eyed the Flame suspiciously as it lingered before them. The landscape had melted further into formless mist: ground and sky had both receded, leaving them suspended in a vast, white space. Thick wind rolled down from above, its taste rich and spicy. The column of light and the crystal which had once been a dragon called Lessen had grown to immense proportions. It was like a dream.

Continuity, he thought suddenly, remembering his earlier intuitions. He looked in turn at the dragons who were with him: Gossamer, Aria and Brace . . . Wist and Lessen. Ledra.

An answer promised itself to him but remained stubbornly out of reach.

'This light!' announced Lessen suddenly. She had indeed grown large, a great dragon sculpted from flowing, red crystal. She beat the dense air with shining wings, a goddess. 'This light opens the way to another world. It is made from charm and, like all charm, it has limited energy. A single breath may pass through it – after that it will collapse, never to be used again. It is a one-way journey, and only one, breathing life may take it. Who shall it be?'

'That's why the Flame can't use it directly,' murmured Aria. 'It is not truly *alive*. It has to travel through on the breath of a living dragon.'

'And Scarn is the only dragon left in the world who can breathe fire!' exclaimed Fortune.

'The Flame bestowed that power on him,' Aria agreed.

'And if Scarn goes through without it, the Flame is stuck here forever.'

'Forced to survive in the glare of what it hates more than anything else – the light of the Cloud.'

'Then what's it waiting for?' muttered Brace.

If the Flame had reason for waiting, Scarn did not, for it was then that he made his leap.

It was a dreadful sight: this once handsome dragon, now crushed and bloodied, jerking forward through the air with weird, spasmodic strokes of his shattered wings. The Flame, a tight knot of energy gliding inexorably towards the dragons, swivelled as if regarding his progress.

It needs Scarn to move first, Fortune realized. *Now it will take him, to ride through on his breath like some evil parasite.*

The Flame did indeed move, with an awful, leisurely air. Scarn was tattered and pathetic – his bold leap had become a pitiful scramble for a freedom he surely could never reach.

Another dragon stepped through the aperture from Ocea. It was Jevell.

'Quickly, mother!' cried Gossamer. 'Join us now!'

Gossamer and Aria took off the instant Jevell appeared, gathering in the dense air, blocking the Flame's approach to the portal.

'No!' shouted Brace, reaching up towards his sister and mother.

'Leave them!' snapped Fortune. 'Trust them!'

Aria directed Gossamer and Jevell with brisk, soundless gestures. Some hidden communication was marshalling them, pulling them close together, adjusting the beat of their wings. Then Aria called out.

'Line of Light!'

Of the three, only she had seen this trick of the mirror-dragons. How the others knew what to do Fortune could not guess, only that some telepathy between them – mothers and daughters – made such intuition possible. However it was achieved, the manoeuvre was performed fast and flawlessly.

Aria's teeth gripped the end of Jevell's tail at the same instant Gossamer's jaws closed on hers; a breath later Jevell took hold of Gossamer's tail. This closed loop of dragons

416

began to spin slowly in the air before the onrushing Flame.

Fortune flicked his eyes across to Scarn and saw that if the Flame were to stand any chance of catching the limping, lumbering dragon in time it would have to pass directly through the centre of the loop.

Through the eye of the storm.

Scarn was very close to the portal now. Lessen had frozen; the light from her back was less like a beam now and more like a hole, a hole in the fabric of the world. Clouds swirled in its depths, tugged by unseen winds. At that instant it looked as though Scarn might yet win the race.

Wist sprang up before him, her eyes afire.

'Stop, Scarn!' she commanded.

But Scarn did not even slow. The Flame launched a tendril of fire *around* the dragon loop, aiming it at Scarn's head. It struck him and immediately a gout of flame erupted from his jaws. The Flame maintained this tenuous connection with its intended host even as it approached the loop – clearly this was how it hoped to ride with Scarn across the boundary between the worlds.

The three dragons – Aria, Gossamer, Jevell – were spinning so fast now that their bodies were a dark blur, a continuous circle.

This *is the Last Circle!* thought Fortune suddenly. *Here, now – the last circle of dragon charm this world will ever know!*

The flames which burst from Scarn's mouth struck Wist squarely on the breast.

Wist fell back, choking and beating at her scales. Scarn lunged again and suddenly Wist's wings were on fire. She screamed in agony. Fortune grabbed her and flattened her body against the crystal wall of her twin sister's flank; Lessen still did not move. Fortune rolled Wist along the smooth cold surface, suffocating the fire. The flames died away, leaving an appalling smell of smoke and burnt flesh.

'I served you once,' howled Wist, her voice breaking. 'Yet you did nothing but lie to me!'

Scarn turned his head. It hung from his neck as though it was not a part of his body at all. Fire continued to crackle between his teeth, pumped there by the fiery ligature connecting him to the Flame.

'I told you stories,' he leered.

'All stories are lies!'

Fortune tried to wrap Wist in his wings, to comfort her, but his every touch brought fresh cries of pain and he was forced to let her go. She crouched between two of her sister's massive claws, floating unsupported in the white void. 'Go then,' she wailed. 'The world is well rid of you, Scarn, and the evil you have brought to it.'

'*There was Evil before Scarn! As your sister well knows!*' boomed the Flame. It was close enough for Fortune to feel its searing heat, barely a tree's height short of the spinning dragon loop. He looked bravely up into its blazing heart, and believed that he was about to die.

Scarn had stopped and turned to face the Flame. For the first time, it seemed, he had noticed the loop the three dragons had made in the air. It held his gaze, fascinating him.

'The Last Circle!' he whispered. Then he actually began to move away from the portal.

The Flame lunged, a sudden burst of acceleration carrying it through the loop. Such momentum would hurl it bodily against Scarn, carrying them both through the portal and out of the world altogether.

The three dragons were a solid, continuous ring.

The Flame passed through with the width of a dragon's claw to spare.

It never reached Scarn.

The dragon ring broke the Flame apart. If the ring was the epitome of continuity, then what happened to the Flame was its exact opposite. It *fragmented*. It had reduced itself to a single ball of fire: now it was separated into a billion or more separate flames, and each broke into a billion more. It emerged the other side of the ring of dragons a diffuse cloud of light. Its countless motes fluttered in the air like so much scintillating blue dust, burning still yet *tiny*.

Then the wind caught them.

The wind blowing out of the portal repelled the motes of fire and whirled them away from its light, out into the depths of the milky-white abyss. The dragons stared into the void, wondering what underworld it was to which they

418

had been banished. The wind continued to carry them far into the distance until nothing remained, not even the strand of fire which had joined the Flame to Scarn.

Scarn!

Fortune spun round, expecting to see the crushed dragon sneaking into the portal while all attention was elsewhere. Instead he found himself looking into the eyes of Volley.

'Volley!' he blurted stupidly. 'How did you . . .'

'Get here?' The big dragon smiled, reminding Fortune achingly of Tallow. He nodded back towards the oval, where the others pressed anxiously against the invisible barrier, still trapped on the other side of the world. 'It saw fit to let me through. It wouldn't before.'

'Do you know why?'

Volley nodded. 'I would have killed him before his work was done.'

He moved aside, revealing Scarn.

A more wretched sight Fortune had never seen. The air was littered with red scales, even now being whipped into motion by the constant wind. Scarn floated before the glowing blue portal, his eyes dull, his body almost completely destroyed.

'What did you do to him?' gasped Fortune. Volley paused before answering.

'Nothing, Fortune. Justice had already been done before I reached him.'

Scarn's breath was a faint gargle. His eyes began to close slowly . . . so slowly.

The whirling ring of dragons had slowed down; now Fortune could make out the individual forms of Aria, Gossamer and Jevell. Presently it stopped altogether and they detached themselves gracefully from each other's grip. Flying without moving their wings, drifting through the void, they joined Fortune and the others. Gossamer and Jevell went straight to Wist, whom Brace and Ledra were trying to comfort in her pain. Aria faced Scarn.

'I do not ask . . . your forgiveness,' croaked Scarn, his voice barely audible.

'I do not give it,' answered Aria. 'The Evil came before you, Scarn, as the Flame said. Nevertheless, you *were* evil.

419

Now it is up to the Cloud: you will be judged before its mercy.'

Scarn frowned. Perhaps he was puzzled, perhaps angry. Whichever state it was, it was how he ended his life on this world. His last gasp might have been a word; if it was, it was not understood by any dragon there. His head dropped imperceptibly and then the wind was carrying not only his scales but his body too, carrying it away from the portal in pursuit of the shattered Flame. He glimmered red against the milky haze, then the haze swallowed him and he was seen no more.

'Help us,' cried Gossamer, trying to lift Wist's head.

They gathered round the badly burned dragon. Gossamer looked at Fortune and shook her head. *She looks so tired*, he realized.

'Did Scarn escape?' croaked Wist.

'No,' said Aria. 'But he has gone.'

'And my sister?'

'I am here with you.' For the first time since the breaking of the Flame, the crystal dragon moved. It flexed its claws, gathering Wist up into its embrace as a mother might cradle an infant. Except this mother was a wall of red glass of mountainous size and the infant was a dragon on the edge of death. Fortune and the others watched as she was carried up out of their reach.

'There is room for you in here,' Lessen said, her voice smooth and kind. 'Now the Flame has gone.'

'Has its evil left you?' they heard Wist ask.

'I am what I am. Will you join me?'

Wist's voice grew fainter as she was lifted up to the level of her sister's face. Fortune watched in fascination as the facets of Lessen's jaw flexed into a smile. The last words they heard Wist utter were these:

'I love you, sister.'

Lessen began to shrink back to her former size. As she did so Wist's body floated free of her claws. It darkened, grew red. Angles began to cut their way out from the scales. Slowly at first, then quicker, it too turned to crystal. Soon both of the crystal dragons were the same size, indistinguishable from each other except for the glowing blue portal which still rose from Lessen's back. They hovered at the same level as the rest of the dragons, shimmering in the haze.

'You must choose now,' came Lessen's voice, practically a whisper. 'The charm is almost spent; the portal must close.'

'What's happened to Wist?' called Brace.

'We are together now,' Lessen answered softly. 'As we shall be for ever. We shall not need our lives any more. We have each other.'

Her words blew away on the wind. Brace looked at Ledra. She nodded, once, and he turned to his sister.

'We will never find a home in the natural world,' he blurted. 'Come with us.'

Gossamer stroked his brow with her wingtip.

'Don't go,' she said. Jevell moved forward and embraced her son.

'A mother wants what is best for her infants,' she sobbed. 'Be happy, Brace.'

'We cannot live without hope,' said Brace. Now he too was crying. 'What hope is left for us here?'

Jevell held him away from her, looking deep into his eyes.

'Hope will outlive us all,' she smiled.

Behind them the portal sighed, a rich, animal sound. Its edges were wavering now; it was visibly smaller.

'Is this what you want, Ledra?' Fortune asked, touching her gently.

'Brace is all I want now,' she replied. 'I will go wherever he takes me.'

'But how can you both pass through? Lessen said . . .'

'That only one, living breath may use the portal?' Ledra smiled. 'Watch, Fortune. You will see why this is the right choice for us.'

Beside her Brace was embracing Gossamer clumsily.

'I hope you find whatever it is you feel you have lost,' she wept. 'Think of me sometimes.'

'I shall.'

Brace looked at Fortune's face. As he held his sister with his wings so he held his friend with his eyes. They stared at each other, both unable to speak.

'Look after her,' choked Brace eventually.

'Always,' said Fortune, touching the young dragon's wingtip with his own. 'And wherever you find yourself, Brace, promise me one thing.'

'What?'

'Seek out the sky, Brace. Fly, and you may one day find your way home.'

Ledra tugged at Brace's wing. 'Come,' she urged. 'Or all these tears will be wasted and we'll look like fools!'

'Hope remains for us too!' called Aria as the two dragons rose swiftly towards the portal. 'There is more than one way to escape!'

The light was bleeding around Brace and Ledra now. They flew close, using their wings though they had no real need to – this strange void seemed to sense dragons' intentions and move their bodies accordingly. Soon they were moving belly to belly, and then Brace's wings enfolded Ledra so that she could barely be seen. They both dipped their necks towards each other then their mouths opened and met . . . and Fortune finally saw how they intended to cheat the magic which had opened a way out of the world.

Sparks began to chase down the edges of the portal, descending until they were absorbed into the crystal of Lessen's back. Brace and Ledra made a vague, distorted shape against the glaring light. Their lungs moved in perfect synchronization: as one inhaled so the other exhaled. Their breath was wholly contained within their twinned form, a loop of life-giving air which carried them on to the very brink of the portal. As they entered, the light flared, sending a shower of charm-laden energy across the faces of the onlookers. None moved, for the touch of the magic was strong and warm. The curve of Brace's wings grew faint, indistinct against the glare. There was a sudden impression of great speed and a chatter of distant noise. Then, for a single breath before the portal snapped shut, the light dimmed and they were afforded a single, tantalizing glimpse of what lay beyond.

It was a sky, vast and blue. Lines of cloud were set against its richness in soaring, vertical bands. A world tipped on its side. A world beyond this. Fortune watched as Brace's wings opened, releasing Ledra into the sky. She rolled over and opened her wings wide. The last Fortune saw they were two tiny dragon motes flying strong and sure against a wall of vivid blue. Then the portal narrowed to a slit and disappeared. The light which had illuminated Lessen from within blinked out.

The white void in which they had been floating grew suddenly dark. Irregular shapes burst outwards, puncturing the featureless space. Pricks of light appeared above them.

The familiar landscape of Mahl re-formed itself around the astonished dragons.

The waves lapped against the shore of the lake, their crests clearly defined by the orange light of the lava flow. Fortune was huddled close with the others: Gossamer and Aria, Jevell and Volley. It was cold, desperately cold, and he could not decide what to do.

Far away yet visible through the oval of charm, Cumber was complaining. 'We still can't get through the barrier,' he said. He pressed his face against the invisible shield which the oval presented, squashing his snout flat. 'See if you can get back from your side.'

'But what if Brace was right?' sighed Fortune. 'What if we really don't have a home any more? Does it really matter where in the world we are when there is no future for our kind?'

'Don't talk like that, old fellow – I mean to say . . .'

Then Velvet's voice piped up. She had just returned from a brief exploratory flight and was breathing hard, clearly excited. 'I've just managed to look over the top of the oval!' she exclaimed. 'And I think something extraordinary is happening in the Last Circle! You've got to come and look, all of you. Quickly! Come back to us here!'

Fortune looked at Gossamer and was surprised to find himself smiling at her: they were smiling at each other. Their smiles were tired but true. Velvet's infectious enthusiasm roused their stiffening muscles and together they led the others back along the rocky shore to the aperture. Fortune paused and looked back.

'Land of fire and ice,' he mused. 'I shan't miss this place.'

'I will come back here one day,' said Aria as she stepped through the oval.

They all followed her, transported across the face of the world by the subtle miracle of the Cloud. They left the twin crystals – once they had been Wist and Lessen – on the shore of the lake. Already the lava was rolling towards them; soon they would be engulfed and buried. *Aeons hence they may be found again*, thought Fortune, *when the land is weathered down to expose their resting place once more.*

'May you share peace together until then,' he whispered.

He was the last to step through, and as the tip of his tail slipped back on to the continent of Ocea the oval aperture contracted into a dimensionless point of light, then vanished.

They were back amid the red rocks, beneath a sky black with ash. In the distance bright fire raged at the centre of the Last Circle, reaching high into the sky.

Something was moving in the flames.

CHAPTER 31

From the Ashes

They flew as near as they dared to the Last Circle. Its heat was beyond that of any normal fire; ribbons of energy chased outwards from the crater, soaking into the ground as they fled into the world. The taste of ash was bitter in their mouths and smoke hung heavy in the air. It was like a cloying, starless night.

'Not pleasant,' grumbled Scoff. 'For a day of creation.'

They landed in a shallow bowl some way short of the crater. Its ragged lip stood out in vivid contrast to the orange of the fire burning inside the crater itself. Every so often, a shadow lifted itself above the dark line, then folded itself back into the flames once more.

'What is it?' whispered Velvet.

'It looks like a serpent of some kind,' answered Smoke, huddling against her. 'A sea serpent breaching the waves.'

'But where did it come from?'

Smoke looked eloquently up into the sky.

The fire belched out a ball of flame which shivered up into the ash cloud. A rounded tail rose into view, trembled for an instant, then slithered away out of sight. It was huge, completely black, though its ribbed surface shone as though slicked with oil.

'It is not of the comet,' said Aria suddenly. 'It is of the world.'

The thing hunched its back clear of the flames then slipped out of view again for a long time. Some of the mirror-dragons began to fidget, growing restless. Presently Wemp came forward.

'We do not want to stay,' he murmured, pitching his voice so that only Fortune would hear. 'We have a home, of sorts.'

'The Rift, of course,' Fortune replied. 'Of course, you

must . . .' He stopped, deliberated. 'No! You must *not* go, Wemp. We are all that is left now. We must stay together, for the time being at least.' He paused. 'Will you stay?'

Wemp appraised him long and hard. 'If you wish it, Fortune, of course we will. But there is danger here.'

'No, Wemp. There is nothing for us to fear.'

There was a collective gasp as the thing in the crater reared up suddenly. Vast and black and shapeless, twisting blindly, reaching up into the dark sky.

A pair of huge, black wings unfurled from the writhing shape. They extended, spreading out across the diameter of the crater. The giant was revealed. Its wingspan exactly equalled the width of the Last Circle; of all the giants they had encountered on this day, it was by far the most awe-inspiring.

'Wyrm,' said Smoke simply, and she began to weep.

Wyrm's jaws opened. Fortune half-expected to see fire blazing in his throat, but he was not disappointed when he saw nothing. The voice that came was no surprise, however.

'*It is time to say goodbye, dear dragons,*' Wyrm boomed. '*There is no longer time for stories. Fly while you can. And watch over my children, for they are your legacy.*'

He smiled, then looked down at each of his wings in turn. Flames reared up, investing them with brief colour, then subsided. Slowly Wyrm folded his tremendous bulk back down into the crater, disappearing beneath the golden aura which had replaced the fire. For many long breaths the dragons watched; above them the sky brightened as the dust cloud thinned. From beyond the ridge there was no further movement.

Fortune exchanged a glance with Gossamer, then advanced tentatively up the ridge towards the crater's lip. Golden light bathed his face with warmth. Close behind him was Aria. They reached the top together and looked down at what lay within the Last Circle.

Beneath their astonished gaze was a huge rainbow ocean, a sea of moving colour, swelling and shimmering. Blue and bronze crashed together, merging with currents of rich crimson, deep cobalt, fluorescing, gleaming. It filled the crater, this colourful tide, obscuring the rock and ash, the debris of the comet. Beads of liquid gold lapped at their claws . . . feathers of gold!

'What do you see?' Cumber's voice floated up from behind them. Fortune jumped at the sound, half-turning. All else was silent.

Of Wyrm there was no sign.

'Father,' whispered Aria, 'look.'

The ocean had lost its liquid appearance. Still it heaved but a multitude of shapes began to separate. Colours condensed, coalescing into individual forms. Living forms.

Without warning they rose on a million soft feathered wings, lifting skywards. A soundless rush of air pressed Fortune back into his daughter's embrace.

Upwards and outwards they spiralled, a new cloud spreading over the land. No cloud of ash but a storm of new and living beings, the infinite variety of their hue and shade bringing dazzling splendour to a sky which, in a world without dragons, would otherwise have been utterly empty.

'They fly as though they are born to it!' exclaimed Fortune.

'That is exactly what they are,' said Aria, hugging him tight. 'Theirs is the sky now. We should honour them. Aren't they beautiful?'

The cloud began to disperse into the revitalized air. A faint line of white trailed towards the horizon: the parent comet, continuing on its voyage through the cosmos, its work on this particular world done. Everything seemed remade, unspoilt and splendid.

'A perfect day,' whispered Fortune, staring at the guttering fire.

The feathered newborns were moving north in a huge flock, abandoning this barren land. Soon they would spread across the world. Fortune picked out the variety of forms already manifesting itself in their midst: tiny, brightly-coloured creatures whose wings moved so fast that they hummed; large, soaring giants, white and narrow of wing; this one raucous and black, that one many-hued, still more cast in simple browns and greys. An entire race, born from Wyrm's ashes, on the day of creation.

Suddenly there seemed no reason to stay.

Fortune located Wemp again. Dragons were beginning to take to the air now that the sky had been made safe. He was concerned that they should stay together. Perhaps they should return to the Rift after all, while the import of all that had happened sank in.

If it ever does . . .

He did not notice Smoke advancing towards the crater, her eyes half-closed, her wings taut and trembling. One by one the others followed her.

'Fortune!' whispered Gossamer, suddenly at his side. 'Look!'

Had he thought the day finished with surprises? He was mistaken.

A faint, yellow aura remained above the very centre of the Last Circle. It hovered there like a patch of golden mist. Eddies rippled through it as though something were moving there.

Fortune caught Volley's eye. He, like Smoke, was staring intently at the curious phenomenon. One by one the other dragons followed their gaze until the entire group was gazing into the crater.

What more can there be? Fortune wondered.

There was a darker area in the heart of the mist. It was made more of motion than of substance, a regular, beating action which was instantly recognizable. It was the movement of a dragon's wings.

The yellow mist started to fade, but as it did so the dark flaw became more solid; at first blurred, it grew tight and narrow, a cross-shape.

A dragon, a flying dragon.

Slowly, so slowly, it emerged from the vanishing mist. Like the newborn fliers – which had by now disappeared into the north – it seemed fresh and untainted.

Not newborn, though, realized Fortune in wonder. *Reborn!*

It was a tantalizing moment. For a breath or two the dragon was too far away to be recognized. It was simply a dark rhythm against the sky.

'Wyrm?' whispered Aria. She shook her head. No – Wyrm was gone.

Fittingly, it was Smoke who recognized him first, though she could not speak his name. Her claws scrabbled through the dust as she launched herself clumsily into the air. The wings which had carried her across the great eastern sea to

428

the shores of Ocea, which had outpaced the blast of the falling comet, served her well on this last, most important flight. They opened wide and cupped the air with strong, backward strokes, accelerating her on to meet the dragon for whom she had been waiting.

'It's Vox!' exclaimed Cumber, then he was flying too, they were all flying towards him, hurrying yet keeping far enough back from Smoke so as not to crowd her.

And it was Vox. As he drew near the purple of his scales shone forth in the brilliant sunlight, the colour which had once marked him as an outcast and which now seemed to represent all that was good about this day, about the coming of the Cloud, about the vanquishing of the Flame and the bravery of the dragons who had lived through the turning of the world and all that had followed since. It was Vox, returned to the world in glory, and there was only one dragon he wanted to see.

'Smoke!' he bellowed. Still Smoke could say nothing. Instead she started to laugh, and then to cry, and the two mingled so that there was no separating them. The distance between them halved and suddenly they were touching, crashing against each other, knocking each other from the sky so that they tumbled hysterically, ecstatically, claws locked, spinning over and over. They recovered just clear of the ground, touching wingtips and swooping flamboyantly back over the line of their approaching friends. Dragons reached up to touch them as they soared high, hoping to share the magic, the miracle which was Vox reborn.

For that brief time, the sky above the Last Circle was empty but for the play of dragons, and the only rain was their tears. The sun drifted by, throwing long, dragon shadows across the flanks of the red pinnacles. As it began to set those shadows became mighty indeed, dark and beautiful wings which stretched across the desert, climbed the towers of rock, embracing and caressing the fabric of the world as though reluctant ever to let it go.

When night fell, however, the dragons were gone. They took their shadows with them, and it was as if they had never been there at all.

CHAPTER 32

Dragonhome

The Rift served as a place to stay for a while. There were physical wounds to be healed, of which Volley's were the worst. Emotionally, these battered and exhausted dragons would take much longer to recover. Perhaps they would never fully be healed.

The days were long and peaceful. The Rift was at once both vast and tiny, a metaphor for the world itself with its varied climates, its separate microcosms, its beauty and its danger. The dragons flew endlessly between its buttresses, beneath its sculpted arches, simple exercise driving away the pain. The fear went quickly, however, and for that they all gave thanks.

The mirror-dragons managed to light fires by using their wings as lenses, but the practice did not last. Such was their distrust of fire in general – and of the Flame in particular – that even Cumber turned away from it.

'I no longer miss the charm,' he announced quietly. 'I shall learn to live without fire well enough.'

There was much discussion about what had actually happened to the Flame. Scarn was certainly dead, and Wemp was not alone in maintaining that the Flame too had been destroyed. But most agreed that the stories which Scarn and Wyrm had woven were indeed true – that although it had been cast down the Flame was cursed with survival.

'It remains for a reason, for only by perceiving the evil of the Flame can we truly know the goodness of the Cloud,' explained Gossamer reverently, as they watched the dying embers of what would prove to be the last pyre ever lit by dragons on the continent of Ocea. 'It will forever live in the shadow of the Cloud. Justice has been served, and the penalty the Flame will pay over the aeons shall be terrible.'

Volley nodded firmly. He was much stronger now, new enthusiasm speeding his recovery.

Above them, in the night sky, Smoke and Vox circled together, laughing.

'I want to go back to South Point,' Fortune told Gossamer. 'Back to the Island of Torr.'

It was ten nights after the Day of Creation. Tiny, chattering shapes fluttered in the night above them: more newcomers to the sky, small, black animals which fed on the flying insects which had begun to invade the Rift. New birth everywhere, creation at work. The sky was becoming a busy place.

'So do I. You have seen my birthplace. I should very much like to see yours.'

Wemp and the mirror-dragons did not come. The goodbyes were stilted, for no dragon imagined they would meet again. The degenerative disease which afflicted the dragons of the Rift, making them age too fast, was still at work and Fortune doubted they would live for many more years. They suited this place though, reflecting the grandeur of the landscape in their shining scales, flying tight and controlled through the canyons and gullies.

'I hope you find what you are looking for, Fortune,' said Wemp. He looked deep into Fortune's eyes as he hugged him tight.

'Fly well, my friend,' answered Fortune. 'And live as long as you dare.'

Wemp looked around at his comrades and smiled a bright, metallic smile. 'We may look old, but we're not incapable of adventure. You may yet hear of us, Fortune, though we might be just legends by then.'

'There's nothing truer than a good story,' replied Fortune warmly. 'Farewell.'

They flew then, Fortune and Gossamer, Aria and Jevell, Cumber and Velvet, Scoff, Volley and Anchre, Smoke and Vox. They flew east across the desert until they reached the great plains and the swathe of forest which led them finally

431

to the sea. They flew on into the east, tireless and unhurried.

After many days of constant flight Volley spotted the distinctive coastline of Mahl far away to the north.

'Torr lies to the south and east,' called Fortune. 'That is, if the world-storm did not bury it beneath the waves.'

He flew over to Aria, sensing her uncertainty.

'You want to go back there, don't you?' he said gently. 'Back to Mahl.'

Aria shivered. 'Oh, I don't know,' she replied. 'I thought I did – I said I would. But now that I see it . . . I just don't know. I thought I had found myself there, but what I found turned out to be only Scarn's lies, making me feel as though I belonged.'

'And now?'

'Now I am content with who I am. That is as good a place as any for a dragon to start her life.'

'The Cloud has brought you that?'

Aria laughed lightly. 'Oh, father! Can't you hide your suspicion any better than that? The Cloud lives in my heart now, of course, but my heart is still my own. Can you understand that?'

Fortune nodded. 'I think so, my dear Aria.'

She smiled, a little sad now. 'Perhaps one day you will see it for yourself too. You have seen a little, I think, but . . .'

'You have found a place for yourself – I have not. Perhaps I should have escaped with Brace and Ledra.'

Aria shook her head, but said no more. They flew on.

Torr had broken apart. Its northern mountains had folded, their central part descending below the surface of the sea so that it was no longer one island but two. Fortune urged them on, praying that the southern regions had been less drastically affected.

Heath and moor gave way to river plain and rolling, green meadows. The terrain seemed simpler here, lacking the spectacle of Ocea yet retaining something of its splendour. Familiar patterns raced by beneath Fortune's wings: the grassy plateau of Sett, the complex folds of land which led eventually to the modest hills north of his beloved South

Point. The dragons rose with those hills now. Cumber grew excited at Fortune's side: this was his home too, after all. The others, even Gossamer, held back, giving them this moment.

They flew low over the grass together, inhaling the salty air in great draughts, anticipating the sudden drop of the cliffs, the first sight of the sea. Granite punched through, scarring the soil. The land rose, then fell away.

It was glorious . . . but it was not South Point.

The shape of the land was similar, but not exactly the same. Sea cliffs still rose from flat, rock shores but they were folded, twisted somehow. Stacks and arches made complex shapes above the waves – the remains of collapsed cliff walls. Water spurted up into their faces from hidden blowholes. It was at once familiar and devastatingly foreign. They hovered together, sharing the updraught from the cliff, drinking it in.

All sign of the old dragon settlement had been erased.

Fortune was unsurprised, but that did not prevent him from feeling sad.

'There's no going back,' he murmured to Cumber.

'No, my friend. But I think we knew that all the time, didn't we?'

They made a temporary camp. On the second morning Volley and Anchre announced that they were setting off on their own. Fortune was pleased to see their burgeoning friendship. Volley had always flown in the shadow of Tallow, and now it seemed he had found a place in a new partnership, one in which he was the leader. Anchre in turn was experimenting with new-found sociability – at last he could be himself among dragons he knew and trusted.

More goodbyes, thought Fortune as he watched them strike out south. They planned to retrace Fortune and Cumber's epic journey across the Heartland, to see what had changed there. Then they would continue south until they reached the fabled continent of Zaren, where the rocks were locked beneath mountains of ice. *Everything divides, everything goes.*

One day he flew out to sea with Vox. They took up station above a small, chalk-cliffed island which Fortune did not remember. Far to the south the land mass which had once been known as the Heartland was clearly visible, much nearer to Torr than it had been in the past.

Vox had said nothing since his miraculous return from the fire. All his time had been spent with Smoke – they had been inseparable and none had interrupted their renewed courtship. Fortune appraised him as they hovered together, facing each other, marvelling at the confidence in his wings, the calmness in his face.

'I remember when you used to stammer, Vox,' he chuckled, breaking the silence.

Vox smiled. 'I remember it too. Much has happened since then.'

'Much indeed.' Fortune hesitated. 'How much do you remember, Vox – about the Cloud, I mean?'

Vox's smile widened, became radiant. 'Everything, Fortune.'

'I envy you,' sighed Fortune, turning away.

'Don't be sad, my friend.' Vox's words floated across to him. Fortune closed his eyes and imagined it was Wyrm talking. 'Despite everything I have seen and experienced, I am still just a dragon. We are all still just dragons, including you, Fortune. And that is the greatest miracle of all. We have survived against all the odds. We are the only ones who lived through it all.'

'Yet we cannot live forever.' Fortune turned back again. Vox's smile remained, reassuring him with its strength, its *certainty*.

'Who does, Fortune? Who does?'

Fortune's melancholy mood lasted for ten more days, during which time he explored the environs of what he was coming to think of as 'New Point'. Nothing seemed familiar beyond the overall lie of the land, and this depressed him. He grew ill-tempered, prone to snapping at any dragon who came near him.

Then, on the eleventh night, something happened to jolt him out of his mood.

He had strayed on to an area of shore he had not explored before. It was tilted at an alarming angle, a flat bed of rock thrown upwards from the sea like an outstretched wing. Alone in the darkness, he ventured out on to it, gripping the water-worn grooves with his claws to avoid slipping. Above him the stars were cool and bright.

At the far end of the sloping shore was a great pile of boulders. They were heaped on top of each other, and it seemed clear to Fortune that they had rolled down the shore to land against the base of the cliff which curved round at its far end. Once they must have littered this rocky shelf, a veritable maze of boulders.

He clambered down towards them. A flash of light caught his eye in a tiny rock pool – the reflection of some event in the night sky. He looked up and saw the trail of a shooting star vanishing into the distant haze. He continued to stare for a while longer, but saw no more.

He looked down, and saw a pair of parallel grooves in the rock.

Bending down, he slipped his claws into them. They fitted perfectly.

He lay there, watching the stars. He was about to get up again when two more shooting stars flashed high above him, a twinned pair, flying higher and faster than any dragon. He thought of his parents, Welkin and Clarion.

Fortune clutched the rock, feeling the press of the grooves against his claws. He knew this place. It had possessed a name once – 'Welkin's Hollow'. These grooves had been made by his father's claws, long ago, before the world had turned. When the night sky had been the territory not of falling stars but of night dragons.

Long ago, in the days of charm.

A voice called him from the clifftop.

'Fortune! It's such a beautiful night. Will you fly with us?'

It was Gossamer. The others were there, all of them, their wings spread.

Fortune needed no urging. His heart felt full and heavy but his wings were strong enough to bear its weight. He rose up the side of the cliff, confident in the grip of the eddies which played there. After all, he had grown up here, hadn't he?

No, it was later that I grew up, much later.

He led them in to the night, taking them high to where the air was thin. The unclaimed land of New Point was tiny beneath them. The far-off horizon was dim and blue, fading to black as it blended with the sky. They were so high that they could see its curve.

Fortune looked around him, saw his friends, the dragons he loved most in the world. Gossamer, and the daughter they shared.

He felt the sky, held it in his wings, and knew at last where it was that he belonged.

'We're here,' he said. 'We're home.'

EPILOGUE

Deep in the ice, she waited. Lines of power – the remains of the trollveins – kept her connected to the rest of the world. Through them she watched and learned. And waited.

Once she had owned a name, but now she did not possess even a body. Deathless, powerless, she ached for the life which had once been hers. A virtual dragon, imprisoned at the crest of the world.

She heard the roar of the Flame, watched its fruitless battle with the Cloud, saw the escape route it had laid for itself. Witnessed its failure at the threshold. Saw what lay beyond.

The sky beyond was endless. There lay a home for an immortal dragon, beyond the confines of this meagre world. There she would journey, if it took her a million years.

There her story would begin again.

Stories end.

Histories, by way of contrast, go on.

The history of the turning world is the history of all worlds, including that which was inhabited by dragons, for a time at least. They, like many others, came to be, and lived, and passed on. The world they left behind is one in which they never existed, even though they knew themselves to be real. Their memories remain, however, and remain still, in the most potent form a history can attain: story.

What, then, of these last dragons?

Wyrm was indeed the last-born of his race, for no dragon thereafter brought forth a fertile egg. Dragon lifespans were prodigious by all the standards of the new, natural world, and they were lived to the full. Many corners of the world

439

remained unexplored by dragon, even by the time of the Turning, and many were the adventures they promised. Many were the adventures that were had.

Dragon lives were lived, and few were empty of heroism. From time to time, those who had been parted met each other again, and shared their tales, enriching their store of memories. They spoke of the past and the future in equal measure, and always when they turned to the latter there was hope.

For, much as they knew their line in this world to be coming to an end, these last dragons knew that two of their number had escaped. The direction of that escape none could guess, even those who had witnessed it directly, nor whether it was to a heaven or a hell. Yet faith sustained the belief that Brace and Ledra lived still, and that they had found a world where dragons were more than just a story.

A world where dragons might live forever.

There was one further time after the Day of Creation when all the dragon survivors were gathered together again. It was on a crisp, autumn night, beneath a full moon. It was in the crater known to them as the Last Circle.

They met and they talked. There were tears, and much laughter, and the telling of tall stories made taller by the mood and the season. There was faith and there was hope.

When the night was done, in the low light of the dawn, they looked to the east, towards the land of fire and ice where their friends had flown into a shaft of blue and vanished into a place where the clouds were turned on their side. They prayed to the Cloud, embraced, parted, and lived out their lives.

And for many years the world still knew the charm of the dragons.

Fire and ice.

At the crest of the world, she waited.

Little remained now that she remembered from her youth. The dragons were gone; the sky was filled instead with tiny flying creatures which buzzed and sang and whistled. Strange creatures roamed the changed land. The natural faeries thrived.

Dragoncharm
Graham Edwards

The ultimate dragon saga

THE WORLD IS TURNING

The bones of trolls are turning suddenly to stone as nature draws apart from the Realm, the mysterious source of charm. It is a young world, but soon it will be old, and no magic is strong enough to resist the onset of a new era.

Instead, a young natural dragon named Fortune, with no fire in his breath nor magic in his power, holds the key to the survival of charm.

The malevolent Charmed dragon Wraith knows this, and he awakens the basilisk in a desperate bid to gain power over Fortune . . .

Myths handed down since the dawn of time tell of dragons, the most strange and magnificent creatures of our mythical prehistory. In this glorious epic fantasy, Graham Edwards captures the terror and the beauty of the days when dragons roamed the sky.

ISBN 0 00 648021 7

The charm of the trolls lingered however, somehow retaining its grip on the fabric of the world, which the Turning had made so slippery. What had once been trollvein became a net, able to catch traces of magic and direct them north to where she lay in her prison. This new gathering was slow, immeasurably so, but she had all the time in the world. Eventually her own power would begin to grow again.

Until then, she would wait.

If only she could remember her name . . .